# By the Light of the Bluff

*A Novel by:*
## Blake Gunnels

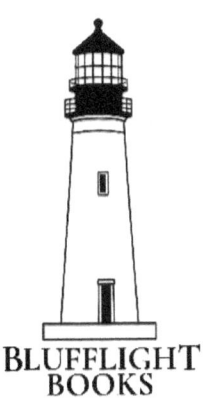

**BLUFFLIGHT
BOOKS**

*"A lighthouse does not warn with fear, nor guide with force. It
simply stands in the storm, steady as memory, certain as grace."*
*— From the journal of a keeper, Saint Simons Island, 1871*

For the ones raised on sandspurs and salt wind,
whose feet remember the ridges of oyster shells and tidal mud.

For those who have stood silent in the marsh,
watching the moon pull secrets through the Spartina.

For the ones who know the hush of Spanish moss,
the distant cry of gulls,
the thunder of summer rain on old tin roofs.

For every soul shaped by soft tide and stubborn memory,
by family names etched in driftwood,
and stories carried by wind and flame.

For those who light the lamp anyway,
even when no one is watching.

This is for you.

For my mother, Royce, and my late father, Bernie.
For my daughter, Mary Grace, and my son, Jack.
For my brother, Darren, and his beloved wife, Karen,
who left us, surrounded by love, during the writing of this book.
For my sister, Susan, and her husband, Pete.
For my niece, Katie, and my nephew, Jacob.
For all the summer vacations we spent together on Saint Simons
Island—or "Simple Simon"—as it became affectionately known
over the years.

And for Tammy,
whose love, support, encouragement, and hope carries me through
more than she knows.

# TABLE OF CONTENTS

# PROLOGUE

## The Storm and the Stranger
### *Saint Simons Island, Georgia—December 1872*

T he sea devoured men on nights like this. Captain Silas Roarke stood atop the highest dune, his greatcoat whipping against his legs, salt spray stinging his weathered face. Brine hung thick in the air, sharp with the coming storm.

The water had turned black and heaving. And there, rising against the sky, stood the unfinished lighthouse.

Federal record-keepers with their tallies. Harbor masters with their manifests. Customs officials with their questions. Silas Roarke had not built his network—his arrangements with harbor pilots in Charleston, warehouse foremen in Savannah, dockmasters who looked the other way—to see it undone by a beam sweeping across the water night after night.

Lightning flashed, illuminating the low clouds over the Atlantic. In that brightness: the silhouette of a schooner, gray against the storm.

"There she is." The wind snatched away his words. The *Miranda* was early, but that was just as well.

Behind him, the maritime forest of Saint Simons Island groaned and swayed, live oaks with their sprawling limbs and Spanish moss blowing wildly in the gale. The wind moved through the marsh grasses. Somewhere in the darkness, a night heron—a single sharp cry, then silence.

Roarke turned inland. The skeleton of what would become BluffLight stood against the churning sky, timber beams jutting upward like bare ribs. Even incomplete, it rose higher than anything else on this stretch of coast.

His jaw shifted. That lighthouse had been the talk of the island for months. The good citizens of Saint Simons believed it would bring safety to their shores and prosperity to their harbor.

"That tower will never be lit," he said.

Twenty years he'd spent building his trade routes. Legitimate merchant captain, then blockade runner during the war, then something else entirely when peace came and prosperity did not. The island families depended on him now—wages paid, favors granted. A lighthouse meant federal oversight. Documented traffic. Cargo holds subject to inspection.

Another flash of lightning revealed the schooner drawing closer, its sails reefed as it battled the mounting waves. The treacherous shoals and sandbars surrounding the island had claimed vessels before, but the *Miranda's* master had made this run in darkness many times.

The rain came then—a sudden deluge that soaked Roarke to the skin in moments. He let it wash over him. Blockade fire during the war had been worse. Federal pursuit after it. The slow years of postwar tariffs.

He remembered the winter of sixty-three, when the Union blockade had strangled the coast so completely that children on this very island had gone hungry. Confederate surgeons in Savannah had run out of chloroform, out of morphine, out of hope. Roarke had been a legitimate captain then—or near enough—with a fast schooner and a knowledge of these waters that no Federal chart could match. The first runs had been medicine, bandages, quinine for the fever wards. Later, other cargo. But it had started with necessity, with island mothers pressing his hands and whispering *God bless you, Captain* as he slipped past the blockade in the dark of the moon.

The island had given him refuge when he had nothing. Now it was his—the coves where boats could anchor unseen, the paths winding through the marshes.

And still they depended on him. The Bellamy boys worked his warehouse. Old Mrs. Crandall's pension came from his accounts, payment for her husband's silence years ago. Half the fishing families owed him for nets, for boat repairs, for loans that kept them through lean winters. They didn't ask where his money came from. They didn't need to. Roarke provided, and that was enough.

Roarke reached inside his coat and withdrew a spyglass, extending it despite the lashing rain. Figures moved on the *Miranda's* deck, preparing to drop anchor in the deeper channel between sandbars.

The unfinished lighthouse drew his attention again. They had begun the project with hope after the war. The original keeper, Henry Miller, had died before seeing it completed, and now his son, with his father's name but none of his caution, had returned to take up the work as if it were his birthright.

"Let your light so shine," the pastor had quoted at last Sunday's service, his eyes on the half-finished tower visible through the church windows. "That men may see your good works."

Roarke had sat in the back pew, his face unreadable.

The longboat would be launching soon. He stood a moment longer, watching the rain lash against the timbers of BluffLight.

"You will fall," he said. "Before you ever throw light."

He turned to descend the dune, then paused. The rain streamed down his face, cold as the sea that had shaped him. For a moment— just a moment—the weight of what he'd become pressed against his chest.

He descended the dune, his boots sinking into wet sand as he headed toward the meeting point. The island's inhabitants were in their homes against the storm, asleep.

In the distance, near the village, a single candle burned in a window.

Roarke lit his own lantern, shielding it with his coat as he swung it once, twice, three times.

He extinguished the flame and waited.

Behind him, the lighthouse skeleton stood black against the storm.

# CHAPTER ONE

## Arrival at the Edge of the World
### *Marsh Cottage, Saint Simons Island—April 12, 1873*

The skiff rocked as it cut through the gray-green waters of Buttermilk Sound, carrying Jessica Whitmore—Jesse to the few who had known her well—and her two children toward Saint Simons Island. Jesse's knuckles ached where they gripped the boat's edge, white beneath her gloves. Her eyes moved constantly—the boatman's hands on the oars, the tree line ahead, the open water behind. The boatman, an elderly freedman with hands like gnarled driftwood, guided them through the tidal creeks separating the mainland from the island.

"Not much further now, ma'am," the boatman reassured, nodding toward the approaching shoreline where the maritime forest rose like a wall of green. "Hampton Point's just around that bend."

Jesse nodded, one arm wrapped around six-year-old Eliza, who dozed against her side, exhausted from the journey that had begun three days earlier on a train from Savannah. Across from them, eleven-year-old Daniel sat upright, spine straight, chin lifted, hands folded in his lap. His eyes tracked the boatman's movements—the grip on the oars, the angle of each stroke. He had positioned himself between Eliza and the stranger without being asked, his slight body angled to shield his sister from the unknown. Jesse recognized the posture. She had taught it to him without meaning to.

"Will there be other children there, Mama?" he asked, his voice barely audible above the gentle lapping of water against the boat's wooden hull.

"Yes, darling," Jesse replied. "The letter said there's a modest school. And there will be plenty of shores to explore."

The April sunlight filtered through live oak branches draped with Spanish moss as they rounded the bend. The distinctive, slightly acrid scent of the marsh filled Jesse's nostrils—a living smell of mud and salt and things growing and dying all at once. Somewhere, a heron's haunting call echoed across the marshes. The pungent tang of oyster beds exposed by the retreating tide mingled with the sweetness of wild jasmine blooming along the shoreline. And there it was—Saint Simons Island. Her refuge, her hiding place, her fresh start. The shoreline was a tapestry of salt marsh grasses in myriad shades of green and gold, dotted with the occasional splash of color from early spring wildflowers. Beyond the marsh rose the trees—towering pines, spreading live oaks, and the occasional magnolia with its waxy, dark leaves and promise of creamy blossoms to come. The wind shifted as they neared, bringing salt, wet earth, and something wild—perhaps honeysuckle or crushed wax myrtle leaves. The water slapped gently at the skiff.

Above them, osprey circled lazily in a sky worn thin by sun and salt, their cries sharp as flint. Jesse inhaled deeply, the air cool against her throat. It smelled unlike anything from Richmond—less soot, more salt.

"You can see Christ Church steeple from here on a clear day," the boatman offered, gesturing toward the southern part of the island. "Been standing since before the war. Yankees didn't burn it down, praise the Lord."

Beyond that, only the undulating line of trees. She had chosen Saint Simons for its seclusion. Tucked away from the main thoroughfares, it offered distance and water on all sides. She had conducted correspondence with the island's solicitor through her late mother's cousin in Charleston. The cottage she had leased sight unseen was at the island's north end, away from the main settlement, backing up to a stretch of forest with the ocean just beyond the dunes.

The skiff eased toward a modest wooden dock that extended into the sound. Two figures stood waiting—a tall, broad-shouldered man with a full beard and a slender woman in a simple gray dress, her hair tucked beneath a white cap.

"That'll be Mr. Lawrence, the solicitor," the boatman informed. "And Miss Haskins, I expect. She looks after properties for folks."

Jesse straightened her spine and adjusted her bonnet, conscious of the impression she must make. Her traveling dress, once fine but now showing wear at the cuffs and hem, had been hastily mended before their departure. The carpetbag at her feet contained a few changes of clothes for herself and the children, her mother's Bible, a box of keepsakes, and nearly all the money she had managed to conceal over the past year.

"Daniel, wake your sister," she said softly. "We've arrived."

Daniel shook Eliza's shoulder as the boat bumped gently against the dock. The little girl stirred, blinking sleepily, her blonde curls tumbling from beneath her bonnet.

"Are we home now?" Eliza's voice was soft with sleep.

Jesse swallowed hard. "Yes, darling. We're home now."

The boatman secured the skiff and offered his hand to help Jesse onto the dock. Her legs, stiff from hours in the boat, trembled slightly as she found her footing on the weathered planks. Daniel followed, solemn and careful, then turned to lift Eliza up beside them.

"Mrs. Whitmore, I presume?" The solicitor stepped forward, hat in hand. His voice carried the smooth cadence of coastal Georgia, warm but formal. "Walter Lawrence, at your service. And this is Miss Amelia Haskins, who has prepared Marsh Cottage for your arrival."

Jesse extended her gloved hand. "Mr. Lawrence. Thank you for meeting us. Yes, I am Mrs. Jessica Whitmore, and these are my children, Daniel and Eliza."

Miss Haskins, a woman perhaps fifteen years Jesse's senior, with watchful eyes and a tight-set mouth, gave a precise nod. "The cottage is modest but sound. I've stocked the pantry with essentials to tide you over until you can make arrangements with the mercantile."

"That's very kind, thank you." Jesse reached for her purse, but Miss Haskins waved her off.

"Already settled in your arrangement with Mr. Lawrence. No need to concern yourself."

Mr. Lawrence gestured toward a waiting wagon. "I've brought transportation. It's a fair distance to Marsh Cottage, especially with your trunks."

Jesse hesitated. "There's only the one trunk, actually. And these bags." She nodded toward the carpetbag and valise the boatman was now lifting onto the dock.

Something flickered in Miss Haskins' eyes—a question, or simple observation—but she made no comment. Mr. Lawrence merely nodded and instructed the boatman to load the luggage onto the wagon.

Jesse took her first deep breath of island air as they settled onto the wooden bench. It was rich with the scent of salt marsh and pine, sun-warmed earth, and distant sea—so different from the coal smoke and closed rooms that had defined her life in recent years. Beside her, Eliza's face had come alive with curiosity, her eyes wide as she took in the unfamiliar landscape.

"Look, Mama! Birds!" she exclaimed, pointing toward a group of white egrets wading in the shallows of the marsh, their slender necks bending in delicate arcs.

"Great egrets," Miss Haskins supplied. "They nest in the tall cypress trees in the marshes. You'll see them everywhere once you know where to look."

The wagon jerked into motion, its wheels crunching on the packed-earth road cutting through the maritime forest. Sunlight dappled the path, falling in golden patches through the canopy above. Daniel's shoulders relaxed slightly as his gaze darted from side to side, taking in every detail of their new surroundings.

"The island has changed since the war," Mr. Lawrence remarked. "Many old plantations lie abandoned or have been sold off in parcels. Hampton, Cannon's Point, and Retreat sit empty now. But the village survives, and some new enterprises have taken root."

"I understand there's ongoing construction of a lighthouse?" Jesse ventured, recalling a detail from the island newspaper she had obtained before deciding on Saint Simons.

Mr. Lawrence nodded. "BluffLight, yes. Been in progress for some time now. Funding comes and goes, but the work continues.

4

It stands on the eastern bluff, not far from your cottage, in fact. Mr. Jonas Miller oversees the project—he's the son of the original keeper, Henry Miller, who passed away before seeing it completed."

A lighthouse meant keepers, visitors, federal inspectors.

As they traveled deeper into the island, the forest occasionally gave way to stretches of former plantation fields, some returning to wild scrub, others showing signs of new, smaller-scale cultivation. Jesse spotted a group of freedmen working a plot of land, bent to their work beneath the spring sun.

"Contracted labor," Miss Haskins explained, following Jesse's gaze. "Some former slaves have stayed on, working the land they once worked in bondage, but now for wages. Others have claimed plots of their own. The arrangements vary."

Moss swayed from the branches like silver-green lace, filtering sunlight into soft flickers across the dirt road. Somewhere nearby, a woodpecker tapped steadily on pine bark, the rhythmic staccato joining the buzzing of cicadas in late-morning song.

The road curved, and suddenly, they were passing the ruins of a grand house. Only the foundation and parts of two walls remained, blackened by fire and partially reclaimed by creeping vines.

"Retreat Plantation," Mr. Lawrence said. "Burned during the war. The Union troops were thorough in their destruction, though they spared the church and a few other structures."

Jesse said nothing. Daniel's gaze rested on her face, questioning. He remembered little of their life before Richmond, before his father's return from the war had changed everything. But he was old enough to understand that they had once been people of means, that the South's defeat had altered their fortunes.

The wagon continued, eventually turning onto a narrower track that wound closer to the eastern shore. The trees thinned, and Jesse caught glimpses of the Atlantic between their trunks, a vast expanse of blue stretching to the horizon. The sea air grew stronger, carrying the tang of salt and the distant roar of surf.

"There," Miss Haskins said, pointing ahead where the track widened into a clearing. "Marsh Cottage."

The cottage was indeed modest, but it appeared sound, with a porch facing east toward the sea. Built of tabby—that distinctive coastal mixture of lime, sand, oyster shells, and water—its walls gleamed pale in the afternoon sun. A brick chimney rose from the cedar-shingled roof, and several windows, though not large, were numerous enough to suggest that the interior would be well-lit. Behind the cottage, a stand of pine and oak offered shelter from westerly winds while the land sloped gently down toward the east, where a stretch of salt marsh separated the property from the dunes beyond.

"It was built before the war as a caretaker's cottage for one of the plantations," Mr. Lawrence explained as he brought the wagon to a halt. "Never suffered damage during the occupation. The property includes the cottage, the barn there, and about five acres stretching from the marsh to where the forest thickens." "Is it very isolated?" Jesse asked, her tone carefully neutral.

Miss Haskins gave her a shrewd look. "Nearest neighbor is half a mile south—the Widow Patterson. Village is three miles beyond that. The lighthouse construction site is about a quarter-mile north along the bluff. You're on your own here, but not entirely cut off."

That suited Jesse.

Daniel jumped down from the wagon first, then turned to help Eliza descend. Jesse followed, the sandy soil giving beneath her shoes.

"Shall we see you settled?" Miss Haskins asked, her tone practical but kind.

The interior was simple but clean. The main room served as both a parlor and a kitchen, with a large hearth on one wall and windows letting in abundant light. A narrow ladder led to a loft divided into two bedrooms. The furniture was sparse but serviceable—a table with four chairs, a settee, a rocking chair by the hearth, beds, and basic storage in the loft.

"The well is just outside the back door," Miss Haskins explained. "Good, sweet water. There's an outhouse behind the barn and a kitchen garden plot that's been turned over for planting."

Eliza had already claimed the rocking chair, setting it in motion with delighted giggles. Daniel stood by the window, looking out toward the distant sea.

"It's perfect," Jesse said. Here, no footsteps would thunder through the night. No fists would pound on tables, walls, or flesh.

Mr. Lawrence cleared his throat. "Your arrangements are paid through September, as agreed. By then, you'll have had time to settle and determine if the island suits your needs. Miss Haskins can direct you to opportunities for income should you decide to stay longer."

Jesse nodded. "Thank you. Both of you have been most kind."

"I'll call again tomorrow," Miss Haskins said. "Show you the path to the village, introduce you to Widow Patterson. She takes in sewing if you're in need."

After a few more practical instructions about the cottage's peculiarities—the chimney that needed cleaning before first use, the north window that swelled shut in humid weather—Mr. Lawrence and Miss Haskins took their leave. The boatman had already departed with the skiff, having been paid for his services. Jesse stood in the doorway of Marsh Cottage, watching the wagon disappear down the sandy track.

Behind her, she heard Eliza's voice, bright with excitement: "Daniel! Come see! There are shells in the walls!"

Jesse turned to find her daughter tracing the embedded oyster shells in the tabby wall with one finger, her face alight with discovery. Daniel examined the hearth with the seriousness of someone twice his age, testing the damper, checking the flue.

"We should unpack, Mama," he said thoughtfully. "And I can gather kindling for a fire before dark."

Jesse crossed to her son and placed a gentle hand on his shoulder. "Yes, we should settle in. But first..."

She walked to the center of the room and slowly turned in a complete circle, taking in their new home—this space that belonged to no one but them.

"First," she said, her voice gaining strength, "let us be grateful for our safe arrival."

She held out her hands to her children, who came to stand beside her in the pool of sunlight that streamed through a window. Together, they formed a circle in the heart of Marsh Cottage.

"Dear Lord," Jesse began, her voice soft but steady, "we thank You for guiding us to this place of refuge. We ask for your continued protection and blessing as we begin anew. Please help us to find peace here. Amen."

"Amen," echoed Daniel solemnly.

"Amen!" Eliza repeated, more enthusiastic than reverent.

Jesse squeezed their hands once before releasing them. "Now, let's make this our home." It wasn't much, this crooked cottage with its peeling shutters and patchwork floorboards, but for now it was theirs. And Jesse would see it through.

The late afternoon light slanted through the western window, washing the worn floorboards in gold. Outside, the first evening frogs struck up their slow, rhythmic chorus, the sound swelling and falling like breath.

The door banged open with a rush of damp air and fleet feet.

"Mama! Look what I found!" Eliza shouted, cupping her hands around something wriggling inside.

Daniel recoiled instantly, knocking over a three-legged stool with a crash. "If it's a snake, I'm moving out!"

"It's not a snake," Eliza said, full of injured dignity. She opened her palms to reveal a squat green frog, blinking solemnly up at them.

Daniel let out a high-pitched wail and scrambled onto the toppled stool.

Jesse bit the inside of her cheek to keep from laughing.

"This is Ferdinand," Eliza announced proudly. "He's going to live with us now. He likes damp places and eating bugs. I read it in a book."

"We already have Daniel for that," Jesse said dryly.

Eliza beamed as she nestled Ferdinand carefully into a chipped teacup she had scavenged from the hearth. She packed damp moss and tiny twigs around him like a throne fit for a marsh king. She leaned close to examine him, breathing in the smell of wet earth and

8

green growing things—nothing like the chalk dust and lamp oil of their Richmond nursery.

"He smells like rain," she whispered reverently. "And mud. Good mud."

The frog croaked once, deep and contented. Eliza clapped her hands with delight.

Jesse smiled and gathered the children close.

As Daniel went to bring in their trunk and Eliza explored the corners of the cottage, Jesse moved to the window and gazed out toward the sea.

Her eyes caught a distant shape rising above the trees to the north—the skeletal frame of the unfinished lighthouse. BluffLight, they called it.

"Let your light so shine," she whispered.

# CHAPTER TWO

## Shadows in the Sanctuary
### *Saint Simons Village—April 19, 1873*
### *(One week after arrival)*

The village of Saint Simons appeared as Jesse rounded the bend in the sandy road, Eliza's hand clasped in hers while Daniel walked a few paces ahead, investigating every stone or leaf. After a week at Marsh Cottage, they were down to the last of the flour and coffee, and the children had grown restless within the cottage walls.

Tall pines gave way to more scattered growth, and the road widened slightly as it approached the cluster of buildings that constituted the island's main settlement. The village had been largely spared the wartime destruction that had claimed many plantation homes. It possessed a worn but dignified appearance, like a once-fine garment carefully mended and preserved.

"Is this the place we'll get sugar, Mama?" Eliza asked, skipping slightly to keep pace with her mother's long strides.

"Yes, and flour and coffee and some ribbon for your hair if Mr. Thatcher's store has any," Jesse replied, adjusting the worn straw bonnet that shaded her face. The spring sun was warm, perspiration gathering at the nape of her neck beneath her pinned-up hair.

Daniel had paused to wait for them, his keen eyes taking in the village layout. "There's the church," he observed, pointing to a white structure whose simple steeple rose above the surrounding buildings. "And that must be the store."

Indeed, the most prominent building fronting the main street bore a weathered sign proclaiming, "Thatcher's General Merchandise." Several men were gathered in conversation outside its broad porch, some seated on benches, others leaning against porch posts. A few wagons and horses were hitched nearby.

Jesse's step slowed. During their first week on the island, they had encountered only Miss Haskins, who had made good on her promise to check on them, and the Widow Patterson, a reserved but kind woman who had sold them fresh eggs. To reach the store, they would have to pass directly by those gathered men.

"Remember what we discussed," she murmured to her children. "We are Mrs. Whitmore and her children, recently arrived from Charleston to take the sea air for our health. Nothing more need be said."

Daniel nodded solemnly. Eliza merely swung their joined hands, more interested in the promise of ribbon than in adult complexities.

As they approached, the conversation among the men faded. Jesse kept her eyes forward, her spine straight, though every instinct urged her to hurry past or turn back. A lifetime of social training took over, and she inclined her head in a polite but reserved greeting as they neared the steps.

"Good day," one of the older men said, tipping his hat. He had the weathered complexion of someone who had spent decades in sun and salt air. "You must be the widow who's taken Marsh Cottage."

Jesse's step hitched at the word "widow."

"Yes, sir. Mrs. Jessica Whitmore," she replied. "My children and I arrived last week."

"Thaddeus Bellamy," the man introduced himself. "Harbor master, such as we have need for one these days. Fine day to be making your first trip to the village."

"Indeed," Jesse agreed. "If you'll excuse us, we have purchases to make."

"Of course, of course." Mr. Bellamy stepped aside as Jesse moved past and guided Eliza up the steps. "Mind your step, ma'am."

Inside Thatcher's store, the door swung shut behind them. Jesse blinked at the cluttered space—ropes beside ribbons, flour next to fabric, nails stacked near small goods. Richmond stores had been tidy and polished. This one felt lived-in. Every inch of wall was utilized for shelves or hooks, from which hung tools, lanterns, coils of rope, and sundry household items. Barrels of flour, sugar, coffee beans, and rice stood in neat rows, while glass cases displayed more expensive or delicate goods—sewing notions, jewelry, stationery, and medicinal items.

A tall, thin man with spectacles and a neatly trimmed beard looked up from the ledger he was studying behind the counter. "Good morning," he greeted them. "You must be Mrs. Whitmore. Word travels fast on our little island."

"So I'm discovering," Jesse replied. "Mr. Thatcher, I presume?"

"At your service." He inclined his head. "What can I help you with today?"

Jesse produced a list from her reticule. "We require these items, if you please."

As Mr. Thatcher examined the list, two women approximately her own age were examining bolts of fabric near a window, occasionally glancing toward her. An elderly woman was selecting from a display of buttons, her experienced fingers testing each one for quality. At the far end of the counter, a man in work clothes was discussing the merits of different types of nails with a store clerk.

"Mama, look!" Eliza tugged at Jesse's skirt, pointing toward a case containing ribbons and lace. "Blue ones, just like you promised!"

"In a moment, darling," Jesse said softly. "Let Mr. Thatcher fill our order first."

Daniel had gravitated toward a shelf displaying pencils, paper, and slates. He ran his finger along the edge of one slate, then pulled his hand back.

"Perhaps a slate and pencils as well," she added to Mr. Thatcher. "And do you carry any books suitable for children's lessons?"

"Some primers and readers," the shopkeeper replied, adjusting his spectacles. "Miss Caroline Jenkins, our schoolmistress, orders them special from Savannah. Your boy looks to be of school age. The island school meets in the old church hall, three days a week."

Jesse hesitated. Sending Daniel to school meant entrusting him to the care of strangers, expanding the circle of those who knew of their presence.

"We shall consider it," she said. "For now, the books will do."

As Mr. Thatcher gathered her requested items, voices rose outside the store—men arguing, their words indistinct but sharp. Daniel moved to the door to peer out onto the porch.

"What's happening?" Jesse asked, joining him at the doorway.

The gathering had grown larger, and at its center stood two men engaged in an increasingly tense conversation. One was Mr. Bellamy, the harbor master who had greeted them earlier. The other was a stranger to Jesse—younger, perhaps in his early thirties, with broad shoulders and a hat dusted pale from the worksite. His face was partially turned away, but he stood with feet planted wide, arms loose at his sides.

"All I'm saying, Miller, is that there are those who question the continued expense," Mr. Bellamy was saying, his voice carrying through the open door. "The lighthouse project has dragged on for years now with little progress to show for it."

"Little progress?" The younger man's voice was controlled but firm. "The foundation is complete, the first tier of the tower stands twenty feet high, and the stone for the next section arrives next week. We're making steady headway despite the limitations of funding and materials."

"And how many more years before it's finished? Before the first ship is guided safely past our shoals by its light?" This from another man in the circle, one whose finer clothes and confident demeanor suggested wealth or position.

"As many as it takes, Mr. Demarest," Jonas replied evenly. "My father began this work because he believed this island deserved a proper lighthouse. I intend to see it completed."

"Noble sentiments," Demarest said, in a tone that suggested he found them anything but. "But one might wonder if there aren't those who prefer our shores to remain... navigable only to those with specialized knowledge. Knowledge that can be bought and sold."

Bellamy looked away. One of the younger men coughed and studied his boots.

Mr. Thatcher appeared at her elbow. "Your items are ready, Mrs. Whitmore. That'll be two dollars and seventeen cents."

Jesse returned to the counter to count out the coins. As she did so, she asked in a low voice, "What was that about? The discussion outside."

Mr. Thatcher glanced toward the door, then back at Jesse. "Island politics. The lighthouse project has its supporters and its detractors. Jonas Miller—that's the younger man—came back from the war determined to finish what his father started."

"And the opposition?"

"Some say it's too costly for a community still recovering from the war. Others..." He hesitated, then lowered his voice further. "Others have more personal reasons to prefer our waters remain hazardous to outsiders."

Before Jesse could inquire further, the store's bell jangled as the door opened. The man named Jonas Miller entered, removing his hat as he stepped inside. Up close, Jesse could see that he was older than she had first thought—closer to forty than thirty—with lines around his eyes that spoke of squinting into sun and wind. He walked with a slight but noticeable limp, favoring his left leg. His hands were broad and weathered, the knuckles scarred—working hands, not a gentleman's hands. When he spoke to Mr. Thatcher, his voice carried a steadiness that seemed rooted somewhere deeper than mere confidence. It was the voice of a man accustomed to giving orders that would be followed, yet without the sharp edge that made such authority a threat.

His gaze swept the store, pausing briefly on Jesse and her children before moving on to Mr. Thatcher. "Morning, Jacob. I need to place an order for those specialty lantern parts we discussed. The ones from the Charleston glassworks."

"Of course, Jonas. I've got the catalog in the back office. Give me a moment to finish with Mrs. Whitmore here."

At the mention of her name, Miller's attention returned to Jesse. His eyes met hers briefly, then moved to Daniel, to Eliza, back to her. Jesse stiffened slightly.

"Mrs. Whitmore," he acknowledged with a polite nod. "Welcome to Saint Simons. I understand you've taken Marsh Cottage."

14

"Yes, thank you," Jesse replied, gathering her packages as Mr. Thatcher wrapped them in brown paper. "We find it quite suitable for our needs."

"It's not far from the construction site," Miller observed. "I hope the noise doesn't disturb you."

"Not at all. We've scarcely heard anything." In truth, Jesse had occasionally caught the distant sounds of hammering and men's voices carried on the breeze, but they had been more reassuring than disruptive—evidence of ordinary life continuing around them.

Miller was about to say more when Eliza piped up: "Are you building the lighthouse, sir? The tall one on the bluff?"

A smile softened Jonas's weather-worn features. "Indeed, I am, young lady. Or trying to, at any rate."

"What's it made of?" Eliza persisted, emboldened by his friendly response. "How tall will it be? Will it have stairs inside?"

"Eliza," Jesse admonished gently, "Mr. Miller is busy with his own affairs. We shouldn't detain him with questions."

"I don't mind," Miller assured her. He crouched down to Eliza's level, wincing slightly as his injured leg bent. "The lighthouse is being built with a foundation of tabby—that's crushed oyster shells mixed with lime and sand, like the walls of your cottage. The tower itself uses brick for the inner wall and cut stone for the outer facing, brought all the way from a quarry near Savannah. When finished, it will stand ninety feet high, with one hundred and thirty-one steps to the lantern room at the top."

Eliza's eyes widened. "That's a lot of steps."

"It certainly is," Miller agreed with a chuckle. "Enough to make a keeper's legs strong."

Daniel had edged closer, watching the exchange. Jesse saw him studying Miller—the way the man held himself at Eliza's level despite the obvious discomfort in his leg, the patience in his voice, the absence of the false heartiness some adults used with children. Daniel's gaze lingered on Miller's hands, then on his face. Whatever her son was looking for, he seemed not to find cause for alarm. His shoulders, which had been tight since they entered the village, eased a fraction.

"My papa was a soldier," Daniel said suddenly. "He had to climb mountains with the army. That's even higher than a lighthouse."

Silence followed this declaration. Jesse's pulse quickened. Daniel had never before volunteered information about his father—and certainly not in the present tense.

Miller's gaze flickered briefly to Jesse's face. "Was he indeed? I served myself with the 26th Georgia. Which regiment was your father with?"

Before Daniel could respond, Jesse intervened. "My husband served with a Virginia regiment, Mr. Miller. He... did not return to us." She placed a hand on Daniel's shoulder. "And now we must return to our cottage before the day grows any warmer. Eliza tires easily in the heat."

Miller rose to his full height. "Of course. Perhaps you'll bring the children to see the lighthouse construction sometime. Many find it interesting to watch the progress."

"Perhaps," Jesse said noncommittally, gathering the last of her purchases. "Good day, Mr. Miller. Mr. Thatcher."

As they left the store, eyes followed them—not just Mr. Miller's, but those of every islander they passed. The widow Whitmore from Virginia, with her well-spoken manner that hinted at better days, and her two children who clearly didn't know what story they were meant to be telling.

"Daniel," she said once they were beyond the village, "remember what we discussed. About the past."

The boy walked beside her, his jaw tight. "But I didn't say he died, Mama. Just that he was a soldier."

"Even so, it raises questions we'd rather not answer." Jesse softened her tone. "I know it's difficult to remember what to say and what to keep private. But it's important for our safety—for your sister's safety—that people believe your father is gone."

Daniel nodded slowly. "Because otherwise he might find us?"

"Yes," Jesse admitted. "That's why."

They walked in silence for a time, the road narrowing as it wound through stands of longleaf pine. The scent of the trees, resinous and clean in the warm air, filled her lungs. Unlike the cloyingly sweet magnolias that had perfumed Richmond's gardens, these pines smelled of something elemental and enduring.

"I liked Mr. Miller," Eliza announced suddenly, skipping ahead of them. "He knows all about the lighthouse. Can we go see it being built, Mama? Please?"

"We'll see," Jesse replied.

Their path took them past Christ Church, standing serene among ancient oaks draped with Spanish moss. The white clapboard building, with its simple steeple pointing heavenward, had survived the war intact—one of the few structures the Federal troops had spared when they burned the plantations.

Jesse paused. "Let's rest here for a moment," she suggested, nodding toward a wooden bench placed beneath one of the spreading oaks. "We can eat some of the corn bread Mrs. Patterson gave us."

As the children settled onto the bench, Jesse unwrapped the corn bread and broke it into pieces. The church door stood open, inviting in the spring breeze. Through it, she could see gleaming wooden pews and light streaming through clear glass windows.

"Your first visit to our church?" a voice inquired, startling Jesse from her thoughts.

A man in clerical dress had approached from the direction of a cottage visible behind the church. He was of middle years, with kind eyes and the weathered complexion of an islander.

"Yes," Jesse admitted, rising from the bench. "We were resting on our way home from the village."

"You are most welcome to rest here," the man assured her with a gentle smile. "I am Pastor David Willoughby. And you must be Mrs. Whitmore and her children."

"Yes," Jesse replied, unable to keep a note of wariness from her voice.

If Pastor Willoughby noticed her reticence, he gave no sign. He addressed the children with genuine warmth. "And what are your names, young ones?"

"I'm Daniel Whitmore, sir. And this is my sister, Eliza."

"Splendid names, both," the pastor said approvingly. "Daniel was a man of great courage and faith, you know. And Eliza means 'consecrated to God.'"

"Mama says it means I was a gift," Eliza piped up, wiping crumbs from her mouth.

Pastor Willoughby's smile deepened. "Your mama is quite right. All children are gifts from the Almighty." He turned back to Jesse. "We hold services each Sunday at ten o'clock. You would be most welcome to join our congregation. It's small but faithful."

Jesse hesitated. Church attendance had once been a cornerstone of her life, but in Richmond, after her marriage soured, the Sunday service had become yet another performance—another public space where she was required to maintain the façade of a respectable wife while nursing hidden wounds.

"Thank you for the invitation," she said. "We are still settling in."

"Of course." The pastor nodded. "There is no hurry. God's house stands open whenever you are ready to enter."

A bell sounded from the direction of the village—not the church bell, but a deeper, more resonant tone that carried across the island.

"Ah, the shipyard bell," Pastor Willoughby explained. "Signals the midday meal break for the workers. They're building a schooner there—the first vessel of size constructed on Saint Simons since before the war."

"The island seems to be recovering well," Jesse observed.

"In some ways," the pastor agreed. "The tides rise and fall, the egrets fish in the marshes. But the war changed much. Old orders collapsed, and new arrangements struggle to take root."

His tone reminded Jesse of the tension she had witnessed outside Thatcher's store. "You're speaking of the lighthouse project?"

"You're perceptive, Mrs. Whitmore. Yes, BluffLight has become something of a symbol here—of progress to some, of unwelcome change to others."

"And which side do you favor, Pastor?"

"I stand with the light," he said simply. "In all its forms." He glanced toward the church. "Will you come inside for a moment? There's something I think might interest you."

Curiosity overcame caution, and Jesse nodded. "Children, stay here on the bench where I can see you," she instructed. "Finish your corn bread."

Inside, the church was cool and hushed, with sunlight filtering through plain glass windows to reveal polished wood and whitewashed walls. Unlike the ornate Episcopal church Jesse had attended in Richmond, Christ Church was austere in its beauty, built for worship rather than display.

Pastor Willoughby led her to the front of the nave, where an open Bible lay on a wooden lectern. "Our text for this Sunday's sermon," he explained, indicating the marked passage.

Jesse leaned forward to read the highlighted verse from the Gospel of Matthew: *"Let your light so shine before men, that they may see your good works, and glorify your Father which is in heaven."*

"A fitting passage for a community building a lighthouse," she observed.

"Indeed." The pastor paused. "But the light Christ speaks of is not built of stone and brick, Mrs. Whitmore. It shines from within."

Jesse said nothing. The words cut closer than she would have liked.

"Some darkness cannot be so easily dispelled, Pastor," she said.

"No," he agreed. "But darkness has never yet put out a flame."

Before Jesse could respond, the church door creaked open wider, admitting a shaft of brighter sunlight. Daniel stood in the doorway.

"Mama," he called. "Eliza's chasing a butterfly again. She's going toward the cemetery."

"Excuse me, Pastor," Jesse said hurriedly. "Thank you for your hospitality."

As she stepped back into the sunlight and hurried to collect her daughter from among the weathered gravestones, she could still see the pastor's kind eyes, the open Bible on the lectern. They resumed their journey home, Eliza chattering excitedly about the orange butterfly that had led her on a merry chase among the tombstones.

By the time they reached Marsh Cottage, the midday heat had given way to afternoon shadows. Jesse set the children to their respective tasks—Daniel to bring in kindling for the evening fire, Eliza to arrange the wildflowers she had gathered along the way in a jar of water—while she unpacked their purchases.

As she worked, her thoughts kept returning to Demarest's insinuation. "Knowledge that can be bought and sold." And the way Bellamy had looked away when he said it.

Through the eastern window, Jesse could make out the distant shape of BluffLight's unfinished tower, silhouetted against the afternoon sky.

As she placed the newly purchased candles in their holders, the verse from the church lectern came back to her. *"Let your light so shine before men, that they may see your good works."*

As Jesse moved about the cottage, preparing their simple evening meal, she began to hum softly.

Outside, the island's evening chorus began—frogs in the marshes, nightbirds in the forest, the distant rhythm of waves against the shore. And somewhere to the north, perhaps men were lighting lanterns at the construction site, working into the gathering dusk to raise BluffLight another few inches toward the sky.

"Mama," Eliza called from the doorway, "come see! The sun is turning everything gold!"

Setting aside her work, Jesse joined her daughter on the porch. The late afternoon sunlight slanted through the trees, transforming the ordinary landscape into something rare. Golden light spilled across the clearing, caught in Eliza's blonde curls, and gleamed on the tabby walls of their modest cottage.

The marsh had turned to molten brass, glinting off still water and catching in the fronds of palmetto. Frogs croaked in a slow harmony, and a pair of dragonflies danced above the surface of a puddle.

Jesse let her eyes fall half-closed, absorbing it all—the hum of life, the breath of the sea on the breeze, the subtle scent of crushed pine needles beneath the porch boards.

"It's beautiful," Jesse agreed, putting an arm around her daughter's shoulders.

Behind them, in the cottage doorway, Daniel appeared with an armful of kindling. "Ready for the fire, Mama," he announced.

Jesse gathered Eliza close for one more moment, then turned back to the cottage.

# CHAPTER THREE

## A Glance from the Past
*The Saturday Market, Saint Simons Village—May 3, 1873*
*(Two weeks later)*

A breeze off the harbor stirred Jesse's bonnet as she stepped onto the village green. Canvas awnings flapped overhead, and the smell of strawberries and fish mingled in the warming air. The Saturday market sprawled across the green, a patchwork of booths and makeshift tables laden with the island's bounty. Jesse kept to the edges of the crowd, steering wide of clusters where conversation might trap her. Eliza skipped alongside her, occasionally reaching out to touch a bolt of cloth or a basket of shells with curious fingers. Daniel walked a few paces ahead, carrying the basket that would soon be filled with their purchases.

Twice weekly now, they ventured to the village—once for market day when the church bells marked ten o'clock, once for Sunday service at Christ Church, where they arrived just before the bell and departed immediately after the benediction. Otherwise, they kept mainly to Marsh Cottage and its immediate surroundings, where Jesse had begun a modest garden with seeds provided by Miss Haskins.

"Good morning, Mrs. Whitmore," called Mrs. Patterson from her stall where she sold eggs, honey, and hand-knit scarves. The widow had proven to be a reserved but reliable neighbor, occasionally stopping by Marsh Cottage with excess produce from her own garden. "Got some fresh strawberries today. First of the season."

"How lovely," Jesse replied, examining the ruby-red berries with appreciation. "We'll take a pint, please."

As Mrs. Patterson measured the berries into a paper cone, Jesse surveyed the market. It had grown livelier with the warming weather, attracting not just islanders but visitors from the mainland who came by ferry for the day. Most were there for commerce, but near the harbormaster's shed, two men stood with their hands in their pockets, watching the crowd rather than the wares. One of them glanced toward her, and Jesse looked away first.

She had seen no one she recognized, yet her fingers tightened on her coin purse. William had connections, resources, a temper that would not abide defiance. She had stolen away his son and heir, after all. His pride, if not his heart, would demand their return.

"That'll be fifteen cents," Mrs. Patterson said.

As Jesse counted out the coins, a ripple of interest passed through the crowd near the village green. She glanced up to see what had caught their attention.

A tall man in a captain's coat stood conversing with several fishermen near the harbormaster's shed. His back was to Jesse, but his bearing sent a cold wave through her body.

It couldn't be William, and yet...

"Mama?" Daniel was tugging at her sleeve. "Mama, are you well? You've gone white."

Jesse forced herself to breathe, to focus on her son's concerned face. "I'm fine, darling. Just a momentary dizziness." She turned back to Mrs. Patterson, who was watching her with shrewd eyes. "The heat, I suppose."

"Happens to all newcomers," the older woman replied, though her tone suggested she didn't quite believe this explanation. "Best get yourself to shade. There's a bench under the oak by the churchyard."

"Thank you. I think we will."

Jesse gathered Eliza's hand and directed Daniel toward the massive live oak that dominated the edge of the green. Her legs trembled, her mouth dry. *Don't run. Don't draw attention. Observe first, then decide.*

Once they reached the bench, she seated herself with Eliza beside her, positioning herself so she could watch the harbor area without being obvious. Daniel remained standing, his young face troubled as he looked from his mother to the man who had caused her distress.

"Is it him?" he asked, his question too steady for a boy his age.

"I cannot see his face. But something in his manner..."

The captain turned then, laughing at something one of the fishermen had said, and Jesse's breath released. It was not William. Beyond the similar build and bearing, this man bore no resemblance to her husband. His face was tanned and lined by years at sea, framed by a neatly trimmed beard with hints of gray. There was nothing of William's cold precision in his easy movements, nothing of his calculated charm in the honest laugh that carried across the green.

"Not him," she whispered. Heat rose in her cheeks.

Her hands were still trembling. She pressed them flat against her skirt, willing the shaking to stop. Her breath came in deliberate measures—in through the nose, out through the mouth—the way she had taught herself during the worst nights in Richmond. The false alarm had cost her more than she wanted to admit. Even now, her pulse refused to slow, her body still braced for flight though the threat had dissolved into a stranger's laugh. This was the tax of constant vigilance: exhaustion that accumulated in the bones, never fully discharged.

She had nearly fled the market over a stranger's silhouette.

The boy's shoulders relaxed, but his eyes remained watchful. "Should we go home now?"

Their list of needed supplies remained largely unfilled, and such an abrupt departure might draw exactly the kind of notice she sought to avoid.

"No. We'll finish our shopping first. But stay close."

She was about to rise when she noticed Jonas Miller making his way across the green, moving with his characteristic slight limp. He nodded to various islanders as he passed, pausing occasionally for brief exchanges, but his path led directly toward them. Jesse wondered if their obvious retreat to the bench had caught his attention.

"Mrs. Whitmore," he greeted her, removing his hat. The spring sunlight caught in his dark hair, highlighting threads of silver at the temples. "I hoped I might find you here today. Miss Haskins mentioned you were in need of work."

Jesse straightened on the bench. "I... yes, I have been considering seeking employment. But I'm afraid my skills are limited to those typically taught to ladies of middling circumstance. Sewing, basic accounting, household management. Nothing that would be of use to a lighthouse builder, I imagine."

Miller smiled, the expression warming his typically serious face. "On the contrary. The lighthouse project requires considerable organization and record-keeping. Supplies must be ordered, inventories maintained, correspondence handled with various officials and suppliers. I find these tasks consume time I would rather spend on the actual construction."

Jesse hesitated. The position would place her at the center of an island dispute she did not fully understand, and in regular contact with Miller himself.

"The hours would not be demanding," Miller continued. "The office is a building near the construction site—not far from your cottage, in fact. Three days each week would be sufficient, and you could bring your daughter if needed." He paused. "Daniel, I understand, has begun attending Miss Jenkins's lessons at the church hall. Your son shows promise, I'm told—especially in mathematics."

This was true. After much deliberation, Jesse had enrolled Daniel in lessons with Miss Jenkins, recognizing his need for education that exceeded what she could provide. Eliza, however, remained her constant shadow.

"It's very kind of you to consider me," Jesse said. "But I'd rather not place myself in the middle of any island disagreements. I understand there are... differing opinions about the lighthouse project."

Miller's expression grew more serious. "There are those who oppose progress in any form, Mrs. Whitmore. Particularly when it threatens certain... established interests. But BluffLight will be built. My father began this work before the war, and I mean to see it completed."

Jesse's hands stilled in her lap.

"May I consider your offer?" she asked. "It would be a significant change for us."

"Of course." Miller reached into his coat and produced a leather-bound book. "In the meantime, I thought your son might have an interest in this. It belonged to my father—his journal from when he first came to the island to survey the lighthouse site."

Daniel's eyes widened as Miller extended the book toward him. The boy looked to his mother for permission before accepting it.

"That's very thoughtful," Jesse said, surprised by the gesture. "You're certain you wish to part with it?"

"It's merely a loan. Though he kept several journals, this one covers the early planning stages of BluffLight. There are drawings and observations that might interest an inquiring mind." His gaze shifted to Daniel with genuine respect. "Miss Jenkins tells me you have a particular aptitude for mathematics and draftsmanship."

Daniel stood a little straighter, clutching the journal. "Thank you, sir. I'll take great care of it."

"I'm certain you will." Miller turned his attention back to Jesse. "The lighthouse office is the tabby building just north of the construction site. Should you decide to accept my offer, you can find me there most mornings."

Eliza, who had been examining a caterpillar on the bench arm, looked up suddenly. "Mr. Miller, how many bricks are in the lighthouse?"

Miller's serious face transformed—the lines around his eyes softening, a warmth entering his expression that Jesse had not seen before. He crouched down to Eliza's level, and Jesse watched him wince as his injured leg bent beneath him. He shifted his weight quickly, trying to mask the discomfort, but not before she noticed.

"That's an excellent question," he said, his voice patient in a way that William's had never been with children. William had tolerated Daniel and Eliza as extensions of himself, props in the performance of respectable family life. He had never knelt to meet their eyes. "We've used nearly twelve thousand bricks so far, and we'll need perhaps eight thousand more before the tower is complete."

"That's a lot of bricks," Eliza said solemnly.

"It certainly is." Miller smiled—a real smile that creased the weathered skin around his eyes and made him look younger, less burdened. "Each one placed by hand, one at a time."

His eyes lifted to meet Jesse's, and for a moment neither spoke. She saw curiosity there, and something that might have been respect. She looked away first.

Miller rose, his hand briefly pressing his thigh where the old injury troubled him. "I should let you continue your shopping. Good day, Mrs. Whitmore. Daniel. Miss Eliza."

With that, he tipped his hat and took his leave, moving through the market crowd with the same purposeful stride that characterized all his actions.

Eliza tugged at Jesse's sleeve. "Can I come too, Mama? To the lighthouse office? I want to see how tall it is now."

"We haven't decided yet, dear," Jesse reminded her. The work would be manageable, the walk short, and the income needed. It was the visibility that concerned her—placing herself in a position where she would inevitably become more known to the islanders, more fixed in their awareness.

Daniel was already leafing through the journal, his expression rapt. "Look, Mama," he said, turning the book to show her a detailed sketch of the lighthouse foundation, with measurements and calculations neatly noted alongside. "Mr. Miller's father was an engineer. Like my... like Papa was before the war."

William had indeed been trained as an engineer, had overseen the construction of bridges and rail lines for the Confederacy. She remembered his drawings spread across the parlor table, the precision of his hand, the same hand that had left bruises beneath her sleeves.

"Yes," she said simply. "Shall we continue our shopping? I still need salt and thread."

As they moved back into the bustle of the market, Jesse found her thoughts divided between practical concerns and the unexpected job offer. It was time to establish themselves more firmly, to build something beyond mere survival.

They were passing a stall selling handcrafted wooden items when a voice called out from behind them—a voice that made Jesse freeze mid-step.

"Mrs. Whitmore! A moment if you please."

She turned slowly, arranging her face into polite inquiry. The man who approached was the bearded captain she had observed earlier. Her jaw tightened, her breath snagging high in her throat.

"Captain Silas Roarke," he introduced himself with a slight bow. His accent carried the liquid cadence of the coastal South, but with an underlying hardness. "I understand you're new to our island."

As he spoke, a young fisherman passed nearby and touched his cap respectfully. "Morning, Captain." An older woman at the nearest stall—the one selling rope and nets—nodded to Roarke with the deference of someone who owed him more than courtesy. Jesse noted it: the web of obligation that surrounded this man, the small gestures of those who depended on his patronage or feared his displeasure.

"Yes," Jesse replied, keeping her tone neutral while placing herself subtly between the captain and her children. "We arrived last month."

"From Virginia, I'm told." Roarke's eyes were keen beneath heavy brows, assessing her with an intensity that made her skin prickle. "I do business in Richmond occasionally. Perhaps I knew your late husband?"

Jesse kept her voice even. "I doubt it. My husband was not involved in maritime matters. He was an engineer with the Confederate Corps of Engineers during the war and afterward worked primarily with rail construction until his passing."

Roarke studied her face a moment longer, then smiled. The expression did not reach his eyes.

"Engineers are valuable men," he observed. "They understand how things work, how they can be built—or taken apart." He glanced toward the northern end of the island, where the lighthouse stood partially constructed. "Your neighbor Miller fancies himself one, though without formal training. More determination than skill, I'd say."

The contempt in his voice when speaking of Jonas Miller—thinly veiled by false civility—made Jesse want to defend the man. She held her tongue.

"I couldn't say," she replied. "We've had limited interaction with our neighbors thus far. Now, if you'll excuse us, Captain Roarke, we must complete our errands before the heat of the day."

"Of course." He stepped aside with exaggerated courtesy. "Welcome to Saint Simons, Mrs. Whitmore. I'm sure we'll have opportunity to become better acquainted."

She had heard that tone from William countless times. The promise wrapped in pleasantry.

"Good day, Captain," she said firmly, guiding her children away with a hand on each shoulder.

They completed their shopping in tense silence, Jesse acutely aware of Roarke's occasional presence at the periphery of her vision as he moved through the market. He made no further approach, but his initial interest had been plain enough to concern her.

Only when they were well away from the village, following the sandy track back toward Marsh Cottage, did Jesse allow her rigid posture to relax somewhat.

"I don't like that man," Daniel declared, breaking the silence. "He reminds me of—"

"I know," Jesse interrupted softly. There was nothing physically similar between William Whitmore and Captain Roarke, yet they shared something essential—that watchful stillness she had learned to fear.

"Is he a bad man, Mama?" Eliza asked, her face pinched with worry.

Jesse considered how to answer. She had promised herself not to lie to her children more than absolutely necessary for their safety. "I don't know him well enough to say. But it's always wise to be cautious around people until you understand their character."

She had sensed, even from her first day at the market, that certain men on the island did not move in easy harmony with one another. She remembered Demarest—the wealthy man whose practiced smoothness she already distrusted—and his comment about waters that should remain "navigable only to those with specialized knowledge."

Could Roarke be among those opposed to the lighthouse? His dismissive remarks about Mr. Miller's engineering abilities suggested as much. Jesse's steps slowed. A lighthouse would be unwelcome to anyone who profited from dark waters and unmarked channels.

"Mama, look!" Eliza's excited cry broke into Jesse's troubled thoughts. The child had darted ahead to where the path curved around a stand of palmettos and now stood pointing toward the marsh. "In the water!"

Jesse hurried forward, alarmed at her daughter's proximity to the marshy edge where solid ground gave way to mud and shallow pools. But Eliza wasn't in danger—she was transfixed by the sight of a large, gray form moving slowly through the water about thirty yards from shore.

"A manatee," Jesse breathed, recognizing the gentle creature from descriptions she had read. "How wonderful."

The sea cow surfaced briefly, its whiskered snout emerging just enough to draw breath before it submerged again, leaving barely a ripple on the water's surface. Eliza clapped her hands in delight. Jesse watched the creature glide through the shallows, unhurried, undisturbed. Something in her shoulders loosened.

"They're rare here," Daniel said, joining them at the marsh's edge. "Mr. Lawrence told me they sometimes come into the warmer waters in spring, but most people never see them."

As the manatee disappeared from view, Jesse found herself humming—a fragment of Chopin's Nocturne in E-flat major that her fingers still remembered from years of lessons. Music had been her refuge long before William, the piano her confidante when words failed. Sometimes, late at night, when the children slept, she would silently position her fingers on the wooden table, playing phantom melodies that only she could hear. Perhaps someday, when the cottage was truly theirs, a piano might find its way home. Until then, her silent playing would suffice.

"Do you think it's a sign, Mama?" Eliza asked, her eyes still following the barely visible shape as it moved further into the marsh. "Pastor Willoughby says God sometimes sends signs to guide us."

"Perhaps," Jesse allowed, surprising herself with the admission. "What do you think it means?"

Eliza considered this, her brow furrowed. "I think it means we should be like the manatee. Peaceful and minding our own business." She paused, then added with a child's perfect logic: "But we shouldn't eat seagrass. That would be yucky."

Jesse laughed, the sound startling in its genuine mirth. "Very wise advice, my love."

They watched until the manatee slipped from sight, then continued home. Jesse's thoughts drifted back to Miller's offer. Perhaps Daniel was right about Captain Roarke. Perhaps the lighthouse stirred something in men that had little to do with commerce or safety.

And yet, as Marsh Cottage came into view, its tabby walls gleaming in the midday sun, Jesse found a curious resolve forming. Her eyes caught on the distant framework of BluffLight, visible above the tree line. In Richmond, she had made herself small— smaller each year, hoping to slip beneath William's notice, to give his anger nothing to grip. His anger found her, no matter how small she tried to make herself.

"Daniel," she said as they reached the cottage door, "what do you think of Mr. Miller's offer—the position at the lighthouse office?"

The boy looked up from the journal he had been carrying with reverent care. "I think you should accept it, Mama. The lighthouse is important. Even Mr. Miller's father thought so." He tapped the journal's leather cover. "And we need the money, don't we?"

Jesse smiled at his directness. "Yes. We do. And you, Eliza? Would you mind spending time at the lighthouse office while Daniel is at school?"

Her daughter tilted her head, considering. "Will I get to climb the tower? And see the big glass that makes the light go far?"

"I imagine that might be arranged, with proper supervision," Jesse replied.

"Then I think you should say yes," Eliza declared. "And we should avoid the captain with the scratchy beard."

Jesse unlocked the cottage door, ushering her children inside. "Sound advice, my dear. Now, who will help me wash these strawberries for our midday meal?"

As evening shadows lengthened across the bluff, Jesse stood at the kitchen window, watching the sky deepen from gold to violet. She would give Miller her answer on Sunday, after church. Yes to the position, but with her own conditions about the children's safety. Yes to learning whatever the keeper's work required.

# CHAPTER FOUR

## Quiet Resistance
*The Lighthouse Office, Eastern Bluff—May 6, 1873*
*(Three days later)*

T he lighthouse office sat thirty yards from the construction site—a squat tabby building with a door that faced away from the water. Jesse counted its two windows, its single door. Work here would keep them fed. Work here would make her known. The morning air carried the mingled scents of salt marsh and fresh-cut pine. The hammers rang out in steady rhythm, the workers calling to one another in the easy cadence of men accustomed to shared labor. Somewhere behind the scaffolding, a man laughed—a deep belly sound that reminded her this was honest work, not smoke and secrets.

"Remember what we discussed," Jesse said to Eliza, who skipped alongside her, a slate and chalk in her hands. "You must occupy yourself while I attend to Mr. Miller's records."

"I know, Mama," Eliza replied with the exaggerated patience of a child who has been reminded too often. "I shall practice my letters and draw BluffLight—and I won't smudge a single mark."

Jesse smiled despite her apprehension. Eliza's earnest attempts at solemnity never lasted long, but her intentions were sincere.

They rounded the stand of scrub oaks that partially shielded the office from the construction site, and Jesse paused to take in the scene before her. The lighthouse tower had risen another eight feet since she had last observed it from a distance. Now it stood nearly thirty feet high, its inner brick wall and outer stone facing taking shape in a graceful taper. Scaffolding encircled the structure, where masons worked with practiced precision, each stone fitted to its neighbors. On the ground below, other men prepared mortar or

33

guided oxen hauling more materials from the nearby landing where supplies arrived by boat.

And everywhere, there was Jonas Miller—checking measurements, consulting with the master mason, examining a shipment of materials, his slight limp barely slowing his constant movement through the organized chaos. The workers looked to him with genuine regard—she could see it in the way they straightened when he approached, not from fear but from respect. In Richmond, men had gone silent when William entered, their eyes finding the floor.

"The office is open, Mama," Eliza tugged at Jesse's skirt, pointing to the building where the door stood ajar.

Taking a deep breath, Jesse straightened her shoulders and resumed walking. The decision had been practical, necessary. Yet the voice of caution still whispered that it might prove unwise.

The interior of the lighthouse office was unexpectedly orderly given the magnitude of the project it served. A large desk dominated the single room, its surface covered with neatly stacked papers, ledgers, and rolled blueprints. Shelves lined the walls, holding reference books, models, and sample materials. A table with two chairs stood in one corner, apparently designated for conferences, while a pot-bellied stove occupied another, cold now in the spring warmth but doubtless essential during winter months.

"Good morning, Mrs. Whitmore."

Jesse turned to find Miller entering behind them, carrying an armload of rolled papers. Sun from the doorway caught the dust motes swirling around him, showed the tan line at his collar where his shirt had shielded his neck.

"Mr. Miller," she acknowledged with a polite nod. "As agreed, I've brought Eliza with me. I trust that won't pose difficulties."

"Not at all." His smile, when it came, transformed his usually serious countenance. "In fact, I've prepared for our young guest." He gestured toward the table in the corner, where Jesse now noticed a box containing pencils, paper, and wooden blocks carved into various shapes. "My father kept these in the office for me when I was a boy. Architectural blocks, he called them. For building models."

Eliza's eyes widened with delight. "May I truly use them, sir?"

"Certainly," Miller replied. "Perhaps you might design your own lighthouse while your mother and I discuss the real one."

As Eliza settled happily at the table, Jesse turned her attention back to Miller, who was now spreading blueprints across the desk.

"These are the current plans," he explained without preamble. "The foundation and first twenty feet of the tower are complete. We're working on the next section now—another fifteen feet that will take us to the first interior landing. The greatest challenge is coordinating materials. The cut stone comes from Savannah, the specialty bricks from Charleston, the timber locally, and the ironwork from as far away as Philadelphia."

Jesse studied the plans with interest. The technical drawings reminded her of those William had often brought home in Richmond—complex renderings of bridges and rail junctions that she had learned to understand during the early, happier years of their marriage when he had still valued her mind.

"You maintain correspondence with all these suppliers?" she asked.

"And with the Light-House Board in Washington, the harbormaster's office, various officials whose permissions or allocations we require." Miller ran a hand through his hair. "It's the paperwork that delays us as much as any material shortage. Letters go unanswered, approvals take months, funds arrive late if at all."

Jesse nodded thoughtfully. "Show me your filing system, please. And your ledgers."

Over the next hour, Miller guided her through the administrative aspects of the lighthouse project. His thoroughness impressed her, even as she noted where efficiency might be improved. He thought like an engineer—every detail accounted for, every measurement precise—but his filing lacked the same order. Letters were arranged by date instead of correspondent, invoices recorded but not cross-referenced to payments, supply inventories kept separate from construction schedules.

"I believe I can establish a more streamlined system," she said finally, closing the most recent ledger. "With your permission, I'd like to reorganize the files first, then implement a new method for tracking supplies against construction needs."

Miller's relief was visible. "I'd be most grateful. My father kept everything in order. I've let things grow tangled since his passing."

"Your father seems to have been a remarkable man," Jesse observed, glancing at the framed survey maps on the wall that bore Henry Miller's signature. "Daniel has been reading his journal with great interest."

"He was," Miller agreed, a shadow passing briefly across his features. "He came to Saint Simons in '58 to complete a survey for the Light-House Board. He fell in love with the island and returned in '60 with a commission to build BluffLight. The war interrupted everything, of course. He joined the Confederate Corps of Engineers but continued planning the lighthouse whenever he could. After Appomattox, he came back determined to complete it." His voice softened. "He died before he could see it rise more than a few feet above its foundation."

Miller's hand found the edge of the desk and gripped it. His jaw tightened, and he turned toward the window—a deliberate movement, giving himself a moment. When he spoke again, his voice had roughened.

"Some mornings I still walk to the site expecting to find him there. Checking the mortar mix. Arguing with Gardner about brick placement." He exhaled slowly. "Two years now. You'd think..."

He didn't finish. The sentence hung in the air, incomplete, honest.

Jesse watched him—the set of his shoulders, the way he kept his face turned toward the light so she couldn't see his expression clearly. This was not the composed project manager she had observed at the market. This was a man who had lost his father and was still learning to carry the weight of that absence.

William had never shown grief. Not when his mother died, not when his brother fell at Chancellorsville. He had attended funerals with the same calculated composure he brought to business negotiations, offering condolences as though reading from a script. Jesse had wondered, in those moments, if he felt anything at all— or if feeling had been burned out of him long before she knew him.

Jonas Miller felt. She could see it in the tension of his hands, hear it in the roughness of his voice. He grieved openly, even clumsily, and did not seem ashamed of it.

"And you've taken up his work," Jesse said, not a question but an acknowledgment.

"It was his legacy to the island. To me." Miller's eyes moved to the window, through which the upper portion of the lighthouse was visible. "The war left so much in ruins. He wanted BluffLight to stand as proof that we could still build something that would last."

Miller's hand tightened briefly on the window frame. Jesse followed his gaze to the half-built tower.

"Yet I understand not everyone on the island shares this vision," she said.

Miller's expression grew more guarded. "There are those with interests best served by darkness," he said simply. "Captain Roarke among them."

"I met the captain at the market," Jesse admitted. "He seemed... overly interested in newcomers to the island."

"Roarke misses little that happens here. He presents himself as a successful merchant captain, but his business extends beyond legitimate commerce." Miller paused, choosing his words. "During the war, he ran the blockade. A necessary service then, perhaps. But now..." He shook his head. "Let's just say that a proper lighthouse, with regular keepers following federal regulations, would complicate certain nighttime activities in our waters."

Jesse had suspected as much after their market encounter, but hearing it confirmed sent a chill through her. Men like Roarke—men who built power in shadows and viewed opposition as a personal affront—were too familiar.

"I see," she said. "And his opposition to the lighthouse is... significant?"

"He has influence," Miller acknowledged. "Money speaks loudly in a community still recovering from war. He employs many, directly or indirectly. And those who might stand against him remember what happened to James Worthing."

"Worthing?"

"A young harbor officer who started asking questions about certain shipments last autumn. He was found beaten nearly to death on the north shore. He survived, but left the island as soon as he could travel." Miller's voice had hardened. "No evidence linked Roarke to the attack, naturally. But the message was received."

Jesse's hands clenched in her lap.

"And yet you continue," she observed. "Despite the opposition."

Miller met her gaze directly. "Some things are worth the risk, Mrs. Whitmore. I believe you understand that better than most."

The implication startled her. Did he suspect her circumstances? Had she been less careful than she thought? But before she could formulate a response, they were interrupted by a commotion outside.

"Mr. Miller!" A young worker burst through the door, his face flushed with exertion. "There's trouble at the landing. The stone shipment—Roarke's men say it can't be unloaded today. Some dispute about dock fees."

Miller was on his feet immediately, his expression darkening. "This isn't the first such 'dispute.' Excuse me, Mrs. Whitmore. It seems I must attend to this. Please continue with your assessment of the records. You'll find the tea things in the cabinet by the window if you desire refreshment."

After he had gone, striding purposefully toward the shore despite his limp, Jesse sat motionless at the desk.

"Mama?" Eliza's voice broke into her thoughts. "Look what I built!" She proudly displayed a structure of wooden blocks arranged in a rough approximation of a lighthouse.

"Very fine, darling," Jesse praised. "Now, shall we see about that tea Mr. Miller mentioned? And then perhaps I'll show you how these ledgers work."

As they busied themselves with these domestic tasks, Jesse turned over the morning's events. She had wanted only distance. Instead, her choices kept drawing her toward the center of things.

By midday, she had reorganized one set of files and begun sketching plans for a new inventory system. Miller had not returned, suggesting the dispute at the landing was proving difficult to resolve. Eliza had grown restless with her blocks and was now standing at the window, watching the construction activity with undisguised fascination.

"Mama, may I go outside to watch them lift the big stones?" she pleaded. "I'll stay where you can see me from the window."

Jesse hesitated. The construction site was no place for a child, with its heavy materials and precarious scaffolding. But the area immediately surrounding the office was cleared and relatively safe. "You may sit on the bench just outside the door," she conceded. "No further. And if any of the workmen speak to you, you must be polite but reserved."

"Yes, Mama," Eliza agreed, already halfway to the door in her eagerness.

Alone in the office, Jesse moved to the framed maps and surveys that lined one wall. Henry Miller's work showed a methodical mind and a steady hand—qualities his son had clearly inherited. One document in particular caught her eye: a rendering of the completed lighthouse as it would appear when finished, with its lantern room crowning the tapered tower and a keeper's house alongside. It was dated 1860, just before the war that would engulf the South and defer this dream for a decade.

Written in a neat hand at the bottom were words from Matthew: *"Let your light so shine before men, that they may see your good works, and glorify your Father which is in heaven."*

The same verse Pastor Willoughby had chosen for his sermon the Sunday after their arrival. Jesse touched the frame lightly and stepped back.

Her contemplation was interrupted by the office door opening. Expecting Miller's return, she turned with a polite greeting on her lips, only to find herself facing Captain Silas Roarke instead.

He filled the doorway with his substantial presence, his captain's coat immaculate despite the island's omnipresent dust and sand. Behind him, through the open door, Jesse could see Eliza still seated obediently on the bench, though her daughter's posture had gone rigid.

"Mrs. Whitmore," Roarke said, removing his hat with elaborate courtesy. "I heard you'd taken employment with our ambitious lighthouse builder. How... resourceful of you."

Jesse remained seated behind the desk, allowing it to serve as a barrier between them. "Captain Roarke. Mr. Miller is currently at the landing, dealing with some difficulty regarding a stone shipment. Perhaps you have information about that situation?"

A thin smile crossed Roarke's face. "Merely a scheduling confusion. These things happen in commerce. But I didn't come to discuss shipments." He stepped further into the office, his gaze sweeping assessingly over the papers on the desk. "I came to offer you alternative employment."

Jesse kept her expression neutral. "I've only just begun this position, Captain. It would hardly be appropriate to consider another so soon."

"Loyalty is admirable," Roarke acknowledged, "but prudence has its place as well. Miller's project is perpetually underfunded, constantly delayed. How secure is your position if BluffLight stands unfinished for another year? Two years?" He settled uninvited into the chair opposite her. "I, on the other hand, manage several profitable concerns. My offices at Hampton Point require someone with organizational abilities and discretion. The wages would be considerably better than whatever Miller can manage."

Jesse glanced past him to where Eliza sat frozen on the bench.

"You're very kind to consider me," she replied evenly, "but I've given my word to Mr. Miller. I intend to honor that commitment."

Roarke's expression hardened almost imperceptibly. "A widow with two children to support might be expected to weigh circumstances more carefully, Mrs. Whitmore. Especially one who arrived with such... limited means."

"I've found that keeping one's word serves well enough in the long term, Captain," Jesse said, rising from her seat to signal the conversation's end. "Now, if you'll excuse me, I have inventories to reconcile."

Roarke did not immediately stand. Instead, he leaned forward slightly, his voice lowering. "You've chosen a side rather quickly for a newcomer, Mrs. Whitmore. I wonder if you fully understand the... implications of that choice."

Jesse hesitated—the same sensation that had so often preceded William's outbursts. But she was not in Richmond now, not isolated

40

within the walls of a house where neighbors politely ignored the sounds of conflict. She was in a public office, in broad daylight, with witnesses nearby.

"I've chosen employment suited to my skills," she replied coolly. "Nothing more, nothing less. If you have business with Mr. Miller, I suggest you return when he's available."

For a long moment, Roarke held her gaze. Then, with deliberate slowness, he rose to his feet. "I'll do that," he said. "Give him my regards when he returns from his... negotiations. And do reconsider my offer, Mrs. Whitmore. A woman in your position should keep her options open."

With that parting remark, he replaced his hat and exited the office, pausing briefly to touch Eliza's blonde curls in a gesture that made Jesse's blood run cold before continuing toward the path that led away from the construction site.

Once he was out of sight, Jesse rushed outside to gather Eliza into her arms. "Are you all right, darling? Did he say anything to you?"

Eliza shook her head, her body trembling slightly. "He just looked at me, Mama. Like he was remembering my face for later. I didn't like it."

"Nor did I," Jesse murmured, holding her daughter close. If Roarke made inquiries in Richmond, if he discovered that William Whitmore's wife and children were not dead but missing...

She forced herself to breathe slowly, to think instead of react. Roarke might suspect she was not what she claimed, but he had no proof. His interest in her might stem from his opposition to Miller, or perhaps something more personal. Either way, she needed to proceed with greater caution.

"Mrs. Whitmore?" Miller's voice carried from the path. He was approaching from the direction of the landing, his expression troubled. "Is everything all right?"

Jesse released Eliza, straightening to face him. "Captain Roarke paid us a visit in your absence," she said directly. "He offered me alternative employment in his administrative offices."

Miller's face darkened. "Did he indeed? And did this offer come with conditions?"

"Only the implicit one that I leave your service immediately," Jesse replied. "He spoke of your project's uncertain future, suggested my position here was equally uncertain."

"A typical Roarke tactic," Miller said grimly. "Undermine, divide, conquer. I apologize that you were subjected to his attention."

"No apology needed," Jesse assured him. "I declined his offer quite firmly."

A hint of admiration showed in Miller's eyes. "Many would not have, faced with Roarke's methods. Thank you for your loyalty, Mrs. Whitmore."

"It was more than loyalty," she clarified. "I dislike being manipulated, Mr. Miller. Almost as much as I dislike veiled threats."

"He threatened you?" Miller's voice sharpened.

"Not explicitly. But his message was clear enough." Jesse hesitated, then added, "He seems to have been making inquiries about my circumstances. About our arrival on the island."

Miller nodded slowly. "Roarke makes it his business to know everyone's history. It gives him leverage." He studied her face. "Is there anything in yours that concerns you, Mrs. Whitmore?"

The question was direct but not accusatory. Miller was offering an opportunity for openness instead of demanding explanations. For a moment, she was tempted to confide in him—to share the truth of her flight from Richmond, her fear of William's pursuit, her desperate need to protect her children. But years of careful concealment could not be undone in a moment of vulnerability.

"Some stories are better left in their graves," she said, brushing the dust from her skirts. "But I assure you, Mr. Miller, there is nothing in my past that would compromise your project or this island's welfare."

He accepted this, nodding once before changing the subject. "The stone shipment has been released, no thanks to Roarke's harbormaster. We should see it delivered by this afternoon."

Their conversation turned to practical matters then—the progress of the construction, Jesse's proposals for reorganizing the files, the schedule for the coming week. By the time she and Eliza departed for Marsh Cottage in the late afternoon, the morning's fear had loosened its grip.

The path home led past the marsh where they had spotted the manatee days earlier. Today, the water lay still and empty, reflecting the lengthening shadows of cypress trees along its edge. But as they paused to look, a motion caught Jesse's eye—not in the water but along its grassy margin, where a red fox emerged briefly from the tall grass before disappearing again, its russet coat vibrant against the green.

"A fox!" Eliza exclaimed in a hushed voice. "Miss Jenkins says they're shy and clever."

"Indeed they are," Jesse agreed, watching the spot where the creature had vanished.

"Like us?" Eliza asked.

"Yes," Jesse admitted after a moment. "Perhaps a bit like us."

# CHAPTER FIVE

### Storm Memory
*Marsh Cottage—May 24, 1873*
*(Two weeks later)*

T he first storm of summer announced itself with a restless wind that rose just after midnight, rattling the shutters of Marsh Cottage and sending dry leaves skittering across the tabby floor. Jesse woke instantly, her body responding to the change in atmospheric pressure before her mind registered the approaching tempest. Years of vigilance had made her sleep light.

She lay still, listening. The children slept in the loft above, their breathing untroubled by the weather's warning. Outside, the wind continued to strengthen, carrying with it the distinctive scent of rain—clean and electric—that preceded coastal storms.

Rising, Jesse moved to secure the cottage against what was coming. She checked the shutters, making certain each was properly latched, then placed buckets beneath the two spots where the roof had proven less than watertight during previous rains. As she worked, memories stirred—other storms, other nights when wind and rain had provided backdrop to events she would rather forget.

By the time she had finished her preparations, the first heavy drops were striking the cedar-shingled roof with increasing frequency. Jesse lit a candle against the darkness, then settled into the rocking chair near the hearth with her mending basket. Sleep would not return easily now.

The wind intensified, driving rain against the eastern windows in sheets. A low rumble of thunder rolled across the island, still distant but drawing nearer. Jesse's hands stilled on her mending as she counted under her breath, measuring the distance the way she had as a girl: one, two, three...

The storm's fury awakened something in Marsh Cottage itself. As thunder cracked overhead, Jesse could have sworn she heard a woman's voice—distant, mournful—carried on the howling wind that forced its way down the chimney. The cottage had stood for generations, weathering hurricanes and war alike. How many others had sought refuge within these tabby walls? How many had found it? The voice came again—or perhaps it was merely wind finding new paths through ancient cracks—a sound like someone calling a name that was almost, but not quite, her own.

The thunder came again, closer now. Four miles, perhaps less.

A particularly strong gust rattled the door in its frame, and Jesse's heart accelerated. The sound was too familiar—that shaking, that demand for entry. Suddenly she was back in Richmond, three years earlier, listening to a different door shake beneath William's fist.

*"Open this door, Jessica!"* His voice, distorted by rage and whiskey, had been almost unrecognizable. *"Open it now, or I swear I'll break it down!"*

She had stood on the other side, one hand pressed against Daniel's mouth to keep him silent, the other gripping the key she had thought to have made in secret. The bedroom door was oak, solid enough to withstand initial assault, but she had no illusions about its permanence. William was strong, made stronger by his fury, and the door would eventually yield.

But she had needed only enough time for the laudanum to take effect—the sedative she had slipped into his after-dinner brandy after seeing that dangerous stillness come over him at supper.

Lightning flashed outside Marsh Cottage, and Jesse blinked against the brightness, her hands still gripping her mending. The rocking chair beneath her. The tabby walls. The smell of salt marsh, not Richmond coal smoke. She inhaled once, deeply, until the trembling eased. Saint Simons. The storm outside was only weather.

Another crash of thunder, almost directly overhead now, sent reverberations through the cottage walls. From the loft came the sound of stirring, followed by a frightened whimper.

"Mama?" Eliza's voice, small and uncertain.

"I'm here, darling." Jesse set aside her mending. "Just a summer storm passing through. Nothing to fear."

But she heard light footsteps on the ladder, and moments later Eliza appeared, her nightgown rumpled and her blonde curls in disarray. The child's eyes were wide, reflecting the candlelight as she moved quickly to her mother's side.

"It's angry," she whispered, pressing against Jesse's knees. "The storm is angry like—"

She stopped. The unfinished comparison hung between them. Even at six, Eliza understood there were things better left unsaid.

"Not angry, love," Jesse corrected gently, lifting her daughter onto her lap. "Just powerful. The warm air and the cool air meet, and neither wishes to yield. But there's no malice in it, only natural forces finding their balance."

As if to contradict her reassurance, lightning struck nearby with a deafening crack, followed immediately by thunder that shook the very foundation of the cottage. Eliza buried her face against Jesse's shoulder with a small cry.

"It's all right," Jesse soothed, stroking her daughter's tangled hair. "We're safe here. The cottage has weathered many such storms."

"Is Daniel afraid too?" Eliza asked, her voice muffled.

"I expect he's still sleeping soundly," Jesse replied. But Daniel rarely slept through storms anymore, not since Richmond. He only pretended, as if silence could keep them safe. "Would you like to check on him?"

Eliza shook her head, clinging tighter as another thunderclap boomed overhead. "Stay with you."

"Very well." Jesse shifted the child more comfortably on her lap and began to rock slowly, humming an old lullaby her own mother had sung during storms.

But the storm was relentless, its fury seeming to focus directly above Marsh Cottage. Rain lashed the windows, wind howled through the chimney, and lightning flashed with such frequency that the room was more often light than dark.

Rain like this, that other night—the night that had finally broken her resolve to endure, to maintain appearances, to protect the family name at all costs. Thunder providing convenient cover for the sounds from the master bedroom that the servants pretended not to hear.

William had returned from his club earlier than expected, his mood already simmering. Something had provoked him—a business setback, a perceived slight. Jesse had learned not to inquire, as questions only provided targets. Instead, she had instructed the cook to serve his favorite dish and sent the children to the nursery.

But her precautions had proven insufficient. The anger had continued to build throughout the evening meal, each of William's movements becoming more controlled, more precise—a warning sign she recognized. By the time they retired to the parlor, she knew what was coming.

The first blow had been almost a relief—the culmination of hours of dreadful anticipation. She had learned to move with it instead of against it, to let her body absorb the impact rather than resist it.

But that night had been different. That night, Daniel had appeared in the doorway just as William's hand connected with her cheek, sending her staggering against the marble mantelpiece. Her son had frozen there, ten years old and suddenly witness to what she had spent years concealing from him. Their eyes had met over William's shoulder—her own filled with shame and desperate apology, Daniel's with shock that transformed rapidly to something harder, older than his years.

"Go back to the nursery," she had managed to say, her voice steady despite everything. "Go now, Daniel."

But William had turned, following her gaze to their son's rigid figure. "Stay where you are," he had countermanded, his tone conversational, reasonable. "It's time you learned how a man maintains order in his household."

And in that moment, seeing her husband turn his attention toward their child, Jesse's spine straightened. Her breath steadied. Her hands, which had been raised to shield her face, lowered to her sides and unclenched. The decision was made—visible in her body

47

before her mind had fully formed the words. They would leave. Tonight. Whatever the cost.

A particularly violent gust of wind shook Marsh Cottage. Jesse blinked, felt the weight of Eliza sleeping in her arms, saw the candle burning lower on the table beside her. The tabby walls. The rain drumming on the roof. The present.

She drew a shaky breath. As thunder continued to roll across the island, Jesse tightened her hold on her sleeping daughter.

A soft creak on the loft ladder announced Daniel's descent. He appeared at the bottom, his expression solemn in the candlelight. His eyes moved first to the shuttered windows, then to the door, then to the darker corners of the room—a systematic sweep Jesse recognized. He positioned himself at the base of the ladder where he could see both the door and the window, his back to the wall, his body angled to move in either direction. The posture of a boy who had learned to anticipate.

"Is she asleep?" he asked, nodding toward his sister.

"Yes. The storm frightened her."

Daniel moved to sit on the floor beside the rocking chair, leaning slightly against his mother's skirts. At ten, he was increasingly conscious of his role as the man of the family, a burden Jesse wished he didn't feel compelled to carry.

"It's a bad one," he observed as another flash of lightning lit the cottage interior. "Worse than the storms in Richmond."

"Different," Jesse corrected gently. "Coastal storms have their own character. They move differently, speak with different voices." She paused. "Not everything that seems familiar is the same, Daniel."

Her son glanced up at her, understanding the subtext. "I know, Mama. This isn't like... before."

They sat in silence for a while, listening to the storm's gradual movement away from the island, the thunder becoming more distant, the rain settling into a steady pattern instead of violent downpours. Eliza slept on, her breathing deep and even.

"I've been reading Henry Miller's journal," Daniel said finally. "About building the lighthouse."

"Is it interesting?"

Daniel nodded. "He describes a storm worse than this one. It came while they were surveying the bluff. The waves were so high they almost reached the top, and the wind bent pine trees almost to the ground." He glanced toward the window. "He wrote that he knew then that the lighthouse was necessary, that it would save lives if it stood strong against such storms."

"Mr. Miller seems determined to fulfill his father's vision."

"He is," Daniel agreed. "The journal says a lighthouse keeper must be someone who doesn't fear the storm but respects it. Someone who understands that light is most important when darkness is strongest."

Jesse let the words settle. She thought of Jonas Miller as she had seen him that first day at the construction site—steady in the wind, patient with his workers, carrying his father's unfinished work without complaint. The kind of man who stood in weather rather than fled from it.

Lightning flashed again, more distantly now, and in the brief illumination, Jesse caught sight of something she hadn't noticed before—a sheet of paper on the table near the door. Eliza's drawing, left there before bedtime.

"Could you bring me your sister's drawing?" she asked Daniel. "I'd like to see what she worked on today."

He retrieved it, his movements deliberate to avoid waking Eliza. "She was drawing all evening," he said, handing the paper to Jesse. "She wouldn't show me until it was finished, but then she fell asleep."

In the candlelight, Jesse examined her daughter's artwork. For a child of six, Eliza showed remarkable attention to detail. The drawing depicted the lighthouse as it would appear when completed—not as it currently stood, half-built and surrounded by scaffolding, but whole and purposeful. A beam of light extended from its lantern room, cutting through storm clouds.

But what caught Jesse's attention most was the group of figures standing at the base of the lighthouse. Three people—herself and the children—facing the storm with the lighthouse protective behind them.

"She sees it as our protector," Jesse murmured.

"Isn't it?" Daniel asked simply.

"Perhaps it is," she conceded finally. "In its way."

Daniel nodded, satisfied with this answer. He sat with her a while longer as the storm's fury diminished to occasional rumbles and steady rain, until his own eyelids drooped.

"Go back to bed," Jesse urged him. "I'll bring Eliza up shortly."

After he had climbed back to the loft, Jesse remained in the rocking chair, her sleeping daughter a warm weight against her chest, the lighthouse drawing resting on her knee. The candle burned lower, its flame occasionally flickering as diminishing gusts found their way down the chimney.

She thought of that night in Richmond, after Daniel had witnessed William's violence for the first time. Waiting until William succumbed to drugged sleep. Gathering the children and only what they could carry. The rain soaking through her cloak as they fled to the home of her mother's oldest friend, Mrs. Eleanor Carrington.

The elderly widow had harbored them in secret, helped Jesse access the inheritance her mother had left in trust—funds William had never been able to touch. And then the necessary fiction: fever, Charleston, a false grave in the Carrington family plot. Bribes to officials. Notices placed in the newspapers.

The journey south. Charleston first, just long enough to establish a paper trail. Then Savannah. Then this remote island where no one would think to look for the supposedly deceased wife and children of William Whitmore, respectable Richmond engineer.

The rain had stopped altogether now, though water still dripped steadily from the eaves outside. Jesse rose, cradling Eliza against her shoulder, and carried her up the narrow ladder to the loft. The girl stirred, murmuring something about the lighthouse, but didn't wake as Jesse laid her on the bed beside her brother's.

"Sleep well," she whispered, smoothing a hand over both children's hair before descending to the main room again.

The storm had left a peculiar stillness in its wake. Jesse extinguished the candle and moved to open the shutters, allowing the first hint of pre-dawn light to filter into the cottage. The air that entered was fresh, cleansed by the storm's passage, carrying the mingled scents of rain-soaked earth, pine, and distant sea.

Far to the north, barely visible against the lightening sky, stood the skeletal frame of BluffLight, apparently undamaged by the night's tempest. A testament to careful building, to foundations properly laid and materials selected for strength. The lighthouse was being constructed to withstand far worse—hurricanes that lashed the coast with deadly force, winter gales that could shatter ships against the shoals.

Henry Miller's journal words, as relayed by Daniel, returned to her: *A lighthouse keeper must be someone who doesn't fear the storm but respects it.*

She stepped to the window. The dawn was still pale, but it had come. And she had weathered the night.

# CHAPTER SIX

## Smoke in the Pines
*The Maritime Forest, Saint Simons Island—May 27, 1873*
*(Three days after the storm)*

Morning fog clung to the pines as Jesse followed the narrow path from Marsh Cottage to the lighthouse construction site. Three days had passed since the storm, and island life had resumed its steady rhythm—birds rebuilding nests damaged by wind, workers returning to the bluff to continue BluffLight's gradual ascent. The masons had resumed work on the inner brick lining while stone cutters prepared granite blocks for the outer facing. Only occasional puddles in low-lying areas suggested the tempest's recent passage.

"Can I collect pine cones today, Mama?" Eliza asked, skipping alongside her mother. The morning was still cool enough to make such exertion pleasant, though the late May sun would soon burn away both fog and comfort.

"You may gather a few, but remember your promise to sit while I finish the correspondence for Mr. Miller." Since accepting the position two weeks earlier, Jesse had established certain rules for Eliza's behavior at the office—necessary compromises that allowed her to work while keeping her daughter close.

"I'll be very good," Eliza assured her earnestly. "And when Daniel comes after school, can we walk to the beach?"

Jesse hesitated. Daniel's lessons with Miss Jenkins ended earlier than her own duties at the lighthouse office, which meant her son often made the journey from the village to the construction site alone—a practice that unsettled her despite the island's relative safety.

"We'll see," she said. "The tide may be too high for safe shore-walking."

As they rounded a bend in the path, the unfinished lighthouse came into view, now standing nearly forty feet tall. Its progress over the past weeks had been steady if not swift, each new layer of stone adding purpose to its emerging form. Jesse watched it rise above the tree line the way Daniel watched it—a structure built in defiance of those who preferred darkness.

The faint sound of hammers carried across the morning air, along with occasional shouts as workers communicated across the scaffolding that encircled the tower. Jonas Miller's figure stood at the base, conferring with the master mason, their heads bent over what was likely a blueprint or diagram.

Jonas had proven to be exactly the kind of employer Jesse had hoped for—respectful of her abilities, appreciative of her contributions, and mindful of the boundaries she had established. He never inquired about her past, though she sometimes caught a look in his eyes that suggested he had drawn his own conclusions. His focus remained on the lighthouse, his father's legacy, and the future it represented for the island.

As they approached the small tabby office building, Jesse noticed an envelope pinned to the door with a brass tack—an unusual sight that made her steps slow. They received correspondence regularly, of course, but it was always delivered to the village post office, never directly to the lighthouse site.

"Wait here a moment, Eliza," she instructed, keeping her voice even. "I need to check something."

The child obediently stopped, distracted by a stand of wildflowers growing at the path's edge. Jesse moved forward alone, removing her gloves as she reached for the envelope. It was plain, unaddressed, secured only by the tack that held it to the wooden door. No official seal or postmark marked its surface.

With steady fingers, Jesse removed the tack and opened the unsealed envelope. Inside was a single sheet of paper bearing three words in a rough, block script:

I SEE YOU.

The note was unsigned. Jesse's hands went cold despite the warming day. How had they been found? Had William somehow traced them to Saint Simons? Or was this something else—perhaps connected to the island politics surrounding the lighthouse, a warning meant for Jonas that she had intercepted?

She glanced over her shoulder. Eliza remained absorbed in the wildflowers, unaware. Jesse folded the note and slipped it into her pocket. Should they flee again? Abandon the cottage, the island, everything they had begun to build here? Her shoulders ached; even her bones felt tired.

"Mrs. Whitmore." Jonas's voice broke into her thoughts. He was approaching from the construction site, his slight limp more pronounced than usual after what had clearly been a morning of active work. "You've arrived early today."

Jesse composed her features. "The children were eager to begin the day. I thought we might organize the supply invoices before the afternoon shipment arrives."

Jonas nodded, his eyes moving over her face in that way of his. "Is everything all right? You seem... concerned."

For a moment, Jesse considered showing him the note, seeking his counsel. But what could he do? If William had found them, no island resident could offer protection sufficient to deter him. And if the note had some other origin, involving Jonas might complicate matters or place him in danger as well.

"Just a small headache," she said. "The changing weather, perhaps."

He accepted this with a nod, though his eyes suggested he was not entirely convinced. "I've left the correspondence from the Light-House Board on your desk. Three letters, actually—one responding to our request for additional funding, though they're offering only half what we requested. Another regarding new specifications for the lamp mechanism from the Lighthouse Service. And a third from the Treasury Department about documentation required for federal inspections."

Jesse unlocked the office door, gesturing for Eliza to join them. As the child ran toward the building, Jonas added in a lower voice, "There have been some... incidents at the construction site. Missing tools, materials disturbed overnight. Nothing serious, but concerning."

"You suspect deliberate interference?"

54

"I suspect Roarke's influence, though nothing can be proven." Jonas's expression darkened. "He seeks to discourage us through a thousand small delays."

The mention of Roarke sent a different chill through Jesse. The captain had made no further direct approach since their encounter in the office, but she occasionally glimpsed him in the village, his gaze following her movements in a way that reminded her too much of William's surveillance. Could the note be from him instead? A warning tied to her present association with the lighthouse, rather than her past?

"We won't be discouraged," she said.

Jonas's expression warmed. "No, Mrs. Whitmore. We certainly won't." He tipped his hat and turned back toward the construction site, where a worker was signaling for his attention.

Once inside the office, Jesse established Eliza at her usual small table with paper and colored pencils, then seated herself at the desk. But the note sat heavy in her pocket. She removed it, studying the crude handwriting for any clue to its author.

If it was from William or someone he had sent, why not be more specific? He had never been one for vague threats—his warnings had always been precise, detailed. This message was different in tone, almost impersonal.

And yet, who else would care that she was hiding? Only someone who knew she had fled.

Jesse folded the note again and tucked it into her desk drawer, forcing her attention to the Light-House Board correspondence. Practical matters required addressing. But as she worked, a plan took shape: maintain their routines outwardly, watch more closely, prepare more thoroughly for genuine danger. No flight. Not yet.

The morning passed in a blur of invoices and requisition forms, letters drafted and documents filed. By midday, when she normally walked with Eliza to meet Daniel at the crossroads where the village path met the shore track, she had managed to convince herself that immediate action was unnecessary. The note might be nothing more than an attempt to frighten.

"Shall we go meet your brother?" she asked Eliza, who had grown restless with her drawing.

"Yes!" the child agreed eagerly, gathering her latest artwork to show Daniel. "Do you think he found any shells at school? Miss Jenkins was going to take them to the shore path during their nature lesson."

"Perhaps he did. We'll ask him."

But Daniel was not at the crossroads when they arrived. Jesse checked her small silver watch—a gift from her mother years ago, one of the few valuables she had taken when they fled Richmond. The school day had ended twenty minutes earlier. Daniel should have reached the meeting point by now.

"Where is he, Mama?" Eliza asked, her initial excitement fading.

"He may have stopped in the village." But a faint unease had begun to build. Daniel was scrupulously punctual, understanding his mother's fear when expectations were not met. "Perhaps Miss Jenkins asked him to help with something after lessons."

They waited fifteen more minutes, Eliza growing increasingly restless. Jesse made a decision. "We'll walk toward the village. We're likely to meet him coming along the path."

They had gone perhaps a quarter-mile when Jesse detected an acrid scent carried on the breeze—smoke, but not the controlled, aromatic smoke of a cooking fire or a pipe. This was sharper, wilder, the smell of pine resin burning. She froze, scanning the forest that lined the path.

A thin column of gray-white smoke rose from among the trees some distance to the west, where a stand of longleaf pines grew particularly dense. Not a major fire, by the look of it, but any flame was cause for concern in the pine forest, especially after several days without rain.

"Eliza, stay on the path," Jesse instructed firmly. "I need to check something."

"Is it Daniel?" Eliza asked, suddenly fearful. "Is he hurt?"

"I'm certain he's fine. But we need to make sure the forest isn't burning. Stay here where I can see you."

She moved toward the source of the smoke, her skirts catching on underbrush as she left the path. The scent grew stronger as she approached, and then another smell reached her—coppery, unmistakable. Blood.

"Daniel!" she called, abandoning caution. "Daniel, are you there?"

A weak cough answered her, followed by her son's voice. "Mama? Here... I'm here."

Jesse rushed forward to find Daniel seated on the ground beside a small, smoldering fire pit. His face was smudged with soot, his school clothes dirty and torn, and most alarmingly, a makeshift bandage fashioned from his handkerchief was wrapped around his right forearm, stained with blood.

"What happened?" she demanded, dropping to her knees beside him. "Who did this?"

"No one, Mama," he said quickly. "It was an accident. I was trying to... to practice making fire like in Mr. Miller's father's journal. For emergencies." He looked down, ashamed. "I didn't do it right. The sparks caught my sleeve, and when I tried to put it out, I fell against that sharp rock."

Jesse examined the wound, unwrapping the crude bandage. The cut wasn't deep, but it was several inches long, running along his forearm where he had apparently scraped it against the jagged edge of a stone. The bleeding had mostly stopped, but the area around the wound was angry and red.

"Oh, Daniel." Relief that he was fundamentally all right mingled with exasperation at the risk he had taken. "This needs proper cleaning and bandaging."

"I know," he admitted. "I was trying to fix it myself before coming to meet you, but it hurt too much to walk very far."

Jesse helped him to his feet, supporting him as they made their way back to where Eliza waited anxiously on the path. As they emerged from the trees, Jonas Miller was approaching rapidly from the direction of the lighthouse, his expression concerned.

"Mrs. Whitmore," he called. "Is everything all right? Your daughter said you went to investigate smoke."

"Daniel has had an accident," Jesse explained, suddenly grateful for Jonas's presence. "Nothing serious, but he'll need medical attention."

Jonas quickly assessed the situation. "Let's get him to Marsh Cottage. We can treat him there. I have a wagon near the construction site—it will be faster than walking. Wait here. I'll bring it."

Jonas returned moments later with the wagon. He lifted Daniel carefully, mindful of the injured arm, and settled him into the back. "You and your daughter ride in the back with him."

The journey to Marsh Cottage passed quickly. Jonas drove the wagon with careful speed along the sandy track, while Jesse sat in the back with both children, maintaining pressure on Daniel's wound with a clean cloth Jonas had provided from his toolkit.

"Almost there," Jonas said as they rounded the final bend and the cottage came into view. "My mother was skilled in treating such injuries. A plantation childhood provides ample opportunity to learn field medicine."

Jesse barely registered his words, her attention fixed on Daniel's pale face. The wound wasn't life-threatening. But her hands wouldn't stop trembling—and not only because her son was hurt. The threatening note. This day of all days.

Was it truly an accident? Or had someone frightened Daniel, caused him to injure himself while fleeing?

Jonas brought the wagon to a halt before the cottage door and helped Jesse get Daniel inside. "Where do you keep your medical supplies?" he asked as they settled the boy on the small settee.

"In the chest beside the hearth," Jesse replied, sending Eliza to fetch fresh water from the well.

With efficient movements, Jonas helped clean and properly bandage the wound, his hands surprisingly gentle for a man accustomed to handling stone and timber. Daniel winced but did not cry out, maintaining the stoic demeanor he had adopted since witnessing William's violence.

"You were fortunate," Jonas told him seriously once the task was complete. "Pine forest fires can spread rapidly. Your quick thinking likely prevented a much worse outcome."

Daniel nodded, his expression a mixture of pain and embarrassment. "I just wanted to learn... to be prepared."

But there was fear beneath the boyish bravado. An urgency that didn't belong to fire-starting lessons. It belonged to the look he'd had the night they left Richmond.

"Prepared for what, Daniel?" she asked.

Her son glanced at Miller, then back to his mother. "In case we had to leave quickly. Like... before."

Jesse's breath caught. Daniel had overheard something, sensed something. Perhaps the note itself, though she had been certain he hadn't seen it. Or maybe it was the way she moved that morning, the undercurrents in her voice.

She looked at her son—really looked—and saw what she had tried not to see. The shoes placed precisely beside his bed each night, toes pointed toward the door. The way he knew exactly where the carpetbag was stored beneath her bed, though she had never told him. The mental map he carried of every exit from every building they entered—she had watched his eyes trace them without understanding what she was seeing. He had been preparing for flight since Richmond. Not consciously, perhaps, but in his bones, in the vigilance that never quite left his young face even in sleep.

Her throat tightened. Her hands, still holding the bloodied cloth, went still.

Daniel was watching her face, reading her the way he read everything—looking for the sign that would tell him whether to relax or run.

"Thank you for your help, Mr. Miller," she said, turning to their unexpected ally. "I don't know how we would have managed without you."

"It was no trouble," he assured her. "I'm just relieved the boy isn't more seriously hurt." He hesitated, then added, "Mrs. Whitmore, if there's anything... that is, if you ever feel unsafe, for any reason..."

The unspoken question hung in the air between them. Jesse considered her response. Jonas had proven himself trustworthy in practical matters, but sharing her deepest fears, her true circumstances, was another matter entirely.

Before she could reply, Eliza approached with Daniel's slate, which she had retrieved from where it had fallen in the forest.

"Look, Mama," she said, pointing to something scratched on its surface. "Daniel found this before he got hurt."

Jesse took the slate, expecting to see one of her son's mathematical calculations or engineering sketches. But what she found were three words inscribed in the same block letters as the note she had discovered that morning:

I SEE YOU.

Jesse went still. Daniel hadn't simply had an accident while practicing wilderness skills. He had found this message—or worse, someone had given it to him—and in his distress had tried to prepare for what he feared was coming: another flight, another desperate escape.

She looked up. Miller was watching her, his expression grave. He had seen the message too.

Something shifted in his bearing. His weight settled forward onto the balls of his feet—a fighter's stance, though his face remained composed. Without seeming to move deliberately, he had positioned himself between Jesse and the cottage door, his body angled toward the window that faced the path.

He didn't ask what the words meant. He didn't demand explanations. He simply stood where a threat would have to pass through him first.

"Mrs. Whitmore," he said, his voice low and even, "I believe it's time we discussed the threats to your family—all of them."

Her careful isolation had cracked. Whatever she said next would shape the kind of safety Daniel and Eliza had—if they had any at all.

# CHAPTER SEVEN

### The Offer on the Bluff
*The Eastern Bluff, Saint Simons Island—May 29, 1873*
*(Two days after Daniel's injury)*

T he eastern bluff caught the first light of dawn, transforming the sandy soil and sparse vegetation to gold. Mist clung to Jesse's face as she stood at its edge, the Atlantic stretching toward the horizon, its surface rippled with gentle swells that caught the morning light like beaten pewter. The air carried the sharp tang of brine mixed with the sweetness of blooming yellow jessamine from the maritime forest behind them. Overhead, brown pelicans glided in formation, dark against the lightening sky.

Behind her rose the skeletal frame of BluffLight, its iron scaffolding creaking in the morning breeze. Beside her stood Jonas Miller, feet planted wide on the uneven ground in a stance that spoke of military bearing despite his civilian clothes. His weathered face turned toward the sea, deep lines carved by sun and salt around eyes that never quite stopped scanning the horizon—a habit, Jesse suspected, from his service days.

They had been standing in silence for several minutes. Below them, the tide was coming in, each wave hissing against the coquina rocks that formed the bluff's foundation. A great blue heron waded through the shallows, its movements deliberate and patient as it hunted breakfast in the receding pools. The bird's reflection wavered in the still water between waves.

"My father stood here often," Jonas said finally, his voice carrying the slight rasp of a man who had shouted orders over cannon fire. "He said the ocean teaches us our proper scale—significant enough to matter, humble enough to know our place."

Jesse nodded. The vast Atlantic had that effect. "It's why I came to the coast," she admitted. "After Richmond, I needed distance."

Jonas shifted his weight, the movement subtle but telling—left leg bearing more burden, the slight hitch in his stance that most wouldn't notice. His hands bore the calluses of both pen and hammer, the nails kept short and clean despite the construction work. A thin scar ran across his left knuckles, pale against his sun-darkened skin.

The wind pulled a lock of hair from her braid, and before she could tuck it back, Jonas reached out and caught it with two fingers, tucking it behind her ear without a word. A man accustomed to storms, steady-handed even with something delicate.

Jesse's breath stopped. The touch had been brief—two heartbeats, perhaps three—but she could still feel the ghost of his fingers against her temple. She looked away before her breath betrayed her, fixing her gaze on the horizon where sky and water blurred into a single pale line.

The morning air grew warmer as the sun climbed higher, bringing with it the distant sound of workers arriving at the construction site—the clatter of tools, the low murmur of voices, the creak of wagon wheels on the sandy path. A mockingbird began its morning repertoire from a nearby live oak.

"Have you thought about my offer?" Jonas asked, turning to face her fully. In the direct light, she could see the squint lines from checking measurements in bright sun, the permanent furrow between his brows from studying blueprints, the weathering that came from standing watch in all conditions.

Jesse turned from the ocean view to study him properly. In the two months since her arrival on Saint Simons, she had grown to respect Jonas Miller's straightforward nature. He spoke without flourish, each word chosen for precision rather than effect—the communication style of a man who had learned that unclear orders cost lives.

"I have," she replied. "Though I still don't understand why you would ask me."

Jonas's offer had been unexpected: to serve as lighthouse keeper once BluffLight was completed. The position would require maintaining the third-order Fresnel lens—cleaning its 168 prisms daily, ensuring the clockwork mechanism that rotated the light completed its revolution every two minutes, trimming the five concentric wicks to prevent carbon buildup, and maintaining the precise oil level that would keep the flame at exactly the right height for optimal magnification through the lens assembly.

"The keeper's primary qualification is reliability," Jonas said, his right hand unconsciously checking the watch in his vest pocket—a gesture Jesse had noticed he repeated precisely every half hour. "The light must burn from sunset to sunrise without fail, every night of the year. The oil reservoirs hold exactly twelve gallons of refined whale oil, which must maintain a flow rate of 2.3 ounces per hour to each wick. Records must document barometric pressure, wind direction and speed, visibility, and every vessel sighted, along with its bearing and estimated distance."

He pulled a small leather notebook from his pocket—worn at the corners, held closed with a length of cord. "See here," he said, showing her pages covered with neat columns of figures. "Temperature affects oil viscosity. In winter, the oil must be preheated to forty-two degrees Fahrenheit to maintain proper flow. Below that, the feeds clog. Above optimal temperature, it burns too quickly, creating soot that dims the light."

Jesse studied the meticulous records, noting how each entry was initialed and time-stamped. "Your father kept similar records?"

"Better ones," Jonas admitted, a note of admiration warming his voice. When discussing his father's work, his shoulders drew back, chin lifted slightly, as if presenting himself for inspection to a man no longer present. "He calculated that BluffLight, once operational, will be visible for twenty nautical miles in clear conditions. The lens will concentrate eighty-seven percent of the flame's light into a beam that sweeps the horizon. Ships approaching from Savannah will pick up our signal before they lose sight of Tybee Island's light."

"And my situation?" Jesse asked. "The risks I bring?"

Jonas's expression shifted—a tightening around his jaw that she recognized as his response to tactical problems. His hand moved to his hip where, she suspected, he had once worn a service weapon. "We all carry risk, Mrs. Whitmore. My determination to complete this lighthouse has earned me powerful enemies. Roarke's men watch our supply shipments, monitor our workers' movements."

He gestured toward the construction site where men were already mixing mortar for the day's work. "Yesterday, they delayed our shipment of iron tie-rods—claimed paperwork irregularities. Cost us six hours of work. The rods are essential; they bind the inner brick wall to the outer stone casing every sixth course. Without them, differential settling could cause the walls to separate during a hurricane."

"Yet the lighthouse rises," Jesse observed.

"Yet it rises," Jonas agreed. "My father began this work because vessels were being lost unnecessarily—twenty-three ships in the decade before the war, four hundred and sixteen souls." His voice carried the weight of those numbers. "He calculated that a light here could prevent seventy percent of those wrecks."

The earnestness in his voice stirred something in Jesse. The lighthouse keeper's position would provide purpose beyond survival. Daniel had been reading about the technical specifications—the clockwork mechanism that required winding every four hours, the delicate balance of the lens assembly that could be disrupted by vibrations as subtle as footsteps on the tower stairs.

"The keeper's cottage," Jonas continued, "should be started now. The federal specifications call for a one-story structure, with eight rooms. A cistern system for collecting rainwater—five-thousand-gallon capacity, lead-lined, with ceramic filters. The oil storage building must be separate, fireproof construction, with capacity for four hundred gallons of winter supply."

He turned to point at a level area near the lighthouse base. "There, thirty yards from the tower. Far enough to avoid any fire risk, close enough for the keeper to reach the light quickly in emergencies. The cottage will have speaking tubes connecting to the tower's watch room. Communication without leaving post during storms."

Jesse considered the practical aspects. "And Roarke? If he is as determined as you suggest..."

Jonas shifted his weight forward. "The keeper's cottage will be visible from the village. Federal inspectors visit quarterly—unannounced. Ship captains pay courtesy calls. The position carries federal authority." He met her gaze directly. "If your former situation ever becomes known, the Light-House Board has significant interest in protecting trained keepers. Federal marshals have jurisdiction here, not local sheriffs."

Jesse understood his meaning. Should William discover she was alive, federal authority would provide protection where local law might not.

Neither spoke for a time. The sun had risen fully now, warming the coquina stone beneath their feet. The morning breeze carried the distant sound of chanties from the dock workers, their rhythm matching the steady pulse of waves against the bluff. A pod of dolphins broke the surface beyond the shoals, their dark backs glistening as they hunted the incoming tide.

"I should return," Jesse said eventually. "Daniel's arm needs tending."

Jonas reached into his coat and withdrew another notebook—this one newer, its pages gilt-edged. "Henry Miller's complete calculations for the lighthouse. Daniel might find them instructive. The mathematical principles behind the Fresnel lens are quite elegant—the curve of each prism calculated to bend light at precisely the correct angle to form a parallel beam."

Their fingers brushed as she accepted the journal. Jonas's hand was warm, roughened by work, and he held the book a moment longer than necessary before releasing it. When Jesse looked up, something had shifted in his expression—a softening around the eyes that made him look younger, less guarded.

She stepped back, feeling the weight of the journal in her hands. "Mr. Miller—Jonas—why me? We are nearly strangers."

For the first time that morning, Jonas smiled—a brief softening of his weathered features that revealed the younger man he might have been before war and loss carved their marks. "I know enough. You arrived with two children and modest means, yet your daughter can identify shore birds by their calls and knows the tides. Your son reads engineering treatises for pleasure and asks questions about load-bearing calculations. You've organized my father's papers better in two months than I managed in two years."

He paused, his hand returning to the watch pocket in an unconscious gesture. "More to the point, you notice things. Every morning, you check sight lines before stepping outside. You note changes—new faces, altered routines. A keeper must possess that awareness."

As they walked back toward the path, Jonas stopped beside a weathered bench his father had built years ago. The wood was silver-gray from salt and sun, worn smooth by seasons of use. "Mrs. Whitmore, I should be clear about one thing more. The position comes with a salary of sixty dollars monthly, plus the cottage and a garden plot. But the true compensation is less tangible."

"How so?"

"Purpose," he said simply. "The knowledge that every night, your light guides souls safely home." He gestured toward the maritime forest where the morning chorus of birds had reached full voice—cardinals, wrens, the liquid notes of a wood thrush. "My father wrote that lighthouse keeping is a calling, not merely employment. It requires someone who understands that darkness must be actively opposed."

Jesse studied his face, seeing in it the reflection of her own hard-won understanding. "When would you need an answer?"

"The cottage construction begins in two weeks. If you accept, I'd like your input on certain design elements—the kitchen arrangement, the children's rooms." He pulled out his pocket watch, checking it with that habitual precision. "Take what time you need, but know this—you'd not be alone in this. The lighthouse community looks after its own."

As she continued along the path alone, Jesse found his words echoing. The morning air was thick with the scent of pine resin and salt marsh. Spanish moss swayed in the breeze, and somewhere in the canopy, a pileated woodpecker hammered its territorial claim.

Marsh Cottage came into view, and she saw Daniel seated on the porch steps, his injured arm carefully supported. His face brightened at her approach—not the unguarded joy of childhood, but the measured relief of a boy who had learned to mark his mother's safe returns.

"Mama!" Eliza burst from the doorway. "Where did you go?"

"Speaking with Mr. Miller about lighthouse business," Jesse replied, gathering her daughter close. The child smelled of sleep and strawberry preserves. "Important business we should discuss."

Later, as they sat around their modest table, Jesse explained the offer. The keeper's cottage would have eight rooms instead of their current two. Running water from the cistern system. Glass windows with storm shutters. A tower room where Daniel could study the stars through the provided telescope—standard equipment for recording weather conditions.

"Would we tend the light every night?" Daniel asked, his eyes bright with interest.

"Every night," Jesse confirmed. "The oil must be carried up one hundred twenty-nine steps. The lens must be cleaned with spirits of wine and chamois cloth. The clockwork requires winding every four hours."

"I could help with the mechanisms," Daniel said eagerly. "Mr. Miller's father's journal explains the governor that regulates rotation speed. It employs the same principles as a clock escapement, but larger."

"What's an escapement?" Eliza asked, tugging at Daniel's sleeve.

Daniel turned to her with the patient expression of an older brother who had explained things many times before. "It's the part of a clock that makes the tick-tick sound. It lets the gears move just a little bit at a time instead of all at once." He held up his hands, demonstrating with his fingers. "Like this—tick, tick, tick. Each tick lets the gear turn one tooth."

"Oh!" Eliza's face lit with understanding. Then, not to be outdone, she added, "I could watch for ships and write their names in the big book!"

"The log," Daniel corrected, but gently, with a half-smile. "It's called the keeper's log."

"I knew that," Eliza said, though she clearly hadn't. "And I'll draw pictures of the ships too. For identification purposes."

Daniel glanced at his mother, his expression caught between amusement and affection. "She'll probably draw them with faces," he said in a low voice.

"I will not!" Eliza protested, having heard. Then, after a moment: "Only the friendly ones."

Jesse watched her children's exchange, seeing in their easy banter something that had been absent in Richmond—the simple comfort of siblings who felt safe enough to tease each other. Daniel's shoulders had relaxed; Eliza's laugh came freely.

"Then we're agreed?" she asked.

"Yes!" Eliza exclaimed, while Daniel nodded with grave approval.

That afternoon, as the children rested, Jesse composed her acceptance:

*Mr. Miller,*

*After careful consideration, I accept the position of lighthouse keeper. My children and I stand ready to undertake these responsibilities with the diligence they require. Please advise regarding preparation and training.*

*Most respectfully, Jessica Whitmore*

As she sealed the note, Jesse glanced through the window toward BluffLight's rising form.

Outside, the red fox appeared at the forest edge—alert, watchful, but no longer retreating at the first sign of movement. It held Jesse's gaze for a long moment before slipping back into the underbrush.

She turned to her work.

# CHAPTER EIGHT

The Keeper's Journal
*Christ Church, Saint Simons Island—June 5, 1873*
*(One week after the offer)*

S unday morning brought a clarity to the air that sharpened every detail of the island landscape—pine needles distinct against sky, Spanish moss in intricate patterns, small wildflowers brightening the path that led from Marsh Cottage to Christ Church. The breeze pressed Jesse's dress against her legs as she walked, Daniel and Eliza keeping pace beside her, all three dressed in their Sunday clothes—modest by Richmond standards but the best of the limited wardrobe they had managed in their hurried flight.

Since accepting Jonas's offer, the days had filled with instruction—three mornings learning to read the barometer, two afternoons reviewing oil flow rates, an evening spent consulting on the keeper's cottage design.

"Do you think Pastor Willoughby will talk about the lighthouse again today?" Eliza asked, skipping slightly in her excitement. The child had embraced the news of their future position with characteristic enthusiasm, already referring to BluffLight as "our lighthouse" in conversations with anyone who would listen.

"Perhaps," Jesse replied with a smile. "He does seem fond of light as a sermon theme."

"I counted," Daniel said. At eleven, he was beginning to develop the studious demeanor of a scholar, his natural intelligence honed by both Miss Jenkins' instruction and his own voracious reading. "Over two hundred times. Miss Jenkins has a concordance."

Jesse gave her son an appreciative glance. Despite the seriousness that life had forced upon him too early, moments like this revealed the curious mind that continued to flourish beneath the protective shell he had built around himself. "You've been counting?"

Daniel shrugged, his injured arm now healing well enough that the sling had been replaced with a simple bandage. "I was curious after last Sunday's sermon."

Their conversation fell into comfortable silence as Christ Church came into view, its white clapboard walls gleaming in the morning sun. The simple steeple pointed skyward, having survived the war that had claimed so many other structures on the island. Around the church, live oaks created a cathedral of their own, their massive branches forming a canopy that dappled the sunlight falling on the weathered gravestones surrounding the building.

Though they had attended services regularly since her conversation with Pastor Willoughby early in their time on the island, wariness still accompanied her into any public space. Her hand moved to her collar, straightening what needed no straightening.

The church doors stood open, releasing the mingled scents of beeswax candles and old wood polish into the morning air. From within came soft murmurs of early arrivals settling into pews— creaking aged pine boards, Sunday dresses whispering against wooden backs, the thump of hymnals being placed on benches.

"Good morning, Mrs. Whitmore," Miss Haskins greeted them at the church steps, her severe expression softened slightly by what passed for a smile on her austere features. The older woman had proven to be a steadfast, if reserved, ally during their months on the island. "Children."

"Miss Haskins," Jesse acknowledged with a polite nod. "A beautiful morning for worship."

"Indeed." The older woman's gaze was shrewd as it rested briefly on Jesse's face. "I understand congratulations are in order. Mr. Miller mentioned your new position."

Miss Haskins had heard from Jonas himself, then—likely at the mercantile, where half the island's business was conducted between the pickle barrels and the bolts of calico. "Thank you. We're honored to accept."

"A fitting choice," Miss Haskins remarked. "The island has lacked a proper lighthouse keeper since Henry Miller's passing. His son has done admirably overseeing the construction, but his talents lie in building instead of maintaining."

Before Jesse could respond, the church bell tolled. Three measured strikes resonated through the morning air, vibrating through the wooden steps beneath their feet. They made their way inside, finding seats in what had become their usual pew—fourth row from the back, left side, near enough to the window to catch the breeze but far enough from the door to avoid drafts.

The interior of Christ Church was cool and hushed, the morning humidity held at bay by thick walls and high ceilings. Sunlight filtered through plain glass windows to cast rectangular patches of light upon the simple altar and polished wooden pews.

Someone had placed fresh magnolia blooms in a simple vase near the pulpit, their waxy white petals already beginning to brown at the edges in the heat.

As the congregation settled, Jesse was aware of the subtle glances cast in their direction. Mrs. Gardner, the grocer's wife, offered a small nod. Thomas Fletcher, the harbormaster, touched his hat brim. She kept her expression composed, her hands folded in her lap.

Pastor Willoughby appeared at the pulpit, his weathered Bible held loosely in his left hand while his right adjusted the simple wooden cross that hung from his neck. His Georgia accent softened the edges of formal liturgy as he began—a drawl that made even scripture sound like conversation between old friends. He had a particular habit of running his thumb along the Bible's spine as he spoke, the leather worn smooth from decades of such gestures.

"Let us pray," he intoned, and the congregation bowed their heads in unison, the collective rustle of movement like wind through leaves.

The familiar rhythms of worship washed over Jesse—"Holy, Holy, Holy" sung in four-part harmony that wavered slightly when old Mr. Tompkins's voice cracked on the high notes, prayers that had sustained her through the darkest nights in Richmond, scripture readings that spoke of endurance and hope. Church had been another performance—smile fixed, posture perfect, bruises hidden beneath long sleeves, voice pitched to suggest contentment she did not feel. Here, her voice joined the hymn without calculation. Her shoulders lowered as the opening prayer concluded. Her hands, which had been clasped tight in her lap, gradually unclenched as the service continued. She was not performing faith; she was, perhaps for the first time in years, simply present within it.

When Pastor Willoughby rose to deliver his sermon, he paused to clean his spectacles with a white handkerchief—a ritual that signaled the congregation to settle more deeply into attention.

His text was not from the passages on light that Daniel had anticipated, but rather from the book of Ruth: *"Whither thou goest, I will go; and where thou lodgest, I will lodge: thy people shall be my people, and thy God my God."*

The pastor's voice rose and fell with practiced rhythm, his hands moving in small, deliberate gestures—never theatrical, but emphatic enough to underscore his points. When he spoke of Ruth's journey, he leaned forward slightly, as if sharing a confidence. When he described Naomi's grief, his voice dropped to barely above a whisper, forcing the congregation to lean in.

"We are all, in some sense, strangers seeking sanctuary," Pastor Willoughby concluded, his gaze moving thoughtfully over the congregation, pausing briefly at each face as if conducting a silent roll call. "And we all have the capacity to create sanctuary for others through the simple act of welcome. As our island rebuilds after the devastation of war, let us remember that the most important structures we create are of community and care."

Around Jesse, several women dabbed at their eyes with handkerchiefs. Mr. Tompkins cleared his throat twice.

The closing hymn was "Blessed Be the Tie That Binds," and Jesse noticed how many voices knew it by heart, not needing to reference the worn hymnals. As the final notes faded and the congregation dispersed, she lingered in the sanctuary's cool peace. Eliza had already slipped outside to join the other children in the churchyard, while Daniel remained beside her, his expression thoughtful in the way that meant something had engaged his mind.

"Mrs. Whitmore," Pastor Willoughby approached their pew, his footsteps echoing on the pine floor—a measured pace that suggested a man who never hurried. "Daniel. I'm pleased to see you both. Eliza appears to have found occupation already." He nodded toward the window where Eliza's laughter could be heard as she joined a game of tag.

"Your sermon was most thought-provoking, Pastor," Jesse said sincerely.

"I'm gratified to hear it." His eyes crinkled with genuine pleasure. "I understand you've accepted a significant position within our community. The lighthouse keeper's role is an honored tradition on coastal islands such as ours."

"Word does travel quickly," Jesse observed, though without the defensive edge such a comment might have carried weeks earlier.

"On an island this size, news is our most abundant crop," Pastor Willoughby replied with a smile. He shifted the Bible to his left hand, a gesture Jesse had noticed he made when preparing to share something of importance. "Which reminds me—Jonas mentioned you might appreciate learning more about our lighthouse's history."

"Indeed," Jesse replied. "Daniel has been particularly fascinated with the technical aspects described in Mr. Miller's journal."

"Henry Miller was a man of remarkable vision," the pastor said, his voice taking on the tone of someone preparing to share a treasured memory. "I had the privilege of knowing him before the war. He attended this very church, sat in that pew there"—he pointed to a spot near the front—"every Sunday without fail when he was on the island."

Daniel leaned forward with interest, his usual guarded posture momentarily forgotten. "What was he like, Pastor?" The question tumbled out before he could stop it, and for a moment he looked simply like what he was—a boy fascinated by a hero, eager for stories the way boys have always been eager.

"Precise in thought and deed, much like his son. But where Jonas is reserved by nature, Henry was reserved by principle. He believed in the economy of words—never saying in ten what could be expressed in five." The pastor's thumb traced the edge of his Bible as he spoke. "Yet when he spoke of the lighthouse, that reserve would crack. His eyes would light up—if you'll pardon the expression—with an enthusiasm that was quite infectious."

"Jonas mentioned his father began the project to save lives," Jesse said.

"Twenty-three ships lost in a decade," Pastor Willoughby confirmed. "Henry kept a list of every soul—416 names. He could recite them from memory. Said it was his duty to remember why the light was needed."

Their conversation was interrupted by the approach of Miss Jenkins, the schoolteacher, who wished to discuss Daniel's exceptional progress in mathematics. As they conversed, Jesse noticed several other congregants lingering in the churchyard, their manner suggesting they were waiting for an opportunity to speak with her—with the simple interest of neighbors toward someone who was becoming a recognized part of their community.

After Miss Jenkins had moved on, Pastor Willoughby reached into his coat pocket and withdrew a small leather-bound book. The leather was burnished to a deep mahogany, worn smooth at the corners where countless hands had held it. Jesse caught the scent of aged paper and leather—a combination that always reminded her of her father's library.

"I've been meaning to give you this," he said, extending it toward Jesse. "It's another of Henry Miller's journals—one he entrusted to me during the war for safekeeping. Jonas has read it, of course, but given your future position, I thought you might find it of particular interest."

Jesse accepted the journal, feeling the weight of it—heavier than its size suggested. The leather was soft beneath her fingers, and when she opened the cover slightly, she could see pages covered with neat handwriting in faded brown ink.

Marginal notes decorated many pages—small diagrams of lens arrangements, mathematical calculations, rough sketches of the lighthouse from various angles.

"This is very kind, but are you certain Mr. Miller wouldn't prefer to keep all his father's writings?"

"It was Jonas who suggested you might appreciate this particular volume," the pastor explained. "It contains Henry's more personal reflections on the keeper's role—the philosophical instead of technical aspects of tending the light."

Daniel's eyes had fixed on the journal with unmistakable longing. "Are there more calculations and diagrams like in the other journal?"

Pastor Willoughby smiled at the boy's enthusiasm. "Some, though fewer. This journal speaks more of storms weathered, solitude endured, and faith maintained—the inner qualities a keeper requires as much as technical knowledge."

"We'll treat it with great care," Jesse promised, already intrigued by this glimpse into the mind of the man whose work they would be continuing.

As they prepared to take their leave, Pastor Willoughby added, "Henry Miller believed the lighthouse to be more than a navigational aid, Mrs. Whitmore." His kind eyes held hers for a moment. "I believe he would be pleased to know someone with your dedication will be keeping the light burning."

The walk home took them along the familiar path through the maritime forest, where afternoon heat drew out pine resin and the earthier smell of decomposing leaves. Eliza chattered about her games with the other children, while Daniel walked beside Jesse, clearly eager to examine the journal more closely.

That evening, after their simple supper of corn bread and vegetable soup, Jesse sat with her children on the cottage's small porch as twilight gathered around them. The journal rested in her lap, its leather cover warm from her hands. Fireflies had begun their nightly display among the trees, their cold light flickering in patterns that seemed almost like coded messages.

"Shall we read some of it?" Jesse asked, and both children nodded eagerly.

She opened the journal, the spine creaking softly in protest. Henry Miller's handwriting was neat, each letter formed with attention—the penmanship of someone who understood that these words might outlive him.

"*April 17, 1860,*" she read aloud. "*Surveyed the eastern bluff today, confirming it as the optimal site for BluffLight. The elevation provides excellent visibility to vessels approaching from both north and south, while the underlying limestone will provide stable foundation for the tower. Standing at the future site, one can observe the channels a ship must navigate to avoid destruction on the shoals. What better vantage point for a beacon of safety?*"

She continued reading, selecting passages that revealed both the man and his mission:

"*September 3, 1860. Construction began today on the foundation. The work will be slow, methodical, each stone laid with care, for upon this base all else depends. The limestone beneath this bluff runs deep—perfect bedrock for a structure that must withstand decades of coastal storms.*"

"*October 15, 1860. Received specifications for the third-order Fresnel lens from Paris. The apparatus weighs nearly three tons and requires a clockwork mechanism with bronze gears to ensure proper rotation.*"

And later: "*December 12, 1860. A gale struck the island today with such force that pines bent nearly to the ground and the surf reached halfway up the bluff. I stood watching from the partial foundation, imagining the completed tower rising strong against such tempests. A lighthouse keeper must be someone who doesn't fear the storm but respects it.*"

Eliza, despite her earlier excitement about the journal, had fallen asleep against Jesse's side, her blonde curls catching the last of the evening light. Daniel remained attentive to every word.

Jesse turned to an entry from the war years when Henry Miller had returned briefly to the island: "*July 23, 1863. Visited the abandoned construction site today while on leave. The war has halted our progress, but not our purpose. The need for the light remains, perhaps greater than before. Ships still founder on the shoals; lives are still lost that might be saved. When peace returns, so shall I, to complete what we have begun.*"

The final entry in the journal, dated just weeks before Henry Miller's death: "*November 30, 1866. My health continues to decline, and I must face the possibility that I may never see*

*BluffLight completed, much less serve as its keeper. This knowledge brings sorrow, yet also determination. I have instructed Jonas in all aspects of the construction. The plans are meticulous, the vision clear. The light will shine, whether or not my eyes behold it.*"

Jesse closed the journal. Daniel sat beside her, his young face solemn in the lamplight.

"He never saw it finished," he said finally.

"No," Jesse agreed. "But he ensured it would be completed nonetheless."

"He trusted the right people." Daniel's brow furrowed. "Mr. Miller. And now us, I suppose."

Jesse nodded, smoothing Eliza's hair as the child slept against her shoulder.

"Time for bed," she said. "Tomorrow will be a full day."

"Yes, Mama." He gathered the journal with careful hands. "May I keep this on my bedside table? I'd like to read more of it."

"Of course."

Jesse tucked her children into their beds in the small loft, the keeper's journal resting beside Daniel's pillow. Outside, fireflies drifted through the pines.

# CHAPTER NINE

## Ghosts on the Docks
*Saint Simons Harbor—June 18, 1873*
*(Two weeks after receiving the journal)*

T he harbor bustled with midday activity as Jesse made her way along the weathered planks of the main dock. The boards groaned under her feet, worn smooth by decades of salt and traffic, gaps between them revealing the dark water below. Fishermen mended nets while exchanging good-natured jests in the lilting coastal dialect—"Y'all see that hammerhead this mornin'? Big as a skiff, I swear't." Merchants haggled over the morning's catch, their voices rising above the constant creaking of hulls against pilings and the rhythmic slap of halyards against masts.

Salt air mingled with tar, fish scales, and the distinctive sweetness of pine pitch from the small shipyard where a new schooner took form. The June heat had already begun baking the dock timbers, releasing the sharp resin scent of old creosote. Overhead, pelicans wheeled and dove, their prehistoric shadows crossing the sun-bleached wood.

Jesse had come to arrange the delivery of specialized glass panels for the lighthouse lantern room—delicate cargo requiring careful handling during the final leg of its journey from the Charleston glassworks. Each panel measured precisely four feet by two feet and weighed nearly forty pounds—thick enough to withstand hurricane winds yet clear enough to allow maximum light transmission. The Charleston glassworks had ground each surface to exact specifications, and even a single fingerprint could create distortions that would weaken the lighthouse beam.

Jonas had entrusted her with this task after she had proven her organizational abilities at the lighthouse office. "The harbormaster should be expecting you," he had explained that morning, demonstrating with his hands the proper lifting technique. "Each panel must be lifted vertically—never tilted. Horizontal pressure causes hairline fractures invisible to the eye until wind stress shatters the glass. They're packed in pine crates lined with horsehair batting, each panel separated by felt padding an inch thick."

She had left the children in capable hands—Daniel at school with Miss Jenkins, Eliza spending the day with the Widow Patterson, who had developed an unexpected fondness for the child's energetic curiosity. The arrangement gave Jesse a rare opportunity to conduct business independently.

"Mrs. Whitmore!" Mr. Bellamy, the harbormaster, hailed her from his office doorway. A stout man with mutton chops gone gray, he moved with the rolling gait of someone who'd spent years at sea. "You keep good time. The *Carolina Maid* is just rounding the point now." He gestured toward a trim vessel approaching the harbor entrance, its sails bright against the blue water.

"Thank you for watching for it, Mr. Bellamy." Jesse joined him on the small dock office porch, shading her eyes against the midday glare. The approaching vessel was a coastal packet, perhaps sixty feet, her hull painted green with a white stripe at the waterline. "I understand the glass panels require special handling."

"Indeed they do." Bellamy pulled a bandana from his pocket and mopped his forehead—the humidity was already oppressive. "I've assigned my most careful men—Murphy and his crew. They handled crystal chandeliers for the Gould mansion last year without so much as a chip." He pointed to where four men waited near massive wooden derricks fitted with block and tackle. "Those panels come off vertical and stay vertical. Murphy's rigged special slings—canvas loops that cradle the crates from beneath."

Jesse studied the derrick apparatus more closely—massive oak beams joined with iron brackets, the rope thick as her wrist running through pulleys that gleamed with fresh grease. A boy of perhaps twelve stood ready with a bucket of water to cool the rope if friction heated it during lifting.

The harbormaster's attention shifted to the approaching vessel. "Captain Morrison's a careful man. He'll have those crates secured topside—won't trust them to the hold where they might shift." He squinted at the vessel's deck. "See there? Those canvas-covered shapes near the wheelhouse? That's your glass, wrapped twice and lashed to pad-eyes."

Jesse watched as the *Carolina Maid* maneuvered into its berth, the captain calling orders in a voice that carried over the harbor noise: "Easy on the spring line! Make fast the bow first!" The crew moved with coordinated precision, barefoot on the wet deck, their movements sure despite the vessel's gentle roll.

"The lantern room is the heart of the lighthouse," Jesse said, echoing Jonas's words. "Proper glass panels are essential for the Fresnel lens to function. The focal plane must be exactly 157 feet above mean sea level—the glass protects the lens while allowing unobstructed light transmission."

Mr. Bellamy gave her an appraising look, one eyebrow raised above his weathered face. "You've taken to the lighthouse business with remarkable aptitude, Mrs. Whitmore. Not every lady would show such interest in the technical aspects."

"I find the mechanisms remarkable," she replied. "Jonas explained that the lens must rotate at exactly one revolution every two minutes—thirty revolutions per hour, while lit. The bronze gears driving it are calibrated to thousandths of an inch. Even a grain of sand in the mechanism could alter the timing."

As dockworkers secured the vessel with thick hemp lines, Bellamy excused himself to oversee the unloading. Jesse remained on the porch, observing the coordinated effort as sailors rigged the derricks. She could hear Murphy directing his men: "Easy now, boys! Those crates are worth more than your yearly wages! Thompson, get them guide ropes ready—we'll walk her in gentle-like."

Her attention drifted to the larger vessels anchored in the deeper water. The harbor water here was green-brown, murky with stirred silt and organic matter from the marshes. Oil slicks created rainbow patterns around the larger ships, and jellyfish pulsed just beneath the surface, their translucent bells catching the light.

A three-masted barque rode at anchor, her crew holystoning the deck, the faint rhythmic scraping carrying across the still water.

A small fishing sloop hauled its nets nearby, the men singing a rough work song as they pulled. Gulls wheeled overhead in hope of scraps, their cries mingling with the creak of rigging and the steady slap of water against hulls.

But it was the sleek schooner beyond them that drew her eye—a vessel whose Baltimore clipper lines suggested speed over cargo capacity.

Jesse could make out the name painted on its stern: *Miranda.*

The ship rode low despite no visible cargo on deck, her black hull glistening in the sun. No crew was visible, though smoke drifted from the galley pipe. The vessel's isolation—anchored well away from other ships, a guard visible at the rail—spoke of deliberate secrecy.

"Admiring Roarke's pride and joy?"

The voice came from beside her, making Jesse start. She turned to find an elderly man studying her with shrewd eyes. His face bore the deep lines of someone who'd spent decades in coastal sun, and he moved with a slight stoop that suggested too many hours bent over charts. His clothes, though clean, showed the casual disregard of someone more concerned with function than appearance— canvas trousers, a faded blue shirt, a straw hat that had seen better seasons.

"I beg your pardon?" she replied, gathering her composure.

"The *Miranda.*" He nodded toward the anchored schooner, then extended a gnarled hand. "Samuel Fletcher, cartographer. I map the changing coastlines for the government—shoals shift every season, channels fill with silt. Have to keep the charts current or ships founder."

Fletcher had a peculiar way of standing—weight always on his right leg, the left held slightly back as if ready to pivot. His fingers moved constantly, as if sketching invisible maps in the air. When he spoke, his eyes never quite met hers directly, instead focusing on points just past her shoulder—a habit, she suspected, from years of sighting distant landmarks.

Jesse accepted his handshake, noting the ink stains on his fingers and the callus on his thumb from holding a compass. "Jessica Whitmore."

"Ah, Miller's new lighthouse keeper." Fletcher's eyes crinkled with interest. "Word travels on an island. That's quite a responsibility you're taking on—tending a third-order Fresnel lens. Three thousand separate prisms, each one ground to precise angles. Beautiful piece of work."

"You know about the lens mechanism?"

Fletcher chuckled, a dry sound like wind through reeds. "Mapped this coast for twenty years, Mrs. Whitmore. Spent many a night studying lighthouse beams to fix my position. The Fresnel lens is a marvel—takes a single flame and bends its light into a beam visible twenty miles out to sea." He gestured toward the construction site. "That light will save lives."

"Is Captain Roarke currently on the island?" Jesse asked, returning her gaze to the *Miranda*.

"Left yesterday for Savannah—business interests, he claims." Fletcher's tone carried skepticism. He shifted his weight, favoring his left leg slightly. "Yet the *Miranda* stays ready. See how her sails are furled loose? She could be underway in ten minutes. Curious for a merchant vessel supposedly loading cargo."

Before Jesse could respond, movement at the far dock caught her eye—a figure whose bearing sent ice through her veins. His face was too distant to distinguish, yet something in his measured stride and the precise set of his shoulders bypassed thought entirely.

The man moved with William's exact gait—that controlled walk that never varied pace, shoulders held at that particular angle that suggested constant readiness for confrontation. Even the way he held his hands, slightly curled at his sides, matched the husband she'd fled.

Jesse's breath caught. The dock tilted beneath her feet.

"Mrs. Whitmore? Are you unwell?" Fletcher's concerned voice came from somewhere distant.

She gripped the porch rail, forcing herself to breathe. "A moment of dizziness. The heat."

Fletcher followed her gaze. "Ah, you've spotted Thaddeus Merrick. Unsettling fellow, isn't he? Got that way of moving that makes folks nervous—like he's measuring everything for later use."

"Thaddeus?" Relief flooded through her, though her hands still trembled.

Her pulse continued to hammer long after the threat had dissolved into a stranger's identity. She could feel sweat cooling on her neck, her jaw aching where she had clenched it without knowing. The body did not release its alarm as easily as the mind— this she had learned in Richmond, where even after William's rages passed, her hands would shake for hours, her stomach would refuse food, her sleep would splinter into fragments of watchfulness.

"Roarke's first mate and enforcer. Handles the captain's less savory business." Fletcher's expression darkened. "Best avoided, especially for those associated with the lighthouse. He was asking questions about Miller's workers just last week—who they are, where they lodge. That kind of interest never bodes well."

The man—Merrick, not William—had moved out of sight, but the shock left Jesse shaken.

"Mrs. Whitmore! The glass crates are ready!" Murphy called from the dock, where four wooden crates now stood upright, each one the height of a man.

Jesse excused herself from Fletcher and made her way to supervise the transfer. The crates bore Charleston Glassworks stamps and warnings in red paint: FRAGILE - THIS SIDE UP - GLASS. Iron bands reinforced the corners, and she could see the horsehair batting through gaps in the pine slats.

"Right then," Murphy said, his Irish accent thick. A burly man with forearms like ham hocks, he wore a sweat-stained shirt and canvas trousers held up by leather suspenders. "We'll use the slings to lift, guide ropes to control sway. Thompson, you and Davis on the ropes. Smooth as silk, boys."

"Mind that splinter on the boom," one of the men warned. "Don't want the rope catching."

"Already sanded it down," Murphy replied, running his hand along the beam to demonstrate. "These crates are worth three months' wages each. We're not taking chances."

The men positioned themselves as the derrick's boom swung over the first crate. The canvas slings slipped beneath, and slowly, with Murphy calling cadence, the crate rose from the dock.

"Heave... steady... heave... hold!" The wooden frame groaned under the weight—forty pounds of glass plus the crate itself made nearly seventy pounds total.

Jesse watched the guide ropes keep it vertical as it swung toward the waiting wagon, where thick straw had been laid to cushion the landing. Sweat dripped from the workers' faces despite the ocean breeze.

"Easy... easy..." Murphy crooned as if gentling a horse. "Thompson, ease your rope. Davis, take up slack. There's a girl."

The crate settled into the wagon bed with barely a sound. Three more times they repeated the process, each transfer accomplished without incident. Between lifts, the men paused to drink from a water bucket, passing the ladle among themselves. The wagon driver, a taciturn man named Josiah, secured each crate with additional ropes, creating a web of support. He'd lined the wagon bed with sailcloth to protect against moisture.

"They'll reach the lighthouse safe," Murphy assured Jesse. "Josiah could keep a wagon steady in a gale."

Jesse thanked the men and signed the shipping receipt Bellamy presented. But as she turned to leave, she found herself scanning the crowd of dock workers and merchants. Every tall man with dark hair made her pulse quicken. Every deliberate gait caught her attention.

The walk back to Marsh Cottage took her through the village, past familiar faces who nodded in greeting. Mrs. Gardner sweeping her store's entrance—pausing mid-stroke to watch Jesse pass. Thomas Gardner touching his hat as he passed with a load of lumber for the lighthouse.

By the time Jesse collected Eliza from Widow Patterson's cottage, her hands had steadied. Her breath had not.

"Mama!" Eliza burst from the door before Jesse could knock, her face flushed with excitement. "Mrs. Patterson showed me the most wonderful thing! There's a nest—a real nest with baby birds— in the jasmine vine by her window. She says they're Carolina wrens and they'll sing the prettiest songs when they're grown. And she let me draw them, very carefully so I wouldn't scare the mother, and she said the babies will remember my face when they're big because birds remember things like that!"

The words tumbled out in a breathless rush, Eliza's hands gesturing wildly to illustrate the size of the nest, the color of the eggs, the way the mother bird had tilted her head.

"Did she now?" Jesse managed, her daughter's joy loosening something that had been clenched tight since the docks.

"And Mrs. Patterson told me a story about a lighthouse keeper's daughter who saved a whole ship just by singing," Eliza continued, grabbing Jesse's hand and pulling her toward the path home. "The ship was lost in the fog and the keeper was sick and couldn't tend the light, but his daughter climbed the tower and sang so loud that the sailors heard her and steered away from the rocks. Mrs. Patterson says it's a true story from a long time ago."

Jesse glanced back at Widow Patterson, who stood in her doorway with something like contentment on her typically stern face. The older woman raised one hand in a small wave.

"I'm going to sing to ships too," Eliza declared. "When we live in the lighthouse. In case the light ever goes out."

"The light won't go out," Jesse said. "That's our job—to make sure it never does."

"But if it does," Eliza insisted with a child's determination to plan for every possibility, "I'll be ready."

"Are we going to see the lighthouse, Mama?" Eliza asked, skipping beside her. "I want to see how tall it is now!"

"Not today," Jesse replied, her throat tight.

That evening, as the children slept, she pulled the carpetbag from beneath the bed. Then she sat at the small table and began a letter she would never send:

*Jonas,*

*Family circumstances require us to relocate immediately. I regret the inconvenience to your construction schedule.*

*The glass panels arrived safely—Murphy's crew handled them well. Josiah will deliver them intact.*

*Please give my regards to Miss Haskins and Pastor Willoughby.*

*J.W.*

She folded the letter and placed it in Henry Miller's journal, which she would leave for Jonas to find.

She touched the worn leather one last time. Then she rose and began to pack.

Her hands moved with the efficiency of practice—folding clothes without thinking, stacking them in the carpetbag in the order they would be needed. She had done this before, in the dark of a Richmond night, and her body remembered the sequence even as her mind drifted elsewhere.

# CHAPTER TEN

### Ashes and Resolve
*The Village, Saint Simons Island—June 20, 1873*
*(Two days after the harbor visit)*

T he acrid scent of smoke hung over the village like a burial
shroud. Dawn had barely broken, the early light revealing the
charred skeleton of what had been Thatcher's General Store. The
blackened timbers jutted skyward, still smoldering despite the
bucket brigade's hours of effort. Wisps of steam rose where water
met hot wood, and the occasional crack of cooling timber
punctuated the morning air.

Where the front wall had stood, only the doorframe remained—
a black rectangle opening onto destruction. The metal hinges had
melted and reformed into twisted drops of iron. The painted sign
that had read "Thatcher's General Goods - Est. 1867" lay in the
street, charred beyond recognition.

A small crowd had gathered to survey the damage—islanders
with soot-streaked faces and exhausted eyes. Their clothing bore
the marks of the night's battle: singed sleeves, water-soaked boots,
hands raw from passing buckets. Some still wore nightclothes
beneath hastily donned coats. Old Mr. Davis leaned heavily on his
cane, his face gray with exhaustion from manning the bucket line
for hours.

Jesse stood to the side, Daniel and Eliza close by. She had not
planned to bring the children into the village so early, but the news
had reached Marsh Cottage before breakfast—a breathless message
from the Widow Patterson that Thatcher's store had burned in the
night, that everyone was needed to prevent the fire from spreading
to neighboring buildings.

The heat still radiated from the ruins, making the morning
humidity even more oppressive. The stench of burned goods filled

the air—charred wood, melted metal, the acrid smell of destroyed fabric and paper. Glass fragments crunched underfoot where windows had exploded from the heat, and ash drifted on the morning breeze like gray snow.

"Was anyone hurt, Mama?" Eliza asked, her voice small in the face of such devastation.

"No, darling," Jesse assured her. "Mr. Thatcher and his family escaped in time."

She spotted the storekeeper himself standing amid the ruins, his normally precise appearance disheveled, his spectacles missing and his beard singed in places. Soot covered his nightshirt, and his bare feet were black with ash where he'd run out without boots. Miss Haskins stood beside him, her thin arm supporting his shoulder. The older woman's jaw was set with barely controlled fury.

Daniel tugged at Jesse's sleeve, drawing her attention to the far side of the square. Jonas Miller was deep in conversation with Pastor Willoughby and Mr. Bellamy. Jonas held a ledger—water-damaged but readable—gesturing at specific entries as he spoke.

"Stay with Eliza," she instructed Daniel. "I need to speak with Mr. Miller."

As she approached the men, their conversation fell silent. "Mrs. Whitmore," Pastor Willoughby greeted her with a nod that carried none of his usual warmth. "A terrible business."

"Indeed," Jesse agreed. "Was it an accident?"

The three men exchanged glances. Jonas responded, his voice low. "The fire began at the rear of the store, near where the lighthouse supplies were stored. We lost two months of specialized materials—brass fittings for the lens mechanism, calibrated weights for the clockwork system. The Charleston foundry can't replace them for six weeks."

Jesse absorbed this. "You believe it was deliberate."

"We know it was," Mr. Bellamy said grimly. "When the first bucket brigade arrived, they found something written in the ashes out back—'I see you,' scratched with a stick beside where the fire started."

The same words that had appeared twice now in connection with her family. Jesse's breath caught. This wasn't random destruction. Someone was sending a message specifically to them.

"Mr. Thatcher had been keeping funds for us," Jonas explained, his voice tight with controlled anger. "After the previous incidents at the construction site, we thought it safer to store valuables elsewhere."

"Roarke's escalating," Pastor Willoughby said. "First threats, then sabotage, now arson."

Before Jesse could respond, a commotion near the ruins drew their attention. Mr. Thatcher had emerged from the smoking debris clutching something to his chest—a metal box, its surface blackened but intact. The small crowd parted as he approached Miller, weary triumph in his soot-streaked face.

"It survived," he said, his voice hoarse from smoke. "The strongbox. I kept it beneath the floorboards behind the counter." He handed the box to Miller.

"The payroll funds?"

Thatcher nodded. "And the correspondence from the Light-House Board. Twenty-eight dollars in wages, plus the contracts."

"You've done more than enough, Jacob," Jonas assured him.

Miss Haskins joined them, her shrewd eyes taking in the recovered strongbox. "The store can be rebuilt," she said firmly. "And it will be." She turned her gaze to Jesse, something like challenge in her expression. "You were planning to leave, weren't you?"

The directness of the question startled Jesse. "How did you—"

"I've been watching young women make decisions about their futures for forty years," Miss Haskins interrupted. "I recognize the look. The careful distance. The calculations behind the eyes." She gestured toward the children. "But consider this, Mrs. Whitmore—what happens when you run? You arrive somewhere new with no references, no connections, no employment. Your funds dwindle. You take whatever work you can find, usually for less than you're worth. And when trouble finds you again—which it always does—you have no one to stand with you."

Jesse had twenty-three dollars remaining from Richmond. Enough for passage to Savannah, perhaps a week's lodging. Then what?

Behind them, the villagers had already begun clearing debris, salvaging what could be saved. Old Murphy was sorting nails by size. The Widow Patterson was washing soot from glass bottles that had survived intact.

"The lighthouse position pays sixty dollars monthly," Jonas said. "Plus the keeper's cottage when it's built. That's steady income, Mrs. Whitmore. More than you'd find elsewhere without recommendations."

Jesse glanced back at her children. Daniel was helping stack salvageable boards while Eliza collected unbroken bottles into a basket. They had made friends here. Daniel excelled in Miss Jenkins's school. Eliza had the Widow Patterson watching over her.

She turned back to Jonas. "The lighthouse position—it's still available?"

The relief in Jonas's eyes was subtle but visible. "It is."

Her spine straightened. Her hands, which had been clenched at her sides, slowly opened. Her breath steadied into something deeper, more deliberate. The decision settled into her body before she spoke it.

"Then we have a store to rebuild first."

Throughout the day, Jesse worked alongside the villagers clearing debris from the store site. The labor was grimy and exhausting—hauling charred timbers that left black streaks on clothing, sifting through ash for salvageable metal, scraping melted tar from stone foundations. By noon, her hands were blistered despite the work gloves someone had provided, her throat raw from breathing smoke-tinged air, and her back ached from stooping.

"Careful with that beam," Murphy called out as four men maneuvered a partially burned support timber. "She's burned through in the middle—might snap."

The beam cracked as predicted, sending up a cloud of ash and forcing the men to jump back. They laughed it off, but they moved more cautiously after that.

The physical details of destruction were sobering. The iron stove had warped from the heat, its door hanging at an impossible angle. Glass had melted and reformed into twisted shapes that looked like frozen waterfalls. Account books were reduced to ash, years of records gone in a night. The smell of burned flour hung heavy where sacks had combusted, mixing with the sharper scent of charred leather from destroyed boots and belts.

Women worked at sorting smaller items—Mrs. Gardner cleaning soot from medicine bottles, the Widow Patterson straightening bent nails with patient hammer taps. A young mother nursed her infant in the shade of an oak while her older children carried water buckets, their usual energy subdued by the destruction around them.

Near the edge of the work site, Jesse noticed a young man—one of the dock workers, she thought—standing apart with his arms crossed. His face was troubled, his gaze moving between the ruins and the harbor road as if expecting someone. When Murphy called for more hands to shift a fallen beam, the young man hesitated before joining. His movements were reluctant, his eyes avoiding Jonas Miller.

Jesse had seen that look before—the conflict of a man caught between loyalties. Roarke's reach extended further than arson and threats; it included the quiet obligations of men who owed him wages, or favors, or debts they couldn't name aloud.

"Found something," one of the workers called out, pulling a cash box from beneath fallen shelving. The lock had melted shut, but when they pried it open with a crowbar, the coins inside were merely tarnished, not destroyed. A small victory, but Thatcher's face brightened at recovering even this much.

By midafternoon, they had cleared the site and erected a temporary structure of canvas and salvaged lumber. The frame went up quickly—four corner posts sunk into the ground, crossbeams lashed with rope, canvas stretched and tied. It wasn't pretty, but it would keep rain off the salvaged goods until proper materials arrived.

"That canvas won't hold if we get a real blow," Thomas Gardner observed, testing the tension on the guy-ropes with a calloused hand.

"It only needs to last until we can get proper lumber from Savannah," Thatcher replied. "Three weeks at most. Maybe less if the weather holds."

The blacksmith had set up his portable forge nearby, straightening bent hinges and brackets. The bellows wheezed with each pump, and every ring of hammer on anvil marked progress.

Mr. Thatcher, recovering from his initial shock, began inventorying what remained. "Lost about three hundred dollars in goods," he said, voice steady despite the loss. "But insurance will cover some. And I've got credit with suppliers in Savannah. We'll have basic supplies within the week—flour, salt, coffee, lamp oil, the essentials people can't do without."

"I can float you a loan if needed," Jonas offered. "The lighthouse fund can spare it."

"Appreciate that, Miller, but I'll manage. Been through worse." Thatcher wiped his forehead with a rag that was now blacker than his skin. "Though I'll take you up on labor. Need help unloading when the supply boat arrives."

"You'll have it," Jonas assured him.

Jesse found a moment's respite in the shade of a surviving oak, watching Jonas direct the placement of support posts for the temporary structure. The man worked efficiently, no wasted motion, delegating tasks based on each worker's strengths.

"Smart decision." Miss Haskins appeared beside her, offering water from a bucket. Her sleeves were rolled to the elbow, her hands as ash-stained as anyone's.

Jesse accepted it gratefully.

"Roarke may be dangerous, but at least here you know who your enemies are," the older woman said. "Out there? You'd be starting blind again. No references means taking whatever work's offered—usually domestic service for half wages. I've seen it too many times."

"The keeper position is good work," Jesse said, watching Daniel help the younger boys stack salvageable shingles.

"Better than good. Federal position means federal protection. The Light-House Board doesn't take kindly to interference with their operations." Miss Haskins paused, then added more quietly, "And you've got Jonas Miller's respect. That's not given lightly or withdrawn easily."

The afternoon grew hotter, the humidity making the work even more difficult. Men stripped to their shirtsleeves, women tucked up their skirts. Someone brought out a barrel of water with a dipper, and workers took turns drinking and splashing their faces. The ash had turned to gray paste on everyone's skin.

The community organized itself without formal direction. The carpenter's wife appeared with a pot of stew and cornbread for the workers. The minister's wife brought bandages and salve for burns and cuts. Even children found tasks—carrying messages, fetching tools, their minds occupied instead of dwelling on the destruction. By the time the stew pot was empty, the first wall frame stood upright, and men were already measuring for the second.

As twilight descended, Pastor Willoughby called everyone to gather. Lanterns were lit, their golden light illuminating tired but satisfied faces. Soot streaked every cheek. Blisters marked every palm.

"Today we have witnessed destruction and rebuilding," he began. "The store will stand again. That is what we do."

A murmur of agreement rippled through the crowd. Jesse, standing with Daniel and Eliza, watched the lantern light play across these faces—the same people who had worked beside her all day.

"The store will reopen," Thatcher announced, voice stronger now. "Three days for temporary operations, three weeks for full rebuilding. Anyone who needs supplies on credit until then, see me."

As the gathering dispersed, Jesse walked her tired children toward Marsh Cottage. Daniel carried the ledger Jonas had given him—lists of supplies needed, workers to coordinate, materials to order. Even at ten, the boy understood the value of steady employment, of being needed. His back was straight despite the day's labor.

"Mr. Miller says I can help with the inventory tomorrow," Daniel said, pride evident despite his exhaustion. "Three dollars for the week if I do it well."

"That's good wages," Jesse replied, knowing it would help stretch their funds.

Eliza, half-asleep on her feet, mumbled, "Miss Patterson says I can help sort buttons and thread when the new supplies come. She'll pay in peppermint sticks."

She unpacked the carpetbag she had filled two nights before and put the clothes back in the bureau.

# INTERLUDE I

## Before the Light

*BluffLight Construction Site—July 4, 1873*
*(Two weeks after the fire)*

I ndependence Day dawned clear and bright over Saint Simons Island, the morning light catching on BluffLight's growing frame. The structure now stood nearly fifty feet tall, its tapered form rising purposefully toward the sky—no longer merely a skeleton of possibility but a tangible presence against the horizon. The whitewashed lower courses gleamed in the early sun, and fresh mortar still glistened between the upper bricks where yesterday's work had ended.

Jesse made her way up the winding path to the bluff, carrying a basket of provisions for the skeleton crew working through the holiday. The smell of fresh-cut timber and lime mortar drifted on the salt breeze. Most islanders would gather later for celebrations in the village square, but the lighthouse work continued. Jonas's quiet determination to maintain momentum after the setback of the store fire kept three men on site even today.

Jonas looked up from his blueprints as she arrived, his expression brightening slightly. "Mrs. Whitmore. You didn't need to bring provisions on a holiday."

"The men still need to eat," she replied practically, setting her basket on the edge of his table. "And the lumber shipment manifest needs checking before the Savannah boat arrives Tuesday. I wanted to verify the board-feet calculations."

"It came this morning—along with the Light-House Board's response. Approval for the additional funds to complete the lantern room."

Daniel and Eliza had adapted to spending more time at the construction site. Her son assisted with simple drafting tasks while

95

Eliza charmed the workers with her enthusiastic questions about their craft.

At the edge of the bluff, Daniel stood with a small notebook, making careful sketches of the water below.

"He's been documenting the tidal patterns," Jesse explained. "After reading Henry Miller's journal entries about navigational hazards, he became interested in how the tides affect the visibility of the shoals. He marks the water level against that post every hour."

Jonas nodded with genuine interest. "A worthwhile study. The lighthouse will guide ships at night, but daylight navigation remains challenging in these waters. The sandbars shift with every storm."

"He hopes to create a reference for captains navigating by day," Jesse said, unable to keep the pride from her voice.

"An engineer's mind," Jonas observed. "Like his father."

Eliza came running up the path from Marsh Cottage, clutching a small arrowhead found in their garden—Timucuan, one of the workers had told her. She bounded over to show her brother, and the two bent their heads together in shared discovery.

"Mr. Miller! Mr. Miller!" Eliza broke away from Daniel and ran toward them, holding up her prize. "Look what I found! It's older than *everything*. Mr. Gardner says Indians used it to hunt deer a thousand years ago. A *thousand*. That's before the church and before the war and before Mama was even born!"

Jonas crouched to examine the arrowhead with appropriate gravity. "A fine specimen. See how the edges are still sharp? Whoever made this was a skilled craftsman."

Eliza beamed, then tucked the arrowhead carefully into her pinafore pocket. "I'm going to keep it forever. Daniel says I should draw it for my collection."

Jonas turned to Jesse. "The keeper position paperwork arrived with the funding approval. Whenever you're ready."

He extended the folded documents. When Jesse reached to take them, their fingers brushed—his hand warm, roughened by work. The contact was brief, incidental, yet she was suddenly aware of the way morning light caught the silver threading his dark hair, the steadiness in his voice that never seemed to waver. She took the papers and stepped back, sliding them into her basket beside the empty dishes.

Jonas nodded, satisfaction in his response. "The light should be operational by late autumn. The keeper's cottage shortly thereafter."

They watched the children at the bluff's edge, Daniel explaining something about the arrowhead's shape while Eliza listened with characteristic intensity. From the village, the pop of firecrackers carried on the breeze.

"There's still danger," Jonas said finally. "Roarke has been unusually quiet since the fire. No interference, no threats. Nothing."

"I'm familiar with that kind of quiet," Jesse said.

Her hands stilled on the basket handle. The silence before the worst nights had sounded exactly like this—William's footsteps stopping outside her door, the held breath before the handle turned.

"We'll do what we can," she added.

Jonas's gaze returned to the rising lighthouse.

Below them, a pelican dove into the waves, emerging with a fish held in its pouch. Above, BluffLight continued its rise.

# CHAPTER ELEVEN

### First Stone, First Step
*BluffLight Construction Site—August 1, 1873*
*(Four weeks after Independence Day)*

The August sun blazed overhead as Jesse made her way up the path, her arms laden with rolled blueprints from the morning packet boat. Perspiration dampened her forehead despite the early hour—the humidity so thick the air felt liquid. She paused at the crest, watching the organized chaos of construction.

The site bustled with activity. A dozen workers moved among stacks of cut stone and barrels of mortar, while overhead, BluffLight rose sixty feet against the cloudless sky. Scaffolding encircled the structure—pine poles lashed with hemp rope, platforms of rough-sawn boards where men worked despite the dizzying height.

The scaffolding itself was an engineering feat—vertical poles sunk three feet into the ground with crossed braces every eight feet, platforms of two-inch planks laid across horizontal supports with gaps between boards to reduce wind resistance. Hemp rope from Charleston bound every joint, swollen tight by salt air and stronger than iron for this purpose.

Workers climbed ladders between levels, carrying tools and materials. Those afraid of heights stayed ground-level, preparing stones and mixing mortar. The brave ones worked the upper tiers, secured by nothing but balance and nerve.

"Mrs. Whitmore." Jonas Miller approached, dust coating his boots. "The revised blueprints?"

"Just arrived." Jesse extended the rolled papers. "The Light-House Board's modifications for the upper tier."

Jonas unrolled them on a makeshift table—planks across sawhorses. "The Savannah granite proved denser than expected. We can reduce wall thickness by two inches without compromising strength."

Jesse studied the modifications. Reducing the wall thickness would decrease the overall weight load on the foundation by nearly fifteen percent—significant for a structure this tall. "That saves material costs too," she noted.

Thomas Gardner, the head mason, joined them. A weathered man with decades of coastal construction experience, his hands bore the permanent calluses of his trade. "Ready for the cornerstone specifications, Mrs. Whitmore?"

Jesse studied the blueprints, noting Jonas's precise calculations in the margins. "The cornerstone dimensions: thirty-six inches by twenty-four, depth of eighteen. The facing stones follow this pattern." Her finger traced the interlocking system that would bind the outer decorative stones to the solid inner core.

Gardner nodded. "We'll need to modify the cutting jig. Robert!" He called to his apprentice. "Bring the template tools."

As Robert hurried off, Gardner explained the technicalities. "The cutting jig uses an iron template—ensures each stone matches the precise angle. Lighthouse tolerances are less than an eighth-inch, otherwise the tower loses vertical alignment over height. Any variation and the salt air gets in."

"Show me the stone selection," Jesse said.

They walked to the granite blocks delivered yesterday—rough-cut pieces awaiting final shaping. The morning heat already radiated from the pale stone. Gardner ran his hand over several blocks, feeling for invisible flaws.

"This one." He indicated a block with minimal veining. "See how the grain runs straight through? No hidden fractures. Veins create weak points—salt water follows them and works its way in, causing spalling over time." He guided Jesse's hand along the surface. "Feel here—smooth texture means it'll take the chisel clean."

The stone was warm beneath her palm, solid and permanent. "Good choice. Have the men position it for cutting."

For the next hour, Jesse supervised the cornerstone preparation. The workers used iron wedges and wooden mallets to split the granite along its grain—a process requiring both strength and precision. One miscalculated blow could shatter the stone uselessly.

"Easy with that sledge, Murphy," Gardner cautioned. "Let the wedge do the work, not brute force."

First, they scored the cutting line with a carbide-tipped chisel, creating a groove for the wedges to follow. Then came the delicate process of inserting the wedges—thin iron shims spaced every six inches along the scored line. Each wedge had to be driven to exactly the same depth, or the stone would crack unevenly.

"Listen to the stone," Gardner instructed his apprentice. "Hear that ringing sound? That means the tension's building even. A dull thud means you're forcing it."

The rhythmic ring of hammer on wedge filled the air—ping, ping, ping in sequence down the line. Granite dust coated everything—tools, clothing, skin. The workers paused frequently to drink from the water barrel, sweat streaming despite the ocean breeze.

The heat made the work brutal. Men stripped to their waists, backs gleaming with perspiration. The metal tools grew hot enough to burn bare skin. Someone had to continuously pour water over the cutting area to keep the dust down and cool the stone.

Finally, with a sound like a rifle shot, the granite split clean along the line. The crack echoed across the construction site—workers paused, heads turning toward the sound. Success. The two halves fell apart, revealing the stone's crystalline interior—white feldspar and clear quartz sparkling in the sun.

"Mortar's ready," announced Thompson, one of the younger workers. He stood beside a wooden trough where three men mixed lime, sand, and crushed oyster shells—the traditional coastal mortar recipe.

"What's the shell ratio?" Jesse asked.

"One part shells to three parts sand, two parts lime," Thompson replied. "The shells add binding strength, help resist salt penetration. We burn them first, crush them fine as flour."

Jesse checked the mixture's consistency—thick enough to hold the stones, wet enough to spread evenly. The mixture had to be used within an hour of mixing, or it would begin to set in the trough.

"Temperature matters too," Gardner added, joining them at the mixing trough. "Too hot and it sets before we can position the stones. Too cold and it won't cure properly."

The men worked the mixture with long-handled hoes, turning it repeatedly to ensure even consistency. Their arms strained with the effort—wet mortar was surprisingly heavy. Lime dust rose from the trough, forcing them to wrap cloths around their faces.

By midday, the cornerstone was ready for placement. The entire crew gathered for the small ceremony. Using a wooden crane with rope and pulleys, four men lowered the stone into position.

The crane consisted of an A-frame structure built from twelve-inch pine beams, rated for loads up to a thousand pounds. The rope—two-inch Manila hemp—ran through three pulleys to create mechanical advantage. Four men could lift what would require twelve without the system.

"Easy now, boys," Gardner called out, guiding the stone with his hands. "Thompson, slack on your side. Murphy, take up the tension."

The 800-pound block descended inch by inch. Gardner had spread a bed of fresh mortar where it would rest—leveled and grooved to ensure maximum adhesion. As the stone touched down, mortar squeezed from the edges.

Gardner checked the level repeatedly—a precision instrument with a bubble in oil, imported from Philadelphia. He tapped the stone with a wooden mallet, making minute adjustments. Thin iron shims, some no thicker than paper, went beneath the corners until the bubble centered perfectly.

"She's true," he announced, wiping sweat from his brow. The men applauded briefly—tradition demanded acknowledgment of a successfully placed cornerstone. Then back to work. No time for extended celebration with daylight burning.

Jonas appeared beside Jesse with a tin cup of water. "The men respond to your directness."

She drank gratefully, throat parched from the dust. The water was warm but welcome—everything turned lukewarm in this heat within minutes. "Gardner's expertise makes it straightforward."

"Still, not everyone can translate blueprints to practical application." He gestured toward the workers laying the next course of stones. "Each tier brings new challenges. The lighthouse narrows as it rises—the math gets complex."

Jesse watched the masons work. Each stone had to be individually shaped to fit its specific position. The outer faces were dressed smooth while the inner surfaces remained rough for better mortar adhesion. It was painstaking work in the crushing heat.

Daniel and Eliza arrived with Miss Haskins, who'd been teaching them botanical identification. Eliza ran toward the cornerstone, fascinated by its fresh chisel marks.

"Is this your stone, Mama? The one you chose?"

"The crew placed it," Jesse corrected. "I simply approved Gardner's selection."

Daniel studied the construction with his characteristic intensity. His gaze moved from the cornerstone to the crane assembly, then up the scaffolding to where men worked on the upper courses. "The new timber supports," he said, moving closer to examine a diagonal brace. "They're for wind resistance?"

Jonas nodded. "Hurricane bracing. We're reinforcing the southeastern exposure."

"The angle looks like forty-five degrees," Daniel said. "Is that optimal for lateral load distribution?"

Gardner, overhearing, turned with raised eyebrows. "Forty-three degrees, actually. The boy's got an eye." He gestured Daniel closer. "Come here, lad. Let me show you how we calculate the stress points."

Daniel followed eagerly, his notebook already open. Jesse watched him crouch beside Gardner as the mason traced lines in the dust, explaining the mathematics of structural support. For a few minutes, her son was simply a boy fascinated by how things were built—no shadows in his face, no vigilance in his posture.

Miss Haskins observed the children's engagement with approval. "Daniel documented sixteen species of dune grass this morning. Quite thorough sketches."

"Thank you for the instruction," Jesse said.

"Knowledge requires transmission," Miss Haskins replied curtly. "I must return—the ladies' auxiliary meets about the store furnishings." She departed with her usual rigid posture despite the steep path.

As the afternoon progressed, Jesse coordinated material deliveries for the next day's work. Twenty more granite blocks were due from Savannah, plus iron tie-rods for structural reinforcement. She checked the inventory ledgers, ensuring sufficient mortar supplies.

The heat had become brutal by three o'clock. Sweat stung eyes, blurred vision. The air shimmered above the stone piles, creating mirages. Men worked in shifts now—fifteen minutes of labor, five minutes in the shade. Someone had collapsed from heat exhaustion the previous week, and Gardner wouldn't risk another incident.

The physical toll showed on every worker. Hands bled from handling rough granite. Backs ached from lifting and positioning stones. The lime in the mortar burned exposed skin—wrists and forearms bore red welts that took weeks to heal. Murphy wrapped a rag around his palm and reached for the next stone.

"We'll need more medical supplies," Jesse noted in her ledger. "Bandages, salve for burns, salt tablets for the heat."

Jonas nodded, reviewing her list. "Order double. August will only get hotter."

The sound of stone on stone continued—a grinding, scraping rhythm as masons fitted each block precisely. They used wooden wedges soaked in water, which would swell to hold stones temporarily while mortar set. Every few courses, iron tie-rods were inserted, running through the entire wall thickness to bind inner and outer faces together.

The workers began securing tools as shadows lengthened. Each tool had its specific storage place—chisels oiled and wrapped against rust, levels stored in padded boxes, trowels cleaned of every trace of mortar. These tools were expensive, some imported from England, and Gardner treated them like surgical instruments.

"Make sure those plumb bobs are properly boxed," he called to Robert. "One dent throws the weight off-center, ruins the accuracy."

The plumb bobs—brass weights on silk strings—were essential for ensuring the lighthouse walls remained perfectly vertical. Even a quarter-inch deviation over sixty feet could compromise structural integrity. Gardner checked the plumb every morning and evening, recording measurements in a leather-bound notebook.

The day's progress was visible—the cornerstone set, the first course of the new tier begun. Three layers of stone now rested above the cornerstone, each one individually shaped and placed. At this rate, the tier would be complete in two weeks, assuming weather held and supplies arrived on schedule.

Pastor Willoughby appeared on the path, making his evening rounds. "Good progress today."

"Consistent work yields results," Gardner replied, cleaning mortar from his trowel.

The pastor studied the lighthouse's rising form. "The Psalmist wrote about rejected stones becoming cornerstones."

He departed without elaborating. The workers dispersed toward their homes, tools cleaned and stored for tomorrow.

Jesse gathered the blueprints and ledgers.

The sound of hammering from the village carried on the evening air. Thatcher's store, rising again.

# CHAPTER TWELVE

New Faces, Old Doubts
*BluffLight Construction Site—August 15, 1873*
*(Two weeks after Jesse's first day on the bluff)*

T he mid-August heat shimmered above the bluff. Jesse wiped perspiration from her brow as she reviewed the supply manifest. Construction had continued steadily—the tower now stood nearly seventy feet tall.

A commotion at the path entrance drew her attention. Five men approached, tool bags slung over shoulders, the weariness of travel evident in their dusty clothing. Jonas had mentioned new workers arriving from Savannah to replace those who had departed after completing the foundation work.

The man leading them caught her eye immediately—perhaps thirty-five, with weathered features that spoke of years exposed to sun and salt. Deep lines bracketed his mouth, and a white scar ran along his left jawline—old but prominent. He moved with the rolling gait of someone more accustomed to a ship's deck than solid ground, his balance automatically adjusting to phantom swells. His hands bore the particular scars of rope burns, the kind that came from hauling lines in storms. When he stopped, he stood utterly still—no fidgeting, no shifting weight—with the patience of a man who had spent long watches waiting for weather to turn.

His eyes, sharp and gray as winter sea, swept the construction site with professional assessment, pausing at structural points—the scaffolding joints, the mortar lines, the crane assembly. This was a man who understood how things were built and, more importantly, how they might fail.

Behind him came the others—a wiry Irishman named Donnelly with arms corded like ship's rope, two brothers from Charleston named Bishop who moved with synchronized efficiency, and an older man called Hayes who kept his own counsel. Each carried the tools of their trade: specialized hammers, chisels wrapped in oiled cloth, measuring strings wound on wooden spools.

"Mrs. Whitmore?" His voice carried the flat vowels of the Carolina coast. "Name's Thompson. We're the crew Miller hired on."

Jesse extended her hand, noting the calluses that marked a working man's palm. "Welcome to BluffLight, Mr. Thompson. Jonas is inspecting the morning's stonework but should return shortly."

Thompson's gaze moved to the lighthouse, studying its structure with obvious expertise. "Impressive structure. Quality masonry—those joints will hold against hurricane winds. Though I hear some islanders don't look kindly on its building."

The observation, casually delivered but pointed, confirmed he'd already heard about the tensions surrounding the project.

"Every harbor has its factions," she replied. "But BluffLight will serve all who navigate these waters."

Thompson held her gaze a moment longer than strictly necessary before nodding. "Where would you have us begin?"

Jesse directed the men to the storage area where they could deposit their belongings before reporting to Thomas Gardner. As they moved away, she studied Thompson's retreating figure. His manner was deliberately opaque.

"New blood," observed a crisp voice behind her.

Jesse turned to find Miss Amelia Haskins approaching, her severe black dress and rigid posture impervious to the summer heat.

"They come well recommended," Jesse replied, falling into step beside Miss Haskins as they moved toward the shade. "Though a man's papers don't always reveal his character."

"Indeed." Miss Haskins settled herself on one of the rough wooden benches. "Which is why I took the liberty of inquiring about Mr. Thompson during my recent visit to Savannah."

Jesse raised an eyebrow. "And?"

"He worked on several vessels suspected of contraband trade during the war. Never charged. Since then, he's maintained a reputation as a skilled shipwright who asks few questions about his employers' intentions."

"You believe this makes him unreliable?"

Miss Haskins considered the question, her shrewd eyes tracking Thompson as he joined the other workers. "A man who's sold his loyalty before may be tempted to do so again."

"I appreciate your thoroughness, Miss Haskins."

The older woman nodded, then abruptly changed the subject. "Your daughter shows remarkable aptitude for botanical identification. Her drawings of salt marsh grasses are quite accurate."

Their conversation was interrupted by Jonas Miller's arrival. "The new men have arrived, I see," he observed. "Thompson among them?"

"Yes," Jesse confirmed. "Miss Haskins has been sharing information about his background."

Jonas listened as the older woman repeated her assessment. When she finished, he nodded. "We'll proceed with appropriate caution."

"See that you do." Miss Haskins rose with the aid of her walking stick. "The Ladies' Auxiliary meets at noon." She departed with her characteristic rigid stride.

After Miss Haskins left, Jonas turned to Jesse. "Our island sentinel remains vigilant."

"Formidably so."

Jonas watched Thompson examining a block of granite. "Gardner says Thompson can read stone grain like other men read books. Knows where it'll split clean and where it'll shatter. That's not learned quickly."

Thompson ran his palm along the surface, then tapped it with his knuckles in three places, listening to the sound.

"Roarke's been quiet lately," Jonas added. "His schooner hasn't docked in two weeks."

"Planning something?"

"Or waiting. The lighthouse grows taller each day. Soon we'll be beyond the point where destruction would stop completion."

Jonas nodded. "Shall we review the lantern room specifications? The updated drawings arrived this morning."

They moved into the lighthouse office, where blueprints were spread across the desk. For the next hour, they discussed the specialized glass panels and focal length calculations—work requiring complete concentration.

By midday, when workers paused for their meal, Jesse emerged to find Daniel engaged in earnest conversation with Thompson. Her son sat on a stone block, notebook open as Thompson demonstrated something with his hands.

"It's called a bowline," Thompson was explaining, his rough fingers moving with practiced precision. "Most useful knot a sailor knows. Creates a loop that won't slip or jam, no matter the strain."

He demonstrated slowly, narrating each step. "The rabbit comes out of his hole, goes around the tree, and back down the hole." The childish mnemonic contrasted oddly with his rough appearance.

Daniel's fingers mimicked the movement, fumbling at first with the sequence. Thompson adjusted the boy's grip without impatience. "Keep the working end longer—you'll need the length for the final tuck."

"And it can be tied one-handed? Even in darkness?"

Thompson held up his left hand, demonstrating the one-handed technique with remarkable dexterity. "Once your fingers know the pattern, they don't need your eyes. Saved my life once, hanging from rigging in a nor'easter off Cape Hatteras."

"With practice, yes. Though let's hope you're never hanging off a yardarm in a midnight storm."

"My father knew sailing knots," Daniel said suddenly. "He was an engineer who built bridges during the war—worked on river crossings, had to understand boats for the pontoon bridges."

Thompson regarded the boy steadily. "Engineers are resourceful men. They understand secure connections."

The response satisfied Daniel, who returned to perfecting the knot. Jesse remained where she was, watching her son speak of William without the usual fear shadowing his features.

Jesse pressed her hand flat against her skirt, steadying the tremor that wanted to start there.

"He's a bright lad," Thompson observed, having noticed Jesse's presence. "Quick hands and a quicker mind."

"Thank you," she replied. Up close, his appearance concealed relative youth—perhaps thirty-five at most. "Daniel has always been drawn to practical skills."

"Useful trait in this world, ma'am." Thompson rose, tipping his hat before moving to join the other workers.

Daniel looked up at his mother. "I was just learning about sailing knots. For when we're living at the lighthouse."

"Indeed. Mr. Thompson seems knowledgeable."

"He worked on blockade runners during the war," Daniel said matter-of-factly, returning to his rope practice. "Fast ships that could outrun the Union navy. But he says now he prefers structures that stay in one place."

Her hand tightened on the stone beside her.

"He told me about one run," Daniel continued, eyes bright with interest. "They were carrying medical supplies through the blockade when a Union frigate spotted them. Had to navigate the shoals in complete darkness, using only sound and current to guide them. The captain wanted to jettison the medicine to gain speed, but Mr. Thompson convinced him to keep it. Said the Confederate hospital in Charleston had children dying of fever."

"What do you think of him?" she asked.

Daniel considered with characteristic seriousness. "When I asked about the Cape Hatteras storm, he said he didn't remember all the details. Most men would have made something up."

"That's a valuable observation," Jesse acknowledged. "Though a man may be honest about some things and not others."

"Like we are?" Daniel's direct gaze challenged her.

"What we face is not simple. But yes, we choose what truths to share."

"Because of Father. Because he might find us."

"Yes."

Daniel nodded, returning to his rope. "He didn't look at me the way some men do. Like I'm too young to be worth the truth."

Jesse smiled despite her concern. "A wise observation."

That evening, Miss Haskins appeared at Marsh Cottage with unexpected news.

"I've made additional inquiries," she announced without preamble. "Through my cousin in Savannah—she keeps house for the port authority clerk."

Jesse set down her mending. "Regarding Thompson?"

"Indeed. My cousin has access to shipping records, crew manifests." Miss Haskins's tone carried satisfaction. "Thompson's name appears on legitimate vessel registrations for the past eighteen months. Before that, a gap during the war years when records were... selective."

"And Roarke?"

"Ah, that information came through different channels. The harbormaster's wife attends my cousin's church. She mentioned an altercation at Donnelly's Tavern three weeks past. Roarke's men approached Thompson with an offer. He broke one man's nose and sent the other back with a refusal."

Jesse absorbed this. "Eighteen months of clean records. And a broken nose for Roarke's man."

"It would appear so. Though a cynic might suggest he's playing a longer game—establishing credibility before revealing true intentions."

"What's your assessment?"

The older woman's fingers drummed on her walking stick as she considered. "My network has served me well for forty years, Mrs. Whitmore. It helped identify Union sympathizers during the war, bootleggers during peacetime. I've cultivated sources in every church congregation from here to Savannah, and half the domestic servants on the coast owe me favors." She paused. "Men playing false usually try too hard to seem honest. Thompson doesn't try at all."

"Meaning?"

A slight shrug. "Draw your own conclusions."

After Miss Haskins departed, Jesse stood at the window. Thompson remained at the construction site, checking rope knots on the scaffolding, testing each one with a sharp tug.

# CHAPTER THIRTEEN

Blueprints and Ghosts
*The Eastern Shore—August 28, 1873*
*(Two weeks after the new workers arrived)*

T he late summer afternoon stretched across the eastern shore, the tide retreating to reveal a wide expanse of packed sand ideal for walking. Jesse followed Jonas along the water's edge, their shadows elongating as the sun sank toward the maritime forest behind them. The lighthouse stood in the distance, its tower nearly seventy feet tall.

These walks had become routine over the past fortnight as they discussed the day's progress and planned the next day's tasks. Today they had left Daniel and Eliza at Marsh Cottage with their studies, taking advantage of the low tide to inspect the shoreline for suitable locations for a small dock that would serve the lighthouse keeper's cottage once completed.

"The cove just north of the bluff path would offer the most protection," Jonas observed, gesturing toward a natural indentation in the shoreline. "Deep enough water for a small boat even at low tide and sheltered from the worst of the northeastern storms." He pulled a folded chart from his coat—one of his father's, Jesse had learned, with Henry Miller's annotations still visible in faded brown ink along the margins. "The depth here runs to at least eight feet at mean low tide—my father's soundings from sixty-two, confirmed by my own measurements last week. The tidal range averages seven feet, which means we need consistent access for supply boats carrying whale oil and lens components even at spring lows."

He crouched at the water's edge, tracing the rock formation with one hand. His fingers moved with precision, following the natural contours. Jesse noticed the scars across his knuckles—pale lines against weathered skin, the accumulated evidence of years working with stone and timber.

"The sand holds firmer here," he continued, tracing the curve of the shoreline with his hand. "Compacted shell beneath the surface. My father noted this stretch specifically—called it 'Providence Point' in his survey notes, though I don't know if the name was his invention or local tradition." He glanced up at her. "The foundation for BluffLight rests on driven pilings and packed substrate much like this. We would still need to bring in stone for a proper breakwater—granite from the mainland, most likely—but the base here would support it. It would give smaller vessels protection during the winter gales when the northeast winds drive straight into this shore."

Jesse studied the site, noting the rock formation that would provide a solid foundation for pilings. "Yes, I believe you're right. Though we'll need to clear a connecting path through that stand of palmetto."

Jonas nodded, making a brief notation in the small book he carried. They continued walking. William had filled every space with words, demanding constant response. Jonas allowed for silence.

A ship appeared on the horizon, its sails bright against the deep blue of the open ocean. Both paused to observe its passage, instinctively tracking its course relative to the dangerous shoals that lurked beneath the seemingly placid surface.

"Heading north to Savannah," Jonas noted. "A good day for sailing."

"Would it be visible from the lighthouse at this distance?" Jesse asked, mentally calculating the range of the future light based on the technical specifications they had been studying.

"Easily. The third-order Fresnel lens carries over twenty miles in clear conditions. That vessel couldn't be more than seven or eight miles offshore."

Jesse nodded.

"Shall we continue to the point?" she suggested, indicating the rocky promontory that extended into the sound at the island's northern tip. "The view might give us a better sense of the shipping lanes."

They resumed walking, the wet sand firm beneath their feet. A formation of brown pelicans passed overhead, their prehistoric silhouettes briefly shadowing the beach before they continued toward their evening roosts in the marsh. The tide pools left by the receding water teemed with tiny life—hermit crabs scuttling between shells, transparent shrimp darting among sea grasses, the occasional flash of a minnow caught in nature's temporary aquarium.

"Daniel mentioned you were a military engineer during the war," Jesse said.

Jonas glanced at her, perhaps surprised by the personal nature of the inquiry. "Yes. With the Confederate Corps of Engineers. We built bridges primarily—temporary structures to move troops and supplies across rivers. And when necessary, destroyed bridges to slow the Federal advance."

The admission carried no pride or remorse, a matter-of-fact acknowledgment of duties performed in a conflict that had reshaped all their lives. William had claimed to have saved a colonel's life at Antietam one night, then at Fredericksburg the next.

"William was an engineer as well," she offered. "Though he worked primarily on railway projects and fortifications."

Jonas received this information with a thoughtful nod. "Similar skills applied to different purposes." He paused. "My father had an engineer's mind as well. He wasn't formally trained, but he understood structural principles intuitively."

"You were close to him?"

"Very much so. He was a shipbuilder who occasionally supplied materials for coastal projects. When he began planning BluffLight, I watched him develop his ideas from the very beginning."

They reached a fallen log half-buried in the sand, smooth and silver from years of salt water and sun. Jonas paused, then gestured toward it with a questioning look. Jesse nodded, grateful for the opportunity to rest. Though her endurance had increased significantly since their arrival on the island, the combination of the day's heat and the distance walked left her glad for the respite.

Jonas lowered himself carefully, favoring his left leg as he settled onto the weathered wood. Jesse had noticed this before—the slight hitch in his gait that became more pronounced over distance, the way he positioned himself to keep weight off that side. He never mentioned it, and she never asked.

As they settled on the weathered wood, a comfortable distance between them, a pod of dolphins appeared in the sound, their sleek bodies arching through the water as they herded a school of fish toward the shallows.

"My father used to watch them hunt," Jonas commented, following her gaze to the graceful creatures. "Said they'd drive fish into the shallows where they were easier to catch."

"He must have known this shoreline well."

Jonas smiled slightly, his eyes still on the dolphins. "He was. A contradiction to those who didn't know him well—the precise mathematician who could quote Shakespeare at length, the methodical surveyor who tracked bird migrations." The smile faded. His hands, resting on his knees, tightened briefly. "He would have approved of the progress."

The shift was slight but visible—a tension in his jaw, a sudden stillness. Then he exhaled and looked away toward the water.

"Some days I still expect to find him at the site," he said quietly. "Checking measurements. Arguing with Gardner about mortar consistency." His voice roughened. "Foolish, after two years."

Jesse said nothing. She understood the way grief ambushed— how the mind could know something the heart refused to accept.

Jonas shook his head slightly, as if clearing it. "Forgive me. You didn't come on this walk to hear an old man's melancholy."

"You're hardly old," Jesse said. "And grief isn't something requiring forgiveness."

He glanced at her then—a quick, searching look that seemed to register something new. The dolphins surfaced again, closer now, their exhalations carrying across the still water.

She looked away, focusing on a sandpiper that darted along the water's edge.

"I'm still learning," she said finally. "Both the technical aspects and what the position requires."

Jonas nodded. They sat in silence as the dolphins completed their hunting circuit and moved back toward deeper water.

"Do you regret it?" Jesse asked. "Taking up this project after your father's death?"

Jonas considered it seriously, his gaze now fixed on the horizon where the ship they had observed earlier was disappearing from view.

"No," he said finally. "Though I questioned it at times." He paused. "It's work he started. Seems right to see it finished."

Jesse nodded.

"And you?" Jonas asked, turning the question back to her. "Do you regret accepting the keeper's role? It's not what most would consider suitable employment for a widow with young children."

The query held no judgment, only genuine interest in her perspective. Jesse considered how to answer truthfully without revealing too much of their circumstances.

"No," she said simply. "The work suits me. And it provides for the children."

Jonas nodded, seemingly satisfied with her response. "We should head back," he observed, noting the sun's position as it descended toward the tree line. "The children will be wondering where you are."

They rose from the log and retraced their steps along the beach. A ship's bell sounded faintly from somewhere in the distance—the evening watch change on one of the vessels anchored near the island's southern harbor. The familiar rhythm of eight bells, marking the end of one watch and the beginning of another, carried across the water.

The lighthouse grew larger as they approached.

As they reached the path that would take them back to their separate destinations—he to his small house near the village, she to Marsh Cottage where the children waited—the path divided. The evening light had softened, casting long shadows across the sandy track.

Jonas stopped. He seemed about to speak, then hesitated—his mouth opening slightly before closing again. His hand rose toward his hat brim, a gesture that went nowhere.

"Mrs. Whitmore," he began, then paused. "Jesse." The use of her given name was new. "I find these walks... useful. For the project."

"As do I," she said. "For the project."

Something flickered across his expression—amusement, perhaps, or recognition of what had gone unsaid. He nodded once, holding her gaze a moment longer than routine required.

"Until tomorrow, then."

"Until tomorrow."

Jesse turned toward Marsh Cottage. She was several steps down the path before she realized she was still aware of him standing there—could feel his presence behind her without looking. She did not look back.

The first stars appeared above the tree line as she walked.

# CHAPTER FOURTEEN

Marshside Market Day
*Western Marsh—September 3, 1873*
*(One week after Jesse and Jonas's beach walk)*

T he western marsh stretched beneath the early September sky, its expanse of cordgrass rippling in the breeze. Jesse followed Miss Haskins along the narrow boardwalk that extended from the island's western shore into the wetlands, careful to match the older woman's measured pace. Behind them, the main island rose in a gentle slope, its maritime forest forming a dark green backdrop to the sun-dappled waters and waving grasses.

"Mind your step," Miss Haskins cautioned, tapping her walking stick against a weathered plank. "This section floods during the highest tides. Even now, it's not entirely stable."

Jesse nodded, grateful for the warning as she felt the slight give beneath her feet. The weekly market held at the marsh's edge was new to her, though apparently a long-standing tradition among the island's inhabitants. Unlike the village market that catered to general needs, this smaller gathering specialized in the unique bounty of the coastal wetlands—items traded among locals instead of offered to summer visitors or mainland merchants.

"I appreciate your invitation," Jesse said, balancing the empty basket looped over her arm. With Daniel at school and Eliza spending the morning with Mrs. Gardner, whose husband continued to oversee the lighthouse masonry, Jesse had accepted Miss Haskins' unexpected suggestion to accompany her to what the older woman had cryptically described as "the real market."

"You've been here nearly five months," Miss Haskins replied. "It's time you learned the island's other economy." She paused at a junction where the main boardwalk branched into three separate paths snaking deeper into the marsh. "This way. The gathering happens at Oyster Point."

They turned onto the leftmost path, which widened slightly as it approached a small island of firm ground amid the wetlands. As they drew closer, Jesse could see a collection of small boats pulled up on the muddy shore and perhaps two dozen people engaged in quiet commerce. Unlike the lively village market, this gathering was quieter—goods examined, words exchanged in low tones, handshakes confirming transactions with minimal fanfare.

Most striking to Jesse was the market's composition. Here, former slaves traded alongside white islanders, the social distinctions relaxed by practical necessity. An elderly Black woman was showing sweetgrass baskets to the village doctor's wife. Nearby, a white fisherman and a young Black man compared cast nets.

"The marsh doesn't recognize human divisions," Miss Haskins commented.

As they stepped off the boardwalk onto the small patch of solid ground, several people nodded in greeting to Miss Haskins, their expressions reflecting various degrees of respect and wariness.

"Miss Amelia," a middle-aged Black woman called, gesturing toward a display of glass bottles containing various liquids. "I've prepared that marsh elder tincture you requested."

"Excellent, Ruth," Miss Haskins replied, making her way to the woman's simple table. "This is Mrs. Whitmore, who will be taking the keeper's position at BluffLight when it's completed. Mrs. Whitmore, Ruth Jackson is our most knowledgeable herbalist. Her remedies are far more effective than those expensive concoctions sold at Thatcher's store."

"A pleasure," Jesse greeted the woman, who studied her with intelligent eyes.

"You'll want something for sea colds. The tower will catch every wind once it's finished, and the damp will settle in your bones on winter watch."

Before Jesse could respond, Ruth was already selecting a small amber bottle from her collection. "Marsh rosemary and pine resin. Three drops in hot water at the first sign of chest tightness."

"You'll also need something for the lamp smoke," Ruth continued, selecting another bottle. "Whale oil burns clean, but the wick trimming creates fumes. This willow bark tincture helps with the headaches. And eye strain—staring into that bright lens for hours each night will tire your vision. Elderberry and marsh tea, twice daily."

"And for the hands," Ruth added, reaching for a small clay pot. "The brass fittings and glass panels—they'll be cleaned with spirits, yes? Dries the skin something terrible. This salve is rendered tallow with sea lavender and calendula."

"Thank you," Jesse said, accepting the bottle and reaching for her coin purse.

Ruth shook her head. "First remedy is always a gift. Builds the proper relationship between healer and patient." Her eyes crinkled slightly. "Besides, anyone standing against Roarke's interests deserves support."

The direct reference to the island's tensions startled Jesse, but Miss Haskins merely nodded.

They moved on after Miss Haskins collected her own purchases, making their way through the small marketplace.

At one table, a weathered man with calloused hands was displaying a collection of carved wooden bird decoys. Miss Haskins stopped, examining the pieces.

"Samuel's work continues to improve," she commented. "Mrs. Whitmore, you should consider these. Both decorative and functional."

Jesse studied the carvings—realistic renderings of ducks, herons, and shorebirds painted in subtle, natural colors. "They're beautiful. Though I'm afraid I don't hunt."

The carver—Samuel—looked up with a slight smile. "Not all decoys are for hunting, ma'am. Some are for watching."

Seeing her confusion, he elaborated. "Place the right bird at the marsh edge, and living ones will often approach, thinking they've found a friend. Lets children observe them up close. Educational, my grandfather called it."

Jesse selected a pair of carved sandpipers. "Daniel and Eliza would love that. How much?"

The transaction completed, they continued through the market.

As they passed a table stacked with mended nets, Jesse noticed a young woman receiving a parcel of salt pork and flour—no coin changing hands. The vendor, an older man with a pipe clenched in his teeth, marked something in a ledger and nodded toward the harbor.

"Roarke's account," Miss Haskins said quietly, following Jesse's gaze. "The widow Marsh. Her husband drowned last winter running cargo for him. Roarke's been providing for her since." Her tone carried no judgment, only information. "He inspires loyalty through such gestures. It complicates matters."

They walked in silence for a moment, passing several more vendors before Miss Haskins spoke again, her voice pitched low.

"You asked about Captain Roarke at our first meeting. It's time you understood who he truly is."

Jesse glanced at the older woman, surprised by the directness. "Jonas mentioned he ran the blockade during the war."

"He did. But it's more than simple patriotism." Miss Haskins paused at the marsh's edge, her eyes following the path of a heron wading through the shallows. "His family lost everything in '57. During the blockade, he ran medicine and munitions." She gestured subtly toward the village. "Half the merchants here still buy from him."

"So the community tolerates him."

"More than tolerate." Miss Haskins's expression hardened. Her gaze moved toward the village, then back.

"Thank you for trusting me with this," Jesse said.

Miss Haskins's sharp eyes studied her. "Men like Roarke are most dangerous when cornered."

Miss Haskins paused frequently to introduce Jesse to various islanders—some she had glimpsed in the village but never properly met, others who rarely ventured from their marsh-side dwellings. A net-mender's widow sold preserved fish; a former field hand traded vegetables from a garden plot reclaimed from the marsh's edge.

They eventually reached the far side of the small island, where the marsh opened into a wider channel. Here, an elderly Black man sat mending a cast net with methodical precision, his fingers moving with practiced ease despite their gnarled appearance. A pipe smoked unattended beside him.

"Solomon," Miss Haskins greeted him. "How does the tide run today?"

The man looked up, his aged face creasing into a smile that revealed several missing teeth. "Coming in strong from the southeast. Third quarter moon pulls sharper than most expect." His eyes shifted to Jesse, curious but not unwelcoming.

"Mrs. Whitmore," Miss Haskins said. "Soon to be keeper of BluffLight. Mrs. Whitmore, Solomon Davis knows the marsh channels better than any man on the island. He was born in a cabin not far from here, before most of these boardwalks existed."

"A lighthouse keeper should understand the waters as well as the land," Solomon observed, setting aside his net. "Come, let me show you something."

He rose with surprising agility for his apparent age and led them a short distance to where the island's elevation rose slightly, providing a broader view across the marsh. From this vantage point, Jesse could see the intricate network of channels winding through the cordgrass—some broad enough for boats, others silver threads reflecting the morning light.

"What do you see?" Solomon asked.

Jesse studied the panorama. "Water and grass. And the patterns they make together."

Solomon nodded. "Most folks just see mud and weeds. But you're right—it's the pattern that matters. Every channel tells a story about where water wants to go. Every stand of grass tells about the soil beneath."

He pointed toward a distant line of darker vegetation. "See that ridge of wax myrtles? Marks an old shell midden—ancient gathering place. And that bend in the big channel there? Deepest hole in the marsh. Holds water even at lowest tide, where redfish hold in winter."

Jesse followed his weathered finger, trying to fix the landmarks in her memory. "How do you know which channels lead safely through and which end in mud?"

"Same way you'll learn to read the sea from your lighthouse. By watching every day, through all seasons. By respecting what you don't understand until understanding comes."

They spent nearly an hour with Solomon, who named each grass and plant visible from their vantage point—cordgrass and needlerush, salt meadow hay and sea oxeye, marsh elder and glasswort. He explained how the different species grew in distinct zones based on how frequently they were flooded by salt water.

"The cordgrass can stand being underwater twice daily," he explained. "The needlerush needs less. The salt meadow hay just occasional splashing." He pointed to the island's slightly higher ground. "And the myrtles and cedars need dry feet most times."

Jesse listened intently. Something in her shoulders loosened as Solomon spoke—the patient rhythm of his teaching, the absence of expectation or judgment.

"And the birds follow this pattern as well?" she asked.

"Each to its own place," Solomon confirmed. "Herons in the deeper channels. Rails among the cordgrass. Sparrows in the high marsh. All finding the spot that suits their nature."

When they took their leave, the sweetgrass Solomon pressed into Jesse's hands smelled of salt and sun. Miss Haskins observed, "Solomon rarely speaks so much. He must have sensed your genuine interest."

"It was genuine," Jesse confirmed. "I've never seen the marsh from that perspective before."

They walked in silence for a while, the gentle rustling of cordgrass in the breeze creating a soothing backdrop. In the distance, a great blue heron rose from a hidden pool, its enormous wings moving in slow, powerful strokes.

"The lighthouse will change things," Miss Haskins said suddenly. "Not just the shipping routes or the island's economy."

Jesse considered this. "Change isn't always harm."

"No." Miss Haskins stopped walking. "But neither is it always improvement."

A mullet jumped in the nearby channel, silver flash against dark water.

As they reached the main shore and turned toward the village path, Miss Haskins' typically severe expression softened fractionally. "You're learning to see, Mrs. Whitmore. That's a promising beginning."

They parted ways at the crossroads, Miss Haskins heading toward her cottage near the church while Jesse turned toward the lighthouse office where she was due to meet Jonas for the afternoon's work.

The village path curved close to the harbor before veering east toward the bluff. Jesse slowed her pace, noting the way the midday haze softened the outlines of ships bobbing at anchor. The smell of tar and salt hung heavy in the humid air. Near a stack of drying nets, a cluster of dockhands lounged in the shade, trading stories in low, familiar voices.

"Best mind your step walking back tonight," one of the old dockhands muttered as Jesse passed, a gnarled hand brushing the brim of his battered cap.

She paused, half-curious. "And why's that?"

The men glanced at each other, faces weathered like old pilings sinking into the marsh. One shrugged and said, "Might see the lights. Marsh lights. Folk say it's the *Sea Wren*, still looking for safe harbor."

Jesse frowned. "A ship?"

"Was," the man said. "Went down near the shoals forty, maybe fifty years back. They say her lanterns still float up on foggy nights, bobbing along the marsh, lookin' for a way home."

The younger dockhand snorted. "Or it's just swamp gas. Science, y'know."

"You laugh now," the older one said, "but you'll laugh less when you're up to your knees in saltwater and no boat in sight."

The others nodded, their weathered faces solemn. One spat tobacco juice into the dust.

Jesse forced a polite smile and continued on.

Later, as she trudged the familiar path toward the bluff, the mist rose thick and silver over the marshes. For a wild moment, she thought she glimpsed a glimmer—a pale flicker where no lantern should be.

Her pulse quickened. She held her breath, every instinct sharpening the way it had in Richmond when footsteps sounded in the hall. The light—if it was a light—wavered and seemed to drift, as if carried by unseen hands across the water.

She walked faster.

She didn't look back until she reached the rise above the marsh. BluffLight's unfinished tower came into view.

# CHAPTER FIFTEEN

## Freight Delay
*BluffLight Construction Site—September 10, 1873*
*(One week after the marshside market)*

"Missing?" Jesse stared at the shipping manifest in her hand, then back at the half-empty wagon that had just arrived from the harbor. "The iron brackets weren't included?"

The driver, a weathered man with salt-stained clothing, shrugged apologetically. "Not on the packet when it docked, ma'am. The harbormaster checked the hold twice. The Charleston shipping agent sent most of the materials, but the brackets weren't included. Likely caught up in the warehouse fire from last week."

The iron brackets were essential components for securing the lantern room to the top of the lighthouse tower. Each bracket weighed nearly fifty pounds and required precise measurements— the mounting holes had to align perfectly with the stone anchors. A single misaligned bracket could compromise the entire structure. Without them, construction would halt once the stonework reached the upper platform—a milestone they were set to achieve within days.

"Any explanation? A note from the supplier?"

"Nothing official-like," the driver replied, shifting uncomfortably.

Jesse nodded. After months on the island, she had grown familiar with the accidents and delays that plagued the lighthouse project. She made a quick notation on the manifest before signing for the partial delivery.

"Please tell Mr. Bellamy I'll be sending a telegram to Charleston this afternoon to inquire about the situation," she said, her tone making it clear the message should be delivered verbatim.

As the driver departed, Jesse turned toward the lighthouse office. Behind her, two dock workers who had accompanied the wagon spoke in low tones near the water barrels. One mentioned something about the harbormaster's logs showing the brackets loaded, then crossed off. She caught only fragments before they moved out of earshot.

She made a note to reach out to Savannah that afternoon—if Charleston couldn't deliver, perhaps the next harbor could. The Savannah foundry had different specifications—their brackets used a wider mounting pattern that would require modifications to the stone anchors already set in place. It would mean chiseling out the existing holes and cutting new ones, risking damage to the fitted stones.

The tower now rose nearly eighty feet into the September sky.

Inside the office, Jesse found Jonas bent over the technical drawings for the lantern room assembly, his expression focused as he made precise measurements with a brass compass. He looked up at her entrance.

"Trouble with the delivery?" he asked.

"The iron brackets didn't arrive," Jesse confirmed, placing the manifest on the desk between them. "Everything else was on board—the glass panels, the copper sheeting, the specialized tools—but the brackets were apparently 'missing' from the shipment."

Jonas's face tightened slightly. "Without them, we can't secure the lantern room. And the foundry in Charleston requires at least three weeks to produce replacements."

"Three weeks during which the upper stonework will be completed, leaving the men without next steps," Jesse added. "We'll lose momentum, possibly even workers if they seek other employment during the delay."

Jonas nodded, his gaze moving to the window where the upper portion of the lighthouse was visible. "Unfortunate timing."

"I'll take responsibility for the situation," Jesse said.

Her jaw tightened as she spoke the words. Every instinct built over years with William whispered the opposite: stay invisible, draw no attention, let others absorb the blame. To stand in the open and invite scrutiny—this was the opposite of survival as she had learned it. Her shoulders squared. Her hands, which had wanted to clench, deliberately relaxed at her sides. She was choosing to be seen. Choosing to be the target.

"The men should direct their frustration at me instead of speculating about outside interference."

Jonas looked at her directly, surprise evident in his expression. "That's unnecessary. Supply management is only one aspect of your role here."

"It's the aspect most visible to the workers," Jesse countered. "Better they question my competence."

Jonas studied her for a moment. "The workers respect you."

"Then let them respect me enough to blame me for this. We'll adjust."

Jonas nodded once, accepting her decision. "We should explore alternatives while waiting for replacements. The Savannah foundry might be able to produce simpler brackets that could serve temporarily."

"I'll draft inquiries immediately," Jesse agreed. "And we should consider projects to keep the men employed once the stonework is complete. Perhaps beginning preparations for the keeper's cottage foundation or improving the bluff path for equipment transport."

Their discussion of contingency plans continued through the morning. By midday, they had outlined several possible approaches.

Jesse stood to leave, intending to check the stonework progress before meeting Daniel after his school session. As she gathered her notes, Jonas spoke.

"My father used to say that when work faltered, someone had to keep it moving."

Jesse paused at the door. "Then we'll keep it moving."

Outside, Jesse made her way toward the base of the lighthouse where Thomas Gardner was instructing his team on the next section of stonework. As she approached, the men paused their discussion, several glancing in her direction.

"Mrs. Whitmore," Gardner greeted her, his weathered face neutral. "We heard about the bracket shipment."

"Yes," Jesse acknowledged directly. "A significant oversight in my coordination with the Charleston suppliers. I apologize for the disruption it will cause to your work schedule."

Gardner's eyebrows rose slightly. "These things happen in construction. Especially on remote islands."

"Nevertheless, it was my duty to verify the complete shipment before the vessel sailed," Jesse continued. "Mr. Miller and I are exploring alternatives, including temporary brackets from Savannah that could allow the lantern room assembly to proceed while we await the proper components."

One of the younger workers—Robert, Gardner's apprentice—spoke up hesitantly. "Begging your pardon, ma'am, but couldn't we fashion something ourselves? There's a blacksmith in the village who might manage simpler ironwork."

Jesse considered this. "That's an excellent thought, Robert. Would the village smith have the necessary equipment for such large pieces?"

"Not alone," Gardner interjected. "But if we combined his forge with the shipyard's metalworking tools..."

The conversation quickly evolved into a technical discussion of local capabilities, the men's initial wariness giving way to engaged problem-solving. Jesse listened, asking questions that demonstrated her growing understanding of construction methods while acknowledging the superior practical experience of the workers themselves.

Gardner turned to her midway through the discussion. "Mrs. Whitmore, what's the maximum tolerance on the mounting holes? If we're modifying the anchor points, we'll need exact specifications."

"Three-sixteenths of an inch," Jesse replied without hesitation. "The Light-House Board specifications require the bolts to seat flush within that margin, or the vibration from high winds will work them loose over time."

Gardner nodded, something like approval crossing his weathered face. "Then we'll need to template the new positions before we start chiseling. Robert, fetch the calipers from the office."

By the time she departed for the village, several workers had volunteered to consult the blacksmith that evening.

The school building came into view, a modest structure adjacent to Christ Church where Miss Jenkins taught the island's children three days each week. Classes were concluding, and Daniel emerged deep in conversation with a boy several years older, their heads bent over a map or diagram.

"Mama," he called upon spotting her. "Benjamin has been telling me about tide calculations. His father was a pilot before the war and taught him how to predict the high water at different points around the island."

"That sounds fascinating," Jesse replied, nodding greeting to the older boy. "Perhaps useful knowledge for a future lighthouse keeper's assistant?"

Daniel's smile confirmed her assessment. "If you know the tide times and heights for the harbor, you can calculate the delay and difference for any other point. It's all mathematics—the Rule of Twelfths. First hour, one-twelfth. Second hour, two-twelfths. Third and fourth hours, three-twelfths each."

"Useful knowledge," Jesse agreed. "Would you like to invite Benjamin to visit the lighthouse construction sometime? He might be interested in the survey instruments Mr. Miller uses."

The suggestion pleased both boys. As they walked toward the crossroads where Benjamin would turn toward his home while Jesse and Daniel continued to the bluff, Daniel talked about how the principles applied to different channels.

"Benjamin says his father used to race the other pilots to incoming ships," Daniel said, grinning. "First one to reach the vessel got the fee for guiding it in. They'd bet on who could read the currents faster."

Benjamin ducked his head, half-embarrassed, half-proud. "Pa says Daniel's got the head for it. Says most folks don't care about the math, but the math's what keeps you off the shoals."

"Perhaps you could teach me sometime," Daniel said. "The racing part, I mean. Not with ships, but—"

"Skiffs," Benjamin supplied. "There's races in the spring. We could practice in the marsh channels. If your mama allows."

Both boys looked at Jesse with identical expressions of hopeful negotiation. She found herself smiling despite the day's frustrations. "We'll discuss it. After the lighthouse is operational."

They crested the path to find Eliza waiting with Miss Haskins at the lighthouse office, displaying a sketch of marsh birds she had made that morning.

By evening, the men had already begun assessing the village forge. Jesse stood at the cottage window, watching the last light fade from the sky. Daniel and Eliza were settled at the table behind her— Daniel copying passages from Henry Miller's journal, Eliza humming softly as she colored her bird sketches.

# CHAPTER SIXTEEN

### Raising the Frame
*BluffLight Construction Site—September 24, 1873*
*(Two weeks after the freight delay)*

T he morning arrived clear and still, a rare occurrence during the
volatile September weather. Jesse arrived at the construction
site earlier than usual, knowing this day's work would require every
hour of available light. In the two weeks since the bracket shipment
had failed to arrive, a collaboration had unfolded between the
lighthouse workers and the island's craftsmen.

The village blacksmith, a reserved German immigrant named
Mueller, had studied Jonas's technical drawings and produced a set
of temporary brackets—simpler than the originals but sturdy
enough to support the lantern room once reinforced with elements
borrowed from ship fittings until the proper components arrived
from Charleston. Meanwhile, Jesse had secured an agreement from
the Savannah shipyard to provide additional metal supports,
creating redundant security for the crucial junction where masonry
tower met iron-framed lantern assembly.

Now, with the stonework completed to the upper platform, they
were ready to raise the first tier of the lantern room framework—an
operation requiring precise coordination among two dozen men
positioned at various levels of the lighthouse.

"The ironwork has been tested?" Jesse asked Jonas as they
conducted a final review before the day's work began.

He nodded. "Each bracket loaded to twice the weight it will
bear. Mueller's work proved excellent—the metal failed at other
points before his welds gave way. He used a technique from his
apprenticeship in Hamburg—overlapping the joints and
hammering them at precisely the right temperature."

"And the weather forecast?"

"Fair through evening, according to Solomon Davis. He reads the marsh birds better than any barometer." Jonas glanced toward the assembled workers, who were checking ropes and pulley systems near the base of the tower. "The men are ready. We should begin."

Jesse moved to her position at the temporary desk established outside the lighthouse office. From here, she would coordinate communication between the teams—those at ground level managing the hoisting apparatus, those at mid-tower securing guide ropes, and those on the upper platform who would receive and place each section of the frame. With the noise of construction and the height of the tower making direct communication impossible, she would relay signals and maintain the choreography of the complex operation.

Daniel had arrived with her that morning, his school lessons set aside with Miss Jenkins' blessing so he could witness this milestone in the lighthouse construction. He now stood a careful distance from the activity, his notebook open as he sketched the scene with growing technical precision.

"First section ready for lifting," announced Thomas Gardner, who oversaw the ground team. "Awaiting your signal, Mrs. Whitmore."

Jesse raised the red flag that would alert the upper platform team to prepare for incoming materials. When Micah Thompson, positioned at the top, responded with a corresponding signal, she gave Gardner the nod to proceed.

The operation began with meticulous slowness. The first section of iron framework—an angular segment that would form one-quarter of the lantern room's base—rose gradually as six men turned the winch in careful unison. The winch system employed a three-to-one mechanical advantage, tripling their lifting power while maintaining control. Two other men steadied the piece with guide ropes, preventing it from spinning or striking the stonework during its ascent.

Jesse maintained a steady count, calling out measurements as the three-hundred-pound section passed marked points on the tower. "Twenty feet... thirty feet... approaching forty..."

"Approaching upper platform," she called as the section neared its destination. "Prepare to secure."

The section's ascent slowed, then stopped precisely at the level where Thompson and three other men waited. Using tools specially designed for working at height, they guided the heavy frame into position against the temporary brackets. Thompson used a plumb bob to verify perfect vertical alignment—even a half-degree deviation would compound as they built upward, potentially making the lens installation impossible. The clang of metal meeting metal carried in the still air, followed by Thompson's signal flag indicating successful placement.

"First section secure," Jesse announced. "Prepare second section for lifting."

The process repeated with the remaining three sections of the base frame, each requiring the same deliberate care, each concluding with confirmation from above. By midday, the entire base was in place—a complete iron ring now crowning the stone tower, secured by Mueller's brackets and additional bracing designed by Miller. The assembled framework weighed nearly a ton, its octagonal shape precisely aligned to distribute wind loads evenly across all eight support points.

As the workers paused for their meal, Jesse joined Daniel, who had moved closer to study the next phase of construction.

"It's exactly as in Mr. Miller's journal," he said, showing her his sketch alongside the historical diagram he had copied from Henry's records. "He designed the lantern room to allow for expansion of the light apparatus without rebuilding the entire structure. The mounting brackets could accommodate a first-order Fresnel lens weighing up to four tons, though they'd start with a third-order lens at just eight hundred pounds."

"Sensible foresight," Jesse observed.

"Mr. Miller says I may accompany him up the interior stairs this afternoon," Daniel continued. "He wants to show me how they'll align the upper framework with the stone beneath."

"A valuable lesson," Jesse agreed. "Just remember to maintain three points of contact at all times, as Mr. Gardner taught you."

"I will," Daniel promised.

After the brief respite, work resumed with the raising of the vertical supports that would extend from the base frame upward to form the walls of the lantern room. These pieces were lighter than the base sections but required even greater precision in placement, as any misalignment would prevent proper installation of the glass panels that would eventually enclose the space.

Jesse returned to her coordination position, once again acting as the communication nexus between ground and tower top. The afternoon proceeded without incident, each vertical support rising and settling into its designated position under the guidance of Thompson's team. By the time the sun descended toward the western marshes, the basic framework of the lantern room stood complete—a geometric skeleton that would soon house the powerful light designed to reach over twenty miles across the Atlantic.

As the workers secured their tools and prepared to descend, Jonas joined her after overseeing the final security checks. "A significant day. The first time BluffLight has looked as my father envisioned it."

Jesse nodded. "And accomplished despite the missing shipment."

"Because of it," Jonas said. "Without that setback, we wouldn't have discovered Mueller's skills or the shipyard's willingness to collaborate."

"There's a lesson in that," she said, "though I'm not certain Roarke would appreciate being the unwitting teacher."

Jonas gave a short nod. "Perhaps not. Speaking of lessons— your son shows remarkable aptitude for engineering principles. His questions during our tower inspection demonstrated unusual insight for his age."

"Daniel has always been observant," Jesse acknowledged. "Though since coming here, he's had more chances to use it."

Jonas nodded. "He's taken well to the work." He looked back toward the lighthouse, where Daniel was descending the exterior scaffolding under Gardner's watchful eye. "The island has been good for him. For all of you, I think."

"Yes," she agreed. "It has."

The construction site emptied, workers departing in small groups toward the village. Lingering conversations carried across the bluff, plans for the tavern later.

"Will you join the celebration this evening?" Jonas asked. "The men would welcome your presence. Your coordination today was essential to their success."

Jesse hesitated. Since arriving on the island, she had maintained careful distance from social gatherings.

The evening light caught Jonas's profile—the strong line of his jaw, the patience in his expression as he waited for her answer. He didn't press, didn't fill the silence with persuasion. He simply stood, the completed framework rising behind him, and let her decide. She became aware of the sawdust on his sleeve, the fatigue around his eyes that couldn't dim the quiet satisfaction there.

"I'd need to settle the children first," she said. "Perhaps I could come for a short while."

Eliza was spending the evening with Widow Patterson, engaged in a project involving shell decorations. And Daniel had been invited to dine with Miss Jenkins and her father.

"I'll be passing the crossroads at seven," Jonas said.

"That works."

Daniel joined them, still recounting the tower ascent, as the last workers departed toward the village.

# CHAPTER SEVENTEEN

## The Drowned Man
*Northern Beach—October 2, 1873*
*(One week after raising the lantern room frame)*

The shout carried on the morning breeze, faint but urgent. Jesse looked up from the tide pools where she and Eliza had been examining tiny crabs and sea anemones. They'd risen early for their weekly shore exploration—an educational ritual begun at Miss Haskins' suggestion.

"Mama, someone's calling," Eliza said.

Jesse shaded her eyes, scanning the beach northward. A figure waved frantically from the shoreline perhaps a quarter-mile distant, where driftwood marked the island's northernmost point.

"Stay close to me," she instructed, gathering their collection basket. As they drew closer, Jesse recognized young Robert Gardner, the mason's apprentice.

The quality of light changed as they walked—or perhaps it was only her perception shifting, her body reading the young man's posture before her mind could name what was wrong. The shore birds that usually worked the tide line had vanished. No gulls cried. No sandpipers darted. The silence pressed against her ears like cotton, broken only by the rhythmic hiss of waves and the crunch of shells beneath her boots.

Her pulse quickened. Her breath came shallow. The sand seemed different here—darker where the tide had recently retreated, and something about the arrangement of driftwood ahead looked deliberate, as if the sea had deposited its burden with purpose rather than chance.

"Mrs. Whitmore!" Robert called, his voice tight. "Please fetch Mr. Miller or the pastor! There's a body—" He broke off, glancing at Eliza.

"Eliza, wait here," Jesse directed, positioning her daughter near a large piece of driftwood. "Count how many different shells you can find within ten paces, but do not approach the water."

The girl nodded solemnly. Jesse covered the remaining distance quickly.

"Show me," she said when she reached Robert.

He led her around salt-bleached logs to where the incoming tide lapped at a dark form half-buried in wet sand. A man lay face down, his clothing sodden, his limbs arranged at unnatural angles.

The smell reached her first—brine and marsh grass and something beneath it, something her body recognized before her mind could name. Copper. Decay just beginning. The wrongness of flesh where it did not belong.

Wet sand clung to the man's clothing, to his hair, to the exposed skin of his hands. His coat was heavy with seawater, dragging at his frame, making him seem smaller than he must have been in life. One arm was flung out as if reaching for something; the other was pinned beneath his body. The waves lapped at his boots—one boot, she corrected herself. The other foot was bare, the flesh pale and waterlogged.

Jesse's stomach tightened. She forced herself to breathe evenly, in through the nose, out through the mouth.

"I was collecting driftwood for my mother's garden," Robert explained. "Found him just as the tide was turning. He can't have been here long—the water would have taken him back out."

Jesse approached. "We should turn him. Identify him if possible."

Together, they rolled the body onto its back. The man appeared to be in his thirties, bearded, weathered. His clothing was that of a sailor—canvas trousers, woolen shirt heavy with seawater, sturdy boots. One boot was missing. Sailors knew to tie their laces in reef knots that wouldn't come loose accidentally.

"Do you recognize him?" Jesse asked.

Robert shook his head. "Not from the island. Might be crew from one of the trading vessels."

Jesse was about to suggest they seek help when something caught her eye—a mark on the man's exposed forearm. She leaned closer, brushing away wet sand to reveal what looked like a brand: an "R" enclosed within a crude circle. Old but deep, likely made with a heated marlinspike.

"What is that?" Robert asked.

Footsteps approached. Jonas was crossing the beach toward them.

"Robert. Mrs. Whitmore." He greeted them before turning to the body. "When?"

"Just found him, sir," Robert replied. "Mrs. Whitmore helped me turn him."

Jonas knelt beside the drowned man. When he reached the marked forearm, his face tightened.

"You recognize it," Jesse said.

Jonas nodded. "Roarke's mark. He brands men who serve on his vessels—an old practice, though illegal now. This man was one of his crew."

The confirmation sent a chill through Jesse. Why would one of Roarke's sailors be washed ashore on the remote northern beach?

"Robert," Jonas said, "return to the village and inform Pastor Willoughby. Ask him to bring men and a cart. Then find Constable Hayes."

The young man departed quickly. Once he was beyond earshot, Jonas spoke more frankly.

"This is no drowning," he said, indicating subtle discolorations at the man's neck. "He was dead before he entered the water."

Jesse had noticed the marks but had hesitated to voice the conclusion. "Why would Roarke dispose of one of his own men?"

"Discipline, perhaps. Or to prevent him speaking of something he witnessed." Jonas surveyed the shoreline. "The northern currents should have carried a body out to sea, not deposited it here. At this time of year, with the equinoctial tides, anything entering the water north of Gould's Inlet would be swept toward Cumberland Sound. Yet here he is."

Jesse said nothing.

Jonas nodded. "And not the first such I've encountered."

A small voice called from beyond the driftwood. "Mama? May I come now? I've counted fourteen different shells!"

Jonas immediately removed his coat and laid it over the dead man's face and upper body. "Yes, Eliza," Jesse called, composing her features. "But stay on this side of the logs, please."

Eliza appeared with her collection basket. She hesitated upon seeing Miller, then approached politely.

"Good morning, Mr. Miller," she greeted him. "Are you collecting shells too?"

"Not today," he replied. "I was inspecting the tides before work begins."

Eliza accepted this, more interested in displaying her discoveries. "Look, Mama! I found a perfect angel wing shell. Miss Haskins says they're uncommon here."

She held it up—a delicate thing, translucent white with fine ridges radiating from the hinge, curved like a wing indeed. The morning light shone through it, revealing the faint pink blush near its center. Eliza's face was bright with uncomplicated joy, her earlier concern about the shouting already forgotten in the pleasure of her discovery.

Jesse took the shell in her palm, feeling its impossible lightness. Her daughter's hands were still sandy, her cheeks flushed from the morning's explorations. She knew nothing of what lay beyond the driftwood. Her world still held only shells and birds and the simple adventure of a beach walk with her mother.

"It's beautiful," Jesse acknowledged, her voice steady through effort alone. "We should take it to show Daniel when he returns from his lessons."

Jonas rose. "I'll remain until help arrives. You should take Eliza home."

Jesse nodded. "Please let me know if there are developments I should be aware of."

The carefully phrased request encompassed her unspoken concern: whether this incident represented a specific threat to the lighthouse project.

Jonas understood. "I'll come by the cottage this evening. Once matters here are resolved."

As Jesse guided Eliza back along the beach, she found herself newly alert to every movement in the dunes, every shadow among the forest's edge.

"Why was Mr. Miller's coat on the sand?" Eliza asked as they climbed the wooden steps. "Was someone sleeping there?"

Jesse hesitated. "A man was injured. Mr. Miller was helping him until more help arrives."

"Oh." Eliza processed this. "Like when Daniel hurt his arm, and Mr. Miller brought him home?"

"Something like that," Jesse agreed.

They walked in silence, Eliza occasionally stopping to examine plants along the path.

At Marsh Cottage, Jesse checked the door latch twice before going inside.

That evening, after the children were asleep, Jonas arrived as promised.

"The man was Roarke's first mate," he said, accepting the cup of tea she offered. "Thomas Merrick. Missing from the *Miranda* for three days, according to the harbormaster's report."

"The same man I saw at the docks." Jesse set down her own cup. "The one Fletcher called Roarke's enforcer."

Jonas nodded. "Constable Hayes examined the body. Death by strangulation, followed by deliberate placement in the water. No attempt to weight the body or ensure it wouldn't be found."

"A public execution," Jesse said.

"And a warning to others in Roarke's employ." Jonas's gaze was steady. "The lighthouse nears completion. His opposition grows more desperate."

Jesse rose and moved to the window, looking out at the darkness beyond the glass. Jonas's reflection appeared beside her own—he had risen too, standing closer than the small cottage required.

"My father suspected Roarke of worse than smuggling," Jonas said quietly. "He kept records—shipments that disappeared, vessels that foundered on routes Roarke's pilots had charted. Men who asked too many questions and then... stopped asking."

"Like Merrick."

"Like Merrick." Jonas's voice was rough. "My father was building this lighthouse to end Roarke's hold on these waters. A proper light means proper shipping lanes, federal inspections, accountability. Everything Roarke has avoided for twenty years."

"And your father's death?"

Jonas was silent for a long moment. "The physician said pneumonia. But my father was hale that autumn—I have letters from October where he describes walking the bluff daily, supervising the foundation work. By December he was dead." His hand, resting on the windowsill, had curled into a fist. "His logbook disappeared the night before we buried him. Someone wanted those records."

Jesse turned from the window. In the dim lamplight, Jonas's face showed the weight he carried.

"We're close now," she said. "Weeks away."

"Yes." He met her eyes. "Which is why I need you to understand what we're facing. This isn't just opposition to a building project. Roarke has killed to protect his operations. He'll kill again if he believes it necessary."

The words hung between them. Jesse became aware of how near they stood—close enough to see the pulse at his throat, to smell the salt air that clung to his coat. The cottage was very quiet. The children slept in the loft above. Outside, the autumn wind moved through the pines.

"I'm not leaving," she said.

Jonas's expression shifted—something that might have been relief, or fear, or both. His hand rose, hesitated, then came to rest briefly on her arm. The touch was light, almost formal, but it lingered a moment longer than reassurance required.

"I know," he said. "That's what concerns me."

"We continue," she said.

Jonas studied her face for a long moment. "Yes," he agreed. "We continue."

He retrieved his hat from the table, pausing at the door. The night air entered with the scent of pine and salt, cold against Jesse's face after the cottage's warmth.

"Lock the door behind me," he said. "And keep the lamp burning until you sleep."

Then he was gone, his footsteps fading down the path.

Jesse stood in the doorway, watching his lantern grow smaller in the darkness until it disappeared around the bend toward the village. The autumn wind cut through her shawl. Above her, she could hear the soft breathing of her sleeping children.

She closed the door and turned the lock. Then she climbed the ladder to check on Daniel and Eliza—both peaceful, undisturbed.

# CHAPTER EIGHTEEN

Saltwater Secrets
*Marsh Cottage—October 5, 1873*
*(Three days after finding the drowned man)*

T he autumn rain fell steadily outside Marsh Cottage. Jesse sat at the small table while Miss Haskins examined the contents of her teacup. Neither woman had spoken for several minutes.

Miss Haskins broke the stillness. "You intend to tell me about the drowned man, I presume. That's why you invited me here while the children are away."

Jesse had arranged for Daniel and Eliza to spend the rainy afternoon at the Widow Patterson's cottage, ostensibly to help with indoor chores but primarily to create the privacy this conversation required. If anyone could help her understand the implications of recent events, it would be this sharp-eyed observer of Saint Simons' hidden currents.

"Yes," Jesse confirmed. "I need to understand what it means— not just for the lighthouse project, but for my family's safety."

Miss Haskins set down her cup. "It means Roarke is desperate. He doesn't dispose of useful men lightly, particularly not one who has served as his right hand for years. Merrick knew too much to be dealt with as simple discipline."

"Then why?"

"Perhaps Merrick was developing a conscience. Or negotiating with authorities. Or he questioned Roarke's opposition to the lighthouse." Miss Haskins adjusted her black shawl. "There is history between Roarke and the lighthouse that precedes your arrival, Mrs. Whitmore. History between Roarke and both Millers— father and son."

This direct reference sparked immediate interest. "What kind of history?"

"War and its aftermath." The older woman weighed her words. "Henry Miller's plans for BluffLight were well advanced before the conflict began. Roarke was nobody then—a few small cargo runs."

"What changed?"

"The blockade. Roarke expanded from marginal trader to major operation within a year." Miss Haskins sipped her tea. "When Henry returned after Appomattox to resume construction, he found the political landscape altered. Opposition was subtle at first— bureaucratic delays, material shortages."

"But it became more direct."

"Drastically so." Miss Haskins' voice took on a harder edge. "Henry began making inquiries about shipments arriving at unusual hours, about discrepancies in the port ledger." She paused. "His death the following winter—pneumonia, the physician recorded. Though there were those who wondered."

Jesse kept her voice neutral. "Wondered what?"

"His personal logbook from that last month disappeared from his study the night before his burial. So did his detailed charts of the northern channels. The housekeeper found the desk drawer forced open."

Jesse had known, in a general way, that Henry Miller had died before seeing his lighthouse completed. But the suggestion of deliberate elimination cast the project—and her own role in it—in sharper relief.

"And Jonas Miller?"

"Jonas served with the Confederate Corps of Engineers, as did his father. He returned from the war to find Henry's health declining and the lighthouse half-abandoned. Jonas took up Henry's work as an engineer honoring another engineer's unfinished work."

The connection explained Jonas's quiet determination, his refusal to abandon the project despite years of setbacks. Jesse had accepted the keeper's position for similar reasons—employment, but also purpose.

"Why tell me this now?" she asked.

"Because Merrick's death changes the nature of your involvement." The older woman's gaze was penetrating. "Until now, you've been peripheral in Roarke's calculations—a widow with children, employed by Jonas but not essential to his plans. That perception protected you."

"And now?"

"Now Roarke knows the lighthouse will be completed despite his efforts. The lantern room frame stands, the glass installation progresses, and within weeks the first light will shine. His focus will shift to the keeper—to you."

The words settled heavily. Outside, rain dripped steadily from the eaves. "You believe my family is in danger."

"I believe Roarke is unpredictable when cornered," Miss Haskins corrected. "And I believe there are aspects of your situation that might become relevant should he decide to investigate more thoroughly."

The subtle reference to Jesse's "situation" made her breath catch. Had Miss Haskins deduced the truth about their arrival on the island?

"What do you know?"

Miss Haskins met her gaze steadily. "I know that women don't flee comfortable circumstances without compelling reasons. I know that a mother who has gone to such lengths to protect her children will not abandon that purpose now. And I know that you are more capable than perhaps you realize."

It wasn't a direct acknowledgment of Jesse's false widowhood, but the understanding was unmistakable. Miss Haskins had drawn her own conclusions but chose to keep them unspoken—a discretion that honored Jesse's privacy while offering tacit support.

"I need to protect them," Jesse said.

"Then you'll need allies." Miss Haskins rose and moved to the window, watching the rain trace patterns down the glass. "The island has factions, Mrs. Whitmore. Those who prosper from Roarke's operations and those who suffer from them. Those who welcome the lighthouse's completion and those who dread it. It's time you knew where everyone stands."

For the next hour, Miss Haskins provided a detailed assessment of the island's power structure. Thomas Fletcher at the general store carried twice the inventory he could afford. The

Harrison brothers ran night deliveries to vessels anchored beyond the bar.

A gust of wind rattled the window. Miss Haskins moved to refill her teacup.

But more importantly, she named those Jesse could trust. Solomon Davis, whose knowledge of marsh channels had frustrated Roarke's operations for years. Ruth Jackson. Pastor Willoughby, whose sermons on justice were more pointed than casual churchgoers realized.

"And Jonas Miller?" Jesse asked, though she believed she already knew the answer.

"As trustworthy as his father before him," Miss Haskins confirmed. "Though perhaps less willing to recognize danger until it confronts him directly. Henry was more politically astute—he understood that corruption often wears a respectable face."

As the rain eased to a gentle mist, Jesse walked Miss Haskins to the cottage door.

"One last question," Jesse said as the older woman prepared to depart. "Why have you chosen to help us? You could live quietly, avoiding involvement."

Miss Haskins adjusted her shawl with precise movements. "I had a brother once," she said, her voice matter-of-fact but carrying an undertone Jesse had never heard before. "A ship's navigator before the war. He specialized in coastal charts—knew every shoal from Charleston to Jacksonville. He insisted that proper charts and signals would save lives, regardless of who profited or lost by their existence." She met Jesse's gaze directly. "He disappeared during a voyage to Charleston in '52. His body was never found."

The words landed like stones dropped into still water. Jesse's hand tightened on the doorframe.

Jesse drew in a breath. "You believe Roarke was responsible?"

"He was newer to his trade then." Miss Haskins' expression hardened briefly before returning to its usual composure. "My brother's logbook showed that he'd mapped certain channels. Three weeks later, he was gone."

With that statement, she departed, her straight-backed figure soon disappearing into the misty afternoon. Jesse remained in the doorway.

When Jonas arrived that evening to discuss the next day's construction schedule, the cottage felt different. He paused at the threshold, sensing the weight of the day even before she spoke.

Jesse saw the rain still clinging to his coat, the weariness in the set of his shoulders. His eyes moved over her face, reading something there, and for a moment neither of them spoke. The evening air entered with him—damp earth, pine resin, the particular coolness that came after rain.

"Miss Haskins visited today," she mentioned as they reviewed the plans for installing the glass panels in the lantern room.

Jonas glanced up. "Did she? I imagine that was informative."

"Very," Jesse confirmed. "She helped me understand certain island histories I hadn't known."

He studied her briefly before responding. "Miss Haskins has observed this island longer than most of us have been alive. Her insights are valuable, if sometimes difficult to hear."

She nodded. They returned to the construction plans.

Outside, the mist had lifted.

# CHAPTER NINETEEN

### Fireflies in the Belfry
*Christ Church—October 12, 1873*
*(One week after Jesse's conversation with Miss Haskins)*

The evening service had concluded, leaving Christ Church lit by oil lamps and candles. Most of the congregation had departed, but Jesse lingered in the back pew, Henry Miller's journal open on her lap. Eliza sat beside her, unusually quiet, while Daniel had remained outside to help Pastor Willoughby extinguish the entrance lanterns.

The sounds of leaving changed the space—footsteps on wooden floors growing fewer, murmured farewells fading to silence, the heavy door closing with a final thud that echoed through the rafters. The settling quiet had its own texture, like water finding its level. Candle flames steadied now that no one moved past them, and the smell of extinguished wicks mingled with the familiar scents of old hymnals, lemon oil on polished pews, the faint mustiness of decades of worship soaked into wood and stone. Jesse's shoulders lowered. Her breathing slowed.

It had become their Sunday ritual to spend these peaceful moments in the empty church, reading passages from the journal. Today, with the lantern room glass panels installed and the light mechanism scheduled to arrive within the week, Jesse had sought a passage Henry had written about practical construction details— one of the few complete entries that had survived intact.

"*October 8, 1860,*" she read softly. "*Today I stood within the lantern room of the Charleston lighthouse, studying how the morning sun brightened its glass panels from various angles. The glass amplifies the light, each panel becoming a conduit that directs the beam outward.*"

Eliza leaned against her mother's arm. "What's a conduit, Mama?"

"Something that carries or directs something else—like the way the creek channel carries water from the forest to the marsh," Jesse explained. "Henry was describing how the lighthouse's glass helps direct light outward."

"Like the prisms Miss Jenkins showed us," Daniel contributed, returning from his lantern-extinguishing duties. "They don't just let light pass—they change its direction."

Jesse nodded. "Exactly. Henry understood that every part of the lighthouse served its purpose—the flame, the lens that focuses it, the glass that protects it, the structure that raises it high enough to see from a distance."

"And the keeper who tends it," came Pastor Willoughby's voice from the church entrance. He approached slowly, his footsteps echoing softly on the wooden floor. "Henry often spoke of the keeper's responsibilities."

"You knew him well?" Jesse asked.

"We arrived on the island within months of each other," Pastor Willoughby confirmed, settling into the pew across the aisle. "His vision for BluffLight was part of what convinced me to accept the position here."

"Like the way he designed the lantern room to allow for technological improvements," Daniel observed, his growing familiarity with the lighthouse's technical aspects evident.

The pastor nodded. "Precisely. He built for the future." His gaze shifted to Jesse. "I understand the lighthouse installation progresses well. Jonas mentioned that the light mechanism should arrive from Savannah by week's end."

"If there are no further delays," Jesse replied, the slight emphasis conveying her awareness that previous shipping problems had been deliberate.

The pastor's expression grew more serious. "Recent events have heightened certain tensions on the island. Merrick's death remains unexplained in official terms, but the unofficial understanding has spread widely." He glanced meaningfully at the children, then back to Jesse. "Perhaps the young ones might enjoy seeing the church belfry while we discuss some parish matters?"

Jesse nodded. "Daniel, would you show Eliza the bell tower? I'm sure Pastor Willoughby wouldn't mind if you carefully explored it before dark."

"Of course," the pastor agreed, producing an iron key from his pocket. "Just be mindful of the ladder's last three rungs—they're awaiting repair."

Daniel accepted the key with solemn responsibility, taking Eliza's hand as they moved toward the small door at the church's western corner.

The ladder was older than Daniel had expected—rough-hewn wood worn smooth by decades of bell-ringers' hands. He climbed carefully, testing each rung, with Eliza following close behind.

"Is it much further?" she whispered, though there was no one to hear them.

"Almost there. Hold tight."

The belfry opened above them—a small square room with louvered openings on all four sides. The great bronze bell hung in the center, its surface green with age, the rope coiled neatly at its base. But it was not the bell that made Eliza gasp.

"Daniel, look!"

Fireflies. Dozens of them, drifting through the dim space like fallen stars. They pulsed their cold light against the whitewashed walls, which caught and reflected each tiny glow until the whole belfry seemed to shimmer.

"They must come in through the louvers," Daniel said, watching one land on the bell itself, its light winking against the bronze. "The white walls make their light seem brighter. It's reflection—like how the lighthouse lens will work."

"It's magic," Eliza breathed.

"It's bioluminescence," Daniel corrected, but he was smiling. "A chemical reaction in their bodies. Miss Jenkins explained it."

Eliza wasn't listening. She had stretched out her hand, palm up, and a firefly landed on her finger. Its light pulsed once, twice, three times before it lifted away to join the others.

"They're talking to each other," she said. "That's what the lights mean. Miss Haskins told me. The boys flash to find the girls."

Daniel watched his sister's face, soft with wonder in the flickering glow. For a moment, he let himself feel only this—the magic of the small space, the ancient bell, the impossible lights. No fear. No watching the door. Just his sister's delight and the silent conversation of a hundred tiny creatures signaling to each other in the dark.

"We should go back down," he said finally. "Mama will worry."

"Can we come again sometime?"

"Maybe. If Pastor Willoughby says yes."

They descended carefully, the fireflies still glowing above them like a secret they would carry home.

Once the children were out of earshot, Pastor Willoughby turned to Jesse with newfound directness.

"Miss Haskins informed me of your conversation," he said without preamble. "I believe she was right to share certain island histories with you."

She nodded. "She helped me understand why Roarke opposes the lighthouse so vehemently. And why Merrick's death represents a significant escalation."

"Indeed." The pastor's normally gentle demeanor hardened slightly. "The war changed many fortunes on this island. BluffLight will shift the balance again."

"What might we anticipate?" Jesse asked. "In these final weeks."

Pastor Willoughby considered her question. "Roarke has eliminated his most trusted lieutenant—a man who knew all his operations. Desperation, not calculated planning." He met her gaze directly. "I would counsel vigilance. Particularly until the light is operational."

"Can you be more specific? What has he done before, when opposed?"

The pastor's expression darkened. "Three years ago, a customs inspector from Savannah began asking questions about Roarke's shipping manifests. The man was thorough—too thorough. He'd found discrepancies in the cargo weights, evidence that Roarke was

151

landing goods that never appeared on any official record." He paused. "The inspector's boat capsized during a routine harbor crossing. Calm water, experienced sailor. His body washed up at Jekyll Island a week later."

Jesse's hands tightened in her lap.

"Before that, there was a merchant who refused to buy from Roarke's suppliers. His warehouse burned. The fire was ruled accidental, but the man left the island within a month." The pastor's voice was quiet but hard. "Roarke doesn't confront directly. He erodes. He waits for the moment when opposition seems like bad luck rather than malice."

"And afterward?" Jesse asked. "After the light is operational?"

"That depends on whether Roarke can adapt." The pastor's expression suggested skepticism. "Men who have held power unchallenged for years rarely do. But once the light shines, the federal government takes interest. Light-House Board inspectors, revenue cutters patrolling the shipping lanes. The darkness Roarke requires for his operations becomes harder to maintain."

"So the danger is now. These next weeks."

"These next weeks," Pastor Willoughby confirmed. "When he has everything to lose and nothing yet lost."

Before they could continue, excited footsteps announced the children's return from the belfry.

"Mama! We saw fireflies in the bell tower!" Eliza exclaimed. "They were all around the bell!"

"The white walls reflect their light," Daniel added.

Pastor Willoughby smiled. "They gather there at dusk."

Jesse gathered her things as they prepared to depart. As they stepped outside into the deepening twilight, the first stars were becoming visible overhead. To the north, the silhouette of BluffLight stood against the darkening sky, its lantern room now fully enclosed with glass that caught the last reflection of sunset.

"I was thinking, Mama," Daniel said as they walked the familiar path toward Marsh Cottage, "about what Henry Miller wrote. The lighthouse will help ships we never see."

Jesse didn't answer. She was watching the darkening tree line.

When they reached the cottage, Jesse paused briefly to look back toward the distant church, barely visible now as darkness settled fully over the island.

That night, a soft knock at the door woke her from uneasy sleep.

Jesse rose quickly, wrapping her shawl around her nightdress, her heart already racing. She checked that the children's breathing remained steady in the loft above before crossing to the door.

"Who's there?"

"Jonas."

She opened the door. He stood on the threshold in shirtsleeves, no coat despite the autumn chill, his hair disheveled as if he too had been roused from sleep. Moonlight caught the sharp planes of his face, the tension in his jaw. Behind him, the darkness was complete—no lantern, as if he had come in haste or in secrecy.

"What's happened?" she asked, stepping back to let him enter.

"Nothing yet." He remained in the doorway, the cold air flowing past him into the cottage. "I couldn't sleep. I've been walking the bluff, checking the site. The guards are in place, the equipment secure." He paused. "I wanted to confirm—we proceed as planned? The mechanism arrives Thursday."

"Yes. We proceed."

But neither of them moved. The cottage was dark save for the embers in the hearth, their glow catching the edges of things—the table, the chairs, the pale fabric of her shawl. Jesse became aware of how she must look, hair loose around her shoulders, feet bare on the cold floor. Of how he looked, coatless and restless, standing at her threshold in the middle of the night.

"You should come in," she said. "You'll freeze."

He hesitated, then stepped inside. She closed the door against the night air.

"Tea?"

"No. I shouldn't stay." But he didn't move toward the door. His eyes moved over the cottage—the children's belongings, the banked fire, the small signs of a life being built. "You've made this place a home."

"It serves."

"More than that." His voice was rough. "When I see you here, with Daniel and Eliza, I remember what this work is for. Ships and navigation. Lives. Families."

Jesse's throat tightened.

"The pastor warned me," she said. "About the next weeks. What Roarke might attempt."

"I know the risks." Jonas took a step closer. In the dim light, she could see the pulse at his throat. "But you need to understand—I won't ask you to face them alone. Whatever comes, we face it together."

"Together," she repeated.

For a long moment, neither moved. Then Jonas reached out and took her hand—not her arm, not her shoulder, but her hand, his fingers curling around hers. His palm was warm and rough with work. He held on as if anchoring them both.

"I should go," he said, but his grip tightened briefly before releasing.

"Yes."

He moved toward the door, pausing with his hand on the latch. "Lock this behind me. And Jesse—" He turned back. The use of her given name hung in the air between them. "Sleep if you can. Thursday will be a long day."

Then he was gone, disappearing into the darkness without a lantern to guide him.

Jesse stood at the closed door, her hand still warm where he had held it. She could hear her own breathing, loud in the silence. From above came the soft sounds of children sleeping, undisturbed.

She crossed to the window and watched the darkness for a long time, but no light appeared on the path—he walked by memory or by moonlight, needing nothing to find his way.

# CHAPTER TWENTY

## The Lantern Lit Within
### BluffLight—October 18, 1873
*(Six days after the evening at Christ Church)*

The autumn wind carried the first real chill of the season as Jesse moved along the bluff path through the pre-dawn darkness. A thin crescent moon cast just enough silver light to guide her steps, though she knew the way so well she could have walked it blindfolded. Wrapped in her heaviest shawl, she moved with purposeful haste.

Yesterday afternoon, the light mechanism had arrived from Savannah—a magnificent third-order Fresnel lens accompanied by the sophisticated clockwork apparatus that would rotate it to create the lighthouse's distinctive flash pattern. The delivery had been met with relief and heightened vigilance, as Jonas had arranged for armed guards to escort the shipment from the harbor and remain with it through the night. Today would see the delicate process of raising the equipment to the lantern room and beginning its installation—a milestone that placed them mere days away from BluffLight's first illumination.

Jesse had risen before dawn. The children slept at Marsh Cottage under Widow Patterson's watchful eye.

As she crested the final rise, BluffLight appeared before her, its completed form outlined against the first hint of gray on the horizon. The stone tower rose nearly ninety feet from its foundation, topped by the glass-enclosed lantern room that caught even the faint moonlight. Two guards were visible at the base, their lanterns small pools of yellow in the surrounding darkness.

"Mrs. Whitmore," one called softly as she approached. "You're out early."

"Couldn't sleep," she admitted. "Is Mr. Miller here already?"

"Since midnight, ma'am. Hasn't left the lantern room since the last inspection."

Jesse nodded, unsurprised. "I'll go up. He could probably use some coffee."

She gestured toward the small pot she carried, wrapped in cloth to maintain its warmth. The guard touched his hat respectfully and returned to his patrol.

The interior staircase spiraled upward through the tower's core—one hundred and thirty-one steps Jesse now knew by heart. By the time she reached the lantern room, dawn light spilled over the sea.

Jonas stood at the eastern window, his back to the stairs, watching the approaching dawn. The lantern room was surprisingly spacious—a twelve-sided chamber not quite ten feet across, with glass panels from waist height to ceiling and a polished brass railing circling the interior perimeter. The floor featured a central mounting platform where the light mechanism would soon be installed.

"Coffee," Jesse announced softly.

Jonas turned, his expression showing surprise. "You're even earlier than I expected."

"Expected?" she echoed, setting the pot down on a small workbench built into the western side of the room.

"I knew you'd come," he clarified, accepting the cup she poured. "Today is too significant to view from a distance."

"I found something this morning," Jonas said after taking a long sip. "I've been reviewing the mounting specifications when I noticed this."

He crossed the room and knelt beside the brass railing. Jesse followed, curious. Jonas pointed to a small inscription engraved into the metal: *H.M. - Let Your Light So Shine.*

"Henry's mark," Jesse murmured.

"I've checked every section of railing," Jonas said. "This is the only marking. The brass arrived with the first hardware shipment— before the foundation was even finished. He must have marked it then, before the war stopped everything."

Jesse traced the letters with her fingertip. The brass was cold, the inscription shallow—carved by hand, not stamped by machine. Henry Miller had held this railing in his hands, years before the war, before his death, before Jesse had ever heard of Saint Simons Island. The tower had been barely begun then, the stairs not yet built—but he had marked it with his hope and set it aside for a lighthouse that might never be finished.

Her throat tightened. He had believed in this light even when he could not see it completed. He had carved his hope into brass, trusting that someone would find it, would understand, would carry the work forward.

Jonas rose. They stood in silence as the sun rose, painting the eastern sky in shades of gold and rose that gradually brightened the entire lantern room.

Before she could say more, a shout from below drew their attention. Looking down through the western window, they could see activity at the base of the lighthouse—the arrival of the first work crew, accompanied by the wagon carrying the carefully crated light mechanism.

"It begins," Jonas said, straightening his shoulders as he prepared to descend. "Are you ready?"

"Ready," she confirmed.

They descended together, emerging into the morning air just as the sun cleared the horizon. The construction site had come alive with focused activity—Gardner directing his men as they prepared the hoisting apparatus, Thompson organizing the unpacking of the mechanism's components, Robert checking the rope system.

"We'll raise the main lens housing first," Jonas announced. "Then the clockwork assembly, followed by the smaller components. Mrs. Whitmore will verify each piece against the manifest before it ascends."

The men nodded acknowledgment. Even Thompson, initially the most reserved of the newer workers, had gradually come to trust her judgment.

As she moved to her position beside the crated mechanism, Jesse caught sight of an unexpected object near the cleared area—a crude driftwood effigy, cloth scorched black, shaped like a miniature lighthouse with a scrap of dark fabric tied around its middle.

Her stomach dropped. For one heartbeat, the morning light seemed to dim, the sounds of the workers fading to silence. She knew what it meant—the burned fabric, the crude shape. A warning. A threat. Roarke's message, delivered in the night while guards patrolled not twenty yards away.

She forced herself to breathe. In, out. Steady.

"When did that appear?" she asked one of the guards, keeping her voice low.

"Sometime in the night, ma'am," he replied grimly. "We found it at first light. Mr. Miller said to leave it where it was."

Jesse studied it for a moment longer—the charred cloth, the rough-hewn wood. Then she deliberately turned her back on it, focusing her attention on the light mechanism being carefully unpacked before her. Roarke wanted her afraid. She would not give him the satisfaction.

"The manifest, Mrs. Whitmore," Gardner said, extending a folded paper toward her.

Jesse accepted it with steady hands. "Thank you, Mr. Gardner. Shall we begin?"

The day unfolded with methodical precision. Each component of the light mechanism was verified, secured, and raised to the lantern room using the pulley system.

The lens arrived in eight separate sections, each a curved panel of hand-polished glass and brass. The main assembly formed a central belt of bull's-eye panels. Jonas personally supervised the positioning of each piece—a delicate operation that required absolute precision. The completed assembly would rest on a circular track lined with brass ball bearings, allowing it to rotate smoothly.

"The weight drops through a shaft in the tower core," Jonas explained as they positioned the clockwork housing. He indicated a brass crank mounted at waist height.

Jesse tested it, feeling the deep, steady resistance of the counterweight system. The mechanism would need regular winding—she would learn the rhythm of it.

Thompson arrived at the top of the stairs carrying a wooden case. "The alignment tools, Mr. Miller."

Jonas opened the case to reveal a set of precision instruments— levels, plumb lines, and optical sighting devices. "The lens must be positioned near-perfect vertical. No margin for error."

By late afternoon, as shadows lengthened across the bluff, the installation was largely complete. The workers began securing their tools and departed in small groups, their usual banter subdued.

Jesse remained as the construction area emptied, drawn to one last ascent to the lantern room before returning to her children. The evening light bathed the glass-enclosed space in golden hues, catching on the brass and crystal of the newly installed mechanism with prismatic brilliance. She circled the Fresnel lens slowly, studying how the angled prisms would direct light outward in a concentrated beam.

As the sun touched the western horizon, its last rays caught the lens at precisely the right angle to send a single beam of intensified light across the lantern room.

# CHAPTER TWENTY-ONE

## A Town Divided
*Saint Simons Village—October 25, 1873*
*(One week after the light mechanism installation)*

T he village square had never seemed so crowded. The smell of salt and fish from the nearby docks hung heavy in the still air. Jesse stood at its edge, watching as islanders gathered for what had been announced as a community meeting. On one side, near the rebuilt Thatcher's store, stood those who supported the lighthouse project—construction workers and their families, merchants, fishermen. On the other side, clustered near the harbormaster's office, gathered those aligned with Roarke's interests—smugglers thinly disguised as traders, sailors from his vessels, families whose livelihoods depended on the shadow economy he controlled.

Between these factions milled the undecided. In one week, according to the public notice posted on the church door, BluffLight would be officially lit for the first time.

"Quite the turnout," observed Miss Haskins, appearing at Jesse's side. "Even those who pretend disinterest couldn't resist attending."

Jesse nodded, noting familiar faces throughout the crowd. "Has the island ever been so divided?"

"During the war, of course. But not since then." The older woman's gaze swept the gathering. "These battle lines are drawn by greed instead of ideology."

The temporary platform at the square's center was mounted by Councilman Howard, the nominal leader of the island's small governing body. A thin man with calculating eyes, Howard had carefully maintained neutrality in the lighthouse dispute despite his financial entanglements with Roarke's shipping interests.

"Fellow citizens," he called, his voice pitched to carry across the square. "We gather today to address concerns raised regarding the lighthouse project. As completion approaches, it seems appropriate to ensure all perspectives are heard."

A murmur passed through the crowd—skepticism from the lighthouse supporters, satisfaction from Roarke's faction. Jesse noticed Jonas standing near the platform, his expression betraying no emotion.

"I'll first recognize Captain Roarke, who has requested an opportunity to address certain economic considerations," Howard continued, stepping aside as Roarke mounted the platform.

"Neighbors," Roarke began, scanning the crowd. "For generations, Saint Simons has prospered through independence— our ability to determine our own commercial relationships without excessive outside interference."

A chorus of approving murmurs rose from his supporters.

"BluffLight, while impressive in construction, represents more than a navigational aid. It brings federal oversight, increased shipping traffic from outside interests, and disruption to the traditional patterns that have sustained many island families." He paused. "Some would say newcomers arrive with ambitious plans for what our island should become, with little regard for what it has always been."

His eyes swept the crowd, lingering briefly on Jesse.

"Federal inspectors will not respect island traditions. They will not care which families have called these waters home for generations. I submit that the project's completion threatens our autonomy and our prosperity."

Jesse watched reactions ripple through the undecided islanders—doubt, consideration, worry. Roarke avoided direct mention of smuggling or illegal activities, instead appealing to community pride and wariness of outside authority.

"Furthermore," Roarke continued, his voice hardening slightly, "we must question who benefits most from this change. Certainly not most islanders, who find their livelihoods increasingly precarious. Perhaps rather, those who seek to remake Saint Simons according to their own vision."

His gaze swept toward Jesse, lingering just long enough to make the personal nature of his accusation clear. Several heads turned, following his attention to where she stood at the square's edge. Jesse maintained her composure, meeting the indirect challenge despite the flutter of anxiety in her chest.

As Roarke concluded to enthusiastic support from his faction, Howard invited Jonas to offer a response.

"I won't pretend the lighthouse won't bring change," Jonas acknowledged. "But change comes regardless of our wishes. The question is whether it arrives as progress or decay."

He spoke without notes or rehearsed rhetoric.

"BluffLight was conceived to save lives—the lives of sailors who would otherwise founder on our shoals, yes, but also the lives of islanders who depend on safe maritime passage for everything from mail to medicine. Henry Miller began this project not to disrupt tradition but to enhance safety."

Jonas's simple eloquence affected the crowd. Even some who had initially gathered on Roarke's side considered his words.

"As for who benefits," he continued, "light benefits all except those who require darkness for their purposes. And I leave each of you to determine what those purposes might be."

The implicit challenge hung in the air as Jonas stepped down. A brief silence followed.

Then Councilman Howard cleared his throat. "Given the strength of feeling on both sides, perhaps a formal vote is in order—among those present—regarding whether BluffLight should proceed with illumination as scheduled, or whether its activation should be delayed until the island reaches greater consensus."

Murmurs passed through the crowd. A ripple of hesitation moved through the gathering.

"Is that how we govern now?" a voice called out—Ruth Jackson's, clear and sharp. "By stalling what's already built?"

Howard raised a hand. "Let us proceed civilly. All those in favor of delaying the lighthouse's operation, raise your hand."

Several hands went up from Roarke's faction.

Howard's eyes moved across the crowd. "And those in favor of proceeding?"

For a moment, the gathering held its breath.

Every instinct told her to stay silent, to let others speak. But she stepped forward.

Her heart hammered against her ribs. Her hands wanted to curl into fists at her sides; she forced them to stay open, relaxed. The words rose in her throat and she let them come, keeping her voice steady through pure will.

"I moved here to escape darkness," she said, her voice steady.

Roarke's gaze locked on her, but she didn't flinch.

"This lighthouse stands not for any one person's agenda, but for the lives it might save—for the future it represents. If we let fear dim it before it even shines, then what message are we sending?"

Miss Haskins's voice rang out next. "Let it be recorded—I vote for the light."

An old fisherman near the platform raised his weathered hand. Then a shopkeeper. Then the blacksmith's wife. And slowly, one by one, more hands rose—not just from the builders and their families, but from merchants, older fishermen, even the quiet seamstress who rarely spoke at public gatherings.

As the meeting continued, voices grew louder and arguments more heated.

"Mrs. Whitmore."

The quiet voice at her elbow startled Jesse. She turned to find Ruth Jackson standing slightly apart from the main gathering.

"Miss Ruth," Jesse acknowledged. "I didn't expect to see you at this display."

The older woman's expression conveyed disdain for the proceedings. "I come to witness, not participate. But there's something you should know." She glanced toward a small group at the edge of Roarke's faction. "The man in the blue coat—newly arrived on yesterday's packet from Savannah. Been asking questions about island residents, particularly newcomers."

Jesse's attention sharpened as she located the stranger—a lean man with city clothes and watchful eyes. His boots were polished to a shine rarely seen on the island, unmarred by salt or mud.

"What kind of questions?" she asked, keeping her voice even despite the sudden tightness in her chest.

"Where people came from. Whether any arrived with unusual circumstances. Asking about any widows with children who arrived in the past year, but now specifically inquiring about the name Whitmore, though he's careful not to mention it directly." Ruth's gaze was direct. "Said he's an investigator from Richmond who represents an attorney seeking distant relations for an inheritance matter."

The pretext was transparent. William had found their trail—or at least enough of it to send someone searching coastal communities.

"I see," she said simply. "Has he spoken with many islanders?"

"Some. Mostly those who frequent the harbor tavern." Ruth's expression conveyed subtle reassurance. "Those who know you best have little to share with strangers."

As if sensing her distress, Miss Haskins spoke quietly. "Don't make decisions in haste, Mrs. Whitmore. Nothing is certain yet."

The meeting had devolved into smaller arguments throughout the square. Jesse noticed Jonas disengaging from a heated exchange, his expression troubled. When his gaze found her, he immediately began making his way toward where she stood.

"Roarke has orchestrated this well," he observed upon joining them, his attention shifting briefly to the stranger. "Who is the gentleman taking such interest in our gathering?"

Before anyone could respond, a commotion erupted near the church path—shouts and the sounds of a physical altercation. Jesse recognized Robert Gardner's voice among those involved.

Two of Roarke's sailors had confronted Robert, taking exception to something he had said. One man shoved the apprentice forcefully, sending him staggering backward into several bystanders.

"Stay here," Jonas instructed, moving quickly toward the developing fight. Pastor Willoughby had also started in that direction.

But their intervention came too late. What began as a confrontation between individuals rapidly expanded, with pushing and shouting quickly transforming into thrown punches. A barrel crashed to the ground, spilling apples across the dirt. The latent tensions of the meeting had found physical expression.

"We should leave," Ruth advised, placing a hand on Jesse's arm. "This is no place for you now, especially with that man watching."

"Go," Miss Haskins urged. "Ruth is right. Your presence here only provides opportunity for that investigator to study you more closely."

Reluctantly, Jesse yielded. "Please tell Mr. Miller I've returned to the cottage," she requested, then slipped away from the square's edge, taking a circuitous route through the village that would make it difficult for anyone to follow.

As she moved between buildings and through narrow passages, a flash of russet fur caught her eye—a red fox pausing momentarily before melting away into the underbrush at the village edge, as if urging her onward. Jesse stayed close to structures, moving with purpose but without drawing attention, alert to any sign of pursuit.

When she reached the cottage, Jesse paused on the porch, looking back toward the village where she could still hear raised voices faintly from the square.

# CHAPTER TWENTY-TWO

## Miss Haskin's Warning
*Marsh Cottage—October 27, 1873*
*(Two days after the town meeting)*

The rain began near dawn, a steady autumn downpour that transformed the sandy paths to mud and shrouded the island in gray. Jesse moved about the cottage preparing breakfast while listening to the rhythmic drumming on the cedar-shingled roof. Daniel sat at the table studying Henry Miller's journal, while Eliza remained curled in her bed above, granted a rare morning of extra sleep by the inclement weather.

Two days had passed since the town meeting. Work on the lighthouse had proceeded despite the tensions, the final adjustments to the light mechanism nearing completion. Yet an undercurrent of watchfulness pervaded every interaction.

"Do you think Mr. Miller will still come today?" Daniel asked, looking up from the journal. "The weather is quite severe."

"I expect so," Jesse replied, setting a bowl of cornmeal porridge before him. "The light testing can't be delayed."

She didn't add her other reason—Jonas's concern about the Richmond investigator Ruth had identified. They had spoken briefly the previous day, Jonas confirming that the man had been making inquiries throughout the village. The storm provided cover for a more detailed conversation.

A soft knock at the door interrupted her thoughts. Jesse approached cautiously, relieved to see Miss Haskins' familiar figure through the rain-blurred window.

"You're about early," Jesse observed as she ushered the older woman inside, noting her drenched appearance despite the oilcloth cape she wore.

"Necessity, not preference," Miss Haskins replied tersely, removing her dripping outer garment. She winced slightly as she moved. A streak of mud marked her normally immaculate skirt. A faint bruise was visible along her jawline.

Miss Haskins—straight-backed, indomitable Miss Haskins—had been struck. Because of her. Because she had offered friendship to a woman running from her past.

"Daniel, would you check on your sister?" Jesse requested.

The boy nodded, closing Henry's journal and heading toward the loft ladder. Once he was out of earshot—Eliza's bed tucked behind the chimney where voices from below rarely carried—Jesse turned to her visitor.

"You're injured."

"Two men thought to discourage my morning walk." Miss Haskins' voice was flat. "Said the island had no room for busybodies. Said a woman ought to mind her place. Said those who encourage troublemakers might find their own troubles multiplying. Hardly worth mentioning except for what they said after."

Jesse guided her to a chair near the small hearth where a modest fire provided warmth against the damp chill. "Tell me."

"Roarke's men—not sailors but those who handle his specialized cargo." Miss Haskins accepted the cup of tea Jesse offered. "They made clear that my friendship with you has been noted."

"They threatened you because of me."

"They attempted to intimidate me. My walking stick may appear ornamental, but hickory wood applied properly leaves a lasting impression." A flicker of something—fear or fury, perhaps both—crossed her features before the composure returned.

Despite the gravity of the situation, Jesse smiled briefly. But concern quickly followed.

"You shouldn't have been subjected to such treatment on my account."

"It provided intelligence." Miss Haskins lowered her voice, glancing toward the loft. "The men were more forthcoming than they intended. The Richmond visitor has made his report to Roarke instead of returning to the mainland. Roarke knows enough to be dangerous. Enough to guess you're running from someone."

Jesse's grip tightened on the chair back. "Then he knows."

"He suspects. The distinction matters." Miss Haskins paused. "But they mentioned your son's daily route to school and your daughter's habit of collecting shells along the north shore."

Heat flashed behind Jesse's eyes. Her breath caught. Her jaw clenched so hard her teeth ached. Her hands curled into fists at her sides before she could stop them—the rage bypassing thought entirely, rising from somewhere deeper than reason. Daniel walking alone each morning. Eliza bent over tide pools, absorbed in her shell collecting, vulnerable. That was a line she would not allow anyone to cross.

"He would target children?"

"Roarke operates by finding pressure points. Your children represent leverage." Miss Haskins' tone was blunt. "You must alter your routines immediately. No more unaccompanied journeys, no predictable schedules."

Jesse's thoughts raced, calculating. Daniel's schooling would need to be suspended or arranged privately. Eliza could not be allowed her usual wanderings.

"There's more," Miss Haskins continued. "The lighthouse illumination is scheduled for five days hence. The Light-House Board requires a continuous burn of twelve hours minimum to certify operational status. Roarke means to prevent it—by disabling the mechanism if possible, but through other means if necessary."

"Jonas must be warned."

Jesse moved to the window. Through the downpour, a figure materialized—tall, moving with that characteristic slight limp, but unusually hurried.

She opened the door before he could knock, noting immediately the tension in his features. Rain dripped from his coat, his footsteps muted by the storm. "You've heard."

"Robinson from the shipyard sent word at first light," Jonas replied, removing his sodden hat as he entered. Water dripped from his coat. "Miss Haskins was accosted."

"I'm perfectly capable of relaying my own experiences," Miss Haskins observed dryly from her seat by the fire. "And the intelligence gathered from them."

As Jonas joined them, Jesse quietly closed the door to the loft ladder, ensuring the children wouldn't overhear. In hushed tones, they shared what each had learned—Miss Haskins' encounter with Roarke's men, Jonas's report from the shipyard about preparations to "inspect" the lighthouse mechanism the following day, Jesse's observations about the Richmond investigator's continued presence.

"Your reasons for coming to Saint Simons remain your own," Jonas said, his gaze holding Jesse's. "But your safety—and your children's—is now inseparable from the lighthouse's completion."

"Which is precisely as Roarke has arranged it," Miss Haskins interjected. "He means to force an impossible choice—abandonment of the project or risk to the family."

"We must accelerate the illumination," Jonas said suddenly. "Advance it before Roarke's planned intervention."

"The mechanism isn't fully calibrated," Jesse objected.

"It's functional. The rotation will run, the lamp will burn—it just won't be perfectly calibrated for the flash pattern." His jaw tightened. "But once the federal registry receives confirmation that BluffLight is operational, Roarke's opportunities to intervene through official channels diminish significantly. It's a risk, but waiting is riskier."

Miss Haskins nodded. "Strategic thinking. But the children remain vulnerable during these critical days."

"They'll stay with me at the lighthouse," Jesse decided. The keeper's quarters were bare, cold, unfinished—but safer than leaving them exposed here. "We'll bring provisions. Though unfinished, they're secure enough."

"I'll arrange discreet transport this evening," Jonas offered. "After dark, when movement near the bluff won't draw attention."

They continued refining their strategy. The rain had lightened to a steady drizzle when Jonas departed an hour later. Miss Haskins remained, insisting on helping Jesse prepare the children for their temporary relocation.

"Daniel will understand the necessity," the older woman observed as they gathered essential items. "But Eliza may find it more difficult."

"I'll present it as an adventure," Jesse replied. "The first night in their future home, a special privilege before official occupancy."

Miss Haskins nodded. "You've become quite adept at navigating these waters, Mrs. Whitmore."

Jesse paused in her packing. Six months ago, she would have fled at the first hint of William's reach. Now she stood her ground.

"We adapt to survive," she said simply.

Outside, the rain continued its steady percussion on the roof. In five days, if their plans succeeded, BluffLight would shine its first beam across the coastal waters.

Something fell from Miss Haskins' reticule as she prepared to leave. Jesse retrieved the small leather-bound book. "You've dropped something."

Miss Haskins hesitated before accepting it, her fingers lingering over the worn cover. "My observations. Twenty years of cataloguing suspicious vessel movements, strange nighttime landings, men who arrived without explanation and departed the same way." She met Jesse's eyes directly. "I may present as a spinster schoolmistress, Mrs. Whitmore, but I've been Saint Simons' most dedicated sentinel since they found my brother's jacket washed ashore in '52."

Jesse understood then why the woman had taken such immediate interest in their family.

# CHAPTER TWENTY-THREE

## The Captain's Chart
*Aboard the Miranda—November 2, 1873*
*(Three days after Miss Haskin's warning)*

The *Miranda* rocked gently against her moorings, the lantern in Captain Roarke's cabin casting steady light across the navigation table. It had been three days since Miss Haskins' warning, and eight days since William's arrival in Savannah. Charts lay spread beneath Roarke's weathered hands—hand-drawn corrections marked over official survey maps, depths penciled in at specific tide stages, notations about seasonal current patterns. A brass sextant sat mounted on the bulkhead beside a coiled lead line marked in fathoms. Outside, the autumn night pressed dark against the ship's windows.

Twenty-three years of corrections on these charts. Twenty-three years of learning every shoal and sandbar, every channel that shifted with the seasons, every approach that federal surveyors had missed or deliberately ignored. His father had started these notations during the Mexican War, trading along the coast when Saint Simons was nothing but plantation ruins and freed slaves trying to scratch a living from exhausted soil. Roarke had inherited the charts along with the obligation—feed the families who depend on you, keep the channels open, maintain the darkness that makes it all possible.

Now a woman with a lamp and a lens was about to erase it all.

"Mrs. Whitmore keeps the light burning despite our previous discouragements," Roarke observed, his finger tracing the penciled line that marked BluffLight's beam across coastal waters. "Impressive determination for a woman in her circumstances."

William Whitmore stood opposite, his lean frame rigid with controlled posture. Unlike the captain's sea-roughened appearance,

William's attire remained impeccable despite the late hour—collar starched, watch chain precisely positioned, not a strand of his dark hair out of place.

"You underestimate her," William replied, his voice measured. "A mistake I made myself, briefly. Jessica has always required structure to remain properly aligned."

Roarke poured amber liquid from a crystal decanter into two glasses, offering one to his visitor. Federal illumination had already cost him three profitable routes and compromised two landing sites his family had used for generations. Every beam she lit erased another shadow his business depended on. "And yet she fled with your children, established herself on this island under false pretenses, and now occupies a federal position that complicates your legal claim."

William's jaw tightened briefly. "A temporary situation. One that requires strategic resolution."

The captain leaned against the cabin wall, studying his unlikely ally. William had arrived unannounced in Savannah with detailed inquiries about Saint Simons Island and its newest residents. Roarke had recognized mutual opportunity in the Richmond engineer's cold determination to reclaim what he considered rightfully his. Roarke trusted Whitmore no more than he trusted federal inspectors. But for now, their goals ran parallel.

"Your legal approach through Virginia courts lacks jurisdiction here," Roarke noted, gesturing toward the documentation William had spread across the table earlier. "Federal lighthouse appointments create complications beyond domestic relations law."

"Legal channels serve as visible strategy, not ultimate solution," William replied. "Filing official claims establishes the necessary impression now and will justify more direct methods later, while undermining her credibility should she raise uncomfortable accusations."

Water slapped against the hull below, a steady rhythm beneath their voices. The captain circled the table, moving to the chart where he had marked specific approaches to the island. His finger traced hidden channels through marshlands, unobserved landing points along the northern shore.

Thirty-two families. That's what these channels represented. The Marsh widow and her four children, fed through the winter when the oyster beds failed. The Harrison brothers, whose boat he'd financed when the bank refused. Old Patterson's medical bills, paid quietly through the general store so the man could keep his pride. The war had broken this island, and Roarke had rebuilt it—not from charity, but from necessity. A man needed loyal crews, reliable pilots, people who knew when to look away. But the obligation had become real over the years. These were his people now, whether he'd wanted them or not.

What would they eat when the lighthouse made his routes impossible? Federal wages wouldn't feed them. Federal inspectors wouldn't care.

William leaned closer, studying the chart.

"The Frederica River channel runs eight feet at mean low water here," Roarke said, tapping a narrow passage. "But the spring tide adds another nine feet. Enough to bring a shallow-draft vessel within a quarter-mile of the bluff. The oyster bars that normally block access will be submerged briefly."

William's eyes followed the narrow passage, calculating distances with an engineer's precision.

Roarke shifted to a second sheet, smoothed its edges flat. "Current runs northeast on the flood, southwest on the ebb. A vessel entering at slack water before the tide turns has ninety minutes before the current strengthens. Enough time to make the approach and return."

William studied the markings. "And the lighthouse beam?"

A rope slapped the mast as the wind shifted. "Creates a shadow zone behind these shoals." Roarke indicated an area marked with cross-hatching. On the chart, the shadow zone looked like a crescent of darkness beneath the sweeping arc of the beam. "The lens is calibrated for open water. Close to shore, the beam passes overhead. A small boat stays invisible in that zone."

"Federal patrols?"

"Revenue cutter makes rounds every third night. Predictable schedule." Roarke's tone was dry. "They post their inspection timetables at the customs house."

William set his empty glass down. "Our interests align, though for different reasons. You require darkness for your operations. I require my family returned to proper authority."

Roarke nodded slowly. "The new moon approaches in five days. Minimal illumination beyond the lighthouse itself. No moon means no reflected light on the water—vessels move invisible against the shore. Tides will expose channel access to the northern shore near midnight."

"And legal documentation arrives tomorrow establishing my claim through formal channels," William added. "Creating proper appearance should direct methods become necessary."

The captain refolded his charts. His hands were steady, but something cold had settled in his chest—the knowledge that he was losing. Twenty years of careful work, and a single lighthouse was dismantling it all. The Miller boy had his father's stubbornness, and this woman had something worse: she had nothing left to lose.

Roarke had always known this day would come. He'd just expected to be dead before it arrived.

"The lighthouse keeper's position provides her certain protections. Federal jurisdiction complicates straightforward recovery."

"Every structure and every law has a place where it bends," William replied, adjusting his cufflinks. "One merely requires proper leverage applied at the correct point."

On deck above them, rigging creaked in the night breeze. The *Miranda's* lines groaned against the dock pilings with the gentle rise and fall of the tide. Footsteps moved across the planking—the night watch making his rounds, boots muffled by the dampness.

Roarke fixed his visitor with a steady gaze. "Your objective is the woman and children. Mine is permanent darkness restored to channels that federal illumination has rendered inconveniently visible."

William returned the gaze without wavering. "I don't care about your lighthouse, Captain. Help me retrieve what's mine, and your channels will remain dark."

Something in the man's voice made Roarke pause. Not the words themselves—reasonable enough, transactional—but the absolute certainty beneath them. No doubt. No hesitation. William Whitmore spoke of his wife and children the way a man might speak of misplaced property: with irritation at the inconvenience, with the assumption that recovery was simply a matter of logistics.

"The keeper's quarters are separate from the tower itself," Roarke said, pulling another sheet from his chart case. His men had been observing the lighthouse since July, documenting every patrol rotation, every construction milestone. "Ground floor, single entrance facing east. Two windows, both accessible. The children have their own rooms."

"You've surveyed the structure."

"I've surveyed everything on this island that matters to my business." Roarke's finger traced the lighthouse grounds on the detailed sketch. "Two guards patrol the base during darkness. They circle the tower on a fifteen-minute interval. The quarters are unwatched for approximately eight minutes during each rotation. My men say the warning was left as instructed."

William's lack of reaction to the effigy confirmed Roarke's suspicion: the man already knew.

William studied the sketch. "Eight minutes."

"Sufficient for entry if one knows the approach and moves efficiently."

"And the woman?"

The ship groaned under the shifting tide. "Will be in the lantern room during the first lighting. Federal regulations require the keeper to remain present during the initial certification burn—twelve continuous hours. She'll be separated from the children."

William's expression didn't change, but his fingers tightened slightly on the edge of the table. Roarke caught the movement—small, but revealing. "When the inspector arrives?"

"November tenth. The new moon." Roarke rolled the charts systematically. "Everything converges that night."

"Coordinated timing."

"Strategic necessity." The captain secured the charts with leather straps, his movements precise. "You take what you came for. I ensure the light fails its certification. Federal funding withdrawn, project abandoned. The waters return to proper management."

William straightened his collar. "The children will require management during transport. They've been encouraged to see me as a threat rather than their father. Jessica's influence, of course."

The words were smooth, reasonable—a concerned father explaining a difficulty. But Roarke heard what lay beneath them: the children's fear was the problem, not its cause. Jessica's influence, not William's actions. The man had constructed an entire architecture of justification, and he lived inside it as comfortably as Roarke lived aboard the *Miranda*.

"Your men can handle reluctant passengers?"

"I've made arrangements. They'll be sedated if necessary— laudanum obtained from a Savannah apothecary. The justification is simple: distraught children needing calm for reunification with their concerned father—and no one questions a grieving father's remedies."

Roarke's expression revealed neither approval nor judgment. "And afterward?"

"I return to Richmond with my family. Jessica will be appropriately managed once removed from federal protection. The children will be properly instructed regarding their mother's perceived instability."

*Appropriately managed. Properly instructed.* The words were careful, clinical. They revealed nothing and everything.

"You'll need to move quickly once you have them. Dawn brings fishermen to the northern channels."

"A carriage waits in Brunswick. We'll be across the state line before anyone raises alarm."

The *Miranda* shifted slightly as the tide changed, the cabin tilting a few degrees before settling. The lantern swung gently on its gimbal, maintaining level illumination.

"Five days," Roarke said. "Everything must be prepared."

William nodded once. "I'll confirm arrangements by the seventh. Your men will have their instructions?"

"They'll have what they need." Principles were luxuries for men with less to lose.

The alliance sealed itself in silence. No handshake, no theatrical gesture. Just two men whose goals briefly aligned, each willing to use the other to achieve what they wanted.

William moved toward the cabin door, pausing at the threshold. "If she resists... the process of retrieval?"

"That's your concern, not mine." Roarke returned to his charts. "The lighthouse is my concern. Your household is yours."

After William departed, his footsteps fading across the deck and down the gangway, Roarke remained at his table. He unrolled the chart once more, his finger tracing the approaches to BluffLight.

The timetable was agreed. The new moon approached.

By November tenth, BluffLight would go dark—and stay dark.

# CHAPTER TWENTY-FOUR

A Wall Around the Heart
*BluffLight Keeper's Quarters—October 29, 1873*
*(Two days after Miss Haskins' warning)*

The keeper's quarters remained unfinished—bare wooden floors, walls awaiting plaster—but the solid stone foundation and sturdy roof provided better shelter than many Jesse had known. She stood at the single completed window watching the predawn mist curl around the lighthouse tower while listening to her children's quiet breathing from the makeshift pallet in the corner. The smell of lamp oil lingered faintly in the cold morning air.

Two days of temporary habitation had established a routine. Daniel had accepted the necessity with solemn understanding, but Eliza's initial excitement at "camping in their future home" had gradually yielded to restlessness. Neither child had been permitted outside since their arrival.

Jesse rolled her shoulders to ease the tension that had settled there. The accelerated illumination—now scheduled for tomorrow night instead of three days hence—had required intense preparation.

A soft scratching at the door brought her instantly alert. She moved silently across the room, checking the children remained asleep before unbarring the heavy wooden door.

"All quiet?" Jonas asked softly as he entered, carrying a covered basket.

"So far." Jesse secured the door behind him. "Any news?"

Jonas set the basket on the rough table. "Roarke's men attempted to access the lighthouse last night. Thompson and Gardner were waiting—a brief altercation, nothing serious."

"And?"

"The Richmond investigator was with them. He carried papers—legal documents, according to Thompson."

The confirmation settled like ice in Jesse's stomach. William knew.

"The papers are meaningless without enforcement," Jonas said. "Local authorities answer to Constable Hayes, who has already made clear he'll not assist Roarke's schemes."

"For now. But if the lighthouse illumination is prevented—"

"Then we ensure the light shines," Jonas replied simply.

A small sound from the corner announced Eliza's awakening. The child sat up, blonde curls tousled from sleep, her expression brightening at the sight of their visitor.

"Mr. Miller! Did you bring more books?"

"Better," he replied, reaching into the basket to produce a small wooden object. "A toy telescope, crafted by Thomas Gardner's father. Proper glass lenses, though modest in magnification."

Eliza scrambled from the pallet, careful not to disturb her still-sleeping brother. "Can I see ships with it? And birds?"

"Indeed. Though for now, only through the window, until matters are settled."

The qualification dimmed Eliza's enthusiasm only slightly as she immediately moved to the window, aiming the small telescope toward the distant shoreline.

Jesse watched with gratitude mingling with renewed determination to restore her children's freedom.

"I should inspect the light mechanism before the day crew arrives," Jonas said. "Gardner reports the calibration was completed yesterday."

"I'll accompany you." Jesse glanced toward Daniel who had begun to stir. "Daniel can watch Eliza for the brief time we'll be absent."

The boy sat up at the mention of his name, immediately alert. Weeks of helping with lighthouse maintenance had taught him to respond to urgency without panic. "I'll keep the door barred," he assured her.

Minutes later, Jesse followed Jonas up the lighthouse's spiral staircase. They emerged into the lantern room still bathed in dawn's amber light. The massive Fresnel lens dominated the circular space, its multifaceted crystal surfaces catching and refracting even the ambient illumination.

"It's ready," Jonas confirmed, completing a quick inspection. "Once lit, it will operate as designed—a two-minute rotation creating the distinctive flash sequence."

Jesse ran her hand lightly along the brass railing, finding Henry Miller's engraved message by touch—*"Let Your Light So Shine."*

"We've come so far," she said softly.

"Too far to retreat. Though I confess concern about tomorrow's illumination. Roarke will expect our acceleration and prepare accordingly."

"We need a diversion. Something to draw attention elsewhere while we complete the lighting."

"Pastor Willoughby has suggested a harvest gathering at the church."

"Roarke won't be deceived by such an obvious tactic."

"Not Roarke himself," Jonas acknowledged. "But it might divide his available men, particularly if rumors suggest you and the children will be present."

Jesse considered further refinements. "We'll need to transport the lamp oil after dark tonight, when—"

Her planning halted abruptly as movement on the path below caught her attention. A small group was approaching from the village direction—five men walking with purposeful stride. Jesse recognized the Richmond investigator among them, his city clothing distinct from the others' island attire.

"Jonas," she said quietly.

His expression hardened. "Roarke's men—before the work crew arrives." He moved quickly toward the trapdoor. "We need to return to the quarters and secure it before they reach us."

They descended rapidly. As they reached the ground level, Jonas secured the lower access door before they moved to the keeper's quarters where Daniel stood watch at the window.

"Men coming," he reported with concise alertness.

"How many?" Jonas asked.

"Five on the path. Two more circling through the dunes. The ones in the dunes are armed—I saw sunlight on metal."

Cold clarity replaced Jesse's earlier apprehension. "They mean to force entry while the others provide official pretext."

"Which Constable Hayes has not granted," Jonas noted grimly, moving to reinforce the door's barring with a length of timber.

Jesse gathered Eliza closer, the child's confusion evident though she remained blessedly silent. Eliza's small body pressed against her, trembling slightly, her fingers clutching the fabric of Jesse's dress. Against her mother's shoulder, Eliza whispered, "When can we go home?" Her voice was barely audible, fragile as the angel wing shell she'd found on the beach. Jesse's arms tightened around her daughter. She could feel Eliza's heartbeat, quick as a bird's, and the trust in that small body nearly undid her.

"What official standing could they claim?" Jesse asked.

Jonas hesitated, glancing at the children before answering carefully. "The investigator has apparently presented documents suggesting guardianship concerns regarding Daniel and Eliza. Implied neglect through removal from their proper home."

The calculated cruelty ignited a cold fury in Jesse's chest.

"They won't take my children," she stated, her voice carrying quiet certainty.

Jonas's jaw tightened. "No," he agreed. "They won't."

Footsteps approached outside. Voices—low, deliberate. A sharp knock at the door followed—three authoritative raps followed by a formal voice. "Mrs. Whitmore? I represent legal interests from Richmond regarding the minor children in your custody. I request civilized conversation regarding these matters."

Jesse met Jonas's gaze. He nodded slightly, understanding her unspoken strategy.

"Daniel, take your sister into the storage room," she instructed calmly. "Remember the small door we showed you yesterday? Use it if necessary."

The boy nodded, understanding without words. He wrapped his arm around Eliza's shoulders and guided her toward the back room.

Once they had disappeared from view, Jesse moved to stand beside the door, positioning herself where she would not be immediately visible. "Remove the bar," she said quietly to Jonas. "Let's hear their supposed authority."

Jonas complied. As the door swung inward, the Richmond investigator stepped across the threshold, flanked by two of Roarke's men. Jesse caught Jonas's eye for a brief moment—the silent plan understood. His confidence faltered visibly upon finding Jonas alone in the room.

Jonas shifted his weight, placing himself squarely between the doorway and the path to the storage room. His hands hung loose at his sides, but his shoulders had squared, his stance widening almost imperceptibly—a man prepared to move quickly if movement became necessary.

"Where is Mrs. Whitmore?" the investigator demanded. "And the children?"

"What legal authority do you present?" Jonas countered.

The investigator produced a folded document. "A writ from the Richmond circuit court regarding the return of Jessica Whitmore and her children to their lawful residence under the guardianship of William Whitmore."

Jesse's pulse quickened at the sight of official seals, but she kept her voice steady. "Virginia courts hold no jurisdiction on a federal lighthouse reservation. Nor does a husband's claim supersede federal appointment."

The investigator turned, startled. He recovered quickly, his expression hardening. "Mrs. Whitmore, your deception regarding your death has caused considerable distress. For your own welfare, madam, your husband—"

"Has no authority here," Jesse interrupted, her voice level. "This lighthouse and its keeper's quarters fall under federal jurisdiction. My position as appointed keeper places me directly under Light-House Board authority."

The investigator's momentary hesitation suggested it had given him pause.

"Furthermore," Jonas added, "any attempt to remove the appointed keeper or her family from a federal installation would constitute interference with interstate commerce—a federal offense."

The investigator glanced between them, reassessing his position. "These matters could be resolved through proper channels. If Mrs. Whitmore would simply agree to discuss—"

"There is nothing to discuss," Jesse stated with quiet finality. "My children and I are exactly where we belong. I suggest you convey to my former husband that any further attempts at interference will be met with federal response."

The investigator looked discomfited. One of Roarke's men shifted impatiently, hand moving toward his coat.

Jonas noticed, his posture subtly changing to place himself between Jesse and potential threat. "I believe this conversation has concluded. Unless you have documentation specifically from the Light-House Board authorizing your presence here, I must ask you to depart immediately."

For a tense moment, no one moved. Jesse held the investigator's gaze steadily.

The investigator inclined his head in reluctant acknowledgment. "This matter remains unresolved. Legal clarification will be sought regarding jurisdictional questions."

"By all means," Jesse replied evenly. "Through proper channels, which begin with the Light-House Board in Washington."

As the men withdrew, Jesse maintained her composed demeanor until the door closed behind them. Only then did she permit herself a single deep breath. The tension drained from her shoulders like water released from a dam. Her hands, which had been steady throughout, began to tremble now that no one could see. She pressed them flat against her skirt until the shaking stopped.

"They'll return," Jonas observed quietly, replacing the door's barring.

"Yes," Jesse agreed. "But not before we light the beacon." She turned toward the storage room to retrieve her children.

# CHAPTER TWENTY-FIVE

Smoke, Plans, and Prayers
*BluffLight Keeper's Quarters—October 30, 1873*
*(One day after the confrontation, one day before the*
*illumination)*

The lamp oil arrived shortly after midnight, delivered by Thomas Gardner and his apprentice Robert under cover of near-perfect darkness. Six brass containers holding ten gallons each passed from hand to hand in silence broken only by waves against the distant shore and the rustle of footsteps beyond the tree line. Padding beneath each tin muffled the weight. Twenty-four hours remained.

"Any sign of Roarke's men?" Jesse asked Gardner in a hushed voice as they completed the transfer.

"Two groups patrolling. One near the village path, another by the shore approach. We circled wide through the pine forest to avoid them."

"And the Richmond investigator?"

"Seen at Roarke's house earlier this evening. A lengthy meeting." Gardner hesitated. "There's talk of additional men arriving from Savannah on tomorrow's packet. Hired muscle."

The convergence of threats—Roarke's opposition, William's legal maneuvers—was reaching its crescendo precisely as they prepared for BluffLight's first illumination.

"The diversion at the church is arranged?" she asked.

Gardner nodded. "Pastor Willoughby has announced a harvest celebration beginning at sunset. Miss Haskins ensured word spread that you and the children might attend."

"Good. That should draw attention away from the bluff long enough for the official lighting."

As Gardner and Robert departed, vanishing into the darkness, Jesse secured the door and returned to the main room where Jonas sat with Daniel, reviewing the lighthouse operation. The boy had absorbed the information with remarkable understanding.

"Oil secured?" Jonas asked, looking up.

Jesse nodded. "Six containers. Gardner reports increased patrols but successful avoidance."

She didn't elaborate further, conscious of Daniel's keen attention.

"We should review tomorrow's sequence once more," Jonas suggested. "Daniel has grasped the mechanical aspects admirably, but timing will be critical."

As they discussed the precise schedule, Jesse's thoughts drifted briefly to the confrontation with the Richmond investigator. The legal strategy had provided temporary respite, but William would find other avenues. The illumination would buy them time. Each night the beacon operated established Jesse more firmly as its legitimate keeper.

"Mama," Eliza's small voice drew Jesse from her reflections. The child had been sitting near the hearth, unusually subdued since the previous day's confrontation.

"Yes, darling?" Jesse moved to kneel beside her daughter.

"I saw smoke in the forest today. From the back room window. It was blue smoke, not like from cooking fires."

Jesse exchanged a quick glance with Jonas. "When did you see this, Eliza?"

"This afternoon when Daniel was reading. It came up from the trees, then disappeared."

Signal smoke—likely communication between Roarke's patrols.

"Thank you for telling me," she said, smoothing Eliza's blonde curls. "It's important to notice unusual things, especially now."

The child nodded solemnly. "Like the red fox that watches our cottage. I saw him again yesterday, from the storage room window. He was sitting very still, looking right at me."

"Did he run away when he saw you?" Jesse asked.

Eliza shook her head. "No. He just watched for a long time, then turned and walked into the trees. But slowly, like he wanted me to see where he was going."

Jonas listened with quiet attention. "Children often notice what adults overlook."

The observation offered a counterbalance to the legal and physical threats closing around them.

"We should finalize tomorrow's preparations," she said. "The children will remain here with Miss Haskins while we conduct the official lighting ceremony. Once the lighthouse is operational, federal recognition becomes immediate."

Jonas nodded, his expression reflecting both determination and concern. "Roarke will make his final attempt to prevent illumination tomorrow."

"And what of you?" she asked quietly. "If he comes for you first?"

"Then I suppose I'll need someone stubborn enough to finish the work in my absence."

He meant it lightly, but the weight of it struck her all the same. She searched his face—lined with sun, marked by labor, but anchored in something unshakable.

"You think I'm that person?" she asked.

"I've never doubted it," he said.

The words hung between them. Jesse held his gaze longer than she intended—long enough to see something shift behind his eyes, something unguarded. Neither of them moved. The fire crackled. Daniel turned a page of Henry's journal, absorbed in his reading. And in that suspended moment, Jesse became aware of the space between them as a living thing—the distance that could be closed, the choice that neither of them was quite ready to make.

She looked away first.

She moved to the small desk in the corner, removing a sealed letter from its drawer. "This contains detailed documentation of Roarke's smuggling operations—specific dates, cargo manifests, names of collaborators both on the island and in Savannah."

Jonas's eyes widened slightly. "How did you obtain such information?"

186

"Solomon Davis has observed Roarke's movements for years, documenting what he witnessed from his fishing routes. Ruth Jackson has relatives working on Roarke's ships who've quietly reported cargo discrepancies and unlogged arrivals. Miss Haskins has kept meticulous records of unusual vessel movements for two decades." Jesse handed him the sealed document. "Together, they've assembled evidence sufficient for federal investigation."

"You've been preparing this for some time."

"Since Miss Haskins shared the island's history with me." The work had taken weeks—quiet conversations at the market, careful questions asked of people who had no reason to trust her until she'd earned it. She had learned the island's hidden architecture: who owed Roarke, who feared him, who had been waiting for someone to ask the right questions. "I recognized that Roarke's power derives from perception as much as reality." Jesse met his gaze directly. "Should anything prevent tomorrow's illumination or threaten my family's safety, this information goes directly to the Revenue Service office in Savannah."

"Insurance," he said, understanding immediately.

"Precisely. Roarke isn't motivated solely by business interests. His opposition carries personal animus against you and, by extension, against me. He won't be satisfied with preventing illumination."

Her hands trembled slightly as she replaced the sealed letter in the drawer. Tomorrow everything converged—every threat, every choice. But she steadied herself. "No," Jonas agreed grimly. "Which is why tomorrow must proceed exactly as planned. Once the light shines, Roarke's ability to operate freely diminishes considerably. And William's legal claims become more complicated when confronting a federal appointee."

As darkness deepened outside, Jesse found herself drawn to the window, gazing toward the forest where Eliza had reported seeing both smoke signals and the watching fox. Somewhere in that darkness, decisions were being made—Roarke finalizing his attempt, the Richmond investigator preparing legal maneuvers, islanders choosing sides.

A lantern moved between the trees in the distance—too deliberate for a casual walker, too slow for someone rushing home. Jesse watched it pause, swing once as if signaling, then disappear.

"We should rest," Jonas suggested, noting the late hour. "Tomorrow will demand full clarity."

Jesse nodded, though she doubted sleep would come easily.

Before retiring to her makeshift pallet near the children, Jesse knelt on the rough wooden floor where the moonlight fell through the single window. The boards were cold beneath her knees. She could hear Daniel's steady breathing from the pallet, Eliza's softer rhythm beside him. Through the glass, the lighthouse tower rose dark against the stars—waiting, as she was waiting, for the flame that would give it purpose.

She folded her hands and closed her eyes.

"Lord, I have learned to ask for the right things. Give me the will to act despite the fear. Give me steady hands and a clear mind. Protect my children. Guide Jonas. And if the light shines tomorrow, let it be enough—for the ships that need it, for the island that has waited, for Henry Miller who believed it would come."

She was quiet for a moment.

"Amen."

# INTERLUDE II

## The Rising Beam

*BluffLight Construction Site—October 30, 1873*
*(The evening before illumination day)*

The construction site lay quiet in the gathering dusk, tools carefully stowed in preparation for tomorrow's illumination ceremony. Jesse stood alone at the base of the lighthouse, her hand resting against the cool stone that had risen, layer by careful layer, through months of labor.

The granite was smooth beneath her palm, still holding the faint warmth of the autumn sun. She could feel the texture of it—the places where chisel marks remained, the joints where mortar had been spread with such care. Around her, the evening came alive with small sounds: crickets beginning their chorus in the grass, the distant rush of waves against the bluff, wind moving through the pines with a sound like breath. The air smelled of salt and cooling earth and the particular dusty sweetness of worked stone.

She gazed upward along the tower's graceful taper. Tomorrow the great lens would catch flame and magnify it across dangerous waters, fulfilling the purpose that had sustained them through delays, sabotage, and outright opposition.

From the forest beyond the bluff came a distant bark—a fox making its nightly rounds. Jesse had come to recognize the sound.

Tomorrow would bring its own challenges. Roarke would not surrender his operations without resistance. The technical demands of the illumination itself required precise execution after months of preparation. The lamp must be lit at exactly the right moment, the clockwork mechanism engaged, the rotation verified. Jonas had walked her through the procedure three times yesterday, but the responsibility would be hers as keeper.

Daniel had asked that morning if he could assist with the lamp lighting. She'd seen the eagerness in his face—the same expression he wore when working through a difficult mathematics problem or helping Jonas align the lens panels.

The first stars appeared overhead as true darkness claimed the island. Soon Jesse would return to Marsh Cottage where the children slept under Miss Haskins' watchful eye. Tomorrow's illumination would transform BluffLight from construction project to operating lighthouse. The lens she had helped install, the mechanisms she had learned to maintain, the lamp she would tend—all would serve the ships navigating the treacherous waters offshore.

She thought of Henry Miller's inscription in the lantern room, those few words carved into brass before war and opposition had nearly ended the project.

The technical checklist ran through her mind: verify oil reservoir level, trim wick to three-eighths inch, check clockwork tension, confirm weight descent clearance, ignite lamp at civil twilight, engage rotation mechanism, monitor beam pattern for first thirty minutes. She had written it down, memorized it, practiced each step.

She pressed both palms flat against the tower's stone, feeling its solidity, its weight, the generations of labor that had raised it from the earth. The darkness wrapped around her, complete now except for the stars overhead and the faint glow of distant cottage windows.

"Stand firm," she whispered. "Whatever comes tomorrow, we face it together."

# CHAPTER TWENTY-SIX

## A Keeper's Oath
*BluffLight Construction Site—October 31, 1873*
*(Illumination Day)*

The dawn broke with unusual clarity over Saint Simons Island, the sky washed clean by an overnight rain that had ceased just before first light. Jesse stood at the base of the lighthouse, watching as the rising sun cast the tower's shadow across the bluff—a long, tapering finger pointing west toward the maritime forest where Roarke's men had been spotted the previous day. The illumination ceremony was scheduled for sunset, less than twelve hours away. After months of construction, delays, and deliberate sabotage, BluffLight would finally fulfill its purpose.

If they could protect it until then.

"The oil is secured in the lantern room," Jonas reported, approaching from the tower's entrance. His expression showed the strain of the past twenty-four hours—the confrontation with the Richmond investigator, the accelerated preparations, the knowledge that Roarke would make one final attempt to prevent the lighthouse's operation. "Gardner and Thompson are checking the mechanism again to ensure there was no overnight tampering."

Jesse nodded, her gaze still fixed on the distant tree line. "And the children?"

"Miss Haskins arrived at first light. They're safe in the keeper's quarters with provisions enough to last the day." Jonas followed her gaze toward the forest. "No sign of movement since the dawn patrol. Perhaps Roarke believes we'll maintain the original illumination schedule."

"He doesn't," Jesse replied. "He knows us too well by now. But he'll wait for the right moment—likely just before the ceremony when attention is diverted."

She had watched Roarke operate for months. The pattern was familiar.

"You understand him," Jonas observed.

Jesse turned to meet his gaze directly. "I understand men who believe power belongs to them by right."

Jonas nodded once.

"I received this at dawn," he said, producing a folded paper from his coat. "It was delivered by Solomon Davis, who found it left at his door during the night."

Jesse accepted the paper, unfolding it to reveal a roughly sketched map of the island with several locations marked by small X's. Most clustered near the village and the church where the harvest celebration would create a diversion, but two marked positions on either side of the path leading to the lighthouse. An annotation in the corner, written in a careful hand: *Roarke's men positioned for midday. Authority papers from Richmond to be served as distraction during illumination attempt.*

"Solomon believes it came from Thaddeus Merrick's former first mate," Jonas explained. "A man who apparently harbored reservations about his captain's drowning but feared speaking openly."

Jesse studied the markings. "They'll block the lighthouse path while serving legal papers. Once I step off federal grounds, they claim I've abandoned the post."

Jonas's jaw tightened. "Invalidates the protection."

"Which is why I stay here," Jesse said, folding the map and tucking it into her pocket. "Whatever papers they bring come to me on federal ground."

Jonas nodded, understanding the strategy.

"There's something else we should discuss," Jesse continued, lowering her voice though no one stood near enough to overhear. "If circumstances become untenable—if Roarke succeeds in preventing today's illumination or the Richmond claims gain traction—I've made arrangements for the children."

Jonas's expression shifted to concern. "What kind of arrangements?"

"Miss Haskins has contacts in Savannah—a women's charitable society with experience helping those in difficult circumstances." Jesse had not spoken of this contingency before, though she had been developing it since their conversation with the Richmond investigator. "If necessary, she will take Daniel and Eliza there while I create a diversion to mask their departure."

"You've thought this through," Jonas said.

"I've had practice," Jesse replied simply.

Before Jonas could respond, Robert Gardner appeared at the lighthouse entrance, his youthful face tight with urgency. "Mr. Miller, Mrs. Whitmore—you should see this."

They followed him inside and up the spiral staircase that wound through the tower's core. The climb had become familiar to Jesse over months of construction, each step bringing them closer to the lantern room. As they emerged into the glass-enclosed chamber at the top, Thomas Gardner stood at the western window, his weathered face grim as he pointed toward the distant village.

A thin column of smoke rose above the tree line—not from the usual location of the village square, but slightly north where Thatcher's rebuilt store stood.

"Fire?" Jesse asked, though she suspected otherwise.

"Signal," Gardner corrected. "The smoke's too controlled, too steady for an actual fire. Someone's sending a message."

As they watched, the smoke changed color slightly—darkening to a blue-gray that Jesse recognized from Eliza's description the previous day. Within moments, an answering plume appeared from the southern marsh, this one paler but equally distinct against the morning sky.

Jonas frowned. "They're moving together."

Jesse studied the distant plumes. "Someone from the construction crew must have shared information."

"Or they've been watching the increased activity," Gardner suggested.

Jesse decided quickly. "Robert, notify Solomon Davis—the diversion needs to begin at midday instead of sunset. Mr. Gardner, check all approaches and post men at intervals along the path. Jonas and I will prepare the mechanism for immediate operation."

The men departed with clear purpose while she turned her attention to the magnificent Fresnel lens that dominated the lantern room. The complex arrangement of prisms and glass panels stood ready to transform a simple flame into a powerful beam visible for miles across the coastal waters—simple in concept but requiring precise calibration for maximum effectiveness.

"You believe Roarke will move before the ceremony," Jonas said as they inspected the mechanism together.

"He adjusts when we adjust. The smoke signals—he's already moving."

Through the western window, she could see activity at the base of the lighthouse—workers moving with increased purpose under Gardner's direction, establishing a perimeter around the structure. Miss Haskins had emerged briefly, her characteristic black dress visible as she surveyed the surroundings before returning inside where the children waited.

"I should check the oil reserves again," Jonas said, moving toward the storage cabinet built into the lantern room's wall.

"Wait," Jesse said suddenly, placing a hand on his arm. The gesture was uncharacteristic—physical contact between them had been limited to professional necessity during their months of collaboration.

"Before events unfold further," she continued, her voice quiet but steady, "I need to tell you something. Something I should have shared earlier."

Jonas turned to face her fully, his expression open despite the tension evident in the set of his shoulders. "I'm listening."

"My husband is not dead," Jesse stated simply. "William Whitmore is very much alive in Richmond, believing his wife and children perished of fever while visiting relatives in Charleston."

Jonas's expression revealed no surprise, only deep compassion. "I suspected as much."

"He had begun turning his attention toward Daniel," Jesse said quietly. "Watching him with that calculating assessment. I could endure what he inflicted on me, but not my son."

Morning light filled the lantern room, refracting through the Fresnel lens into prismatic patterns across the brass floor.

"The investigator's presence confirms William has discovered our survival," she continued. "The legal papers mentioned in Solomon's warning are likely assertions of his claim under Virginia law."

"Which holds no jurisdiction here," Jonas reminded her.

"Not on a federal reservation," Jesse agreed. "But once the light operates, it strengthens everything."

Jonas held her gaze for a long moment. Then, with characteristic deliberateness, he reached into his coat and withdrew a small object that gleamed dully in the morning light—a key, simple but obviously important.

"The key opens the clockwork housing—it must be wound every four hours to maintain the lens rotation." He extended the key toward her. "The lighthouse keeper traditionally takes an oath. Not a formal legal ceremony, but a personal commitment to the responsibilities the position entails. Henry Miller wrote of it in his journal—the private moment when purpose becomes covenant."

Jesse accepted the key, its weight settling in her palm. "The oath isn't recorded anywhere?"

"It exists between the keeper and the light," Jonas explained. "Words chosen to express one's understanding of the duty undertaken."

Jesse looked from the key to the magnificent lens. The brass was warm where morning sun struck it. Beneath her feet, ninety feet of Georgia granite anchored them to the earth. Through the glass, the Atlantic stretched endless and gray.

"I swear to maintain this light with consistent attention," she said quietly, the words forming naturally as she spoke them. The key pressed into her palm, its teeth leaving small indentations in her skin. "To ensure proper operation for ships navigating these waters. To fulfill the keeper's responsibilities regardless of weather or circumstance."

A shout from below drew their attention back to immediate concerns. Looking down from the western window, they could see Robert Gardner running toward the lighthouse from the direction of the village, his speed suggesting urgency.

"They're coming," Jonas assessed grimly. "Roarke has moved earlier than expected."

Jesse pocketed the key and moved toward the stairs. "We adjust. The light goes up today."

They descended the spiral staircase quickly.

# CHAPTER TWENTY-SEVEN

## Ambush in the Salt Flats
*Eastern Marshlands—October 31, 1873*
*(Illumination Day, midday)*

T he midday sun hung directly overhead as Jesse made her way along the narrow causeway that connected the eastern bluff to the salt marshes beyond. The tide had retreated, exposing vast expanses of cordgrass and mud flats stretching toward the distant sound. Solomon Davis's urgent message had been delivered with Robert Gardner's insistence that only she could retrieve what waited at the shell mound—something too dangerous to bring to the lighthouse with Roarke's men watching every approach.

*A package hidden at the old shell mound,* he had whispered to Robert Gardner that morning. *Something Mrs. Whitmore must see before sundown.*

She moved cautiously along the raised path constructed generations earlier by plantation owners. The tabby-and-shell walkway, crumbling in places but still navigable, provided the only safe passage. On either side, the glutinous pluff mud could swallow an unwary traveler to the knee or deeper.

The shell mound rose in the distance—a massive heap of discarded oyster shells left by generations of Guale Indians who had harvested the rich waters long before European settlement. Wax myrtles and stunted red cedars clung to its slopes.

As Jesse approached, a movement among the vegetation caught her eye—a flash of russet against the pale shells. A red fox paused on the mound's crest, then disappeared over the far side.

"Solomon?" she called softly, scanning the mound's perimeter. No answer came.

Jesse began climbing the shell mound, her boots crunching softly on the compacted shells. At the crest, she found a recently disturbed area—shells moved aside to create a shallow depression where an oilskin package rested, partially concealed by overhanging myrtle branches.

The package was roughly the size of Henry Miller's journal, wrapped securely against moisture with twine binding its contents. Jesse knelt to retrieve it.

As she reached for the package, a voice spoke from among the cedars at the mound's far side—not Solomon's familiar coastal drawl but a cultured tone that sent ice through her veins.

"Mrs. Whitmore. Finally a moment alone to talk."

The Richmond investigator emerged from the vegetation, his city attire incongruous against the wild backdrop of marsh and sky. Unlike their previous encounter at the lighthouse, he made no pretense of official purpose now.

"You left the federal reservation," he observed, gesturing toward the distant bluff where BluffLight stood. "An unfortunate decision, given the protections you claimed so confidently yesterday."

Jesse rose slowly, the package secured in one hand as she assessed her surroundings. The investigator was alone, at least visibly so.

"Where is Solomon Davis?" she asked, her voice steady.

"The old marsh guide? I believe he's entertaining my associates near the village." The investigator's smile didn't reach his eyes. "He proved surprisingly resistant regarding your whereabouts. Fortunately, there are other sources of information on this small island."

"What is it you want?" Jesse asked.

"To return valuable property to its rightful owner," he replied. "William Whitmore has been quite distressed by the theft of his wife and children. Upon learning of their miraculous survival, he naturally sought their recovery."

"Naturally," Jesse echoed.

"The situation can be resolved," the investigator continued. "My carriage waits at the mainland crossing. Tomorrow evening, you could be back in Richmond."

"And if I decline?" Jesse asked, taking a measured step toward the mound's western slope, away from both the investigator and the path she had traveled.

His expression hardened. "You've abandoned federal property. Removed minor children from their father."

"Without justification," Jesse repeated softly.

"The courts recognize a husband's authority," the investigator stated.

Another step backward brought Jesse closer to the mound's western edge. From this vantage point, she could see movement along the causeway—two men approaching from the direction she had come, effectively blocking her return path to the lighthouse.

"You seem to have arranged matters thoroughly," she observed, still clutching the oilskin package.

"Mr. Whitmore is a thorough man," the investigator confirmed.

Jesse took another step backward, approaching the mound's western edge where the marsh stretched toward the distant forest. No clear path presented itself—only the treacherous mud flats and scattered patches of cordgrass that might or might not support a person's weight.

"There's nowhere to go, Mrs. Whitmore," the investigator observed. "The tide has begun returning. Even if you crossed the mud, you'd be cut off within an hour."

Jesse glanced toward the distant channel. Water crept back across the exposed mud.

"I'm not returning to Richmond," she said simply.

The investigator sighed, reaching into his coat to produce a small pistol—compact but lethal at this range. "I had hoped for cooperation. But Mr. Whitmore anticipated this. He made arrangements for every possibility, including the regrettable one that only the children might be recovered."

Jesse stepped backward off the shell mound directly into the marsh, her body angling toward a patch of needlerush. The investigator's shout of surprise was cut short by the report of his pistol, the bullet striking shell where she had stood moments before.

Cold mud seized her legs as she landed knee-deep, the firmness beneath the needlerush preventing her from sinking further. The cold shocked through her stockings, into her bones. She pushed toward a stand of cordgrass twenty yards distant, each step requiring immense effort to extract her boot before placing it carefully forward. Her sodden skirts dragged against her legs like hands trying to pull her down.

She pressed onward, following a pattern of vegetation that Solomon had trained her to recognize—spartina giving way to needlerush. The oilskin package remained clutched against her chest, protected from the marsh mud that soaked her skirts.

Shouts carried on the wind from the direction of the causeway. Jesse did not look back.

After twenty minutes of progress, Jesse reached a small hammock—an elevated island surrounded by marsh. Sweet bay and wax myrtle created a natural screen around its perimeter, while a massive live oak at its center spread gnarled limbs outward.

She stopped beneath the oak, breathing hard, her skirts sodden and heavy with marsh mud. The lighthouse stood visible in the distance, its white tower stark against the blue autumn sky, but at least a mile of marsh separated her from its safety.

Jesse rose on trembling legs. At the hammock's western edge, the vegetation opened to reveal a narrow but distinct path leading westward—not toward the lighthouse but toward the maritime forest. The path appeared deliberately maintained, marsh grass trampled and cut back.

Solomon had shown her these routes during their botanical excursions. Paths used by those who knew the marsh.

Jesse pressed forward, watching her footing on the narrow track. The tide continued its return, water now visible in the lowest areas to either side, but the path remained above water level.

After nearly thirty minutes, the path entered the forest's edge, transitioning from marsh to solid ground as pine trees replaced cordgrass. Jesse paused to catch her breath.

Jesse clutched the oilskin package. With trembling fingers, she untied the twine binding and carefully unwrapped the protective covering to reveal a leather-bound ledger, its pages filled with neat columns of figures and annotations.

A small note tucked inside the front cover, written in Solomon's careful hand: *Roarke's smuggling accounts, recovered from Miranda's last cargo. Names, dates, bribes.*

Jesse leafed through the pages. Detailed records of illicit shipments, payments to collaborators, notations regarding "complications"—situations like Thomas Merrick's drowning.

A twig snapped somewhere behind her. The investigator and his associates could be following, though the complex marsh path would slow anyone unfamiliar with it.

As Jesse rose to continue, a human figure emerged from the trees—tall, lean, with the measured movements of someone accustomed to wilderness. Her hand tightened around a nearby branch.

"Mrs. Whitmore," the man said, keeping a respectful distance. "Samuel Fletcher. Solomon sent me to guide you back to the lighthouse by a safer route."

Jesse studied him carefully, recalling their brief interaction at the docks. "How did you find me?"

Fletcher gestured toward the forest. "Solomon and I have mapped every path through these woods. The investigator and his associates have been delayed. But we should move quickly."

"The lighthouse must be lighted by sunset," Jesse said, tucking the ledger under her arm.

Fletcher nodded. "Then we'll get you there. This way—there's a path along the old plantation boundary."

They moved through the forest's dappled shadows toward the distant bluff where BluffLight rose.

# CHAPTER TWENTY-EIGHT

## Fall of the Scaffold
*BluffLight Construction Site—October 31, 1873*
*(Illumination Day, late afternoon)*

T he afternoon sun cast long shadows across the construction site as Jesse and Samuel Fletcher emerged from the forest path. BluffLight's white tower rose against the sky. Mud caked her skirts. The leather ledger was secure in her grasp.

"Jonas's men have established a perimeter," Fletcher observed, gesturing toward the workers positioned around the lighthouse base. "They're expecting trouble."

Jesse nodded, scanning the activity surrounding the tower. The scaffolding that encircled the upper portion rose like a wooden skeleton against the stonework, with workers moving across its planks as they made final preparations. At the top, the newly installed lantern room caught the last of the afternoon light.

"Samuel Fletcher," a voice called. Thomas Gardner approached quickly. "Solomon sent word you'd found Mrs. Whitmore. We'd begun to fear the worst."

"The Richmond man set a trap at the shell mound," Fletcher explained. "Mrs. Whitmore escaped through the marsh, but they may be following."

"Roarke's men have been gathering since midday—more than usual, and some unfamiliar faces among them." He turned to Jesse. "Mr. Miller has been searching for you since we realized you'd left the grounds. He's in the lantern room now, making final adjustments to the mechanism."

"I need to speak with him immediately," Jesse said, indicating the ledger under her arm.

As they approached the lighthouse entrance, Jesse noticed the workers. Tools kept close at hand.

Inside the tower, Jesse paused to catch her breath in the relative coolness of the stone interior. The spiral staircase stretched upward.

"I'll inform the perimeter guards about potential pursuit," Fletcher said. "The tide will have covered your trail by now, but Roarke's men know these marshes nearly as well as Solomon." He nodded once and left through the entrance.

Jesse began her climb, the leather ledger clutched firmly against her side. Each step carried her higher toward the lantern room. The afternoon light filtered through narrow windows cut into the tower walls.

At the top landing, she paused. Through the open trapdoor above, she could hear movement—the soft scrape of tools against metal, the murmur of low voices.

"Oil flow needs to be consistent," Jonas was saying as she emerged into the lantern room. "Once lit, the flame must maintain steady intensity regardless of—"

He broke off mid-sentence, turning as Jesse appeared.

"Report. What happened at the shell mound?"

"The Richmond investigator was waiting at the shell mound. To return us to William."

"You're injured?"

"Only my pride and my clothing," Jesse said, glancing down at her mud-encrusted skirts. "But I've brought something." She extended the ledger toward him. "Solomon left this. Roarke's smuggling records."

Jonas accepted the book and leafed through its pages. He paused, reading. "Merrick's name appears here."

"If we can deliver it to the authorities," Jesse said.

Robert Gardner appeared through the trapdoor. "Mr. Miller, Mrs. Whitmore—riders approaching from the village road. At least a dozen men, moving fast. Carrying torches despite the daylight."

Jonas closed the ledger. "How long until they reach us?"

"Ten minutes, perhaps less," Robert replied. "Father has positioned men at the base and on the first landing with whatever implements might serve as defense."

Through the western windows, Jesse could see them moving fast along the sandy track. The setting sun at their backs cast long shadows ahead of them.

"We proceed with the illumination as planned," Jonas decided, handing the ledger back to Jesse. "This evidence must be protected. Keep it with you."

Jesse tucked the book securely into the inner pocket of her jacket. "The children—"

"Are safe with Miss Haskins inside," Jonas assured her. "She's barricaded the door and has Solomon's son standing guard. Our immediate concern is protecting the lighthouse until sunset."

From below came the sounds of preparation—men moving into position, implements being distributed, instructions called in terse phrases that echoed up the spiral staircase.

"The harvest celebration at the church should have drawn some of Roarke's men away," Jesse observed, moving to the western window.

"It may have, but he's gathered reinforcements," Jonas replied, joining her. "Likely men from Savannah who don't know the island's politics."

As they watched, the group of riders divided, several breaking away to circle toward the southern approach while the main body continued directly toward the lighthouse.

A shout from below drew their attention to the western base of the tower, where Thomas Gardner was directing workers to reinforce the main entrance. The men had improvised barricades from construction materials—stacks of stone blocks, timber beams, empty barrels filled with sand.

"We should join them," Jesse decided. "The defense will be at the base, not here in the lantern room."

Jonas nodded, but as they turned toward the trapdoor, a tremendous crash shook the tower, accompanied by shouts of alarm from the scaffolding outside. Jesse staggered, catching herself against the brass railing that encircled the Fresnel lens.

"They've brought the east scaffolding down!" Robert Gardner's voice carried up from the staircase. "Men are trapped beneath it!"

Jonas moved immediately to the eastern window. "The entire scaffold has collapsed."

Jesse joined him at the window. Several men moved amid the wreckage, pulling their comrades free from broken planks and supports.

She turned toward the western window. The main group of riders now approached at full gallop.

Even as she spoke, the first riders reached the lighthouse perimeter. Despite the defenders' preparation, the sheer number of attackers forced them back toward the tower entrance. Jesse could see Roarke himself among them, directing the assault.

"We need to secure the entrance," Jonas said, moving quickly toward the trapdoor. "Once they breach the tower, the narrow staircase limits how many can ascend at once."

Jesse followed him onto the spiral staircase, descending as rapidly as safety allowed. The sounds of conflict grew louder with each turn—shouts, impacts of improvised weapons, the crash of barricades being moved. By the time they reached the base level, Thomas Gardner stood at the tower entrance with a heavy wooden mallet in hand, directing younger workers to position themselves in the narrow doorway.

"They've breached the outer perimeter," he reported as Jonas and Jesse approached. "At least twenty men, armed with clubs and torches."

Through the partially open door, Jesse could see Roarke's men advancing across the cleared area that surrounded the lighthouse.

A flurry of activity at the periphery caught her attention— several of Roarke's men dragging wooden barrels toward the western side of the tower. One was broached, its contents splashing against the lower stonework.

"Lamp oil," Gardner said grimly. "They're spreading it along the stone."

The reek reached her through the narrow window—sharp and acrid, the unmistakable tang of whale oil. She watched it darken the pale granite, spreading through the mortar joints like veins. Her stomach dropped. The setting sun had warmed the tower's western face all afternoon; she could feel the stored heat radiating even from here.

Jonas turned to Gardner. "Take six men and prepare to rush them when I give the signal. The rest defend the entrance if we fail."

Jesse watched as Gardner selected men from among the defenders, distributing tools—mallets, iron pry bars, lengths of sturdy timber.

"Jesse," Jonas said, turning to her. "If the tower is breached, take the ledger up the staircase. The light must be lit at sunset."

"I understand," she said simply.

Jonas nodded once, then turned to join Gardner's men at the door. Jesse caught one last glimpse of the western sky through the narrow windows—the sun just above the horizon.

The defenders readied themselves at Jonas's signal.

# CHAPTER TWENTY-NINE

## The Father's Dream
### *BluffLight Tower—October 31, 1873*
### *(Illumination Day, sunset approaching)*

T he clash at the lighthouse entrance lasted mere minutes. Wood struck against iron. Men grunted with effort. Jonas led the defenders in a desperate charge against Roarke's men, their improvised weapons meeting the attackers' clubs with crashes that echoed through the stone tower.

The sheer surprise of their sudden advance drove Roarke's forces back several paces—long enough for Gardner and two others to overturn the barrels of lamp oil before they could be ignited. But Roarke's superior numbers forced Jonas and the defenders to retreat, step by hard-won step, back toward the lighthouse entrance.

Jesse saw Jonas stumble as a heavy blow caught him across the shoulder. Her breath stopped. She moved toward him before she could think, but Gardner's son was already there, pulling Jonas back into the defensive circle. Blood stained his shirtsleeve.

"Back inside!" Gardner shouted. "Bar the entrance! Get the injured men to safety!"

The defenders withdrew in orderly retreat, carrying two unconscious workers between them. Jesse moved forward to help Miller, who was now leaning heavily against the stone wall, his face pale. Without a word, she slipped her shoulder beneath his uninjured arm, taking some of his weight as they moved deeper into the tower's interior.

"Bar the door," Jonas instructed.

Gardner and his men were already sliding heavy timber beams through the iron brackets mounted on either side of the entrance. The solid oak door, reinforced with iron strapping, would not yield easily. Three inches of white oak with diagonal iron bracing built to withstand hurricane winds.

"Get Mr. Miller upstairs," Gardner directed Jesse as he positioned men at the narrow windows flanking the entrance. "First landing has the medical supplies. Robert, go with them—you've the steadiest hands for bandaging."

The spiral staircase presented a challenge with Jonas's injury, but between Jesse and young Robert, they managed a careful ascent to the first landing. This small chamber, built into the tower's thick walls as a rest point, contained storage shelves stocked with emergency supplies.

"Sit here," Jesse instructed, guiding Jonas to a wooden bench built along the curved wall. His breathing was labored, his face drawn with pain as Robert cut away the bloodied shirtsleeve to expose the wound beneath.

"Not as bad as it looks," Jonas said. "Glancing blow."

Robert's expression told a different story as he examined the injury. "The skin is split to the bone, sir. Without stitching, you'll lose use of the arm by morning."

Jesse located the medical chest on a nearby shelf—a sturdy wooden box containing the supplies lighthouse keepers required for emergencies far from conventional medical help. She set it beside Robert, then assessed the situation outside through the small window.

Roarke's men had surrounded the lighthouse base, their attempts to breach the door audible even through the tower's thick walls. Others had gathered the scattered timbers from the collapsed scaffolding, piling them against the western side of the structure.

"The stonework won't burn," Jonas replied, wincing as Robert began cleaning his wound. "But the smoke would make the interior uninhabitable."

From below came the sound of splintering wood—not the main door giving way, but something smaller. Jesse heard Gardner shouting instructions, followed by the crash of furniture being moved.

"They've broken through the side window," Robert explained, not looking up from his work. "Father will hold them at the narrow passage. The staircase is still secure."

In the lantern room far above, the Fresnel lens waited, its complex arrangement of prisms and glass ready to transform a simple flame into a beacon visible for miles across the dark water.

"How long until sunset?" Jonas asked, his voice steady despite Robert's ministrations with needle and catgut.

The sun hung just above the tree line. "Less than half an hour."

"The illumination happens regardless of what occurs at the base. That's your responsibility now."

"I can't leave you here," Jesse protested.

"You must," he insisted, meeting her gaze directly. "This lighthouse has stood incomplete for too long. My father's vision must be fulfilled tonight. That light must shine."

Jesse nodded slowly. "I'll return once the lamp is lit. Robert will stay with you."

Jonas reached inside his bloodied coat with his uninjured arm. "Take this," he said, producing a small leather-bound volume that Jesse recognized immediately as another of Henry Miller's journals. "You should have it with you in the lantern room. It contains his reflections on the first lighting ceremony."

Jesse accepted the journal with careful hands, tucking it alongside Roarke's ledger in her pocket. "I'll guard them both."

"See that you guard your own life," Jonas replied. "The lighthouse requires its keeper."

With a final glance at his bandaged arm—Robert's work efficient despite his youth—Jesse continued her ascent. The sounds of conflict below grew more distant with each turn.

Oil lamps mounted in iron brackets lit each landing. Jesse paused at each to light them with the tinderbox kept nearby, creating a path of illumination that spiraled upward through the tower's heart.

By the time she reached the lantern room, the sun had slipped below the horizon, leaving only a band of crimson fire along the western sky. Through the glass panels that encircled the chamber, Jesse could see the first stars appearing overhead.

The Fresnel lens dominated the circular space, its brass fittings gleaming softly in the fading light. Beside it stood the oil reservoir that would feed the lamp at its heart—a precision mechanism designed to provide consistent fuel flow for uninterrupted illumination throughout the night.

As Jesse moved to begin the lighting preparations, she became aware of a new sound from below—not the crash of attempted entry or the shouts of combatants, but a steady, rhythmic chanting. Peering from the western window, she could see a gathering approaching along the shore path, their way lit by lanterns carried high.

For a moment, she feared reinforcements for Roarke's assault. Then she recognized Pastor Willoughby at the group's head, his tall figure unmistakable. Behind him came shopkeepers, fishermen, craftspeople, and their families—Solomon Davis among them, Ruth Jackson, the Thatcher brothers, Miss Haskins's nephew. Moving with deliberate purpose toward the lighthouse.

Roarke's men turned to face this unexpected development, their assault on the tower temporarily abandoned. The villagers carried no visible weapons beyond their lanterns, but their numbers told the story—at least sixty people, perhaps more. Three times Roarke's force.

Jesse could not hear the exchange between Pastor Willoughby and Roarke, but she saw the moment shift. Several of Roarke's hired men from Savannah looked between their employer and the advancing islanders, then backed toward their horses. Roarke gestured sharply, but two more men withdrew.

Jesse stepped to the window so he could see her clearly— silhouetted against the lens, the lantern room's brass fittings framing her like a portrait. She didn't speak. She didn't need to.

Roarke's face turned upward toward the lantern room.

For a long moment, neither moved. She could see his expression even at this distance—the cold fury, yes, but something beneath it.

He knew she held the ledger. He knew the Revenue Service would come. He knew the darkness that had sheltered him was about to be burned away.

Then he turned his horse and rode away, the last to mount.

The islanders continued their advance, surrounding the lighthouse base. Their lanterns created a ring of light in the gathering darkness.

Jesse turned her attention back to the task at hand, opening Henry Miller's journal to draw guidance from the original keeper's words. The entry Jonas had marked described the procedures:

*The illumination ceremony acknowledges that darkness is not banished by accident, but by deliberate, sustained effort. The keeper commits to maintaining a flame and ensuring it reaches those who navigate dangerous waters.*

Jesse carefully filled the lamp's reservoir with oil from the supply stored in brass containers against the wall. With methodical precision, she trimmed the substantial wick, adjusting it to the exact height Henry's notes specified for optimal flame.

Through the glass panels, she could see the villagers still gathered below, their lanterns circling the tower's base. The Light-House Board required at least two witnesses for any official illumination ceremony—tonight they had the entire village. From among them, several people had entered the lighthouse—she could hear their footsteps on the spiral staircase, ascending steadily toward the lantern room.

Jesse struck a lucifer match—the special wind-resistant type the Light-House Board supplied—heads dipped in phosphorus and sulfur. The smell of sulfur rose sharp in the enclosed space. With steady hands, she touched it to the lamp's wick, which caught immediately, the specialized oil producing a clean, intense flame. Warmth bloomed against her face.

The third-order Fresnel lens caught the light, its hundreds of prisms arranged in concentric rings magnifying and directing it outward through each precisely arranged panel. The single flame transformed into a powerful beam that swept outward across the darkened sea—a corridor of light cutting through the night, reaching toward ships that might otherwise founder on the treacherous shoals.

As the clockwork mechanism started its measured turning—one complete revolution every two minutes as specified by the

Light-House Board, creating the distinctive flash pattern that would identify BluffLight to mariners—Jesse heard the door to the lantern room open behind her. She turned to find Miss Haskins entering, followed by Daniel and Eliza. The older woman must have brought them up during the confusion of Roarke's retreat. Their faces were alight with wonder as they beheld the lens in operation.

"It's beautiful, Mama," Eliza whispered, moving to stand beside Jesse. "Like sunrise and stars together."

"Indeed it is," Jesse agreed, drawing her children close as the great light continued its rhythmic rotation above them.

Beyond the glass walls, darkness surrounded them. Below, the villagers' lanterns formed their ring of protection.

The light turned. The children watched. The night deepened.

# CHAPTER THIRTY

## Boxes Half-Packed
*Marsh Cottage—November 3, 1873*
*(Three days later)*

The morning light filtered in through the windows of Marsh Cottage, illuminating the half-packed trunks and scattered belongings that covered every surface. Jesse stood in the center of the small main room, a folded dress in her hands, paused mid-gesture.

How many times had she packed like this? The muscle memory was automatic—fold tight, stack flat, leave nothing that couldn't be carried at a run. Her fingers knew the weight of fabric, the economy of space, the calculation of what was essential and what could be abandoned. Richmond. Charleston. The night boat to Savannah. Each departure had carved these movements deeper into her body until packing had become its own language, spoken without thought.

The dress in her hands was cotton, faded blue, practical. It could stay or go. She stood holding it, suspended between the trunk and the shelf.

Outside, a mockingbird called its varied repertoire from a nearby branch.

Three days had passed since BluffLight's successful illumination.

The evidence from Solomon's package—Roarke's detailed smuggling ledger—had been dispatched to Savannah via trusted courier the morning after the illumination. By the following day, Revenue Service officers had arrived on Saint Simons, their cutters anchored in the sound.

Roarke himself had disappeared before they could serve their warrants. Witnesses reported the *Miranda* slipping away in predawn darkness, likely bound for Caribbean waters. Several of his associates had been taken into custody.

The Richmond investigator had likewise vanished, his lodgings at the island's boarding house abandoned, no forwarding address left. Whether he had returned to William with news of their survival and location remained uncertain.

"Are we truly leaving, Mama?" Daniel asked from the loft ladder, his young face solemn as he observed the packing preparations below. "Now that the lighthouse is lit?"

Jesse set the dress aside, turning to face her son. "I don't know. We may have to leave again before your father sends more men."

"But the lighthouse needs its keeper," Daniel countered, descending to stand beside the trunk. "Mr. Miller said the federal appointment provides protection. And you lit the first flame—that matters, doesn't it?"

"It matters," Jesse acknowledged. "But your safety matters more. Both yours and Eliza's."

At the mention of her name, Eliza appeared in the doorway, her arms filled with wildflowers gathered from the cottage garden. "I picked these for Mr. Miller," she announced. "Miss Haskins says flowers help healing, especially those gathered with intention."

Jonas's injury during the confrontation had proven more serious than initially assessed. The blow that struck his shoulder had fractured the bone beneath, leaving him temporarily incapacitated. Physical recovery would require weeks.

"That's thoughtful, darling," Jesse said, taking the colorful bouquet and setting it in a jar of water. "We'll visit him this afternoon."

Eliza's gaze moved to the half-packed trunks. "Are we going away?"

Before Jesse could answer, a knock sounded at the cottage door. Her shoulders tensed. Her hand moved instinctively toward the drawer where she kept a small kitchen knife.

"Mrs. Whitmore?" Miss Haskins' crisp voice dispelled immediate concern. "I've brought your mail from the village office."

Jesse opened the door to find Miss Haskins holding several envelopes and a small package. Behind her, sunshine warmed the sandy soil along the path.

"You're packing," Miss Haskins observed as she entered, her sharp eyes taking in the cottage's disrupted state. "I suspected as much when you sent inquiry to the Savannah stagecoach office."

Jesse accepted the mail.

"The children might benefit from some fresh air while we speak," Miss Haskins continued, seating herself on the single chair not occupied by clothing or books. "Solomon Davis mentioned turtle eggs hatching near the south dune this morning. With the Revenue officers on patrol today, the children will be safe."

Jesse nodded to Daniel. "Take your sister to the dunes. Stay within sight of the cottage and remember what Solomon taught you about approaching wildlife."

Once the children had departed, their voices fading as they followed the path toward the shore, Miss Haskins fixed Jesse with her penetrating gaze. "Before you decide, there are matters you should know."

"Concerning Roarke?" Jesse asked.

"And other matters." Miss Haskins removed her gloves. She smoothed them across her lap before continuing. "Revenue officers found documents at Roarke's home—correspondence indicating your husband had indeed discovered your survival. The investigator was acting on specific information, not mere speculation."

A cold weight settled in Jesse's stomach. "Then William knows we're here."

"He suspects," Miss Haskins corrected. "But his primary agent has now abandoned the pursuit, and more importantly, the legal landscape has shifted considerably since the lighthouse illumination."

From her reticule, the older woman produced an official-looking document bearing federal seals and signatures. "This arrived by special courier this morning. Your formal appointment as BluffLight's keeper, signed by the Light-House Board commissioner and countersigned by the Treasury Department. A federal position with federal protections that substantially

214

complicates any claim your husband might make under Virginia law."

Jesse accepted the document with careful hands, scanning its formal language. Her thumb paused over the printed words: *Keeper of BluffLight Station*. William would have to petition federal courts, not simply claim marital rights under Virginia law.

"The Revenue Service officers were quite impressed by your role in exposing Roarke's smuggling operation," Miss Haskins continued. "Combined with your demonstrated competence during the illumination, it created sufficient impression for the commissioner to expedite your formal appointment. A woman keeper remains unusual but not unprecedented."

Jesse's fingers tightened on the paper's edge.

"And the children?" she asked.

"Are listed in the supporting documents as residential dependents of the keeper," Miss Haskins replied. "Federal lighthouse reservations function as distinct jurisdictions. While not absolute in legal terms, it creates significant procedural barriers to any attempt at removal without federal court involvement—a process that would expose your husband's treatment to uncomfortable scrutiny."

Jesse set the document aside, moving to the window where she could see Daniel and Eliza in the distance, kneeling beside something in the sand. Eliza's laughter carried faintly on the morning breeze. Daniel gestured broadly, likely explaining some natural phenomenon to his sister.

Jesse's fingers pressed the window frame. Richmond. William's study door opening at three in the morning. The careful retreat up the servants' stairs with the children, silent in their nightclothes. The years of mapping escape routes through their own house.

Her breath caught. "I'm not certain I know how to stop," she said quietly.

The words hung in the air between them.

"Perhaps that's not what's required," the older woman observed. "BluffLight requires vigilance—steady hands and watchful eyes." She glanced toward the window where the children played. "You've shown those qualities since you arrived."

Jesse turned back from the window.

"There's another consideration," Miss Haskins continued. "The keeper's cottage will be completed within the month. Its location on the lighthouse reservation provides both practical security and symbolic protection."

Through the window, Jesse could see her children returning, something cupped carefully in Daniel's hands. Daniel's shoulders were loose. Eliza skipped beside him.

"They're flourishing here," she observed softly.

"As are you," Miss Haskins replied with uncharacteristic gentleness. "Last week you addressed the village council without hesitation. That would have been unthinkable when you first arrived."

"I need time to consider," Jesse said finally.

Miss Haskins rose, smoothing her perpetually pristine black skirts. "Of course. But the light requires proper tending. You're capable of that."

After Miss Haskins had departed, Jesse remained by the window, watching as her children approached with their discovery—a small sand dollar, perfectly formed and bleached white by sun and tide. Eliza's face shone with excitement as she presented this treasure.

Jesse accepted the delicate disc, its intricate pattern a natural marvel unique to these shores.

She crossed to the larger trunk. The wood grain pressed against her palm as she gripped the lid. Then she lifted it. The smell of cedar and old fabric rose. Her hands were steady. One by one, she removed the contents, placing each garment back on the nearby shelves. A dress. A shawl. Daniel's spare shirt. Each movement deliberate, unhurried. Daniel and Eliza stood watching as the shelves filled again.

"We're staying?" Daniel asked hopefully.

Jesse looked at her son—at his eyes that had witnessed too much, at his young shoulders that had carried burdens beyond their years.

"Yes," she said simply. "We're staying."

Outside, the mockingbird continued its varied song.

# CHAPTER THIRTY-ONE

## A Daughter's Candle
### Christ Church—November 5, 1873
### (Two days after the decision to stay)

The interior of Christ Church lay hushed in late afternoon shadows, light streaming through plain glass windows in golden shafts. Jesse sat alone in the back pew, her hands folded in her lap and her gaze on the wooden cross at the altar. Two days had passed since her decision to remain on Saint Simons, to accept the keeper's position formally.

She pressed her palm against the worn pew. William had sent an investigator—the man's disappearance offered reprieve, not security. Her fingers traced a groove in the wood.

The church door opened behind her, admitting a brief breeze that stirred the hymnal pages before settling again. Jesse didn't turn, assuming Pastor Willoughby had come to prepare for evening prayers. But it was Eliza. Her small figure appeared at the end of the pew, her blonde curls glowing in the slanting sunlight.

"I thought you were with Daniel at Widow Patterson's," Jesse said, surprised to see her daughter alone.

"I was," Eliza confirmed, sliding onto the bench beside her mother. "But I needed to come here." She held up a small candle, the kind used in the church's side chapel for personal devotions. "Miss Haskins gave it to me. She said sometimes we light candles for personal prayers."

Jesse studied her daughter's solemn face. At six, Eliza delighted in marsh creatures and island flowers while remaining alert to sudden shifts in atmosphere.

"What would you like to pray for, darling?" Jesse asked.

"For our home," Eliza replied simply. "For the lighthouse to keep us safe. For the bad men not to come back."

Jesse's breath caught. She reached for her daughter's hand.

"That's a worthy prayer," she acknowledged. "Shall we light it together?"

They moved to the small side chapel where a stand of sand held unlit candles, waiting for the faithful to add their personal prayers to the church's collective worship. A single taper burned perpetually at the center—what Pastor Willoughby called the vigil light, maintained by the Altar Guild who took turns ensuring it never extinguished.

Jesse lifted Eliza so she could reach the taper. The vigil flame wavered as Eliza leaned close, her small hand cupped around her candle's wick to shield it. The flame caught—a tiny spark that grew steady as Eliza drew back, her eyes wide with the seriousness of the task. The warmth of the vigil light touched Jesse's face, carrying the faint smell of beeswax and burnt wick.

Together they placed Eliza's candle among the sand, her small fingers pressing it firmly upright, making certain it would stand.

"Now our prayer stays here even when we leave," Eliza explained, repeating what Miss Haskins had evidently told her. "It keeps burning until God answers."

"A beautiful thought," came Pastor Willoughby's gentle voice from behind them. He had entered silently, his clerical collar loosened in the day's heat, his kind eyes moving from the newly lit candle to the mother and daughter who had placed it. "The light that continues in our absence—rather like a lighthouse, wouldn't you say?"

Eliza nodded solemnly. "That's why I wanted to light it. Because we're staying to keep the lighthouse shining, and I want God to help us do it right."

The pastor's smile deepened at this straightforward explanation. "I believe He will, Miss Eliza." He turned to Jesse. "I was hoping to find you here. There's something I'd like to show you if you have a moment."

Curious, Jesse followed as he led them to the church's small vestry, where records and sacred vessels were stored. From a drawer in the ancient oak cabinet, Pastor Willoughby withdrew a leather-bound volume, its binding cracked with age and sea air.

"The parish registry dates to 1760," he explained, opening it carefully on the vestry table. "Baptisms, marriages, deaths—the island's history written in individual lives." He turned yellowed pages with careful fingers until finding the entry he sought. "I thought this might interest you, given recent events."

Jesse leaned closer, Eliza pressing against her side in shared curiosity. The entry Pastor Willoughby indicated, written in faded brown ink in a careful clerical hand, recorded the baptism of one "Henry Miller, son of Samuel and Margaret Miller" in the spring of 1820.

"Henry was island-born," the pastor explained. His finger moved to another entry, this one dated 1845. "He married here—Catherine Bishop, daughter of the mercantile owner."

Jesse ran her palm along the old ledger's edge, the leather cool beneath her hand. Her finger traced the entry—the ink faded to brown, the letters formed by a hand long since still.

"I didn't realize his connection to the island was so deep," she said.

Pastor Willoughby's hand rested on the registry. "Henry understood that a lighthouse serves both passing ships and the community that maintains it." He closed the ancient volume with careful hands, his expression growing more solemn. "I understand you've decided to remain as keeper."

"Yes," Jesse confirmed, her hand tightening on the vestry table's edge. "Though not without concerns."

"Understandable," he acknowledged. "Standing firm often proves more challenging than continuing flight. Yet I believe you've chosen wisely, Mrs. Whitmore." His gaze moved to Eliza, who had wandered to the vestry window to watch birds gathering in the live oak outside. He nodded once. "Deep roots withstand storms."

Jesse adjusted her skirts, considering his words. Each connection formed—with Miller, with Miss Haskins, with Solomon Davis and others who had proven reliable—had anchored them more securely.

"I've spent so much time watching for dangers," she admitted quietly, "that I'm not certain I remember how to be still."

"A habit developed from necessity," Pastor Willoughby replied without judgment. "One that might evolve now that circumstances have changed."

Through the vestry window, the spire of BluffLight was just visible above the tree line, its white tower catching the late afternoon sun with pristine brilliance. Soon dusk would fall, and Jesse would need to ascend its spiral staircase to light the lamp that would guide vessels safely through the night.

"We should return to Marsh Cottage," she said, gathering Eliza from her birdwatching. "Daniel will worry if we're not home before dark, and I must prepare for the evening lighting."

As they stepped from the church into the golden hour that preceded sunset, the ancient oaks draped with Spanish moss caught the slanting light, the distant chorus of marsh birds settling for the night, the salt-tinged breeze carrying whispers of both sea and pine forest.

"Look, Mama," Eliza said, pointing toward the eastern sky where the first evening star had appeared above BluffLight's distant tower. "The star is keeping watch with our lighthouse."

"So it is," Jesse agreed, taking her daughter's small hand as they followed the familiar path toward Marsh Cottage.

Later, as she climbed the lighthouse tower alone with lamp oil and matches, the sky dimmed into full night. She touched flame to wick. The magnificent Fresnel lens caught that single light and magnified it across miles of dangerous water.

# INTERLUDE III

### Keeper's Vigil
*BluffLight—November 7, 1873*
*(Two days after Eliza's candle)*

T he lantern room of BluffLight stood silent in the predawn darkness, its massive Fresnel lens temporarily dormant after a night of steady illumination. Jesse sat on the narrow bench built into the curved wall, watching as the first hint of gray touched the eastern horizon. This quiet moment before extinguishing the night's flame had become her favorite part of the keeper's duties—a peaceful time to check the equipment and prepare for the day ahead.

The air held the particular stillness of the hour before dawn— the smell of warm brass and lamp oil, the faint metallic tang of the lens mechanism, the salt air that seeped through every seam in the glass. The lantern room ticked softly as metal cooled and contracted. Through the windows, the world existed only in shades of gray and black, the horizon a promise rather than a presence.

Below, the island slept. Marsh Cottage—soon to be exchanged for the keeper's residence nearing completion at the tower's base— stood empty this morning, the children staying with Miss Haskins while Jesse maintained the overnight watch. In the village, shopkeepers and fishermen would soon stir to begin their day, many glancing eastward to confirm BluffLight's beam had guided vessels safely through another night.

The ledger that had exposed Roarke's operations now rested in federal hands in Savannah. Revenue Service officers continued their investigation, methodically dismantling the smuggling network that had flourished in darkness for so many years. The captain himself remained at large, his whereabouts unknown but his influence on the island dramatically diminished.

Of the Richmond investigator, no further word had come. Whether he had abandoned his pursuit or merely regrouped to attempt a different approach remained uncertain—a shadow that occasionally darkened Jesse's thoughts but no longer dominated them.

She rose as the horizon brightened further, preparing to extinguish the lamp as daylight rendered its beam unnecessary. This daily ritual—lighting at sunset, extinguishing at sunrise—had become the framework around which her life now organized itself.

Through the window, she watched as the sun breached the horizon, sending its first golden rays across the Atlantic. The lighthouse's shadow stretched westward across the bluff, reaching toward the forest beyond.

She extinguished the lamp. The day watch had begun.

# CHAPTER THIRTY-TWO

## Broken Bones, Unbroken Will
*The Keeper's Quarters—November 8, 1873*
*(One day later)*

The morning light filtered through the unfinished window of the keeper's quarters, casting geometric patterns across the makeshift bed where Jonas Miller lay, his injured shoulder bound tightly in clean bandages. Jesse organized medical supplies on the nearby table while monitoring his sleep. The Revenue Service physician had pronounced the shoulder fracture "severe but not irreparable" before returning to Savannah, leaving detailed instructions for care that Jesse now followed precisely.

A week had passed since BluffLight's successful test during the storm, seven nights of the great beacon sweeping its guiding beam across the coastal waters. Seven days of gradual adjustment to new routines as Jesse balanced her keeper's duties with tending to Jonas's recovery. The tower itself functioned flawlessly, the magnificent Fresnel lens transforming a simple flame into a corridor of light visible for miles across the dark Atlantic.

Jonas stirred, his eyes opening slowly as awareness returned. "What time?" he asked, his voice rough with sleep.

"Just past seven," Jesse replied, pouring fresh water from the pitcher into a cup. "You've slept nearly five hours. The laudanum seems to be helping."

He accepted the water with his uninjured arm, managing a smile. "Sleep is preferable to consciousness when every heartbeat sends fire through one's shoulder."

Jesse noted the pallor beneath his tan, the tightness around his eyes. The physician had been honest about the recovery's challenges—at least eight weeks of immobilization followed by months of careful rehabilitation before the arm might regain its former strength.

"Daniel brought the construction reports from Gardner," she said, helping Jonas sit more upright against the pillows. "The keeper's cottage foundation is complete. They'll begin framing the walls next week if the weather holds."

"Progress continues despite my absence," Jonas observed with a mixture of satisfaction and what might have been melancholy. "As it should."

"Under your direction," Jesse reminded him, spreading the architectural drawings across the foot of the bed where he could see them. "Gardner follows your plans precisely. The men refer to your specifications as if they were biblical commandments." Jesse smiled at that, but her eyes strayed to the window, where Daniel's small journal sat beside his shell collection.

"He's been drawing the tower," she said. "Sketching it from every angle. He wants to keep the logbooks someday."

"He will," Jonas said simply. "In time."

Jesse nodded, the moment catching her off guard with its quiet certainty.

This drew a more genuine smile from Miller. "Gardner has been with the project since the beginning. He knew my father before the war, understood his vision for BluffLight even when others saw only functional navigation."

A knock at the door interrupted their conversation. "Mrs. Whitmore?" Miss Haskins' crisp voice carried through the wooden panels. "I've brought the children and provisions from the village."

Jesse opened the door to find not only Miss Haskins and the children but also Pastor Willoughby and Solomon Davis, each carrying baskets or parcels. Behind them, Thomas Gardner and several other construction workers stood waiting, their expressions a mixture of concern and determination.

"We thought it time for a council," Pastor Willoughby explained as they entered. "Recent developments warrant collective consideration."

Apprehension flickered through Jesse. "What developments?"

The pastor glanced meaningfully at Daniel and Eliza, who had moved immediately to Jonas's bedside to show him their latest collections of shells and botanical specimens. Understanding his reluctance to speak openly before the children, Jesse turned to them. "Why don't you take your treasures to the workshop table? Mr. Gardner might help you identify the unusual specimens."

Once the children were settled at the far side of the room, absorbed in their natural history lessons with Gardner, Pastor Willoughby spoke in lower tones. "The Revenue Service officers returned to Savannah yesterday with their initial arrests. Captain Roarke remains at large, but his network has been significantly compromised."

"Good news, then," Jesse observed, though the grave expressions surrounding her suggested otherwise.

"Partially," Miss Haskins agreed. "But the dismantling of established operations often creates unexpected consequences. The morning boat brought word from Savannah that's troubling in its implications."

Solomon Davis continued the explanation, his deep voice kept carefully quiet. "Three of Roarke's men released on bail have disappeared. Their bondsman found their lodgings empty this morning, with indications of hasty departure."

"You believe they've joined Roarke?" Jonas asked, pushing himself straighter despite evident pain.

"Or been eliminated to prevent testimony," Miss Haskins said bluntly. "Either possibility carries implications for those responsible for their arrest and prosecution."

Whether seeking revenge or attempting to reclaim control, Roarke had ample motivation to target both the beacon and its keepers.

"There's more," Pastor Willoughby added. "The Richmond investigator was observed in Savannah yesterday, making inquiries about maritime law and federal jurisdiction. He has not abandoned his mission, adjusted his approach."

The familiar chill that accompanied any mention of William's agent settled over Jesse. The illumination ceremony had established BluffLight's official operation, creating federal protections that complicated any legal claim on the keeper or her family. But William's determination matched his resources—both considerable enough to warrant continued vigilance.

"We face potential threats from two directions," she assessed calmly, years of managing William's volatile moods having prepared her for clear thinking amid danger. "Roarke's retaliation and William's legal maneuvering."

"Three directions," Solomon corrected quietly. "The winter storms approach. The almanac predicts harsh weather this season."

Jesse nodded, acknowledging this additional challenge. BluffLight had been completed in autumn's relatively mild conditions. Its resilience against winter gales remained theoretical instead of proven, as did her own ability to maintain the light through such conditions.

"Hence the necessity for council," Pastor Willoughby concluded. "Individual vigilance has its merits, but coordinated preparation serves better against multiple challenges."

Jonas's voice, stronger now despite his injury, drew their attention. "What do you propose?"

"Rotation of watchers at the lighthouse," Thomas Gardner replied. "My men will take shifts observing approaches from village, shore, and forest. Solomon's people know every path through the marsh—nothing moves there without their knowledge."

"The village women have organized household supplies," Miss Haskins added. "Preserves, dried fish, medical necessities—stored in multiple locations instead of centralized where they might be targeted."

Pastor Willoughby continued. "The church will maintain continual occupation. Prayer, yes, but also practical observation of who passes the churchyard crossroads. No approach to the lighthouse goes unnoticed from that vantage point."

The comprehensive nature of these preparations—already organized without her knowledge—left Jesse momentarily speechless. During their months on the island, she had maintained careful distance from community involvement, sharing minimal information about their circumstances while focusing on survival through self-sufficiency. Yet somehow, connections had formed regardless—tendrils of mutual support extending beneath her conscious awareness like the complex root systems that stabilized marsh grasses.

"You've prepared all this without being asked," she observed, unable to keep wonder from her voice.

"The lighthouse serves all who navigate these waters," Pastor Willoughby replied simply. "It's keeper deserves similar consideration."

"Besides," Miss Haskins added with characteristic directness, "you and the children have become integral to this island despite your initial reluctance. Your welfare concerns us beyond practical lighthouse operation."

Jesse glanced toward Daniel and Eliza, still absorbed in conversation with Gardner at the workshop table.

"We've received much from this place," she acknowledged quietly.

"And given much in return," Solomon added. "The lighthouse stands because you remained when flight might have been wiser. That light guides vessels beyond your awareness every night, saving lives you'll never meet. Such service merits protection."

Jonas's voice joined the conversation, his tone reflecting the gravity of their situation yet carrying unexpected hope as well. "When I first showed Mrs. Whitmore the lighthouse plans, I described it as renewal after destruction, purpose sustained through opposition." His gaze met Jesse's across the room. "I did not anticipate how fully that would manifest through its keeper."

The simple statement carried layers of understanding that brought unexpected warmth to Jesse's cheeks. Jonas had never pressed for details about her past, had respected the careful boundaries she maintained around certain subjects. Yet his observation acknowledged what he had discerned about her journey from Richmond to Saint Simons. Their eyes held for a moment longer than necessary—no words required, none offered— before Jesse looked away, her pulse quickening in a way that had nothing to do with fear.

"Then we proceed together," Jesse decided, looking around at these people who had transformed from strangers to allies to something approaching family. "The light continues its nightly operation. The keeper's cottage construction advances. Normal routines maintain, but with heightened awareness of potential threats."

"And multiple eyes watching in all directions," Solomon added with quiet confidence. "Roarke may know these waters, but my people know the marshes where solid ground meets tide. The Richmond man may understand legal documents, but he doesn't comprehend island ways."

The tension that had accompanied their initial discussion eased as practical plans emerged—adjustments to work schedules, communication systems between village and lighthouse, arrangements for the children's continued education and safety.

Daniel approached from the workshop table, a piece of paper in his hand. "Mr. Gardner helped me draw the cottage layout," he explained, showing Jesse the careful diagram. "He says we can adjust the interior walls before they're plastered if we have specific requirements."

# CHAPTER THIRTY-THREE

## Building Sanctuary
*BluffLight Keeper's Cottage Construction Site—November 15, 1873*
*(One week after the council meeting)*

The rhythmic sound of hammers filled the morning air as workers raised the timber frame of the keeper's cottage. Jesse stood out of the way, a steaming cup of coffee warming her hands. November's chill crept through her shawl. Pine scent drifted on the breeze.

Seven days had passed since the council meeting. The lighthouse continued its nightly illumination without incident, though Revenue Service officers had reported no success in locating Roarke or his vessel. Of the Richmond investigator, there had been no further sightings since his appearance in Savannah.

"The north wall is nearly complete," Thomas Gardner announced, approaching with his measuring rod in hand. "We'll have the frame finished by week's end if this weather holds. Then comes the real challenge—tabby walls eighteen inches thick at the base, tapering to twelve at the top, with crushed shell aggregate comprising at least forty percent of the mixture."

Jesse's gaze followed his gesture toward the skeleton of what would become their permanent home. It was larger than Marsh Cottage, with rooms arranged so she could always see the lighthouse. The wood frame rose solid and intentional against the November sky.

"You've made remarkable progress," she observed. "Even with reduced manpower."

Gardner smiled briefly. "More hands arrive daily. The Widow Patterson's sons returned from Savannah yesterday. Samuel Fletcher brought three men from the mapmaking office. Even

Robert Jenkins—the schoolmaster's youngest—has joined us after classes."

"We received word from the Light-House Board this morning," Jesse said, handing Gardner the official letter that had arrived on the dawn packet. "The quarterly inspection is scheduled for December third. They'll require complete demonstration of all operational aspects—the lamp mechanism, oil consumption records, weather log, and lens rotation."

Gardner scanned the document. "Standard procedure for a new installation. We'll have the cottage habitable by then, though finishing work will continue through winter."

"Habitable is sufficient," Jesse assured him. "The children and I have managed with far less."

"Mama!" Eliza's voice carried across the construction site as she emerged from the path leading to Marsh Cottage. Behind her came Daniel with a basket covered in cloth. Further down the path, the Widow Patterson followed.

"We baked sea biscuits for the workers," Eliza announced as they reached the cottage foundation. "With dried blueberries that Mrs. Patterson preserved over the summer."

"How thoughtful." The tired shoulders of nearby workers straightened as the scent reached them—warm bread and dried fruit cutting through the sharper smells of sawdust and sweat. "Perhaps Mr. Gardner would help you distribute them during the mid-morning break."

As Gardner led Eliza toward the supply tent, Jesse turned to Widow Patterson. "Thank you for including her in the baking. She thrives with such practical instruction."

"The child has natural talent," the older woman replied. "Steady hands and patience beyond her years." Her gaze softened as she watched Eliza carefully presenting the first biscuit to an elderly worker whose arthritic hands had confined him to lighter tasks. "She'll make a fine keeper one day, should she choose that path."

Jesse watched her daughter move among the workers.

Daniel had moved to examine the timber framing, his expression thoughtful as he studied the joinery at the corner posts.

"Mr. Gardner's using mortise and tenon connections," he observed as Jesse approached. "Like in Henry Miller's original drawings."

"The southeast bedroom will be yours," Jesse told him, pointing toward the framed space nearest the lighthouse tower. "Windows facing east for sunrise, south toward the forest."

Daniel nodded, visibly pleased. "And yours?"

"Western, for watching storms come in. Northern for the lighthouse." She paused. "We'll all share the night watches once you're older."

This brought a smile to Daniel's face.

A commotion at the site entrance drew their attention. Miss Haskins had arrived with unexpected accompaniment—Jonas Miller, his first appearance outside since his injury. He leaned on a walking stick, his injured arm bound against his chest. His eyes were clear as he surveyed the construction progress.

"Mr. Miller insisted on inspecting the work himself," Miss Haskins explained as Jesse approached them. "Against medical advice and simple common sense."

"The physician suggested moderate activity would aid recovery," Jonas countered mildly. "Observing others at work should be moderate enough."

Miss Haskins kept close as they made their way toward the framing. Jesse noted the improvement in his color since the council meeting.

"The framing follows your specifications precisely," she assured him as they reached the partially enclosed structure. "Gardner referenced your father's original drawings for the joinery techniques."

Jonas studied the corner post where Daniel stood. "Fine craftsmanship," he acknowledged. "Though I expect nothing less from Thomas Gardner. Three generations of his family have built structures on this island."

They continued a careful circuit of the cottage foundation. Jonas paused to steady himself, then continued, stopping occasionally to examine particular details. His builder's eye remained sharp, identifying potential improvements that less experienced observers might have missed.

"The additional south-facing windows were your suggestion?" he asked Jesse as they examined what would become the cottage's main living area.

"For winter sunlight," she confirmed. "And cross-ventilation during summer."

Jonas nodded. "Henry's journals served you well."

As midday approached, the workers gathered at the supply tent where Eliza's sea biscuits had been supplemented by additional provisions from the village—smoked fish, corn bread, preserved fruits. Eliza paused to listen as one of the older workers told her something, her face bright with interest.

"She belongs here," Miss Haskins observed quietly, following Jesse's gaze. "As do you."

Nearby, Samuel Fletcher lifted a bucket of nails. The Widow Patterson handed a water ladle to one of the workers.

"One nail at a time," Daniel said, joining them as they watched the cottage construction.

"What was that, darling?" Jesse asked.

"Mr. Gardner told me that's how you build something meant to last," he explained. "By placing each nail with care and purpose. One after another until the structure stands complete."

Jesse turned back toward the rising frame. The hammers kept their steady rhythm.

# CHAPTER THIRTY-FOUR

### The Lightning Trial
*BluffLight Tower—November 22, 1873*
*(One week after the cottage construction began)*

T he storm announced itself with distant flickers on the horizon hours before the first clouds reached Saint Simons. Jesse stood in the lantern room, watching as lightning illuminated the far reaches of the Atlantic. The barometer mounted beside the logbook had been falling steadily since midday, its needle now pointing toward "Storm" as the instrument recorded the approaching pressure change.

"It's moving faster than predicted," Solomon Davis observed from beside her, his face reflecting the lightning as he studied the darkness beyond the glass panels. The elderly marsh guide had arrived an hour earlier, bringing warning from fishermen who had spotted the weather system forming offshore. "A northeasterly gale, driving hard toward the coast. We might have an hour before it strikes, no more."

Jesse nodded, mentally reviewing the preparations already completed—oil reserves secured, tools and maintenance equipment stowed, storm shutters installed on the windows. The children were safe with Miss Haskins in the village, where stone structures offered better protection than the partially completed cottage near the bluff.

"I should complete the logbook entries before the storm arrives," Jesse said, moving toward the small desk built into the lantern room's western wall. "The Light-House Board requires detailed weather observations during first-year operation."

Solomon nodded. "I'll check the lower windows once more, ensure the shutters are secured properly." He departed down the spiral staircase.

Jesse turned to the operational logbook, recording the barometric reading, wind direction, and visibility conditions with measured precision. The Revenue Service investigation into Roarke's network continued, with additional arrests reported, though the captain remained at large.

The storm struck within the hour. Wind pressed against the tower with sudden force, rain lashing the glass panels in horizontal sheets. The lamp flame wavered but held steady within its protective housing, the lens continuing its measured rotation that sent BluffLight's pattern across the churning waters.

The tower flexed slightly beneath her feet—confirmed by water rippling in the drinking glass on the service table. The lighthouse had been designed to allow minimal movement during high winds, preventing the structure from cracking under pressure.

Footsteps sounded on the stairwell below. Thomas Gardner appeared moments later, rain glistening on his shoulders from his inspection of the lower levels. "Normal structural response," he assured her. "My father helped build the Tybee Island lighthouse in '38. During its first hurricane, he described the tower breathing with the wind—a necessary adaptation."

They maintained careful watch as the storm intensified. The operational logbook received precise entries documenting wind velocity estimates, precipitation patterns, and barometric readings that continued falling. Through it all, BluffLight's beam cut through the darkness, visible between squalls.

"The foundation remains stable," Gardner noted, his hand pressed against the lantern room wall to monitor vibrations. "Henry Miller's calculations were precise. The base is absorbing and distributing force exactly as designed."

Lightning struck offshore, the thunderclap following instantly—less than a second's delay, meaning the bolt had landed within a quarter-mile. The flash illuminated the surrounding landscape: the maritime forest bending beneath the gale, the partially constructed keeper's cottage straining against the wind but holding firm due to Gardner's reinforced framing.

"Look there," Gardner said, pointing toward the southwestern horizon where a break in the cloud cover had appeared. Through this window, a distant light flickered—too regular for lightning, too persistent for coincidence.

"A vessel caught in the passage," Jesse identified, moving to the southwestern window. A cold tightness formed beneath her ribs. The light appeared again—a ship's lantern raised and lowered in the recognized vertical distress pattern used by coastal vessels.

"They're too far into the shoals," Gardner assessed. The vessel was approaching from the southeast, drifting dangerously toward the rocks. "The channel shifts during northeastern gales, creating false passages. Without precise knowledge of the alterations—"

"They'll founder on Griffin's Teeth." Jesse named the rock formation that had claimed numerous vessels over the decades. "Unless they can navigate by BluffLight's beam."

The distant vessel's lantern moved slowly northward, following the safe channel that BluffLight illuminated even through the storm. The ship's progress was painfully slow, each advance threatened by waves that could drive it back toward the waiting rocks.

Jesse checked the lamp's flame and oil supply with renewed attention. This was practical salvation—lives depending directly on the beacon's unwavering guidance.

"The flame holds steady," Gardner confirmed. "The lens rotation mechanism is functioning at proper speed. They have the best guidance possible under these conditions."

For nearly an hour, they watched as the distant vessel navigated toward safer waters. The storm continued, lightning illuminating their vigil in irregular flashes.

"They're past the shoals," Gardner announced finally, his keen eyes having tracked the ship's progress. "The channel deepens there, providing better protection from crosscurrents. If they maintain that heading, they'll reach the harbor inlet by dawn."

Jesse gripped the service table, her knuckles white against the brass edge. The breath she'd been holding released in a long, shuddering exhale. Somewhere out there, men she would never meet were alive because this light burned steady. Her hands had trimmed the wick, filled the reservoir, wound the clockwork. Those same hands had pulled them through.

As dawn approached, the storm's fury diminished. Rain continued falling steadily, but the wind subsided to forceful gusts. Gardner departed to inspect the tower's lower levels for potential water infiltration, leaving Jesse alone in the lantern room.

The first lightening of the sky became visible—not true dawn, but the gradual diminishment of darkness that preceded sunrise. The storm clouds remained, yet even this muted illumination signified endurance, purpose fulfilled.

Jesse completed her logbook entry with measured precision, documenting the vessel's safe passage in the same careful hand that recorded barometric readings and wind velocities.

# CHAPTER THIRTY-FIVE

Face in the Fog
*The Maritime Forest—November 30, 1873*
*(Eight days after the lightning storm)*

Morning fog shrouded the maritime forest, transforming familiar paths into passages visible only yards ahead. Jesse moved cautiously along the narrow track connecting the lighthouse to the village, her steps guided more by memory than vision. Behind her, BluffLight's beam scattered through the mist, its pattern blurred but still pulsing faintly.

The storm had passed eight days earlier, leaving saturated ground that now released moisture as the morning air warmed. Jesse had delayed her weekly village journey hoping the fog might lift, but the Light-House Board inspection tomorrow demanded specific supplies—fresh lamp wicks, polishing compound for the brass fittings, regulation logbooks.

She paused at the forest crossroads, listening. The village path continued straight; the right fork led to old tabby ruins. Sound traveled strangely in fog—sometimes muffled, other times carrying with unnatural clarity.

Brush rustled to her left. Not on either path but in the undergrowth where travelers rarely ventured. Jesse turned toward the sound. Through the swirling mist, a darker shape appeared briefly before melting back into white obscurity.

"Who's there?" Her voice stayed steady despite the tension in her shoulders.

No response came, but faint sounds suggested movement deeper in the forest—deliberate steps through sodden underbrush. Jesse remained motionless. The construction workers knew the direct path. Village residents kept to established tracks, particularly in conditions where orientation could easily be lost.

The fog shifted slightly, revealing a figure perhaps twenty yards distant—a man standing utterly still among the pines.

Not Roarke, whose powerful build was unmistakable even at distance. Not the Richmond investigator, whose formal attire distinguished him from islanders. This silhouette carried greater menace than both—the lean height, the precisely squared shoulders, the characteristic tilt of head.

Her mind supplied the name before she could stop it. *William.*

Jesse's breath caught. Her hand tightened around her basket. Her body knew before her thoughts could form—the old familiar tightening in her throat, the ice spreading through her limbs, every muscle tensing toward flight. Years of listening for his footsteps had carved these responses into her bones.

Their gazes locked across the distance. Then the figure stepped forward, emerging from the mist. Jesse turned and moved swiftly back toward the lighthouse path, her feet finding the track through instinct as fog closed around her. Running on the slick ground risked a fall—and running would confirm she had recognized him.

No sound of pursuit reached her ears, but William rarely rushed. His strategies involved careful positioning, ensuring escape routes were compromised before revealing intentions. His presence in the forest suggested reconnaissance—observing, gathering information.

Jesse reversed direction and took the path back toward BluffLight, knowing the established track offered safer return than trackless forest in blinding fog. Each step carried her closer to sanctuary established through federal appointment, to the community organized for their protection.

As the path climbed toward the bluff, the fog thinned slightly. Jesse felt her breathing steady. William's presence confirmed what the investigator's appearance had suggested—he had discovered their survival and located their refuge.

Yet his solitary presence instead of official approach with legal representatives suggested uncertainty. Federal jurisdiction complicated the marital claims that Virginia law supported. The William she had known would never confront a situation without comprehensive understanding of his advantages.

BluffLight's base emerged from the mist as Jesse reached the clearing. The keeper's cottage construction had progressed since the storm, walls now framed and partially enclosed with tabby. Several workers moved across the site despite limited visibility.

"Mrs. Whitmore," Thomas Gardner called, approaching. "We didn't expect you back so soon."

"I decided against continuing," Jesse replied. "But I observed someone in the forest—moving parallel to the path instead of on it."

Gardner's expression sharpened. "Can you describe them?"

"A tall man, lean build. Not dressed as an islander. Moving deliberately but cautiously."

"Which direction was he heading?"

"Deeper into the forest. Away from the path."

"I'll send Robert to alert the village watchers," Gardner decided. "This fog provides cover for those with harmful intentions."

Jesse entered the lighthouse, closing the heavy door behind her. The solid stone walls provided immediate security. She climbed the spiral staircase, muscle memory guiding her steps.

The children remained safe with Miss Haskins in the village. The Light-House Board inspector would arrive tomorrow. The cottage construction continued with witnesses present throughout daylight hours.

The lantern room welcomed her with familiar stillness, its glass panels misted with condensation. Jesse moved to the operational logbook, recording the fog conditions and reduced visibility with characteristic precision. The formal procedure grounded her.

The fog lifted as midday approached, sunlight burning through to reveal the island in increasing clarity. Jesse remained in the lantern room, watching as visibility improved—the cottage, the forest's edge, the distant village rooftops.

No further sign of the man appeared. The question was not whether he had found them, but what approach he would take. Direct confrontation seemed unlikely given BluffLight's federal status. Legal maneuvering would require time and public scrutiny he had always avoided.

Once the last of the mist burned away, she descended to inform Gardner of William's specific identity. The master mason received this with characteristic calm.

"We'll adjust the watch schedules," he decided. "Solomon's people know every approach to this bluff. Nothing will reach the lighthouse unobserved."

# CHAPTER THIRTY-SIX

## Judgement Below the Lantern
*BluffLight Tower—December 3, 1873*
*(Three days after the fog encounter)*

T he Light-House Board inspector arrived precisely at noon, his black frock coat and official cap marking him as a federal representative even before he presented credentials at the tower entrance. Jesse received him in her keeper's uniform—a tailored navy dress with brass buttons, adapted by Miss Haskins to match Lighthouse Service specifications exactly.

"Mrs. Whitmore," the inspector acknowledged, removing his hat as he stepped inside. "Commander James Reeves, United States Light-House Board, Fifth District. I'm here to conduct the quarterly inspection of BluffLight Station."

"We've been expecting you, Commander," Jesse replied, gesturing toward the spiral staircase. "All logs and operational records are prepared for your review. Mr. Miller will join us shortly to address structural questions."

The inspector followed her up the spiral staircase. Jesse noted his impressed expression as they emerged into the lantern room where midday sun brightened the Fresnel lens in all its crystal complexity.

"Remarkable installation," Reeves acknowledged, moving to examine the lamp mechanism. "Third-order French lens system, if I'm not mistaken."

"Correct. Manufactured in Paris, transported via Charleston. The optical precision allows twenty-mile visibility in clear conditions."

For the next hour, the inspector conducted methodical evaluation of every aspect of lighthouse operation. He examined the logbook entries, tested the whale oil reservoir system, verified the clockwork mechanism powered by falling weights that drove the lens rotation.

"The mechanism requires rewinding every four hours," Jesse explained, demonstrating the procedure as the heavy weights descended through the tower's central shaft. Reeves consulted his pocket watch, timing the flash pattern as the beam completed its characteristic two-minute cycle—the distinctive signature that distinguished BluffLight from other coastal installations.

"Precisely calibrated," he noted with approval. "Mariners will recognize this pattern from considerable distance."

"Your record-keeping is exemplary," he continued, reviewing the operational logbook where Jesse had documented the storm-tossed vessel's navigation through dangerous shoals. "Most newly appointed keepers require months to develop such comprehensive documentation."

"Henry Miller's journals provided guidance," Jesse acknowledged. "His attention to detail established the standard we've maintained."

The inspector made a formal notation in his official ledger—the physical record of federal assessment that would become part of BluffLight's permanent administrative file in Washington. "Miller's reputation remains strong within the Service. His designs incorporated innovations we've since implemented in other installations." He closed the logbook with a decisive movement. "The lighthouse appears to be functioning precisely as designed."

A knock at the lantern room door announced Jonas Miller's arrival. The construction supervisor entered carefully, his injured shoulder still bandaged but his appearance significantly improved. Jesse performed brief introductions, noting the professional respect that formed between the two men.

"The tower has weathered its first significant storm without structural concerns," Jonas reported. "The foundation remains stable, masonry intact, lantern room watertight despite driving rain from the northeast."

"And the keeper's cottage?" Reeves asked, moving to the western window where the partially completed structure was visible.

"Proceeding ahead of schedule. Exterior walls complete, roof framing in progress. Living quarters should be habitable within two weeks."

The inspector made several notations, then returned his attention to Jesse. "I understand there have been security concerns. The Revenue Service forwarded reports about smuggling operations disrupted by BluffLight's illumination."

"Captain Roarke's activities have been curtailed," Jesse acknowledged. "Though he remains at large, his network has been largely dismantled through federal prosecution."

"And the other matter? The Richmond situation mentioned in supplementary reports?"

Jesse glanced at Jonas, who nodded. "My former husband has apparently discovered our location. I observed him near the lighthouse grounds three days ago, though he has made no direct approach."

"The Lighthouse Service takes security of its personnel seriously," Reeves said. "Any threat to the keeper creates potential compromise to navigational safety."

The lantern room door opened without preliminary knock.

"Commander Reeves," Thomas Gardner said, his voice carrying unusual urgency. "There's a situation requiring your immediate attention at the base."

They descended the spiral staircase. As they reached ground level and stepped outside, the cause became apparent. A small group stood at the lighthouse entrance—Solomon Davis and two Revenue Service officers flanking a man whose presence sent recognition through Jesse.

Several construction workers had stopped their tasks, watching from near the cottage framing.

William Whitmore stood straight-backed and impeccably attired, though a flicker of tension passed through his jaw. His eyes fixed on Jesse, assessing her keeper's uniform with visible surprise.

"This man attempted to approach the lighthouse unannounced," Solomon explained. "He presented documents claiming legal authority regarding Mrs. Whitmore and her children."

William stepped forward. "William Whitmore, Commander. I'm attempting to rectify a misunderstanding regarding my wife and children, who were reported deceased but appear to have established residence here." His tone suggested assertion, not reconciliation.

"Your documentation, sir?" Reeves requested.

William produced folded papers from his coat—documents bearing Virginia state seals. "Marriage certificate, birth registrations confirming paternity, court declarations of my rights as husband and father under Virginia law."

The commander examined each document. "These appear to be legitimate Virginia state documents, Mr. Whitmore. However, you are standing on federal property administered by the United States Light-House Board, where state jurisdictions have limited application."

"Surely federal authorities recognize established family law," William countered. "A husband's right to reunite with his family supersedes jurisdictional technicalities."

"Federal authorities recognize properly appointed lighthouse keepers," Reeves replied. "Mrs. Whitmore holds official commission from the Light-House Board, with all protections such position entails."

"My wife has no training or qualification for such position," William observed.

"The quarterly inspection I've just completed suggests otherwise," Reeves countered, his official ledger still in hand. "BluffLight's operation meets all Service standards. The logs demonstrate exceptional care, the maintenance is exemplary, and the recent storm response saved lives."

William's expression tightened. "Family matters must surely take precedence over temporary employment. The children require proper household and educational opportunities beyond this isolated location."

Jesse stepped forward. "The children attend formal lessons with Miss Jenkins, the island schoolteacher. Daniel has developed aptitude for mathematics and engineering. Eliza studies the island's plants and animals under teachers who know these marshlands better than any scholar in Richmond."

William's gaze sharpened. "Jessica," he said, using her full name with precise intonation. No one but William ever used it. "You've been through significant strain. Your judgment reflects understandable confusion following your illness. I've made arrangements for medical consultation in Richmond, where specialists can address your condition."

Commander Reeves interjected. "Mr. Whitmore, any claim regarding the lighthouse keeper's status must be submitted through formal channels to the Light-House Board in Washington. Local representatives lack authority to modify federal appointments without procedural review."

He continued, "Attempts to interfere with lighthouse operation or personnel constitute federal offense under maritime safety statutes. I would advise against any action construed as disruption or intimidation."

"Federal jurisdiction over lighthouse personnel is clear," Reeves added. "Domestic cases follow separate appeals channels. What I can offer is process—time and official standing while courts determine these matters."

"I've filed for visitation," William said. "The court in Richmond will rule in my favor."

Jesse's spine straightened. Her hands hung still at her sides—no trembling, no clenching. The words came clear and unhurried. The woman who had once flinched at his footsteps, who had learned to read his moods from the weight of his tread on the stairs, now met his gaze without wavering.

"Then I'll see you in court," Jesse answered. "But not here. The children are not present on lighthouse grounds, and I do not consent to their engagement with you under any circumstances."

William's composure faltered briefly. His eyes moved over her face as if searching for the woman he had known—the one who lowered her gaze, who softened her voice, who made herself small in his presence. He did not find her. Something shifted behind his expression: confusion giving way to calculation, then to something colder. He was reassessing. Recalibrating.

"This matter is far from resolved. I'll use every legal avenue available."

"As is your right," Reeves acknowledged. "Until proceedings reach conclusion, Mrs. Whitmore's federal appointment stands."

The Revenue Service officers escorted William from federal property. Jesse watched his retreating figure, her posture steady. The workers near the cottage had resumed their tasks, hammers resuming their rhythm.

Jonas watched William's departure with the calm, assessing focus he used on unstable structures.

Gardner approached. "Solomon's people will maintain watch on all approaches. Nothing reaches this bluff unobserved."

Jonas had descended with them, standing quietly to one side. "The federal position is stronger than he expected," he observed. "State courts move slowly when federal jurisdiction is contested."

Jesse nodded. The confrontation had established a critical reality: William's usual methods had met resistance instead of acceptance. His documents held weight in Virginia. They held less weight here, on federal ground, with federal witnesses recording every exchange in official ledgers.

She returned to the tower and climbed the spiral staircase. The lantern room waited, the Fresnel lens catching afternoon light through the western windows. She opened the operational logbook and recorded the inspection results in her careful hand—date, time, Commander James Reeves, U.S. Light-House Board, Fifth District, assessment rendered satisfactory.

# CHAPTER THIRTY-SEVEN

Reckonings

*The Village Square—December 7, 1873*
*(Four days after William's confrontation at the lighthouse)*

Sunday morning brought the island community to Christ Church, the white clapboard building standing beneath ancient oaks draped with Spanish moss. Jesse sat with Daniel and Eliza in their regular pew—midway along the right side, positioned for quick exit if necessary. The habit remained despite Commander Reeves's endorsement four days earlier and the Revenue Service officers from the cutter *Vigilant* now patrolling the village perimeter.

William's appearance at the lighthouse had resolved nothing. His presence on Saint Simons confirmed what the Richmond investigator's activities had suggested—he had discovered their survival and located their refuge. Yet the Light-House Board inspection had established federal jurisdiction that complicated his legal claims, creating procedural barriers between his intentions and their implementation.

As the congregation rose for the final hymn, Jesse noted the positioning of island men throughout the sanctuary—Thomas Gardner near the main entrance, Solomon Davis at the side door, Samuel Fletcher in the balcony overlooking the space. William had not appeared at the church service.

"Mrs. Whitmore," Miss Haskins greeted them as the congregation dispersed onto the churchyard following the benediction. "A brief word before you return to the lighthouse, if convenient."

Jesse directed the children toward the ancient oak where several island children had gathered under the Widow Patterson's eye. When they were out of earshot, Miss Haskins spoke with characteristic directness.

"The Revenue Service officers report unusual activity at the southern harbor. A two-masted schooner matching the *Miranda's* description—approximately eighty feet with black hull—was sighted offshore yesterday. A small boat was lowered that made landfall near the old tabby ruins."

"Roarke has returned?"

"So it would appear," Miss Haskins confirmed. "Though he has made no public appearance. The significant detail is the timing—coinciding with your husband's arrival on the island."

"You believe they're coordinating efforts?"

"I believe desperate men with aligned interests often form alliances," the older woman replied. "William Whitmore seeks legal means to reclaim what he considers his property. Roarke desires revenge against those who exposed his operations. Both view BluffLight as an obstacle to their objectives."

"What practical measures would you suggest?"

"Maintain the children at the lighthouse instead of Marsh Cottage until the keeper's residence is habitable," Miss Haskins advised. "Double the night watch, particularly during low tide when the marshes can be crossed on foot. And accelerate the remaining cottage construction—completed walls provide more security than exposed framing."

Jesse nodded, the recommendations aligning with her own assessment. "You believe they'll act soon?"

"Both men operate from wounded pride as much as calculated advantage," Miss Haskins observed. "Neither tolerates perceived defiance without response. I would anticipate movement before the new moon—three nights hence, when darkness provides maximum cover."

Their conversation concluded as Daniel and Eliza returned from the churchyard oak. Jesse studied their faces—Daniel's watchful assessment of surrounding adults, Eliza's careful positioning close to her brother.

"We should return to the lighthouse," she decided, gathering their prayer books.

As they walked the village path toward BluffLight, two *Vigilant* officers followed at a discreet distance. Jesse noted Solomon's network had expanded its vigilance, watchers positioned at key junctions throughout the forest and marsh approaches.

"Mrs. Whitmore!"

The call came from behind them at the forest crossroads. Jonas Miller approached, carrying a leather portfolio similar to those he used for construction documents. His injured shoulder remained bandaged but his movements had grown more fluid.

"A development requiring your immediate attention," he explained, falling into step beside them as they continued toward the lighthouse. "The Revenue Service delivered these documents this morning."

Inside the portfolio Jesse found official papers bearing Department of Treasury seals—formal confirmation of her keeper appointment, documentation of federal jurisdiction over the lighthouse reservation, and legal opinion regarding her status relative to Virginia state claims.

"The Light-House Board's counsel has rendered preliminary assessment," Jonas explained as she scanned the documents. "While not dismissing your husband's legal standing under Virginia law, they establish clear jurisdictional barrier to any attempt at removing you or the children from federal property without proper judicial review at the federal level."

Jesse read the crucial passage: *"The appointment of Mrs. Jessica Whitmore as keeper of BluffLight constitutes federal commission that takes precedence over conflicting state claims within the designated lighthouse reservation."*

The practical import was clear—William's Virginia court orders held no immediate force on lighthouse property. Federal proceedings would require months and allow equal consideration of evidence.

"This provides substantial protection," Jesse acknowledged.

They reached the lighthouse grounds, where construction of the keeper's cottage continued even on Sunday—additional workers having volunteered their day of rest in light of recent developments. The walls now stood fully enclosed, the roof nearly finished.

"Gardner believes the cottage will be habitable within five days," Jonas informed her, nodding toward the structure. "The children's bedroom has been prioritized, with reinforced shutters and secondary exit through the storage room."

Near the cottage foundation, one of the workers called to Gardner. "Someone's been here. Boot prints in the mud—not any of ours. Fresh from last night, by the look of them."

Gardner examined the ground, then exchanged a glance with Jonas. The prints led from the marsh edge toward the cottage, circled the foundation, then retreated the way they came. Someone had approached in darkness, observed the construction progress, and withdrawn.

# CHAPTER THIRTY-EIGHT

Letters Never Sent
*BluffLight Keeper's Cottage—December 10, 1873*
*(Three days after the Sunday revelation)*

T he keeper's cottage carried the scent of new construction—
fresh-cut pine, lime from whitewash, the mineral tang of tabby
walls still curing in winter air. Jesse moved through the main room,
lighting oil lamps as evening shadows gathered outside the newly
installed windows. The space remained sparsely furnished—a table
with four chairs, a settle near the hearth—but the solid roof
overhead and enclosed walls embodied security they had not known
since fleeing Richmond.

"The trunks have been brought up from Marsh Cottage," Jonas
reported, entering through the exterior door nearest the lighthouse.
His shoulder had healed enough to permit limited use. "Gardner
stationed men at both structures overnight, though I doubt they'll
approach by expected routes."

Jesse nodded. William's methodical nature would ensure
thorough surveillance before any attempt. Roarke's knowledge of
the island's hidden approaches would complement this calculated
patience. "The new moon rises tonight—just as Miss Haskins
predicted."

"We've stationed watchers at all approaches," Jonas confirmed.
"Particular attention to the marsh paths Solomon identified as
navigable during low tide." He paused at the door. "The island feels
tight tonight. Everyone senses it."

She felt the familiar tightening beneath her ribs—the instinct
that danger had drawn close.

As Jonas departed to inspect BluffLight's mechanical systems,
Jesse settled at the small writing desk near the window. She drew

paper from the drawer and began writing with measured strokes—
the habit formed in Richmond, writing unsent letters as survival.

*December 10, 1873,*

*William,*

*You have found us, as perhaps you eventually would despite our precautions. The investigator was thorough in his pursuit, and your resources considerable when directed toward specific purpose. Yet what you've found is not what you left behind in Richmond.*

*The woman who fled under cover of fabricated death no longer exists. The desperate mother who prioritized her children's safety above all else remains, but she now stands within federal jurisdiction rather than Virginia's domestic sovereignty. The wife who endured your calculated "corrections" with outward submission has been replaced by a lighthouse keeper whose official responsibilities extend beyond personal circumstances.*

*I wonder if you recognized these changes during our brief confrontation beneath the tower. Your expression suggested recalculation—the slight narrowing of eyes that always preceded adjustment to unexpected variables. The formidable mind that designed bridges and railway junctions now confronts obstacles more complex than mere physical distance.*

*The children flourish here in ways Richmond never permitted. Daniel's natural intelligence finds constructive outlet instead of fearful suppression. Eliza's vibrant spirit expands instead of contracting under your critical assessment. They breathe sea air instead of coal smoke, study natural wonders instead of proper deportment, experience community support instead of isolated watchfulness.*

*Whatever legal channels you pursue, whatever alliance you form with Roarke, whatever resources you direct toward reclaiming what you consider rightfully yours—know this: I will not return to Richmond. The children will not resume life under your control. The light will continue shining across these waters despite whatever darkness you attempt to cast,*

*Jessica.*

She folded the paper carefully, tucking it within Henry Miller's journal where William would never see it.

From the children's bedroom came the soft murmur of Eliza's prayers.

"Time for sleep," Jesse said as Eliza's prayers concluded. "Tomorrow brings the supply delivery from Savannah. You both need rest if you're to help with inventory."

"Will you read from Henry Miller's journal tonight?" Daniel asked.

Jesse retrieved the journal and sat between their beds. The leather binding had softened with repeated handling, pages marked where meaningful passages had been identified.

"December 12, 1858," she began, selecting an entry from years before the war. "Winter settles over the island, bringing quieter days between storms. The lighthouse foundation remains incomplete, awaiting materials delayed by shipping schedules. Yet the concept remains intact, the purpose undiminished. We build not for present navigation alone but for future generations who will guide their vessels by light we establish through current perseverance."

Daniel and Eliza listened as Jesse continued reading Henry's reflections on purpose and patience.

The children settled as she finished, their breathing soft and even, the journal's calm settling Jesse as well. She returned to her desk where another blank page awaited.

*My beloved Daniel and Eliza,*

*Tonight, you sleep beneath BluffLight's protective beam, your dreams guarded by both lighthouse vigilance and community watchfulness. You cannot fully comprehend recent developments, nor would I burden your young hearts with complete awareness of approaching challenges.*

*Know simply this: everything done since our departure from Richmond has been directed toward ensuring your safety, securing your futures, and preserving possibilities that William's control systematically eliminated.*

*Whatever occurs in coming days, remember that light persists even when temporarily obscured. The beacon continues its rotation regardless of conditions, guiding ships hidden beyond the horizon—those unseen, but still in need of light.*

*With enduring love, Your Mother.*

The letter joined others in the journal's pages.

Outside, the night had gone quiet. Too quiet. The usual chorus of marsh frogs had fallen silent—as they often did when something moved through the marsh that did not belong.

Jesse rose and moved to the window. BluffLight's beam swept its arc through the darkness, steady as heartbeat. Tonight would bring whatever approached on new moon darkness.

She prepared for her midnight inspection of the lighthouse—the routine that defined her role regardless of what surrounded it.

# CHAPTER THIRTY-NINE

A Light That Does Not Burn Out
*BluffLight Lantern Room—December 11, 1873*
*(Night of the new moon)*

Midnight arrived, the new moon offering no light to break the perfect darkness. Outside, the wind had begun to rise, carrying the scent of an approaching storm that her morning observations had not foretold. She stood alone in the lantern room, her fingers tracing the cool brass edges of BluffLight's magnificent Fresnel lens. The mechanism rotated with hypnotic precision, transforming a single flame into a powerful corridor of light that cut through blackness for twenty miles across the increasingly choppy Atlantic.

The logbook lay open before her. "All appears in order," she wrote, the scratching of her pen loud in the silence. "Weather clear, wind from northwest at fifteen knots, barometric pressure falling rapidly. Storm front approaching from offshore. Visibility excellent despite new moon conditions, but deteriorating."

The island had fallen into unnatural hush. Jesse paused, pen suspended. The marsh frogs had gone silent. No night herons called. Even the hunting owls had abandoned their territories. Only the waves persisted, striking the shore with increasing violence as the tide fell toward midnight low, revealing hidden channels that led straight to the lighthouse bluff.

A figure emerged from the keeper's cottage—Jonas, his silhouette unmistakable even in darkness. Jesse checked the lamp's flame, verified the clockwork weight had sufficient descent remaining, and made a final notation before closing the logbook. The spiral staircase echoed with her rapid descent. Jonas waited at the tower's base, expression grim.

"Solomon reports movement along the southern marsh path," Jonas said without preamble, voice low. "At least three men approaching by water route instead of established tracks. Gardner's watchers have positioned themselves along the bluff perimeter, with Solomon's people covering the marsh approaches."

"The children?"

"Secure in the cottage with Miss Haskins and the Widow Patterson. Shutters barred, additional guards at both entrance and rear exit. No approach can reach them without confronting multiple defenders."

Relief, brief as a candleflame, stirred within her. This was not Richmond. They were not alone, not unprotected.

"The lighthouse?" Jesse asked, keeper's duty asserting itself.

"Fully functional with additional oil reserves secured in second-level storage," Jonas reported. "The lamp could maintain operation seventy-two hours without replenishment."

The beam would continue its rotation regardless of what happened below. Strange comfort in that thought.

Thunder rumbled distant, confirming their fears. "This storm wasn't indicated by this morning's observations," Jesse said. "It's coming faster than it should."

"We should return to the cottage," she decided. "Consolidated defense instead of divided attention. And the children will be frightened by the storm."

They crossed via the covered walkway Gardner had insisted on building, wind tearing at their clothing with hungry fingers. Inside the cottage, Miss Haskins sat near the hearth like a black-clad sentinel, spine straight as a church pew. The Widow Patterson moved between windows with military precision, checking latches with hands that betrayed no tremor.

"The children sleep," Miss Haskins reported. "Eliza required additional reassurance, but Daniel maintained remarkable composure given his awareness of surrounding preparations."

Jesse nodded, bittersweet ache blooming beneath her ribs. Daniel's composure was hard-won through years of watching for William's moods, learning to read danger in the set of shoulders. A child should not need such skills, yet hers had mastered them.

The Widow Patterson returned from her circuit, voice dropping to near whisper. "Word from the southern watchers. Two boats through the tidal creek behind the tabby ruins—the storm surge had deepened it enough for passage. At least five men, though darkness limits accurate count."

"How long until they reach the bluff?" Jonas asked.

"Perhaps an hour if they maintain current progression. Longer if they encounter Solomon's obstacles along the route." Lightning lit the cottage interior, thunder shaking the windows. "Or much sooner if they use the storm as cover."

Minutes stretched like pulled taffy. Outside, BluffLight's beam swept with mechanical constancy—flash, darkness, flash—while inside, they waited between heartbeats.

A tremendous crack of thunder shook the cottage walls. The clock on the mantel ticked past one when Daniel appeared in the bedroom doorway, nightshirt rumpled but eyes sharp with awareness that broke her heart anew.

"They're coming," he said simply. Two words that should never come from a child's lips with such certainty.

"Yes," Jesse confirmed, refusing to insult his intelligence with false reassurance. "But we're prepared, and not alone in facing them."

Daniel nodded, processing with gravity beyond his years. "Should I wake Eliza?"

"Not yet. Let her rest. You might help Miss Haskins prepare lamp oil for the lighthouse—we'll need to refill the reservoir before dawn regardless."

Relief crossed his features—not from fear avoided, but from having a task worthy of him. He moved to assist with the solemn dignity of a boy determined to be useful instead of protected.

A massive gust tore at the roof, ripping shingles free with a sound like teeth being pulled. Rain poured through the new opening.

A soft knock at the back door sent hands to concealed weapons. Solomon Davis entered, water cascading from his clothing.

"They've reached the bluff base," he reported, voice steady as if delivering news about weather. Only the tightness around his eyes betrayed gravity. "Five men total—Roarke himself leading, with your husband among them according to Gardner's identification."

Jesse's breath caught. William's presence was expected yet landed like a physical blow. She recognized the timing instantly—he had always waited until circumstances felt most desperate before striking, letting fear do half his work. The same pattern from Richmond, when he would time his worst "corrections" for moments when she was already exhausted or isolated. Now he approached under storm and darkness, confident that desperation would make her compliant.

"They carry both weapons and legal documentation," Solomon continued. "Dual strategy—physical intimidation supported by claimed authority." The papers meant nothing here—a shield William held because he understood nothing else.

Jonas checked the pistol Gardner had provided, thumb brushing the hammer back just enough to test its smooth movement. "Their most likely approach?"

"The front path. Advancing directly instead of further concealment. Confidence in either their claimed authority or superior force."

The straightforward advance suggested Roarke's influence—a captain accustomed to direct confrontation instead of William's subtle manipulation.

Boots scraped on the porch—several sets—before a sharp, demanding knock at the front door shattered the quiet. Eliza appeared beside Daniel, hair tousled but eyes instantly alert—the learned response of a child who had been woken by violence before.

"Mrs. Whitmore." Roarke's voice carried through the heavy wood, confidence bordering on arrogance. "We can settle matters peaceably. No need for this to turn ugly. Your husband has business with his family."

*Business with his family.* The phrase landed with particular menace.

Jesse caught Jonas's glance, reading his assessment in the slight nod. Ignoring the demand would provoke immediate assault. Better to engage while maintaining defensive position.

"I'll speak with them from the window."

She opened the shutter just as BluffLight's beam swept across the bluff. In that flash of illumination, she saw them clearly— Roarke standing with the confidence of a man accustomed to command, William slightly behind with controlled posture that had once seemed dignified but now revealed only calculation. Three rough-looking men flanked them, hands resting on visible weapons.

BluffLight completed another rotation, casting stark light across this confrontation unfolding in its shadow.

Behind her, Daniel whispered to Eliza, "Don't worry. Mama knows what to do."

The certainty in his voice nearly broke her. She didn't know. Not for certain. Outside, men who wanted to drag them back into darkness waited. Above, the storm threatened their only protection. The old fear pressed at the edges of her resolve.

The storm and the men had arrived on the same dark tide.

The light kept turning.

# CHAPTER FORTY

## The Bluff's Truth
*BluffLight Keeper's Cottage—December 12, 1873*
*(Continuation of the new moon night)*

"Captain Roarke. Mr. Whitmore." Jesse's voice cut through the midnight air, betraying none of the trembling in her hands as she gripped the windowsill. William's silhouette—so painfully familiar even after all these months—sent ice through her veins, but she forced her chin higher. "State your purpose."

BluffLight's beam swept over the scene, illuminating Roarke's face for one second before plunging him back into shadow.

"A matter requiring resolution, Mrs. Whitmore." His voice carried casual menace. "Certain cargo arrives tonight. This light makes that... inconvenient."

Behind her, Jesse heard Daniel's sharp intake of breath. Jonas shifted position, moving closer to the children while keeping his hand near the pistol at his waist.

"Federal jurisdiction supersedes state domestic claims within the lighthouse reservation," Jesse responded, her words emerging with steadiness. "BluffLight's operation continues under Light-House Board authority."

William stepped forward, his shoulders settling into that stance she knew. "Jessica." Her full name, that precise intonation. "The children's welfare remains the primary consideration."

The mention of her children sent heat through Jesse, burning away cold fear. She glanced back at Daniel and Eliza beside Miss Haskins. Daniel's fists were clenched, Eliza pressed close to his side.

"The children's welfare has guided our every decision since Richmond," she replied, emphasizing "our" with deliberate force. "Their current circumstances reflect significant improvement, as the federal inspection has officially confirmed."

William's face tightened as BluffLight's beam passed over him again—revealing something Jesse had never seen there before. Uncertainty. He had expected tears and pleas, not documented federal authority.

A massive lightning strike illuminated the entire scene. In that flash, Jesse saw movement beyond the cottage—a figure slipping toward the lighthouse tower itself. The same dread she'd felt in the fog returned, cold and certain.

"Jonas," she whispered urgently. "They're trying to reach the lighthouse."

His eyes narrowed. "The oil supply."

The three men behind William and Roarke shifted, hands moving to visible weapons.

Roarke cut in, impatience tangible. "BluffLight must be shut down. Tonight. For the safety of vessels approaching these waters."

"Curious assertion," Jonas observed, his tone deceptively mild. "The harbormaster expects no vessels until tomorrow's packet from Savannah." He paused. "Unless perhaps some vessels prefer to arrive unannounced."

The accusation hung in the air. Even in darkness, Jesse saw William's expression flash with alarm.

A terrible cracking sound came from above—a section of the walkway had torn free in the gale, splintering as it crashed below.

Jesse turned to Jonas. "I have to get to the lighthouse. The beam must not go out."

"Jesse, no." He gripped her arm. "It's too dangerous."

"The children are protected. Miss Haskins and the Widow Patterson will keep them safe. But no one else knows how to maintain that lamp if the oil supply is cut off." Her eyes met his. "A ship could be out there right now, depending on that light."

Daniel stepped forward. "I can help with the lamp, Mama. I've watched you."

Solomon moved beside Daniel. "The boy stays. But someone must protect the light." His eyes met Jesse's. "This home you have made—it is what that light represents. If it goes dark tonight, something irreplaceable is lost."

Jonas's military training overrode personal feeling. "I'll create a diversion," he said finally. "Draw their attention to the far side of the clearing near the marsh edge. Use the storm's cover to reach the tower through the broken walkway."

He glanced at Solomon. "Keep the children safe."

"This community protects its own," Solomon replied.

Jonas turned to Jesse. "Ready?"

She looked at her children—Daniel with his hands protective on Eliza's shoulders. The wind howled against the cottage walls.

"Ready."

Shouts erupted from the far side of the clearing—the diversion working as William and Roarke's attention snapped toward the commotion.

Jesse slipped out the side door into the raging storm. Wind nearly knocked her from her feet as she dashed through darkness toward the lighthouse. Rain lashed her face between lightning flashes. She stumbled over the fallen walkway section, pain lancing through her ankle, and pressed on.

The lighthouse door hung partially open, moving eerily in the wind. Jesse slipped inside, the relative silence after the storm's roar disorienting. She knew every inch of this tower—every step, every landing, every turn of the spiral staircase. She climbed, wet skirts heavy around her legs, breathing controlled to minimize sound.

Halfway up, she heard footsteps above—moving with purpose instead of care. The saboteur, making his way toward the oil reservoir. If he cut the flow, the lamp would begin to dim within the hour.

BluffLight's beam still swept through the night—she could see its reflection flickering in the tower's small windows. Still burning.

Jesse increased her pace, weeks of twice-daily climbs giving her advantage despite the throb in her ankle. She knew which steps creaked, which turns offered concealment. Three-quarters up, she paused, listening. The footsteps had stopped.

He had reached the oil storage room. She heard the clink of metal—tools working at the reservoir fittings. Jesse looked around desperately for a weapon, finding nothing but an old broom propped against the wall. It will do.

263

She continued her ascent, silent now as a hunter rather than prey. The oil room door stood ajar, a lantern casting eerie shadows as the man pried at the copper piping that fed oil to the lamp above. His back was to her.

Jesse raised the broom and brought it down across his shoulders. He cried out, spinning with fury and a wrench raised to strike. She ducked, but her wet shoes slipped, sending her crashing against the reservoir tank.

The saboteur advanced. "Shoulda stayed below."

A shot rang out, deafening in the confined space. The man stumbled, clutching his shoulder as blood welled between his fingers. Jonas stood in the doorway, pistol raised in his left hand, rain dripping from his sleeve onto the iron floor.

"Are you hurt?" he asked, not taking his eyes from the wounded man.

"No. The reservoir—he was trying to drain it."

Jonas secured the saboteur while Jesse examined the oil system. The copper piping had been loosened but not severed. Oil still flowed to the lamp above, though it seeped from the damaged joint—enough to dim the light within the hour if left unrepaired.

"The lamp will start to dim if I don't tighten this," she said, reaching for tools.

A tremendous crash from above cut her off. Both turned upward as shattering glass rained down the stairwell.

Jesse was already moving, hauling herself up the stairs as fast as her wet skirts and throbbing ankle would allow.

The scene stole her breath. One massive glass panel had shattered, allowing the storm's full fury into the chamber. Rain and wind whipped around the Fresnel lens, still rotating despite the chaos. But the flame at its center flickered dangerously.

Jesse moved without thought, her keeper's training overriding fear as she positioned herself to block the wind and spray from reaching the lamp. Rain soaked through her dress as she steadied the oil flow with one hand and used her body to shield the glass chimney from the gale. The cold cut through her soaked clothing to the bone, but against her face the lamp radiated warmth—the flame she protected giving back what heat it could. Her hands moved by instinct: adjusting the wick, cupping the chimney, her body a wall between the storm and the light.

Jonas appeared, coat already removed. "We need to seal this breach! The lens will be destroyed if water reaches the hot glass!"

Together they secured a spare canvas over the broken panel, lashing it to the iron frame with rope, fighting wind determined to tear it from their hands. The flame stabilized as Jesse adjusted the reservoir connection.

A shout from below drew their attention. Through intact windows, they saw lanterns appearing through the trees—not one or two but dozens.

"The islanders," Jonas breathed. "Gardner's messengers reached the village."

Jesse watched as familiar figures emerged—Thomas Gardner, Pastor Willoughby, Solomon leading island men. They surrounded William and Roarke's group with overwhelming numbers.

"This private matter requires no additional complication," William's voice carried faintly, his controlled facade cracking as tactical advantage shifted.

Roarke assessed the situation with a captain's eye, recognizing the numbers faster than William. Five men against twenty. No way through.

"This matter remains unresolved," he stated loud enough to carry to the tower. His eyes found Jesse through darkness and storm, and held.

As they retreated, the storm's fury began to abate. Wind dropped from screaming to howling, lightning moved offshore, rain lessened to steady downpour.

Jesse sank to her knees beside the lamp. She pressed her palms flat against the iron decking. The flame continued to burn, the lens continued to rotate, the beam continued to sweep across increasingly calm waters.

Jonas knelt beside her, his hand finding hers in the semi-darkness. "Are you alright?"

She nodded, breath still uneven. "The children. I need to—"

"They're safe. But yes, they'll need to see you."

Together they descended past the secured saboteur, who glared with impotent hatred as they passed. Outside, the storm had diminished enough for safe passage. Daniel and Eliza burst through the cottage door the moment they saw her approach.

"You saved the light," Daniel whispered against her shoulder, his fingers clutching the fabric of her dress. "I knew you would."

Eliza clung to her, small fingers gripping Jesse's dress. "The storm was so loud. But we saw the light keep shining."

Gardner reached them first. "They've taken the southern marsh path. Solomon's men will track them until dawn."

Pastor Willoughby entered. "The lighthouse?"

"Damaged but functional," Jonas replied. "One window shattered, temporary repairs in place. The lens appears unharmed. And one saboteur secured in the oil room."

A figure emerged from the lighthouse into BluffLight's sweeping beam—the Richmond investigator, his expression taut with conflict. He stopped between retreating shadows and advancing light, visibly torn.

"Mrs. Whitmore. A word, if you please."

Jesse tensed, her hand finding Jonas's arm as she moved to the door.

"I've seen enough," the investigator said quietly. He looked older than he had that first day on the docks. "Mr. Whitmore hired me to find his family. He said nothing of what I've since learned."

He withdrew a folded paper. "Records from Richmond. Physicians' notes. Three years." His jaw worked. "I've seen this in my own family."

He placed the document on the doorstep and walked into the darkness.

Jesse picked up the paper. It was damp at the edges from the rain.

Later, when the villagers had departed and watches were set, Jesse stood at the cottage window. Jonas returned from a final lighthouse check.

"The lamp is secure. Gardner takes the morning watch."

"Jonas," she said, and something in her voice made him pause.

She crossed the room and stood before him. Wordlessly, she reached out and straightened the collar of his shirt where it had folded during the night's commotion. Her fingers lingered there.

His hand rose to cover hers.

"When I saw you in the tower tonight," he said quietly, "standing between the storm and the flame—" He stopped. "I've never been more certain you belong here."

"Thank you," she said simply. She did not pull her hand away.

"Always," he replied.

After Jonas left, Jesse remained at the window. The windowpane was cold, but behind it the lamp still burned. The beam turned, as it had all night. She stood there until the first gray of dawn touched the horizon. The air smelled of salt and rain.

# CHAPTER FORTY-ONE

Morning on the Bluff
*BluffLight Tower—December 21, 1873*
*(Nine days after the midnight confrontation)*

T he winter solstice brought the longest night of the year. Jesse climbed the spiral staircase toward the lantern room, counting the one hundred and thirty-one iron treads by habit. Her footsteps echoed in the tower's hollow core, steady as a heartbeat. She watched dawn break from her elevated vantage.

The nine days since William and Roarke's midnight confrontation had transformed the keeper's cottage from structure to sanctuary. The children now moved through rooms that felt truly theirs—Daniel's lighthouse manuals beside his bed, Eliza's shells arranged on the windowsill beside the potted herbs Miss Haskins had brought. Home.

As Jesse reached the lantern room, dawn had just begun transforming the horizon from perfect darkness to deep indigo. Slowly, impossibly slowly, indigo yielded to rose, then rose to pale gold. The magnificent Fresnel lens continued its measured rotation, the flame burning steadily within the precision mechanism that magnified its illumination across twenty miles of coastal water. Through the glass panels that enclosed the circular chamber, she could observe both the maritime approaches and the island landscape emerging from night shadow into winter morning clarity.

Frost had settled overnight on the glass panes, delicate patterns that caught the strengthening light. The air inside the lantern room held the warmth of the lamp—the faint warm smell of the lamp mixing with the cold salt wind that found its way through the minute gaps in the ironwork. Jesse pressed her palm against the brass housing. Still warm from the night's work.

The lantern room still bore scars from the midnight battle—one window replaced with new glass from the Savannah ironworks, small scratches on the brass housing where tools had scraped during emergency repairs. Gardner's craftsmen had worked three days to properly restore the damaged sections, ensuring the lens mechanism operated with its original precision despite the trauma it had endured.

Jesse completed her morning inspection with practiced efficiency, recording oil levels and notes on the workings of the light in the official logbook. The flame burned steady, the oil reservoir three-quarters full after yesterday's replenishment, the clockwork mechanism maintaining its rhythm. She could hear it—the subtle tick and whisper of gears, the measured breathing of the lamp. The flame danced within its glass chimney, protected, constant. William might pursue federal courts instead of Virginia authorities, and Roarke might be offshore or hiding his movements—no one on the island could say. But BluffLight's beam would continue its sweep across dark water.

As she made final notations, dawn transformed the sky from tentative lightening to genuine illumination. The winter solstice sun emerged reluctantly over the horizon. Today marked the turning— the slow return toward longer days. From this moment forward, each day would claim back minutes from the darkness.

Jesse looked up as sunlight cleared the horizon, casting golden light across the island landscape still bearing winter's muted colors. The maritime forest stretched toward inland marshes where mist lingered among cordgrass and needlerush, rising like spirits in the cold morning air. Egrets picked their way through the shallows, their white forms stark against brown grass. The village rooftops appeared in the distance beyond the tree line, chimneys releasing thin ribbons of smoke into the cold air. The island was waking, life continuing.

Below, the keeper's cottage stood solid—tabby walls enclosing spaces they now called home. The covered walkway connecting cottage to lighthouse—repaired after the storm damage—now provided sheltered passage. Jesse could see the garden beds where

Eliza had planted bulbs under Miss Haskins's watchful instruction. Come spring, there would be flowers.

Movement near the cottage door drew Jesse's attention as Daniel emerged onto the winter-browned grass. Her son carried the journal she had given him for recording lighthouse observations. He moved with more confidence now than he had in Richmond, where every gesture had been calculated to avoid notice.

She watched him pause at the spot where, during the midnight confrontation, he had helped Solomon Davis barricade the door. The old Richmond instinct flickered again—his hand drifting to his side, checking for danger that existed only in memory. Jesse's throat tightened. The body remembered what the mind tried to forget. But he was learning new reflexes here: how to read the tide, how to adjust a lamp wick, how to walk without flinching.

Eliza appeared behind him, her blonde curls catching morning sunlight as she carefully transported a potted plant that Gardner's wife had provided for the windowsill. She was humming something tuneless and happy—a sound Jesse had not heard from her in Richmond. It drifted up to the lantern room, faint but unmistakable.

As Jesse descended the spiral staircase toward the cottage, she heard sounds of activity below. Her hand trailed along the iron railing, cool and solid beneath her fingers. Each step down felt lighter than the climb up had been months ago, when everything had been uncertainty and fear. Miss Haskins had arrived and was instructing Eliza while Daniel sat at the table, transcribing observations into his journal with the careful penmanship she had taught him.

"The Light-House Board correspondence arrived on yesterday's packet," Miss Haskins informed Jesse, indicating several official envelopes on the small desk. "Commander Reeves has expedited your permanent appointment."

Jonas arrived shortly after breakfast, his injured shoulder now healed. He carried firewood for the stove, moving with the easy strength that had returned in recent weeks.

"Watchers saw the *Miranda* slip southward yesterday afternoon," he informed them. "No sign of Roarke aboard. Full-sailed for open waters."

"And William?" Jesse asked.

"He's taken a room at a hunting lodge near the south shore. Preparing legal documentation for federal court."

This aligned with Jesse's understanding of William's methodical nature—measured adjustment of plans instead of emotional reaction. He would pursue her through proper channels now, having learned that direct confrontation on Saint Simons meant facing the entire island. It gave her time. Not peace, but time.

"The children should continue their routines," Jesse decided. "Daniel can keep his lighthouse journal. Eliza can help Mrs. Gardner in the garden."

Later that morning, Jesse stood at the cottage window, watching her children in the garden. Frost still clung to the shaded portions of the grass. She reached for Henry Miller's journal from the small bookshelf where it stood alongside official lighthouse manuals. She opened to a passage she had marked during the first weeks after the illumination ceremony:

*"A lighthouse stands for safe passage and human determination. The keeper tends the flame that illuminates surrounding waters regardless of storm or calm, standing visible upon the shore while guiding vessels unseen beyond horizon."*

"Mama," Eliza called from the garden, "can we visit the lighthouse now? I've finished planting the bulbs Miss Haskins brought."

Jesse smiled at her daughter's eager expression. "Yes, we can. The southeastern windows need cleaning before tonight's illumination. And Commander Reeves will expect updated shore observations when he arrives next week for quarterly inspection."

The children accepted these tasks with the seriousness they'd learned—Daniel understanding how the mechanisms worked, Eliza recognizing patterns in weather and water. They were becoming lighthouse keepers themselves.

"Mama," Eliza asked as they walked toward the tower, "if we move away someday, will the lighthouse still shine?"

Jesse smiled, her hand resting on her daughter's shoulder. "Yes, love. Because it doesn't shine for us alone. It shines for everyone who needs it."

Together they crossed the short distance between the keeper's cottage and lighthouse base, entering the tower whose solid stone construction had weathered both physical storms and human opposition. The spiral staircase carried them upward.

The lantern room welcomed them with its familiar circular space enclosed by glass panels. The magnificent Fresnel lens dominated the chamber's center, its crystal prisms catching the midday light and bending it into soft color.

Daniel had already begun cleaning the windows with methodical care, his cloth moving in steady circles across the glass. Eliza arranged her shore specimens on the service table neatly, the way Commander Reeves preferred—dried cordgrass, a fragment of whelk shell, a piece of driftwood shaped by tide and time.

As midday sunlight brightened the lantern room, Jesse completed her inspection of the workings of the light. The lens mechanism turned with the precision Gardner had restored, each turn marking time's passage. William would pursue his federal court case, Roarke might return with revised plans, but BluffLight would continue its work—the lens kept turning, the beam reaching across dark water to guide vessels she would never see toward shores she would never know.

# EPILOGUE

## By the Light of the Bluff
*Saint Simons Island, Georgia—February 15, 1874*
*(Two months after the winter solstice)*

T he long winter nights had begun to shorten since the solstice, though February still carried its chill. Jesse sat at her writing desk, the official lighthouse logbook open before her, its ruled pages filled with the careful notations that had become her daily practice.

Two months had passed since the winter solstice confrontation.

Outside, BluffLight rose against the February sky, its white tower gleaming in the morning sun. Later, sunset would bring the nightly ritual of illumination—lamp lit, mechanism checked, beam sweeping across coastal waters to guide vessels she would never see toward shores she would never know. But for now, the lighthouse waited, a silent sentinel watching over the life being rebuilt in its shadow.

The sound of children's voices drifted through the open window—Daniel explaining some mechanical principle to Eliza as they worked in the small garden plot Miss Haskins had helped them prepare. Their confident tones carried none of the hushed caution that had marked their first months on the island.

She glanced at the second chair drawn close to the hearth, where Jonas's coat hung on its familiar peg. His boots stood by the door, his mug rested on the windowsill catching morning light. In the evenings, he would take that chair without ceremony, and they would talk—sometimes until midnight, other times in comfortable silence that required no words.

Jesse closed the logbook and moved to the window where she could observe her children without interrupting their focused activity. They knelt in the winter-pale grass, Daniel's hands demonstrating some principle while Eliza listened with rapt attention, her blonde curls catching sunlight.

Daniel had grown an inch or two since their arrival, his eleven-year-old frame filling out with the steady meals and island air. The occasional quick smile that had been unimaginable during their final Richmond months now came easily, transforming his serious face.

Eliza knelt beside a newly prepared flower bed, carefully positioning the spring bulbs Miss Haskins had provided. At seven, her natural brightness had matured into genuine enthusiasm—for gardening, for shore specimens, for the endless questions about tides and stars and lighthouse mechanisms that she peppered the adults with daily.

A flash of orange caught Jesse's eye. Something fluttered near Eliza's garden bed—unusual for February. A single monarch butterfly circled the child before landing delicately on a stone marker.

Eliza froze, then turned slowly toward the cottage. "Mama!" she whispered excitedly, as if afraid to startle the visitor. "It's so early for monarchs!"

Jesse smiled. Unseasonable, perhaps impossible, yet there it was—wings the color of sunset, impossibly vivid against the winter-brown grass. The butterfly lifted away on the breeze, its meandering path taking it toward the lighthouse before it disappeared from view, a small miracle witnessed and gone.

Eliza immediately reached for her specimen journal, already sketching the unexpected visitor with focused intensity.

A knock at the door drew Jesse from her contemplation. Jonas entered at her invitation, bringing several letters delivered on the morning packet from Savannah.

"Commander Reeves sends updated operational protocols," he reported, setting the official Light-House Board envelope on her desk with its familiar wax seal. Then, with the slight tension of someone delivering news of consequence, he added, "And this arrived from the federal courthouse in Charleston."

He extended another envelope bearing legal seals that sent immediate alertness through Jesse's calm exterior.

She accepted the document with steady hands that belied the flutter of tension beneath her ribs. Two months had passed since William had established residence at the hunting lodge near the south shore for the express purpose of pursuing a federal challenge to her keeper appointment and custody of the children. Two months of legal maneuvering through official channels instead of midnight confrontations. This envelope likely contained the response to his initial filing—the first formal engagement in a procedural battle that would determine their standing beyond temporary federal protection.

Jesse opened the document carefully, scanning its formal language with practiced efficiency. The content brought unexpected lightness to her chest.

"The federal court has denied William's motion for emergency custody order," she summarized, looking up to meet Jonas's attentive gaze. "Judge Harrington requires a comprehensive evidentiary hearing before any modification to current arrangements, noting that under maritime law, lighthouse keepers' children are considered wards of the Light-House Board during their parent's term of service."

Jonas's expression reflected measured satisfaction rather than premature celebration. "The burden has shifted. The children's welfare must now be proven deficient rather than automatically subordinated to paternal rights."

"The hearing is scheduled for April twenty-first," Jesse continued, noting the date with careful attention. "In Charleston rather than Richmond, with opportunity for testimony from neutral parties regarding the children's welfare."

The procedural shift moved the battle from Virginia jurisdiction—where wives and children existed as legal extensions of a husband's authority—to federal maritime context where individual welfare received consideration. Not victory itself, but an essential precondition that might eventually establish permanent protection.

Among the documents delivered with Commander Reeves' correspondence, Jesse found something unexpected—a faded map she hadn't noticed initially tucked between official pages. Her fingers hesitated above the yellowed paper, sensing its significance before her mind fully comprehended what she held.

A partial rendering of underground passages beneath the old plantation ruins. Henry Miller's distinctive handwriting marked cryptic notations in the margins: *'Secondary location confirmed'* and *'Documents secured in third chamber.'* Along the bottom edge, barely legible through time's erosion: *'BluffLight is only the beginning. The greater truth remains buried.'*

This was not mentioned in any of the journals she had read.

She studied the map briefly—the precise measurements, the faded ink suggesting decades of concealment—then carefully folded it and placed it inside the keeper's journal for safekeeping. The mystery would wait. They had secured their present. The past's secrets could remain buried a while longer.

She returned her attention to the logbook's more immediate concerns. "Oil consumption averaged forty-one ounces per night this week," she noted to Jonas, grounding herself in the practical rhythms of lighthouse keeping. "Within normal range for February temperatures."

"The Light-House Board quarterly inspection is scheduled for next week," she added. "The maintenance you completed on the rotation mechanism should address Commander Reeves' remaining concerns."

Jonas nodded. "Gardner reports the replacement glass panels will arrive tomorrow for the northwestern section. The winter storms caused minor warping, though the light remains fully functional."

As Jonas departed to continue his work, Jesse returned to her post at the window. Miss Haskins had arrived with additional garden supplies, her severe black dress a familiar sight now. From the kitchen came the gentle sounds of Widow Patterson, who had begun visiting twice a week to help with meals. Outside the cottage window, island life followed its established rhythm—BluffLight's white tower a constant reminder of what they'd built here.

William remained on the island, his continued residence at the hunting lodge a persistent reminder that threats don't simply vanish. Roarke's position remained ambiguous—the *Miranda*

276

occasionally visible on the distant horizon before disappearing beyond sight.

Jesse moved to the western window and looked out toward the marshes and maritime forest, toward the mainland that lay beyond. Somewhere further still, Richmond waited—but now, several layers of protection stood between her family and those old threats: federal jurisdiction, community support, island geography itself.

As dusk approached, the lighthouse stood silhouetted against the darkening sky. The island held secrets, yes—but unlike those she had fled in Richmond, these were mysteries that invited rather than threatened.

As twilight deepened across Saint Simons, Jesse stepped onto the cottage porch. The children were inside with their books, the day's work complete. She had a moment to herself before Jonas would return from his final inspection of the tower.

She settled onto the top step, her skirts gathering around her as she drew her knees close. The first stars were beginning to pierce the darkening sky, and BluffLight's beam had started its nightly vigil, sweeping steadily across the darkened waters. A cool breeze carried the scent of salt marsh and the distant sound of waves against the shore.

Jesse bowed her head toward her knees, letting the weight of gratitude settle over her shoulders like a shawl. "Lord," she whispered into the evening breeze, her voice barely audible even to herself, "I hardly know where to begin."

Her voice caught slightly. "Thank you for bringing us safely to this place. For giving my children ground to grow on again."

The lighthouse beam swept across the water, its rhythm as steady as breath. From inside the tower came the faint mechanical whisper of the clockwork mechanism, the subtle tick and turn that kept the light rotating through the darkness.

"Help me to be worthy of this peace we've found," she added softly. "And to have the courage to believe it can last."

Raising her head, she saw Jonas appearing from the base of the lighthouse, his familiar silhouette outlined against the tower's glow. Jesse rose gracefully from the steps, smoothing her skirts as she moved to stand at the porch railing. A gentle flutter stirred in her chest—anticipation, warmth, something she was only beginning to name.

She watched him approach across the bluff, his familiar stride now as much a part of this place as the tide itself. The lantern above cast its rotating glow across the darkening landscape.

Jonas stepped onto the cottage porch where Jesse stood watching the first stars emerge above BluffLight. The tower's beam had begun its nightly rotation, casting its light across dark water.

"The children are settled with their books," she said as he joined her at the railing. "Eliza's determined to identify every butterfly species that might visit her garden come spring."

Jonas smiled. "She has your persistence."

"And Daniel spent an hour explaining to Miss Haskins how the lighthouse mechanisms could be improved with his proposed modifications."

"That boy has engineering in his blood," Jonas observed, a note of pride in his voice that required no biological connection to feel genuine.

They stood in comfortable silence as darkness claimed the island completely, save for the rhythmic sweep of light above them. The air carried the first hint of spring—salt marsh and night-blooming jasmine mingling in the cool evening breeze.

Jonas gazed at the lighthouse and then back to her, his voice softening. "I came here to build a tower, Jesse. I never expected to find a home."

Jesse smiled, meeting his eyes with newfound certainty. "We could build both. Together."

In the months since their arrival, they had built a relationship composed of small, meaningful gestures—coffee prepared exactly as she preferred each morning, books left open to passages he thought might interest her, hands briefly touching when passing lighthouse tools between them. A foundation laid slowly, carefully, with the patience of those who'd learned that lasting things cannot be rushed.

From the garden below, Eliza's laughter drifted up—she must have slipped outside to check on her bulbs one final time before full dark. Daniel's voice followed, patient and explanatory, teaching her something about the stars.

Jesse listened to her children's voices, then turned back to Jonas. "Eliza wants to plant sea lavender along the walkway. She asked if you'd help her build a border."

"I'd like that," he said.

She reached out, her fingers finding his where they rested on the railing.

The movement between them was unhurried, as natural as the tide. Jonas's hand gently framed her face, his thumb brushing across her cheekbone with reverence. Jesse closed the remaining distance between them, her lips meeting his in a kiss that held no demands—only a quiet acknowledgment of what had been growing between them through shared duties, quiet evenings, and the gradual building of trust.

When they separated, the night air cool against her face where his warmth had been, neither spoke immediately. The lighthouse beam swept across the water beyond them, and somewhere in the marsh a night heron called. Something fundamental had shifted without requiring dramatic declaration or grand promises.

"We should check the lamps before full dark," Jesse said softly, practical even in this moment.

Jonas nodded, his hand still holding hers as they turned toward the tower. "Together, then."

Together, they walked toward the tower, fingers interlaced, BluffLight's steady beam sweeping above them.

By the light of the bluff.

## THE END

# REFLECTIONS

*Offered for personal contemplation or group conversation.*

1. Jesse arrives on Saint Simons seeking refuge, but finds something more—purpose. When have you discovered that what you were running toward mattered more than what you were running from?

2. Daniel positions himself between his sister and the world, a posture Jesse recognizes because she taught it to him without meaning to. What have you taught the people you love—without intending to?

3. Henry Miller's journal says a lighthouse keeper must be "someone who doesn't fear the storm but respects it." What does it look like to respect a storm you're living through?

4. Jesse learns to shield the flame with her own body, letting the lamp give back what heat it can. Where in your life have you protected something that also protected you?

5. Eliza draws the lighthouse as it will be—whole and purposeful—before it's finished. What are you building that only you can see completed?

6. Miss Haskins tells Jesse that the nearest neighbor is half a mile through the woods. Sometimes distance is danger. Sometimes it's sanctuary. How do you know the difference?

7. Jesse thinks: "Not safety—she had learned that safety was illusion—but legitimacy. Standing." What gives you standing when safety cannot be guaranteed?

8. The islanders appear with lanterns in the storm—dozens of lights answering one. Whose lights have answered yours when you needed them most?

9. Daniel's Richmond instincts still flicker—his hand drifting to check for danger that exists only in memory. But he is learning new reflexes. What old reflexes are you unlearning? What new ones are you building?

10. Jesse watches the beam reach across dark water to guide vessels she will never see toward shores she will never know. What light are you tending that may help someone you'll never meet?

# HISTORICAL NOTES

*By the Light of the Bluff* is a work of fiction grounded in real places, historical contexts, and cultural truths. While liberties have been taken in service of story, this section offers insight into the historical framework that shaped the novel.

**Saint Simons Island in the Reconstruction-Era**— Located off Georgia's southeastern coast, Saint Simons is believed to have been named by Spanish explorers in honor of Saint Simon the Zealot. The novel's marshes, tidal creeks, moss-draped oaks, and golden sands reflect the island's enduring beauty—much of which can still be experienced today. The story takes place in 1873, during Reconstruction, a period of profound national transition. Rights for newly freed Black Americans were legally established but remained under constant threat, while the region faced economic hardship and deep social realignment. Daily life along the coast carried both quiet continuity and constant tension beneath the surface.

**BluffLight**—The lighthouse depicted is fictional but inspired by real Southern coastal lighthouses of the 19th century. Its architecture, Fresnel lens, and construction timeline reflect accurate lighthouse-building practices of the post–Civil War era. The historic Saint Simons Island Lighthouse, built in 1872, is open to the public and well worth a visit.

**The Gullah-Geechee Culture**—Characters like Solomon Davis reflect the vital heritage of African Americans in the coastal Lowcountry. The Gullah-Geechee people preserved African traditions in language, spirituality, and community despite centuries of enslavement. These characters are written with reverence for this enduring legacy.

**Plantations and Place Names**—Many plantations mentioned are composites inspired by real antebellum properties. Great care was taken to avoid misrepresentation, especially given the sensitive nature of this history.

# HISTORICAL NOTE ON CHRIST CHURCH

Readers familiar with the history of Saint Simons Island may note that Christ Church, originally built in 1820, was destroyed during the Civil War and not rebuilt until 1884. During the years between, the congregation continued to gather—often beneath the oaks or in private homes—but no permanent structure stood on the site.

In *By the Light of the Bluff*, the church appears in its restored form as early as 1873. This is a conscious use of poetic license, included to preserve the symbolic and narrative weight of Christ Church as a place of gathering, reflection, and renewal. While the physical building did not yet exist at the time of the story, the faith and fellowship it represented most certainly did. This portrayal is meant as a tribute to the enduring spirit of the congregation and the sacred history of the place.

# AUTHOR'S NOTE

Some places leave a mark on the soul. For me, that place has always been Saint Simons Island. I've spent countless summers beneath its oaks, walked its shoreline, climbed its lighthouse, and listened to the wind whisper through the marsh grass. Over time, the island became more than a vacation spot—it became a keeper of memory, a living storyteller. Writing *By the Light of the Bluff* was a way of honoring those stories, both imagined and rooted in truth. I've long been drawn to Southern historical fiction—tales where land, legacy, and light all carry weight. This book is my letter to both the island and the spirit of those old stories: resilient women, weather-worn men, and the slow arc of redemption beneath a Southern sky.

I hope you felt something true in these pages. And I hope, like Jesse, you find your way toward whatever light calls you forward.

With gratitude,
Blake Gunnels

# IN MEMORY OF LOLA

*(2009–2025)*

Faithful soul. Gentle shadow. Keeper of the quiet hours. She spent sixteen years beside me—steady, soft-footed, and always near. Though she is gone, I still catch the shape of her spirit in the corner of a room, in the silence of the morning, and in the stillness in the places where she used to be. She is missed.

# OTHER COASTAL STORIES

While the BluffLight series is set along the historic Georgia coast, Blake Gunnels also writes contemporary thrillers set on the coastal waterways of North Carolina.

***THE CHRISTMAS KEEPER*** – Free Holiday Story
On Christmas Eve 1876, lighthouse keeper Jonas Miller finds a stranger face-down in the marsh—feverish, hollow, wearing a cavalry coat worn to nothing. What the Miller family does next is the whole story.

***WHAT THE TIDE KEPT*** – Free Short Story
Meet Nora Banks at fifteen—before the marina, before the job, before she knew what silence cost. A prequel set on the Cape Fear River.

**GET ONE OR BOTH FREE STORIES HERE:**

***WHAT THE TIDE TOOK***
A Nora Banks Novel
Cape Fear Thriller Series Book 1
Nora Banks is the harbormaster of Southport Marina on the Cape Fear coast of North Carolina. When her cousin surfaces with evidence that a deadly accident was no accident at all, Nora is pulled into an investigation that reaches deep into the power structure of Brunswick County.

**Available now at www.blakegunnels.com**

# ABOUT THE AUTHOR

Blake Gunnels is a designer, coastal explorer, and writer whose work is shaped by a lifetime of returning to the shores of Saint Simons Island, Georgia. His memories of the island span decades of family traditions—early morning kayak trips with his son along quiet marsh creeks, fishing off the village pier, biking beneath ancient oaks, exploring Fort Frederica with his daughter, sharing meals at beloved local restaurants, wandering the village shops, and searching for the Tree Spirits hidden in the island's live oaks. These moments became the fabric of seasons spent together, all under one roof, filled with stories, laughter, and the enduring rituals of coastal life.

It is from this love of place that the BluffLight series was born—stories rooted in lighthouse history, maritime life, and the quiet grace found along the Georgia coast. *By the Light of the Bluff* won the 2025 International Firebird Book Award for Southern Fiction and is the first novel in the BluffLight series.

By profession, Blake is a practicing landscape architect specializing in the renovation of apartment and condominium communities, resorts, and commercial properties. His design work—restoring worn places and helping them thrive again—mirrors the themes of renewal and redemption that run through his fiction.

When he isn't writing or designing, Blake can be found hiking pine-lined trails, boating through tidal estuaries, traveling to new landscapes, or chasing waterfalls with his long-time girlfriend, Tammy. Together, they seek out hidden corners of nature, search for the perfect margarita, and savor the quiet beauty of the world—whether spotting a winter manatee grazing in the shallows or standing together in the hush of a cold December sunrise.

# A NOTE TO THE READER

Thank you for reading *By the Light of the Bluff*. If Jesse's journey resonated with you, I would be grateful if you shared your thoughts by leaving a review. Reviews help other readers discover stories like this one.

# CONNECT WITH THE AUTHOR

Website: blakegunnels.com
Email: blake@blufflight.com
Facebook: facebook.com/BlakeGunnelsAuthor

**Until we meet again—*let your light so shine.***

www.ingramcontent.com/pod-product-compliance
Lightning Source LLC
Chambersburg PA
CBHW052026240626
47153CB00006B/1972